... **WILLIAM BOYLE**

D1374752

'Deploying an inimitable tone that packs sardonic storytelling atop action and adventure, with a side of character development, Boyle's voice works even when it feels like it shouldn't. It's just the right kind of too much – *Kirkus*

'An excellent sequel with a superb plot, matched by its realistically shaped characters' – *Washington Post*

'Powered by brilliantly realized characters, a richly described and grittily realistic backdrop, and subtle yet powerful imagery, this is crime fiction at its best; immersive, intense, and darkly illuminating' – *Publishers Weekly*

'Boyle's writing is raw, poetic, unflinching, nostalgic, and perverse. Urgency inhabits his pages and the characters live on weeks after you put the book down. *Gravesend* is a novel to read in a day, and then again, slowly' – *LA Review of Books*

'Boyle gives us an intimate portrait of a neighborhood in vivid, evocative prose, and explores how place and the past make us who we are' – **Melissa Ginsburg, author of *Sunset City***

'A Jacobean revenge tangle in a Brooklyn where all the players have survived the same nuns. Even the most desperately lost of William Boyle's characters retain a hungry heart'
– **John Sayles, author of *Yellow Earth***

'*The Lonely Witness* is a map of Brooklyn's genome. Amy Falconetti is that rarest of noir characters, a woman redeemed and a redeemer. Walking in her shoes for only a few blocks is worth the price of admission' – **Reed Farrel Coleman, author of *What You Break***

'William Boyle delivers some choice laughs and a terrific trio of felons in *A Friend is a Gift you Give Yourself*'
– *New York Times*

'Boyle has quietly proven he can take on any number of kinds of crime fiction, from a screwball farce to a hardboiled noir to a heartfelt examination of lonely people whose lives cross'
– *CrimeReads*

'A brave and gripping novel from start to finish' – *Big Issue*

'William Boyle has created intensely tangible characters, their voices, thoughts and feelings almost become physical, touchable, and are so very, very believable' – *LoveReading*

'This book is a gift you need to give yourself. Or someone you love. Or everyone you know' – *The Book Spine*

'If you like the richly nuanced novels of George Pelecanos or Dennis Lehane, be prepared to add Boyle to your regular reading list' – *BookPage*

'Fans of American noir will love this novel'
– *New Books Magazine*

'Characters who feel so lived-in and real that their decisions, whether catastrophic or joyful… ring authentic and true'
– *Buzzfeed*

SHOOT THE MOONLIGHT OUT

WILLIAM BOYLE

NO EXIT PRESS

First published in the UK in 2022 by No Exit Press,
an imprint of Oldcastle Books
Harpenden, UK
noexit.co.uk
@noexitpress

ISBN
978-0-85730-493-3 (Paperback)
978-0-85730-494-0 (eBook)

2 4 6 8 10 9 7 5 3 1

Typeset in 11 on 14pt Minion Pro
by Avocet Typeset, Bideford, Devon, EX39 2BP
(UK) Ltd, Croydon, CR0 4YY

n go to @crimetimeuk

For Eamon and Connolly Jean,
keep the hoping machine running.

Shoot the moonlight out
Baby, there ain't no doubt
'Cause tonight we're gonna
Shoot the moonlight out

– Garland Jeffreys,
'Shoot the Moonlight Out'

Anything you don't see
will come back to haunt you.

– Enid Dame,
'Riding the D Train'

SOUTHERN BROOKLYN
JULY 1996

Prologue

Bobby

Once a week this summer, Bobby Santovasco and his best pal Zeke head down by the Belt Parkway to throw things at the cars getting off at the Bay Parkway exit near Ceasar's Bay shopping center.

Bobby's just turned fourteen. Zeke is thirteen. They like stealing CDs from Sam Goody and cigarettes from Augie's Deli and playing video games in Zeke's basement. They both have a crush on Carissa Caruso from Stillwell Avenue. They're both headed into eighth grade at St. Mary Mother of Jesus on Eighty-Fourth Street. Bobby was left back in third grade, so he's older than everyone else in his class. Their teacher is going to be Mrs Santillo, who Bobby heard fart during the Pledge of Allegiance one day. Bobby lives in a small apartment on Eighty-Third Street, a block from St. Mary's, with his father; his stepmother, Grace; and his sixteen-year-old stepsister, Lily. He and Lily don't talk. Grace is just kind of there. His mother moved to California when he was six. He never heard from her again. Zeke lives in a big house on Twenty-Third Avenue. His real name is Flavio, but Bobby started calling him Zeke in fourth grade and it stuck. Zeke's dad owns a pork store. He has four sisters and two dogs. One of his sisters, Giovanna, looks like the Virgin Mary mixed with Marisa Tomei. Bobby thinks about her at night.

They come down here because there's always action. The cars funneling off the parkway, pausing at the traffic light. Ceasar's Bay, with Toys 'R' Us and Kmart and other chain shops. The bazaar, with its stalls, closed down the year before. Shore Parkway Park. The tennis complex. Gravesend Bay itself, stretching from Coney Island Creek to the Narrows. The bike path. The Verrazano Bridge looming. Nellie Bly amusement park, where they used to go as kids, right nearby.

They started small, with little cups of ketchup and mustard they filled at the Wendy's on the opposite corner.

The first day had been the best day, which is why it quickly became a ritual. That day, they had clomped a couple of cups against the wind-shield of an Olds simultaneously, the ketchup and mustard flinging itself across the glass. The driver had slammed on his brakes, abandoned his car in traffic, and chased them behind the tennis courts and onto the bike path by the bay. The guy caught them. Mustache. An L&B Spumoni Gardens T-shirt. The body of someone who played softball as an excuse to drink beer. He grabbed them by their shoulders and screamed at them for a solid two or three minutes, an eternity given the situation, spit flying from his mouth like bird shit. He said he was a cop and they were lucky he didn't bring them down to the station. They nodded, stifling laughs. Eventually, they coughed up apologies and he let them go and told them to smarten up. They turned, ran, and yelled for him to go fuck himself, and all the guy could do was blow angry breaths through the bristles of his mustache and storm back to his stupid little condiment-splattered car.

After that, they tried water balloons, filling them beforehand and hauling them in a bucket, but that was too much work and the balloons didn't last long. Some even broke in their hands as they released them.

It was Zeke's idea to try tennis balls next. They could always find a dozen or so scattered in the grass on the other side of the fence by the courts. The nice thing about tennis balls was how fast and hard they could be thrown. Bobby had a better arm than Zeke, but they didn't have to worry as much about falling short. The downside was the overall effect. Tennis balls just dinged against the cars and no one really thought twice about them. Could've been raining tennis balls for all anybody cared.

That was how they settled on rocks.

Before heading over to their spot now, they stop at Wendy's for orange sodas. They stand outside and drink them, paper cups beaded with condensation. It's a hot day. July-in-the-city hot. The heat's rising up off the sidewalk. Bobby can smell himself. Sweat and the neighborhood. He's wearing a Knicks tank top and his gym shorts, the high-tops he'd inherited from his cousin Jonny Boy. No socks. A Mets cap turned backward on his head. Zeke has no shirt on. Jams. His expensive new Air Jordans.

'With a rock,' Bobby says, 'we could really bust a windshield.'

'That'd be sweet,' Zeke says.

'We gotta be ready to bolt, though. This ain't ketchup.'

'Word.'

'I tell you what I told Carissa?'

'What?'

'That I was gonna throw a rock up at her window one night. Break the glass, climb up the drainpipe, and come into her room.'

'What'd she say?'

'She said, "You try that, my dad'll chop you to pieces in the garage."'

'Chop you up? Oh, shit. He chops you up, you're out of the way and I got a clear path for Carissa.'

'Dream your dreams. She's mine.'

'We'll see,' Zeke says.

'Okay, you take Carissa. I'll take Giovanna.'

'Giovanna wouldn't put you out if you were on fire. You're shit on the sidewalk to her, kid. She's *seventeen*. You should see the guy she's dating now. Serge Rossetti. Muscles up the ass. He goes to Bishop Ford. Plays baseball. Pretty sure he's on steroids.'

They suck down the rest of their sodas. The ice has mostly

melted away, so Bobby's last sip is watery. Zeke's must be too – he spits it out. They drop their cups to the sidewalk. An old lady who has just come out of Wendy's curses them.

They charge across Bay Parkway, dodging cars, and then walk past the tennis courts, hunting in the brown grass for good rocks. Bobby finds one. He's only been to a lake once with Jonny Boy in Jersey, but it's the kind of rock that's good for skipping. Flat and sharp. Fits right in his palm. Kind of pinkish. Zeke collects a couple of smaller ones. Glorified pebbles. Then Bobby finds an almost perfect rock, shaped like a ball, smooth and heavy but not too heavy to throw. Zeke laughs. What a score. He finds a few others that'll work, including a rock that's not a rock at all but a broken hunk of brick.

Zeke throws first and misses. He was aiming for a church van, but the rock sailed over the roof, skittering up against the orange cone propped in front of the divider between the parkway and the off-ramp.

Bobby tries and wings the first rock he found against the passenger door of a rusty red Chevy Lumina. It lands with a thud. The driver slams on the brakes and leans on his horn. They can see him. A man with a beard, looking all around, trying to figure out what hit his car. They can see how sweaty he is from where they are. He doesn't notice them. Finally, he takes off, making a left at the light onto Bay Parkway.

Bobby and Zeke laugh their asses off.

'That dude was like, "What the fuck?"' Zeke says, miming the driver's reaction.

They throw a couple more each, hitting tires and hoods and trunks, eliciting no panicked responses from drivers, which remains their ultimate goal. If someone gets out and chases them again, they have their getaway route all set. Last time, when the guy with the mustache popped out after them, they took the long way around the fenced-in baseball field in Shore Parkway Park. It gave the guy time to catch them as they hit the bike path. Now they know where there's a hole in the fence, and – since no one's playing on the field – it'll be easy to cut through and come out one of the dugouts. A shortcut that will make for a smooth escape up the bike path. Right around Seventeenth Avenue, Bobby knows, a pedestrian bridge crosses the Belt and goes to Bath Beach Park. From there, they can scurry home via the streets, lost in the maze of blocks, of cars and buses and people with shopping carts and boomboxes, kids on stoops, of trees and cracked sidewalks and telephone wires.

'You know what'd be hilarious?' Bobby says. 'Get one in an open window. Hit a driver. Thousand points for that.'

'First one who hits a driver gets to be king for a day.'

'Fuck you mean?'

'I mean I hit a driver, I get to tell you what to do for the day. "Bobby, steal me a tall boy from Augie's." Or: "Steal me three porno mags."'

'You're on. When I win, what I'm gonna make you do is go into that new Chinese restaurant over by Bay Thirty-Fourth and eat an egg roll or something off somebody's plate. Just walk up to their table, snag some food, and eat it right in front of them.'

'You're king for a day, all powerful, that's what you're gonna make me do?'

'Hell yeah. That and then I'm gonna make you bring me a pillowcase full of Giovanna's bras and underwear. I'm gonna sniff those shits until Mrs Santillo farts again.'

Zeke holds up a rock. 'Next one's coming right between your eyes.'

Bobby takes a defensive position, grinning wide. 'What? I love Giovanna. Sue me. You know what I picture? When she pops a squat on the toilet, instead of normal everyday logs, I bet she squeezes out perfect, cold Italian ices. Chocolate, lemon, watermelon, whatever you want. Do me a favor. Look in the bowl one day. Bet I'm right.'

Zeke takes a playful swing at Bobby. 'You wish. I been in the can after her. She lights it up, son. A three match operation. I'm like, "G, what'd you eat?" She's pretty, but she makes a good stink.'

'Not my Giovanna.'

'You're a dumb motherfucker. Ain't a single gorgeous girl who don't drop treacherous deuces.'

More wild laughter. They ready their next round of ammunition. Bobby has his almost perfect rock. Zeke has a good one too, not quite as round and smooth but it has some nice heft to it. Both rocks could probably do the work of a hardball or worse. Bobby's thinking about some guy behind the wheel taking his perfect pitch right in the arm or chest and getting surprise-winded. Like a batter crowding the plate, clobbered by a fastball. Goofy look on the dummy's face. The pain of a fool who couldn't get out of the way. Bobby could've been a starting pitcher on his Little League team if he still played. He'd given it up in sixth grade. He didn't like practice. Girls and after-school fights and scoring beer and cigarettes were way more important. Anyhow, the St. Mary's team sucked donkey dicks. Stupid powder-blue uniforms. Like the goddamn Kansas City Royals. Who wants a uniform like the Royals? Bobby had enjoyed playing from second grade to fifth grade, had been a good second baseman and hitter, but he really wanted to pitch. The coach, Gene Grady, who gave out communion on Saturdays at church, had two sons, Jeff and Matt, who he let pitch all the time. They were okay. Bobby's dream was to get on the mound, a little Vaseline on the brim of his cap, and really start mowing down batters with his good greasy junk. *Fuck baseball*, Bobby thinks now. *Throwing rocks at cars is more fun.*

A shambolic little cherry-red Toyota Corolla gets off at the exit. It's going slow, like the engine's struggling, coughing and burping along. Bobby notices it first and nudges Zeke. The windows on the car are open. The driver's a woman. A girl really. Probably a high school senior or something. She's smoking a cigarette and singing along to whatever's on the radio, stealing glances at herself in the rearview mirror.

As the Corolla rattles toward the changing light at the corner, Bobby and Zeke work in perfect synchronization, taking aim at the open passenger window and throwing the rocks as hard as they can.

What happens next is a blur. One of their throws is perfect. The other sails wide. But the rock that goes into the car doesn't hit the girl on the arm or chest. It smashes into the side of her head. Her body jolts, the cigarette knocked from her hand, and she loses control of the wheel as she barrels toward the yellow light.

Bobby and Zeke don't hesitate. They drop the other rocks, turn around, and run toward the bike path, cutting through the baseball field.

They don't look back. Bobby's not worried that someone's chasing them so much as he's worried that something beyond terrible has happened.

It was a joke, that's it.

For kicks.

They're running at full speed up the path, weaving in and out of the few distracted pedestrians in their way, being passed on the left by asshole bikers once or twice. It's hotter than ever. Sweat stings Bobby's eyes. The bay smells pungent. Salt. Seaweed. Deep darkness.

When they get to the overpass, they cut across into Bath Beach Park and stop to catch their breath and hit up a water fountain.

'Did you see what happened after it hit her?' Zeke asks.

'No, I just bolted immediately,' Bobby says.

'Me too. Anyone see *us*?'

'I don't know.'

'Fuck,' Zeke says. 'Was it the one I threw or the one you threw?'

Bobby puts his head in his hands. The girl's maybe three or four years older than them, tops. Nobody they had it out for. Not someone who was cruel or unkind even. A stranger. Smoking. Singing in her car. A normal afternoon for her. Nothing special. Getting off at her exit and probably going home, wherever home was. Then they came along with their big fucking stupid game. That's all it was. A game. He swears.

'I don't know,' Bobby says to Zeke, unable to stop seeing the girl. 'I don't know anything.'

Jack

Jack Cornacchia grew up in this house on Bay Thirty-Eighth Street, and he knows he'll die here one day. He's sitting on the ramshackle front porch with a can of cold beer. It's early afternoon. He's off work today. He's a customer field representative for Con Ed, goes around knocking on doors, led down to basements and cellars to read gas and electric meters. He never really got what the difference between a basement and a cellar is. Some people say one, some the other. He says basement mostly. He guesses there's a distinction, but he doesn't know or care to look it up. He could. He has a dictionary around. He likes not knowing. Either way, his job allows him to see the private lives of people, to see them in all their loneliness. It's very personal.

His father was a mechanic. His mother worked at Woolworth's before he was born and then stopped to raise him. He was their only child. They bought this house the year they were married for ten grand, a lot of money then. It's a two-story house with a sloping roof, four bedrooms, a wide front porch, and a pine tree out front they brought back from their honeymoon upstate. Jack went to St. Mary Mother of Jesus on Eighty-Fourth Street for grade school. Next door to the school is the church, where he was baptized and confirmed and attended mass every Saturday night with his parents until he was sixteen and made up his mind that mass was no longer for him. He believed and still believes in God but in his own way. High school was Our Lady of the Narrows on Shore Road in Bay Ridge. All boys. He hated it. He didn't go to college. For a while he bounced around from shit job to shit job. Considered taking the civil service test.

Thought about maybe being a postal worker. Finally, his father scored him the job with Con Ed through a guy he knew from the garage, Connected Benny.

At twenty-one, Jack met Janey at a coffee shop on Avenue U. He'd dated a few girls. Nothing too serious. He'd broken his cherry unceremoniously at seventeen in the back of a borrowed car with Mary Concetta Stallone. He'd dated Dyana Petrillo for a few months – that was the most serious things had ever been up to that point. He learned the ropes in the sack with her. She was a good teacher. Gentle with him. Experienced. Of course, that experience wrecked him. He got jealous and called her a puttana, and it was over. He learned how not to be with girls from that. He learned to leave the past in the past. With Janey, things were different right away. He was cool and collected. It was love at first sight. That brown hair. Those soft brown eyes. She looked like a saint mixed with a movie star. She hadn't had any serious boyfriends because her family was religious as hell, so there was not much of a past to excavate out of envy. For a Catholic boy, she was the dream. They got married six months after meeting, against the wishes of her parents. His folks were overjoyed. Jack and Janey moved in with them. Amelia was born the next year, in March 1978. They were so happy. Janey was a perfect mother. Mom and Dad became Nonna and Nonno. Amelia was their sweet girl. A decade passed. Things were better than he'd ever thought they could be.

Then the bottom fell out. Little by little at first. His mother tripped on the way home from shopping at one of the fruit stalls on Eighty-Sixth Street. Her trusty old cart slipped out of her grasp and she toppled hard to the sidewalk, busting her hip. He looks back and thinks of that as the inciting event, the moment when things started going sideways. While she was in the hospital getting better, his old man developed a bad hacking cough that quickly turned into something worse. When he finally went to the doctor, the diagnosis was pneumonia. They were both laid up for a while, incapacitated, but they got better. Then Janey got sick. Cancer. She battled for three years and lost. She was so frail at the end. Thank God his parents were there to help with Amelia, to give her some sense of normalcy. They took her to shows in the city, made birthdays and Christmases special. Janey's parents had remained out of the picture, and they didn't return – not even after Jack called to let them know how bad it was – to make amends with their only daughter. Jack knew Janey was a goner before she was gone. It was just a feeling he had. Things had turned rotten. Everything had gone too good for too long. It was bound to break down.

Janey died on September 13, 1992. Days didn't get much worse than that. Amelia lost her happy glow. Her school suggested therapy. They clung to each other. They depended on his parents for everything. He and Amelia wouldn't have made it out of that time alive if not for Nonna and Nonno, Mom and Dad to him, lifesavers, life-givers. The next two years were tough. A whir of sad days. Amelia started high school at Fontbonne Hall Academy in Bay Ridge, where Janey had wanted her to go. Jack worked his routes. His parents started going to Atlantic City one day a week for a break. They loved it. They were comped meals. They went and came back on the same day via a bus on Bay Parkway. They never stayed over, even though they probably could've been comped rooms too. The Golden Nugget was their joint. Mom liked slots. Dad preferred blackjack. On one of their return trips, his mother took a spill getting off the bus and broke her other hip. They rushed her to the hospital, and she died in surgery. His father died of heartache three months later. They were both buried at a cemetery on Long Island they'd never visited – his father had scored a good deal on graves there many years before. The cemetery wasn't far without traffic, but it was rare not to hit traffic going to the Island and the hassle of getting there kept him and Amelia from frequent visits.

When his folks died, the world really started feeling like a cruel joke to Jack. That decade of good days had merely been a preamble to this decade of death and destruction. He and Amelia struggled on. They clung to each other even harder. The house was empty and sad. It took Jack months to deal with everything he needed to deal with. His father had put Jack's name on the deed to the house, thank Christ, but he needed to update it to include Amelia. He knew he needed a will and a health-care proxy. He had everything his parents had left behind to go through – bank accounts, safe-deposit boxes, insurance policies, crates of stuff. He had to transfer all the bills to his name.

The house is run-down these days. Needs a new roof. The railing on the porch is rotting. The front steps need to be redone. Rogue squirrels have busted two windows in the attic. The oil tank in the basement is fifty years old, and Jack's always worried it's going to blow up. The linoleum in the kitchen is cracked and peeling from the edges. The bathroom sink makes loud clanging noises. The upstairs and downstairs showers have good water pressure, but the grout is full of mold and the drains are clogged. There's a spot on the floor in the upstairs bathroom where water is somehow leaking through and bubbling the ceiling in the dining room below. The ceiling in the bedroom's in rough shape too.

Amelia's eighteen now. She just graduated from Fontbonne. It hadn't been cheap. She's going to Fordham in the fall. She wants to be a writer. She took a creative writing class her senior year and loved it. She's been getting guidebooks, trying her hand at stories and even starting work on a novel. High school is tough under any circumstances – figuring out who she is, who she might want to be – but add tragedy to the mix and it was a million times more brutal. Amelia has had enough tragedy to last her a lifetime. Jack hopes more than anything that she can have a peaceful and happy existence from here on out. He'll do everything he can to keep trouble from her door, and he hopes she's smart enough to steer clear of trouble. She is. She's a bright kid. Good head on her shoulders. He's only forty, but he hopes he lives to see her marry someone nice and have a kid or couple of kids, write that novel, do all the things she dreams of doing. She keeps a map of the world on her wall, and she sticks pins into the places she wants to visit. Italy, Jamaica, Brazil, Hollywood. So many places she wants to see. He doesn't want to tell her she can't do it all, might not even do any of it. What's the point? Let her dream.

Jack hasn't been with anyone since Janey, hasn't dragged any girlfriends or stepmoms into the picture, but he does have a secret life. Something he can't tell his daughter about. Won't ever tell her about. It's given him some purpose – other than just being a dad – these past few years.

It started one day at the Wrong Number, the dive where he sometimes hangs out. He was drinking heavily right after Janey died. Starting early on his days off while Amelia was at school. His buddy Frankie Modica, who he'd gone to St. Mary's and Our Lady of the Narrows with, asked him to hurt the priest who'd molested his son. His son was ten. The priest was at Most Precious Blood. To no one's surprise, the diocese was protecting him. Word was that soon they'd move him to a parish in Western New York, Buffalo maybe, where no one knew of his crimes. His name was Father Pat. Frankie said he couldn't do what he wanted to do, he didn't have the chops, but he knew Jack was tough. He could give him some money, not much in the end, maybe a grand.

'What are you asking me?' Jack said.

'To hurt him,' Frankie said. 'You don't have to kill him. Just hurt him. I want to see the guy pay. Right now all he's being is protected.'

Jack thought about it. He wasn't violent by nature but he was definitely capable of violence when necessary. He'd been in bar fights where honor was on the line. He thought about a bad guy like this Father Pat getting away with what he'd done. He was sick to his stomach over the fact that someone like that kept right on living in the world when Janey didn't get that chance, when she got ripped away. He'd learned that much was true in life. Bad people often lived easier and better than good people. They endured, while good people dropped like flies. He figured what the hell. He could pour his anger and sadness into it. He got the address where the priest was hiding.

Since time was a concern – they weren't sure when Father Pat was being moved – he went there the next night with a baseball bat, wearing a ski mask, and beat the bad priest within an inch of his life. He was surprised how easy it was. He went to this cold place in his head where it didn't even feel like he was doing what he was doing. He'd seen movies about detached hitmen and that's what he felt like. All business. In and out. He split when it was over, left Father Pat bleeding and moaning on the floor. The bastard hadn't even protested. He probably figured he had it coming to him.

Frankie said he was a saint. Jack wanted to refuse the money – he wanted to say he'd done it on principle – but he figured he could put it away for Amelia's future. Start the college fund he'd always meant to start. Make sure he'd set her up in case something happened to him too. He put the cash in a safe-deposit box at his bank.

What he hadn't expected was that word would spread. People started coming to him with their problems, telling him about somebody who'd wronged them, stolen from them, hurt somebody close to them. There'd been fifteen jobs. The fifth one was when he started bringing a gun he bought out of Slim Helen's trunk on Avenue X. He keeps it wrapped in a cloth in the basement, tucked in a nook in the open ceiling over the oil burner, the bullets in a nearby cookie tin. On his seventh job he used the gun, killed a guy who'd raped a girl from the parish. He'd proceeded with the same cold detachment. It was a few months after his parents died, and he found it to be cathartic. The rapist didn't even look afraid. He seemed thankful. Jack was taking poison out of the world. Now he has enough in the bank to help Amelia make a good life for herself. Somewhere down the road, he figures he'll stop. What if Amelia gets married and has a kid and he has to hold that kid, be a grandpa, and know in his heart that he's hurting and killing people on the side? Sure, they're bad people, but that's still a lot of blood on his hands. Plus, he's getting worried that Amelia's going to find out. There's a network of secrets that's been built and maintained, but it only goes so far. All it takes is one violation of trust, one person saying something to a cousin who can't shut up. He hopes Amelia doesn't find out, but he'll deal with it if she does. He'll lay out his case. He'll explain that he did it because he wants a better world for her.

Amelia comes onto the porch with a can of Diet Coke. She lives on Diet Coke. She hardly eats anymore. Melba toast, half a grapefruit, maybe a scrambled egg a couple of times a week. The girl who loved pasta fagioli and spedini and semolina bread and sfinge is gone. She eats like a bird, sucks down her canned diet sodas. She has a streak of pink in her brown hair. That's something they wouldn't let her do at Fontbonne. She's wearing a black T-shirt and jean shorts and her red Chucks. Eighteen. He's wondering, as he always does when he looks at her now, how it got here so fast, her being an adult. He blinks and she's a baby in his arms. That big heavenly smile. Those brown eyes that came right from her mother.

'What's up, kid?' Jack says. He likes their banter. He likes that she likes to banter with him. A lot of kids, they don't give their folks the time of day, but Amelia's always got time to shoot the shit.

She sits on the rickety chair across from him, setting her can on her leg, trying to balance it. He can see the ring of condensation it leaves on the denim.

'Not much,' she says.

'Lazy summer day,' he says.

'Yeppers.'

'You working on your schedule for the fall?'

'I'll get to it.'

'When's that orientation?'

'A couple of weeks, I think. I've gotta find the letter they sent.'

'Let me give you a piece of advice, okay? As your old man and as somebody who speaks from personal experience.'

'Here we go.'

'I'm serious. Be organized. That's it. That's my advice. Be organized. Start a folder. Have a drawer where you keep important stuff. Use that file box of Nonno's I gave you. Trust me. I learned the hard way how important it is.'

'Groundbreaking advice, Pop.'

'Okay, be a smartass. I'm trying to teach you what I've learned so you don't make the same mistakes I did.' He nudges her foot with his foot. 'You were up late again last night, huh?' He'd heard her pecking at the keys of his mother's old Royal typewriter. Digging that up in the basement had been one of the best days. The glow in her eyes. His mother had taken care of it. Kept it under a cover. Had a hefty backup stash of ribbons. Had brought it to the typewriter shop on Stillwell Avenue for maintenance. She'd always liked writing letters on it, his mother. It was massive, heavy as hell. When they got it set up on the desk in Amelia's room, she'd hugged him hard and then she'd run straight to Genovese for typewriter paper.

'The work's never done,' she says.

'How's the novel coming? You gonna let me read it?'

'Maybe when it's finished.'

'And you're still not gonna tell me what it's about?'

'Nope.'

'You know Ron Redden from the Wrong Number? He used to write. He says to me a couple of weeks ago he's got a million stories from the bar. All these drunks across the decades. Guys puking on the bar, pissing on the floor. This one guy – they called him Phil the Mustache – shitting on the pinball machine. I guess he thought it was the toilet. Then, he says, there's love affairs gone wrong. Fights. The time Sancho Stern stabbed Gene Carcaramo. The hit that happened there. The Brancaccios whacking Robbie Guttadoro. He says someday he's gonna put all these stories in a book. I says, "Ron, who wants that?" You want bar stories, you go to the bar. I wanna read about a guy shitting on a pinball machine? Give me James Clavell, Larry McMurtry, Stephen King. I need a story. Not scraps.'

Amelia finishes her Diet Coke, rattling the can over her open mouth for the last few drops and then holding it up, sunlight glinting off the silver. 'What would you do if I just crushed this can on my head right now?' she asks.

'I mean, I guess I'd be impressed,' he says.

They laugh together. There's nothing he likes more than hearing their laughter in harmony like this.

'So, what've you got planned today?' Jack asks.

'Picking up Miranda. She's got a doctor's appointment in Bay Ridge, and then we're gonna get coffee or something.' Amelia got her own car about six months ago. It cost two grand – he'd gotten them a good deal from the guys at Flash Auto. Amelia had paid about half with money she'd saved up from her part-time gig as a file clerk at a dermatologist's office in Dyker Heights. He covered the rest.

'You're a good friend.'

'What're you doing?'

'Just sitting around, taking it easy. Maybe I'll go to the Wrong Number for a drink later.' But that's not true. He has one of his side jobs lined up.

Amelia gets up, struts over, and gives him a kiss on the head. She takes her car keys out of her pocket. On her key chain, there's a thing of pepper spray he bought for her and a crimson Golden Nugget key chain from Nonno. 'See you later, Pop.'

'Love you,' he says.

'You too.' She takes her empty can and bounces down the front steps, dropping it in the garbage as she heads out the front gate to her car, parked up the block in front of Teddy and Sandra Dasaro's house.

The job he has is one he's on the fence about.

Mary Mucci, who Jack knows from West Fourth Street, got wind of the types of services he's been providing and asked him to do something about Max Berry in Bay Ridge. Max has been running what's turned out to be an elaborate Ponzi scheme, where 'investors' deposit money in return for high interest rates. Max is holding Mary's money hostage, and she's essentially been bankrupted by the venture. Money she intended to pass down to her kids and grandkids. Same thing's happening to a lot of other working-class folks across Southern Brooklyn. Max is preying on vulnerable people. In one way, he deserves what's coming to him – stealing from those who have very little to steal. In another way, Jack isn't sure he should go through with this. Max hasn't killed or raped anyone or molested a kid. He deserves jail time but not necessarily vigilante justice. Mary didn't specify what she wants him to do to Max, but Jack's thinking just a warning shot across the bow will do. Let him know this is real. Let him know he's ruining real lives. Show him the gun. Maybe jab him in the guts. A dead Max won't help Mary. He's a degenerate but maybe he just needs to be compelled to reconsider what he's been doing.

Jack goes inside and boils some water in a pot on the stove for coffee. He's got this way of making coffee that grosses Amelia out. He boils the water, adds a couple of tablespoons of grounds, some crushed eggshells that he keeps in a Ziploc bag in the fridge, and a pinch of salt. He stirs it all together and then strains it into his mug. It's how his grandmother taught him to make coffee. She was a good lady. Tall for a grandmother. Strong hands. She died when he was seventeen, before Janey, before his life really got going. He thinks of her every time he makes coffee. He's never really decided how he feels about death, what he thinks the dead are doing with their time. He's always found it strange that people seem to predominantly believe that the dead are spending their time watching over the living. That notion always brings the image of a dead loved one perched in front of a bank of security TVs, watching live-feed footage of happenings on earth. Sure, check in now and again, he gets that, but he hopes being dead isn't all about lusting after living. He isn't comforted by thinking of Janey just constantly having to watch over him and Amelia. He'd rather think of her relaxing, no agony whatsoever, no worries, just peace as far as the eye can see, as loud as the ear can hear. He likes to think that she's just totally overwhelmed by the feeling of love and happiness that she felt at their best moments: their wedding at the Riviera; Amelia's birth at Victory Memorial; Amelia's first steps in this very kitchen. He likes to think that she's powered by that feeling in the afterlife.

It's dead quiet in the house. He shuts off the gas and lets his muddy mixture slow from a boil. Once it's cooled, he goes through the elaborate straining process over the sink. He tosses the shell-spotted grounds into the garbage and rinses the strainer.

He sits with his coffee at the table and watches the clock.

When he's done, he rinses his cup and puts it upside down on a folded dish towel on the counter next to the sink. He grabs his car keys from a hook by the kitchen door and goes down to the basement for his gun. It's a .38; that's what Slim Helen told him anyhow. He doesn't know anything about guns, doesn't have any room in his brain for that kind of information. It works when he needs to use it. He stuffs it in his waistline and heads out of the house, locking up.

His car is out on the street too. The house has a shared driveway but the neighbors have taken to blocking it, and he thinks it's a fight not worth fighting. Sometimes it's hell to find a spot, but it's easier than creating tension with the Yugoslavian family that moved in next door a few years back. He takes the gun out of his waistline and puts it in the glove compartment with his maps and retired air fresheners and receipts from Flash Auto.

Max Berry's office is in Bay Ridge. To get there, Jack takes Bath Avenue to Bay Parkway, makes a left, and then hops on the Belt Parkway right before Shore Parkway and Ceasar's Bay. It always bugs him that *Ceasar* is spelled that way, but it's not named for Julius Caesar, it's named for the fucking guy who started the bazaar in 1982, Ceasar Salama. Back then, it was a big flea market, but it's pretty much just become a strip mall.

The Belt thrums with traffic. Jack turns on WINS for news and weather. He changes it when a piece of bad news sets his mind in the wrong direction and puts on WCBS-FM for oldies instead. He grew up loving Jimi Hendrix and the Doors, stuff like that, but he has a soft spot for some of the oldies, especially Dion and the Belmonts, Elvis Presley, and all the girl groups. The Shangri-Las and the Ronettes, they were something.

Things are stop-and-go all the way to the Verrazano. They open up after that, but he's only on the parkway for another few seconds before getting off at the exit for Fourth Avenue. His history with Bay Ridge is long, and coming here – though it's only a couple of neighborhoods over – always feels so far away. He went to high school at Our Lady of the Narrows on Shore Road. Amelia just graduated from Fontbonne Hall Academy, also on Shore Road. His father used to bring him to Hinsch's for egg creams. He had a job for a summer cleaning out a carpet warehouse on Colonial Road. He was born at Victory Memorial Hospital and so were Janey and Amelia. His first drink was at O'Sullivan's on Third Avenue. When he was in his late teens, he'd take long walks here from Gravesend, look into storefronts, dreaming up different lives for himself.

Max's office is on the corner of Fourth Avenue and Eighty-Fourth Street. St. Anselm Church is only a couple of blocks down, and Jack remembers going there in the mid-seventies for the wedding of a high school friend, Gary Colkin, who was a hell of a three-point shooter. Gary married a girl called Ruby. Jack wonders whatever happened to them. So many people have drifted through his life and now they're just floating faces in his mind. Gary used to do a killer Richard Nixon impression.

It's hard to park on Eighty-Fourth Street, so Jack finds a spot near St. Anselm and walks back over to Max's office. Just as he's about to knock, he realizes that he left the gun in the glove compartment and goes back for it. He reaches around behind his back and tucks it into his waistline under his shirt on the sly, careful that no one is watching him. Last thing he needs is some priest spying on him from a secret window and calling the cops. He goes back to Max's and knocks hard. A forceful knock meant to deliver a message: *This is not good news.*

Jack knows from Mary that Max also went to Our Lady of the Narrows, but he's only in his mid-thirties, so he must've started right after Jack graduated. He's never seen Max in person that he knows of, and he'd never heard of him until Mary. She showed him a newspaper clipping from some Republican fundraiser where Max was holding a plate full of pigs in a blanket while chatting up some white-haired Jack Kemp wannabe. The black-and-white image was fuzzed out, but Jack got his general vibe: slovenly conservative money guy. It amazes him that Max is able to operate so openly, running what's clearly a Ponzi scheme and just getting away with it, that people keep it on the hush-hush because they really believe they're going to get rich. Jack wonders who Max is paying off or if someone's bankrolling the operation. The mob maybe. There has to be more to the story.

Max opens up. He's tall and goofy and pale, wearing a yellow short-sleeved dress shirt with a pocket protector stuffed full of pens. The buttons on the shirt aren't buttoned properly – somewhere he missed a hole. He has deep, dark, summer pit stains blooming under his arms. His shirt isn't tucked into his knockoff Dockers pants. His shoes are flimsy, the laces undone. His glasses have cheap rectangle frames. He has a little red carton of whole milk in his hand, the kind kids get at school for lunch. He's been drinking it. There's a white ring on his upper lip. His hair is poofy, uncombed, dotted with dandruff. This does not look like a rich man, does not even look like a man who's doing particularly well. If he's stealing from people like Mary Mucci, he must be funneling the money out elsewhere. Either that or he's sitting on it. Could just be about the game. That's one form greed takes.

'Can I help you?' Max asks.

'We need to talk,' Jack says. 'Let me in.'

'Who are you?'

'Mary Mucci sent me.'

'Oh, come on, sir. I told Mary ninety-five times that I'll have her money soon. The wheels are in motion. She thinks I don't want to get her dough to her? What's that do to my reputation? I have many clients. Everyone's in the same boat right now. They think I'm a cash machine, but it's a complicated system I've got going.'

'Let's talk inside.'

'Right here's okay with me.' Max takes a swig of milk.

Jack muscles past Max into the office. It's a real dive. Stacks and stacks of file folders on top of old filing cabinets trimmed with rust. A desk with a computer and phone that's otherwise covered in bills, statements, and manuals. Instead of some fancy ergonomic office chair, there's a folding chair, the kind they have in church basements. A wastepaper basket full of empty little milk cartons is right next to the desk. The carpet is thin, worn through to the wood below in several spots. Dust speckles the air, caught in the shafts of light coming through the broken blinds on the window. There's no art on the walls. Just framed certificates. A boxy black safe, about the size of a small dorm fridge, sits in the corner on top of a sagging table. Towers of CDs line the walls. The office smells like a bachelor pad, vaguely moldy and rotten. It's only one room in what's ostensibly a much bigger space. As far as Jack can tell, Max owns the whole corner building. A battered door – a pin up calendar from the seventies hung crookedly at its center, around eye level – must lead to the next room, but it's closed.

'You own the whole building, huh?' Jack says.

'Yes.' Max stays on the threshold of the front door, clutching his milk with nervous force, looking like he's thinking seriously about skittering outside for help.

'What's in the rest of the place?'

'Not that I need to give you an answer, but it's storage. Mostly CDs. I run a CDs-through-the-mail business on the side. Like BMG. You want some CDs? I can hook you up.'

Jack looks around, examining some of the certificates on the wall. Max's degree from St. John's. An accounting license. A notary public certification.

'What can I call you?' Max asks, taking in Jack's work boots, jeans, and his old Brooklyn Battlers softball shirt with blue sleeves that he wore for six seasons back in his mid-twenties when playing on hot concrete in a beer league was a fun thing to do on weekends. The shirt's tight now. 'You don't dress for summer. How about Mr Blue Sleeves? That's what I'll call you, okay?'

'Shut the door and come take a seat.'

'I don't play rough games, Mr Blue Sleeves. You give me a sec, I'll call my friend Charlie French and get him over here. He likes rough games.'

Jack vaguely remembers the name Charlie French from the papers. A regular Bay Ridge shitbird. A nobody who'd built up some kind of air of importance around him. He'd inherited a bunch of dough from his wife; there was speculation he murdered her. Figures that Max is pals with him.

Max continues: 'Charlie's headed down to Florida in a few weeks. Business venture. But he's still around right now, and he'd love to meet you, I'm sure.'

'All that money you steal from single working moms and little old ladies, does it go to Charlie? Or you in bed with the Brancaccios?' Jack motions around the office. 'Because you obviously aren't spending it here. Or on fine clothes.'

'I'm an honest guy,' Max says.

'Shut the door. I just want to talk.'

Max huffs and finally closes the door. He storms over to his desk, dropping his milk container in the wastepaper basket, and sitting dramatically on the rinky-dink folding chair. He puts his elbows up on the edge of the desk, touching the dusty keyboard for his computer. His glasses fogged from all the exertion. 'Okay, talk,' he says. 'I'll give you five minutes.'

'You'll give me however long I want,' Jack says.

Max clasps his hands together and sighs. He looks like an exhausted principal of a decaying middle school sitting there like that. 'Fine.'

Jack reaches around for the gun. He pulls it and shows it to Max. 'It's not much, but it'll get the job done.'

'You're threatening my life in my own office?' Max says.

'I'm telling you you're gonna get Mary her money. I know you've probably fucked over hundreds of people, maybe thousands, but Mary's my concern right now.'

'That's not the way this operation works.'

'I know how Ponzi schemes work, and you're gonna take the hit if you have to. Personally, I mean. You can take that money out of your own pocket. You can borrow it from your folks or some other relative. I don't give a shit.'

'You don't understand.'

'I guess I don't. All that dough, where's it go? It's numbers on paper for you, but where's the physical money?'

Max sighs again. He takes off his glasses and rubs his eyes. 'I've got people I've gotta give it to,' he says.

'So, you're a front for something?'

'I'm not a front. I started this as a legit thing. Look at me, I'm not making out. It just got out of control.'

Jack's starting to understand. Max got in trouble – not unlike the trouble he's in right now – and he asked the wrong people for help. Now he's permanently in bed with them. That's Jack's guess anyway. He doesn't need the whole story.

'Look,' Jack says, 'you're a guy – a smart guy – who's done some dumb shit. Maybe it was out of greed. Maybe you honestly thought you could make it work. Whatever the case, you got in over your head, and it's collapsing all around you. I know you're not the lowest of the low because I've seen the lowest of the low. You don't deserve to die like a dog, but that's how you're gonna wind up. I'm not saying me. I'm saying somebody. I'm sure there are plenty of somebodies out there fed up with you.'

Max is on the verge of tears. 'Are you gonna hurt me? Please don't hurt me, okay? I live with my parents. I'm all they've got. I've got to give my mom her medicine tonight. High blood pressure. I bring my old man a Twinkie one special night a week too. Tonight's Twinkie Night. If I don't bring it, what's he gonna do?'

'"Twinkie Night," huh?'

'Right.' Max lets loose and starts bawling.

'Stop crying,' Jack says.

But Max keeps right on. He's like an Italian grandmother at a funeral, the kind who throws herself on the casket, who revels in making a scene. Here he is, this weasely, milk-drinking Irishman going for the goddamn Academy Award. He has snot hanging from his nose, his lips flecked with spit. 'My work's everything,' Max says.

Jack walks toward him, turning the gun over in his hand.

He's not going to shoot the guy, but he's got to at least give him a little something to let him know he's serious. If he just lets him off the hook, what's Max take away from this? Crying gets him everywhere, that's what.

Max backs up in his chair, or he tries to anyway. It's proving tough to move in reverse on the cheapo folding chair, its legs sunk in the carpet. 'Come on, Mr Blue Sleeves,' Max says.

Just as Max is about to say more, to plead for a reprieve, Jack clocks him in the face with the butt of the gun. He makes good contact, smashing him right in the nose. Max lets out a whine. His left hand goes to his face instinctively, like a kid in school sitting at his desk and tending to an unexpected bloody nose. There's blood everywhere, dripping from his chin onto his yellow shirt and into his pocket protector, splattered across the bills and statements and manuals on his desk. Jack can also see that he's busted Max's glasses. He must've caught him on the bridge. One lens has popped out, and the other is cracked. The whining continues.

'You're gonna straighten things out with Mary, right?' Jack says, backing away.

With his free hand, Max reaches for the handle of a desk drawer just to the right of him and thrusts it open.

At first, Jack figures he's going for tissues, but then it occurs to him that Max might have a piece stashed there. Jack flips the gun around in his hand.

Max does come out holding a piece. It's not much, but it's enough. One of those little jobs. Kind of a purse gun. Max aims it at Jack, though he's clearly having a hard time seeing through his broken glasses, his other hand covering half his face, the blood flowing. His hand is shaky, the gun panning from Jack to the window to the wall and back again. Jack wonders if Max has even held the thing before, let alone fired it. 'You think you can just walk in here and threaten me?' Max says, his tone gone from desperate to angry.

'Take it easy,' Jack says. He steps slowly toward Max, the gun out in front of him. 'Put the gun down.'

'You put yours down.'

Jack moves in quickly. With his free hand, he wrestles the little gun from Max. He steps away, looks at the piece, and checks to see if it's loaded. It's not. He tosses it on the desk. It lands with a light thunk like a plastic cowboy gun from a dollar store. 'Now you're really on my bad side here,' Jack says.

'I'm sorry,' Max says. 'I'm so stupid.'

'Fix things for Mary,' Jack says. He reaches around and tucks the gun under his shirt and then heads out of the office, leaving Max bleeding at his desk. He hears more elaborate moaning from inside as he turns the corner. He pictures Max wadding some of the bills up against his face. He looks across the street at a woman with a shopping cart collecting bottles from a garbage can. It feels especially bright out after being in that dingy office.

Back at his car, Jack opens the door and settles behind the wheel. The oldies station is playing Dion's '(I Was) Born to Cry.' He puts his gun back in the glove compartment and sits there listening. Turning the music up until it rattles the windows. He likes the Johnny Thunders cover of this too. Somewhere he has that record. Johnny Thunders and Patti Palladin, *Copy Cats*. Probably up in the attic. He must've bought it at Zig Zag Records. He's always gone there if there was some new Lou Reed or Johnny Thunders to get. That stopped when Janey got sick. Music seemed so much less important. He's getting back to feeling some comfort from it now, able to sit here and listen.

When the song's over and WCBS goes to commercial, he drives away up the block. A couple of lefts and he's back on Fourth Avenue and soon enough he's cruising on the Belt Parkway, headed home, windows down. He's not sure what he's going to do. Maybe go to the Wrong Number for a beer. Maybe go up to the attic and dig through some of his old records. He wonders if the turntable even works anymore – it's buried under a big cloth in the basement. Probably needs a new needle at least. There might be a few on his old man's workbench. For a brief spell in the seventies, he repaired turntables on the side. At some point tomorrow, Jack guesses, he'll pay Mary Mucci a visit and tell her Max is going to make good.

Music's back on now. Bill Withers, 'Lean on Me.' One of those songs that – no matter how many times he hears it – doesn't lose any of its luster. If anything, it gets better and better. It means more to him now than it could have ever meant to him back when he first heard it.

Sailing along turns into light congestion and then that, suddenly, becomes dead-stop traffic. He regrets not taking the streets. He's stuck now between the Fourteenth Avenue exit and the Bay Parkway exit – probably less than a mile, but it could take forever. He could get out of his car and walk home faster. Those are the goddamn breaks.

He lowers the radio and tries to see what's going on up ahead. It's not rush hour yet, so it must be an accident.

A sudden burst of sirens tells him he's right. Probably some dope was doing ninety and flipped. A regular thing on the Belt. You get these cugines in their souped-up shitboxes, thinking they're on a racetrack, and that's what happens.

It takes a while, but he inches closer and closer to the Bay Parkway exit. He sees now that whatever's happened has happened at the off-ramp. The cops are diverting traffic into one tight little lane, forcing cars to make a left on Bay Parkway. They've blocked off the right lane to try to create some kind of order. One cop is out in the street, controlling traffic, looking frazzled. The accident itself is obscured by a fire truck and ambulance, but it's pretty clear that two cars crashed right under the traffic lights at the intersection of Bay Parkway and Shore Parkway. Probably whoever was getting off the exit tried to beat a yellow, blew through a red, and slammed into an oncoming car. Or something like that.

Jack blesses himself. A habit he picked up from his mother. Every time they drove past an accident, even if it was just a fender bender, she'd bless herself. 'Let's just pray everyone's okay,' she'd say.

As he gets closer yet, squeezed into the narrow left lane now, he gets a look between the fire truck and ambulance. He sees two cars, both totaled. It takes him a second, but he recognizes one as Amelia's car. It's upside down, half on the sidewalk in front of Wendy's.

His heart jumps into his throat. He throws the gear stick into park, the car jolting forward, undoes his belt, and hops out of the car. The guy behind him leans on his horn, screams out his window, 'Buddy, what the fuck you doing?'

Jack races over to the accident. A cop, who practically clotheslines him, stops him. 'That's my daughter's car,' Jack says.

More beeping from the guy stuck behind Jack's car. And then, suddenly, the whole line of cars behind that guy start beeping wildly. Burping and blaring horns. A steady stream of nightmarish wailing. So much terrible noise.

'You gotta move your car, chief,' the cop says over the din.

Jack pushes past him. A couple of firefighters are just getting Amelia out of the car.

'That's my daughter,' he says again, seemingly to no one.

The world buzzes hot, bright, and loud all around him. The firefighters put Amelia down on the blacktop. A couple of EMS workers take over. Jack falls to his knees next to them. Amelia's face is a mask of blood. He barely recognizes her. Her eyes are closed. Her body broken, bent unnaturally. That pink streak in her hair is something electric he hangs onto for a second. She's gone, he can tell. They're trying to coax her back to life, performing CPR, trying hard to get a spark, just a little spark. But she's gone, she's gone, she's gone. Jack's world stops.

JUNE 2001

PART 1

Charlie

Charlie French has Greg Brancaccio pinned down on his living room floor. Greg's the black sheep of the Brancaccio crew, a sketchy low-level punk. He's brought shame to his whole family. First, it was the junk. Then the massage parlor incident made headlines. Stacks really didn't like that. His youngest son tied up with Times Square hustlers and strippers. The *Daily News* and the *Post* had a field day: A SAD DAY FOR MOB BOY and JUNKY GREG'S TIMES SQUARE DEBACLE. Strangers shouted at him from open car widows: 'How's your boyfriend?'

Charlie has one hand on the kid's shoulder and one on his neck. Greg's maybe twenty-seven or twenty-eight but he looks like he's in his forties. Dark smudges under his eyes. A week or two of black scruff on his face. Eyebrows that are way too big for his little mousey face. Snot-welded hairs protruding from his nostrils like fucking stalactites. He's sweating hard. Dying for a fix.

His apartment's the kind of dump everyone who looks like him lives in. Barely any furniture. A wooden chair. A card table. Mattress on the floor. A boombox and some tapes. The kitchen's bare. Glowing red light leaks in from the neon sign above his second-floor window for the pork store downstairs. Charlie's not sure what people think about when they think about Bay Ridge, but a place like this probably doesn't come to mind.

'Where's what you owe me?' Charlie says.

'Next week,' Greg says, his voice strained. 'Just give me until next week.'

'Sure, yeah, let me wait like an idiot. I'm an idiot to you, huh?'

'You're not an idiot.'

Two grand's not a ton but it's enough, and if Charlie lets Greg slide, no matter whose son he is, word gets out to every shitheel in the neighborhood that he's gone soft before he's even really gotten going again in this racket. He never asks what the loan was for or where the money went. He probably shot it straight into his veins, the scumbag. Whatever. Charlie doesn't feel bad that Greg's old man cut him off and he needed to come knocking on his door. He's owed, that's that.

'Charlie, please,' Greg says. He says it like this: *Cholly, please.* Nails on a goddamn chalkboard.

Charlie plays through his options. One thing's for certain. Killing the kid wouldn't be smart. No matter how disgusted Stacks is with Greg, he's still blood. More than blood. A son. A lost son is still a son. A flop of a son is still a son. In fact, killing Greg might finally give Stacks some sort of purpose when it comes to his outcast youngest, allowing him to forget all the ways the kid had let him down and focus on revenge.

'What do you have?' Charlie says. 'You have something for me.'

'I don't, I swear. Next week.'

'I mean, something else.' Charlie lets go of Greg. He goes over to the boombox on the floor in the corner and sits down next to it. He picks up the stack of tapes and traces his finger over the spines. 'Poison, Warrant, Tesla, Ratt, Scorpions, Slaughter, Kix. This is the shit you like? You're washed-up, kid, huh? This stuff's been out of fashion for a decade.'

'It's what I liked growing up.' Greg sits up. He puts his hands around his neck, seems to confirm with himself that he's still breathing.

'That's sad. And you never made the switch to CDs? CDs are it. Tapes are for idiots.'

'Yeah, well, I like tapes. CDs are too futuristic. Tapes, they feel like they fit my world.'

'Your world? That's funny.' Charlie pauses. 'What else you got for me? In lieu of what I'm owed.'

'Like collateral?'

'Nah, not like that. Consider it a gift for my trouble.'

'I don't have anything, man.'

'Nothing? No junk squirreled away? No check your mother wrote you so you could make rent?' Charlie sets the tapes down and reaches under his shirt, taking out his piece, just so Greg can see it.

The punk doesn't blink. He's been around guns his whole life. Probably sat down to spaghetti more than once and clinked his fork against a hidden weapon. 'You're not gonna kill me,' Greg says, somehow sweating harder. It's like a movie trick. Sweat just gushing from his pores, his hair shower-wet. 'Sure, my old man hates me right now, but he'll still dump your ass in a vat of acid.'

Charlie smiles. 'I guess I'll take your tapes and your boombox. That'll have to do for now.'

'Aw, don't take my music, man. That's my only company right there.'

Charlie looks around. Scans the bare floor and the dirty walls. His eyes come back to the stack of tapes. He notices that one of the cases, Poison's *Flesh and Blood*, is missing an actual cassette. But there's something else in there. He puts the gun in his lap, reaches over, and grabs the tape case, knocking the others out of the way. He opens it. A red bowling pin key chain drops out, attached to a small brass key. In yellow curlicue script on the fob is the name of the bowling alley a few blocks away, Ridge Lanes. A blocky faded number six is printed under that, followed by the address and phone number for the dive joint. 'This is a key to a locker. What do you have stashed in there?'

'Nothing. I didn't even know that key was in there.'

'I look like about ten different kinds of asshole?'

'Shit, man.' Greg laces his fingers through his wet hair and lets out an exhausted breath. He looks like he's been gambling for twenty-four hours and he's got nothing left. He looks like he just got fired from a substitute teaching gig for being a degenerate. 'Man,' he says again, following the exhausted breath with an even more exhausted breath that becomes a flittering laugh.

'Where'd you learn to talk like that?'

'Like what?'

'Like some burnout hippie.'

'I mean, I am who I am, you know? I'm how I got made.'

'How you got made is stupid.'

'I don't know squat about that key.'

'Walk over to Ridge Lanes with me. Let's see what's in this locker.'

'I can't do that.'

'You're going to. Stand.' Charlie flips the Poison tape case onto the floor, the two halves shattering apart. He puts the locker key in his shirt pocket and grips the piece in his right hand. He gets up and watches as Greg makes a production of rising first to his knees and then to his full height, huffing and puffing the whole time. Greg's probably about five-five tops, a tiny bastard like his old man, six inches or so shorter than Charlie. Charlie remembers another *Post* headline about Greg: THE NAPOLEON OF BAD DECISIONS.

'You want me to go over to Ridge Lanes with you and open this locker?' Greg asks.

'I got, what?' Charlie says. 'Shit in my mouth? I'm speaking another language? Let's go. Now.'

Greg shakes his head and lets out one more dramatic sigh. 'This is a real spot you're putting me in here, man.'

'You don't even know about this key? It's a mystery to you? What kind of spot?'

They leave the apartment, walking down a long dark corridor full of smells from the pork store – sandwiches and sawdust and fried cutlets – and then down the stairs through a heavy black door stickered with ads for nearby car services. Charlie tucks the gun back under his shirt. On the sidewalk, a woman with a shopping cart is collecting soda cans from the trash. It's late afternoon, the light in the neighborhood gone pink and hazy.

They walk down Fourth Avenue, crossing over to the other side at Seventy-Sixth Street. Charlie half expects that Greg will bolt, but he doesn't. He continues to walk and sweat. They don't talk.

Ridge Lanes is on the corner of Fourth Avenue and Seventy-Fourth Street. The painted sign out front is decrepit. A bowling ball with two pins crossed over it on one side. The name of the place in the same curlicue script from the key chain in the middle. A small, sloppy panel depicting the view from the neighborhood's high ridge of New York Bay. Charlie read somewhere once that way back the neighborhood was called Yellow Hook before the yellow fever ruined that. He thinks that Yellow Hook Lanes would be a much better name for a bowling alley.

They go in. It's all sad sounds. Balls rolling. Pins clanging. Tinny music over bad house speakers. It's not crowded but it's not empty either. Three men standing around a high table with a pitcher of beer look up at them. They know Greg. They laugh. One of them pours beer into three plastic cups. It's late afternoon. The bowlers of the world are getting drunk.

Greg leads the way to a wall of blue lockers next to a small arcade full of ancient pinball machines.

'What are we gonna find in here?' Charlie asks. He takes the key out of his pocket and inserts it into the number six lock.

Greg is jittery.

Charlie turns the key and pulls open the locker door. A black duffel bag is crammed into the little space. He pulls it out and drops it to the floor. 'What's this, huh?'

'Man, it belongs to these guys in Jersey,' Greg says.

'Why do you have it?'

'It's just, like, a thing that happened.'

Charlie kneels and unzips the bag. He looks inside and smiles. Dough, lots of it. Banded stacks. Bricks of junk. A goddamn windfall if ever there was one. 'Jesus Christ, Greg. What is this?'

Greg thrusts his hands into his wet hair. 'Man, you know, we were gonna use it to get back into my old man's good graces. We knocked off these guys in Jersey.'

'What guys?' Charlie zips the bag closed and stands. He picks it up, putting his arm through the shoulder strap.

'Some fucking nobodies.'

'This belonged to some nobodies?'

'Yeah. You know the types. Rich kids. Me and Rainey did it. Nothing's ever been easier. I was gonna pay you what I owed you. I just had to figure some things out. You can't take it, man. It's my old man's now, okay? You take it, I'm fucked, Rainey's fucked, and you're fucked.'

'Your old man knows about it?' Charlie asks.

'Kind of.'

'How's he kind of know?'

'He doesn't know, okay? Not yet.'

'And these rich kids, tell me about them.'

'Their names are Don and Randy. We blackmailed them. Had this hard drive full of incriminating shit. Their fathers are big-shot politicians.' Greg pauses. 'Come on, man. Please. I'll give you a cut.'

'Who else you tell about this? Maybe your brother Vito?'

'I didn't tell nobody else. Just Rainey knows. Like I said, we were gonna use it to get back in my old man's good graces.'

'By stashing it in a bowling alley locker?'

'The wheels were in motion before you fucked everything up. I worked hard on this scheme. You can't just stroll in and commandeer everything. I still got a couple of people's ears, money or no.'

'I'm gonna hold on to this,' Charlie says.

'Please, man,' Greg says. 'I'm begging you. No. That's it. That's my life right there. Take what I owe you. Take double. Take triple. But leave the rest.'

Charlie's got the bag balanced on his back, the strap cutting into his shoulder. It's heavy. It's the best thing that's happened to him in a long time. It was the best thing that had happened to Greg in a long time too. He doesn't feel anything for the guy.

'Rainey's gonna be pissed,' Greg says.

'I'm not worried about Rainey,' Charlie says.

'Please, dude.'

Charlie reaches out with his free arm and pats Greg on the elbow. 'I knew something good would come of you.'

Greg sits down on the carpeted floor. The carpet looks like a million little golden mazes. He leans his back against the blue lockers.

The radio is playing a song that gets blasted at every wedding. Charlie can't place it. A song idiots line up and dance to.

Greg cries into his hands. The open locker above him, emptied of its treasure, must remind Greg what it's like to have nothing where he should have brains. He's crying and sweating. A bum if ever there was a bum. A place like this, it's full of losers. He's just another one. The worst of all.

'Come on,' Charlie says. 'Let's go.'

'Go where?' Greg asks.

'Back to your place.'

Greg gets up. They walk the few blocks back to his apartment. Greg's nervous in a different way now. He's muttering the whole time. Charlie's not sure what he's going to do, but he knows he needs to do something. If he leaves with the bag, there's no way Greg doesn't call Rainey and his brother Vito straightaway. Rainey's not much, but Vito's trouble. Greg keeps begging to split the dough. Fifty-fifty, he's saying now. He's shaking, like he needs a fix worse than ever.

Back in the apartment, Charlie tells Greg to relax. He tells him to go ahead and shoot up. Greg nods. He gets his stuff and sits on the floor. A baggie of dope, a spoon, a lighter, a needle, a tourniquet. He ties off his arm and cooks the junk on a spoon, holding a lighter under it with a shaky hand. He shoots up right there. Charlie watches his eyes roll back. Greg goes limp against the wall. He finally looks peaceful. Charlie wonders if it's junk from the stash he's shooting up. Probably. He bets it's top-notch. Whatever the deal is with these rich Jersey kids, they don't peddle in street-level shit.

Greg's off in junkland now. The needle is in his lap. Lighter and spoon on the floor next to his leg. Charlie has to deal with him. The Brancaccios won't know it was him. They're probably waiting for the call that tells them Greg has OD'd.

Charlie goes into the kitchen and looks under the sink. A spray bottle of multipurpose cleaner. A bucket with some brushes. Stiff sponges and overturned bottles of knockoff-brand dish soap. Behind all that, he finds a tray of rat poison. Blue rocks. He pinches up a few of the rocks and holds them in his palm. He goes over to where Greg is. He crouches next to him and picks up the spoon. Charlie shot up in the old days. He knows the steps. He places the poison on the spoon in a heap with a few drops of water, letting it dissolve, and then uses the lighter to cook it like he's cooking dope. When it's transformed into hot liquid, he grabs the needle and sucks it all up. The tourniquet is still on Greg's arm. He's dazed. Way out of it. Charlie lifts his arm by the elbow and he uses his free hand to find a clean injection site among the trail of track marks. He finds a spot. The vein's ready. He shoots the rat poison into Greg's blood.

Almost immediately, Greg convulses. Charlie takes the needle out and wipes it down. He wipes the spoon and the lighter down next. He wipes the cassette tapes down. He wipes down everything he remembers touching. Greg is dying, and Charlie's covering his tracks. When he's found eventually, it'll look like suicide. It'll look like Greg couldn't take being a junky fuckup anymore so he shot up poison. The cops won't spend much time hunting for clues.

Charlie knows he needs to take care of Rainey next. And then he needs to find these Jersey guys. He doesn't want them to come hunting for what Greg and Rainey stole.

Lily

Lily Murphy is standing outside the bodega on the corner of Eighty-Sixth Street and Twenty-Fourth Avenue, around the corner from St. Mary's church, where she's due in ten minutes. She's smoking a cigarette from the fresh pack of Parliament Lights she just bought inside. She had hastily taken off the cellophane and watched it blow away up the sidewalk. With her free hand, she's drumming her fingers against her thigh. She's nervous. She's stupid for doing this. It was a stupid fucking idea. If she could go back a couple of weeks and talk herself out of it, she absolutely would.

Two weeks ago, to the day, was her twenty-first birthday. She'd come back home to Brooklyn that morning – her mom wanted to throw her a party. She'd just graduated from York College of Pennsylvania in May. Her lease in York had run out, and she was crashing on a friend's couch. A townie named Christine. They were getting wasted a lot. Most of her friends who'd graduated had moved on, gone back to their hometowns for summer jobs or started jobs elsewhere or, worst of all, had gone off to get married and start families. Lily was floating. The truth was she would've preferred to stay in York for her birthday, see some live music and get drunk with Christine, but her mom had begged her to come home. What her mom probably hadn't realized was that she was *coming home* coming home. That is, she was putting the little she'd accumulated in her four years at York in her dumpy car and coming back to Brooklyn indefinitely. She and her mom never talk things through. It's a problem.

Her mom split up with her former stepfather, Danny, three

years ago. Lily was glad she no longer had to return from college to share a space with her squirt of a stepbrother, Bobby. Bobby and Danny are still around, living in the same apartment where they'd all lived previously. Her mom was distressed when Lily arrived and said she was coming home to live because her mom had a new apartment and new boyfriend but also because she was worried that Lily had no prospects. Being back in Brooklyn was, at least, better for work possibilities, Lily argued. Maybe she could get something in the city, temp or otherwise. What was her mother going to do, turn her away?

Lily moved in. There was a room for her. All her childhood stuff from the old place boxed up and ready to be unpacked. A new single mattress on a cheap, ancient frame. A small window overlooking the alley next to the three-family house on Eighty-First Street where the apartment was, only a couple of blocks from their old place with Danny and Bobby. She sold her car for three hundred bucks.

The problem is that Lily doesn't want the kind of jobs her friends are getting. She's not interested in business or law or medicine or whatever. She was an English major, and she wants to be a writer. *Is* a writer. She knows she can get a job waiting tables, but she'd done that at a pub in York, McMartin's, and she'd been a pretty terrible server, the kind that people tipped a lot because they pitied her. What she wanted and wants is time to work on the novel she's writing.

Nor does Lily want to find a partner and settle down. She had a bad breakup with a college boyfriend, Micah, and she's had no real interest in dating seriously since. They'd gone together for over a year, spanning the spring semester of sophomore year to the summer after junior year. The first two months were okay, but then he slowly revealed himself to be a psycho. After they broke up he dropped out of college and moved back to Westchester County to take a job in his father's landscaping business. He called her a lot for a few months and then quit. She thought it was over. As soon as she came back to Brooklyn, though, he started calling again. Fifteen, twenty times a day on her mom's new line. She's not even sure how he got the number. Her mom keeps insisting that all Lily has to do is tell him to back off, insinuating that she's been wishy-washy or even leading him on. She feels like she's been clear, but Micah keeps right on bugging her. Lily's uneasiness about him is clawing at her subconscious constantly. He was never violent, but he came close a few times, and she knows that boys like him often cross the line.

The birthday party – which was just Lily; her mom; her mom's new boyfriend, Dave; Father Andy from church; the Santangelos; her high school friend, Martha; and the Pentavecchias – had turned into a brainstorming session. *What could an aspiring writer, just out of college, do for work in Southern Brooklyn?* That was the question on the table. And, oh, all these motherfuckers took such pleasure in her situation, how lost she was. There were the ones, like Gianluca Santangelo, who aimed to convince her that a good old-fashioned city job couldn't be beat. He worked for the EPA. 'I just hang out half the time,' he said. Laura Pentavecchia suggested getting part-time work at Flash Auto – they were looking for a new secretary. Her mother and Dave said they had an in at some urologist's office in Dyker Heights, where she could easily get a gig answering phones and shelving charts. None of that was for Lily.

Her mom said, 'That's all well and good, but you need to do something to make money. You can't just loaf around.'

It was then, after four ice-cold Miller Lites, that Lily pitched an out-of-the-blue idea to Father Andy. She explained that she got really into creative writing in college and took every creative writing class there was to take. She'd written dozens of stories. Even won a prestigious contest for one. The award was publication in a magazine called *Spiral*, a thousand bucks, and a phone meeting with a literary agent. The agent told her to start working on a novel and get back to him. She'd done that, but she was struggling. Novels are tough, she explained. Her idea – an attempt to make a little cash and do something that could pass as a proper job (since her mother didn't consider writing a novel to be 'real work') – was a community writing class in the basement of the church once a week. She'd lead it. They could charge a hundred bucks a person for five weeks and split the haul. It wasn't a permanent fix, but it'd at least buy her some time. After all, summer break wasn't really summer break anymore. It was the beginning of the future. There was no school to go back to. She needed to figure out her life. The class would be a good distraction, sure, but it might open up some new avenues, too.

To her great surprise, Father Andy went for it. She was excited. She'd have one day a week where she could talk about writing and impart some of what she'd learned to an assortment of neighborhood chumps, if there were even people around interested in taking her class. She figured there would be. There wasn't much going on in the neighborhood, and people went nuts for things like this. She remembered when that community theater on Bath Avenue opened and she thought no one would go to auditions, that there'd be no actors or audience for their production of *Come Back, Little Sheba*. She'd been dead wrong. Suddenly, everybody wanted to be Burt Lancaster and Shirley Booth.

The day after her birthday party, Lily made up some flyers and posted them on the church bulletin board, and she wasn't surprised that she got several calls right away.

And so here she is. The first class starts in a few minutes, and she's hiding out by the corner bodega, shaky and smoking. She should've gotten there early. She should've introduced herself to everyone individually beforehand. She should've taken out her books and gotten everything in order. What business does she have teaching a class? Father Andy was stupid for agreeing to this.

'Fuck it,' she says. She butts the cherry of her cigarette out against the cement wall of the bodega, checks to make sure there are no more embers, and then pockets the filter. She doesn't want to be one of those millions of people who just flicks her cigarette butt down on the sidewalk, letting it become part of some great river of trash under everyone's feet, realizing that losing the cellophane the way she did pretty much cancels out her good intentions. She looks quickly at herself in the reflective glass of the bodega's window, seeing her shadow self in outline over the bright posters for beer and canned iced tea. She's wearing her favorite jeans, which she's had for four years, bought at a vintage clothing shop in York. They're light, stretchy denim, brandless, very seventies. The shirt she got new from her mother as a birthday gift. It's a plain white button-up from H&M, the kind of shirt she would've worn when she was waiting tables. On her feet are her scuffed, black Mary Janes. She's pulled her hair back in a ponytail. She's wearing makeup and lipstick at her mother's suggestion. She doesn't much like wearing either. She has a backpack hanging from one shoulder. She should've borrowed one of her mom's real bags. Something more grown up. A backpack makes her seem like such a kid. She takes a deep breath and then hustles around the corner to St. Mary's.

St. Mary's is where she's gone to church her whole life. Baptism, First Communion, Confirmation. Confessing her sins in a shadowy box that smelled of regret. When her father died they had his funeral mass there. She was nine and remembered the darkness of the day, the shocked looks on the faces of his friends, the cries that sounded like screams in the echoey space. She and her mother had gone to church there every Saturday night together, sometimes with Bobby and Danny in tow during the Remarriage Years, but it had stopped when she went away to York. In fact, she'd stopped altogether. She'd had the whole thing figured for bullshit by junior year of high school, but it took moving away for her to break free from feeling like she had to go. She's fallen back into attending now that she's home, out of a desire not to disappoint her mom in every possible way. As with most things, they don't have conversations about how they really feel.

The church is right next door to the school she went to from kindergarten to eighth grade. The front entrance is on Eighty-Fifth Street and the backside is on Eighty-Fourth. It's shaped like an upside-down funnel and has stained glass windows that are kind of druggy and strange. To get to the basement, she hustles through the parking lot wedged between the church and the school, and enters through the side door. It goes straight downstairs. She's been in the church for mass hundreds and hundreds of times, but she's only been in the basement twice. Once for some kind of 'Catholic singles' mixer that her mom dragged her along to after her dad died but before remarrying. The other time was eighth grade when she did a 'lock-in.' The lock-in consisted of everyone in her class staying up all night, listening to Father Paul and Father Greg and all the nuns from the school talk about Jesus. The goal was to make it through the whole night. They had board games and activities and music mixed in with the Jesus talk but most of that stuff was Jesus-related too. It was the first time she ever had coffee. She'd disappear to the bathroom with her Walkman for long stretches, listening to Madonna's *The Immaculate Collection*.

The door to the basement has been propped open, probably by Father Andy. That's a relief. It would've been awfully embarrassing if she had to bang on it until one of her 'students' opened up. She enters and rushes down the stairs, nearly tripping. The place smells like the frankincense priests burn in the thurible during a service. It's overwhelming at first, hitting her in the back of the throat.

The basement's main function is for AA meetings and as a place for church ladies to gather and play bingo, but it looks kind of like a school auditorium, except in the round. There's a small empty stage, some tables and folding chairs scattered about, and boxes full of Styrofoam plates and cups. It's a sad space.

Close to the stage, someone has arranged a bunch of chairs in a circle. Seven people are gathered there, none of them sitting. Instead, they surround a nearby urn of coffee, drinking nervously from Styrofoam cups. One of the people is Father Andy. Lily wasn't expecting him to be here. She hopes he doesn't intend on staying.

'Here she is,' Father Andy says, clapping his clammy little hands together.

'Sorry,' Lily says. 'I'm not late, am I? I forgot a book.'

'You're right on time,' he says. 'Everyone, this is Lily Murphy. She'll be teaching the class. She's a really wonderful writer. We're very proud of what she's accomplished. She won a prestigious literary prize just a few months ago. What's it called, Lily?'

'The Marsden-Bellwether Prize,' she says.

'Right. And she's working on a novel. We're very lucky she's doing this. Now, as much as I want to learn the ins and outs of making fiction, I'll leave you to it. I have some important matters to attend to back at the rectory.'

'Thanks, Father Andy.'

He smiles – a kind of doltish, phony smile – and walks out the way she came in, stopping once to remind her to shut the lights and yank the door shut when they're done.

Lily looks around at the others. A couple of nearly identical women in their fifties or sixties who seem like they're expecting this to be a bingo thing in disguise. A precocious high school–aged kid. A man in his seventies in a tracksuit who might very well be a retired mobster. A woman who's not that much older than Lily but has lived harder. And – finally – a guy in his forties with this heavy, serious vibe emanating from him. Lily raises her hand and gives them all a little wave.

'I like Danielle Steel,' one of the older women says. 'What a gift to entertain she has.'

Her near twin agrees enthusiastically and then says, 'I work in a podiatrist's office. I have so many stories, I could write a million books. Crazytown, that's what I call it there. This one's got a fungus, this one's got corns up the wazoo. You never met so many nuts in your whole life. Maybe you want to write the book?'

Lily feels sick to her stomach. 'Maybe we should, um, sit down and get started?' she says, turning it into more of a question than she meant to.

They do what she asked, sitting down on the folding chairs in the circle. Lily wishes that she had a desk in front of her. She feels exposed. She puts her backpack on the floor between her feet and riffles through it, coming out with a notebook and a pen. She's kicking herself for not photocopying a story by Alice Munro or Tobias Wolff or Alice Walker. That would've been nice to set the tone. Instead, she figures that they'll just do some introductions and a writing exercise, in preparation for their first workshop next week.

She feels sicker suddenly. She's a fraud. They can see right through her. She has absolutely no authority as a teacher, no right to do this. They're spending what little money they probably have on a joke. She might as well pick their pockets. 'I was thinking, if it's cool with you guys, that we'd just start by introducing ourselves to each other. I have your names here in my book, but I want to make sure I match names to faces. Maybe, when it's your turn, you can talk about your life and why and what you're interested in writing. That sound okay?'

A bunch of half-hearted nods.

She's feeling better. She thinks that what she just said sounded like something a teacher would say. Maybe she has the chops for this after all.

The Danielle Steel lady takes some initiative and starts the ball rolling. It makes Lily feel good that she didn't have to beg. 'I'm Jenny Cappello,' she says. 'I come to church every morning.

Father Andy's probably sick of me. I saw the flyer and I thought, "Oh, that's different." I like to read. I like to watch my soaps. There's almost nothing I like more than writing letters. I get my special paper and my nice pen, and I write long letters to my cousins, old friends, whoever. *Whomever.* My husband thinks I'm whacked out. He's a funeral director. He's too serious all the time. "Lighten up," I says to him. "It's not all death."'

'Thanks, Jenny,' Lily says, putting a neat little blue check next to her name in the notebook. 'It's nice to meet you.'

The other woman, Jenny's pal, the one who works in a podiatrist's office she's dubbed Crazytown, introduces herself as Shelley Simineri. She talks more about her job, about wanting to write down all the absolutely nutty stuff she sees on a daily basis. The doctor she works for thinks he's Jerry Lewis. He does these pratfalls and he has a flower he wears on his lab coat that squirts water. He's also a bad drunk with a mistress. Shelley says that if she were him, she'd have a mistress too because his wife's a real piece of work. Thinks she's a big shot, the wife. Comes strutting into the office with all her fancy jewelry on, wearing some expensive mink, ordering people around. 'Never have I ever wanted to hit somebody like I want to hit her,' Shelley says.

'Wow, okay,' Lily says. 'It's fun to get out your frustrations with work on the page. And your aggressions toward people who make you mad. It's healthy even.'

'Healthy I need,' Shelley says. 'What I don't need is some two-bit garbage man's daughter acting like she's the second coming of Princess Diana. I know her story. I know where she grew up. She's a nobody too.'

'Sounds like my ex-wife,' the old man in the tracksuit says, expecting laughter and getting none. The church basement is not conducive to laughter, apparently. 'I'm kidding. I'm Dino Loreti. I saw the ad, I thought, "Oh, I got stories to write." Stuff I seen on the streets. I did unsavory work for many years. Perturbing work, you might say. I saw bad things. I participated

right on the block. My whole
outside. I remember the old
old man used to take me to
way back. I got Brooklyn in my
ooklyn, I think, "Where they
my language.'

lds back. This Dino, he's one
ome kind. Probably low-level.
ns from him, the floodgates
been able to spill just breaking
She says it's nice to meet him
ries. She says she likes hearing
he knows that Thomas Wolfe
ooklyn.' She read that in her high
school ... ays stayed with her. He shakes
his head and says he never read it but it sounds wrong to him
because he knows Brooklyn inside and out.

'Nobody knows Brooklyn like me, believe it,' Dino says.

'I believe it,' Lily says.

The high school kid seems pretty shy and reserved. His name is Josh Rubin. He lives up the block too but on the other side of Twenty-Third Avenue. He doesn't come to church here, but he likes to write and he saw the flyer when he was cutting through the lot and he doesn't know anybody else who likes to write, so he figured he'd give it a shot. He says he's not Catholic, he hopes that's okay.

'Of course it is,' Lily says. 'This class is for anybody and everybody. I went to church here my whole childhood, but I lost my faith in college. So, I'm not Catholic anymore either.'

'I think that's terrible, losing your faith in college,' Jenny says.

'People find their own truths,' Lily says, and it sounds like some new-age horseshit, but she believes it. Besides, she doesn't want to get into any arguments about religion with these folks, especially on the first night. She's trying to squash it, let it be.

'I know God too,' Dino says. 'Like I know Brooklyn.'

'I like to write about Vikings,' Josh says, switching the conversation back to where it should be. 'Is that okay?'

'The Minnesota Vikings?' Dino asks, as if Josh had directed the comment solely at him.

'No. The, you know, invaders and settlers from Scandinavia. Way, way back. The eighth to eleventh centuries. I like historical fiction. Adventures. Epics.'

'I don't know about any of that stuff.'

'Of course it's okay to write about Vikings,' Lily says. 'You can write about whatever you want. I'm just here to help. I don't like writing classes where the teacher's like, "No serial killers. No first kisses. No this or that." Why put restrictions on it? Write about what excites you. Write about your obsessions.'

'I knew a serial killer,' Dino says. 'In the flesh. Staten Island guy. Bruno Borgia. Big monster of a guy. Lived in a tiny house with his mother. I used to go over there when I was running numbers. Bruno made big bets. He was also killing people and burying them in his cellar. He wasn't eating them or making time with the corpses or anything. He was just knocking them off and burying them. A regular burial-type situation. The whole cellar was graves. It was how he blew off steam. You look at him, okay, he's no normal guy right off the bat, but two-to-one you don't take him for a serial killer.'

'Wow,' Lily says.

'That's very disturbing,' Shelley says.

'I think I remember reading about that,' Jenny says. 'He dressed the bodies up in Santa outfits, right?'

'Yep, that's him,' Dino says. 'Maybe not so regular, after all. Where'd he get all these Santa outfits in all these different sizes? That's what I want to know. He collects them and then finds a body to fit each one?'

Lily tries to regain control. 'Okay, let's get back to intros.'

Next up is the guy with the heavy, serious vibe. He's been

quiet the whole time. When he called to sign up, Lily thought his name sounded familiar, but she can't remember from where. It's been bugging her. 'My name's Jack Cornacchia,' he says.

She looks at his name in her book and checks it off. She'd checked off Jenny but then she'd forgotten to check off the others, until Jack. She realizes why. Because he's not talking. He said his name and now he's just letting the silence sit there. 'Any ideas on what you want to write or why you want to write, Jack?' Lily asks him.

'I'm doing this for my daughter,' he says.

Again, Lily expects him to elaborate, but he just lets the silence hang.

'Okay, that's great,' she says.

The last student is the woman who's probably not much older than Lily, though she looks like she's been hitting the bottle or is living in the aftermath of a tragedy. Her name's Sarah Kwong. She explains that she's just had her heart busted. She's the new organist at St. Mary's. The guy she planned on marrying, he was running around behind her back and broke things off a couple of months before the wedding. She's angry and sad, she's been drinking a lot, she's put on ten pounds, and she thought that writing about it all might help. She used to like to write in college, which wasn't that long ago. She's still young, she says, but she feels so old.

'I get that,' Lily says. 'Writing about pain is so important. It's a great way of processing it. I had a bad relationship not too long ago, and writing was the only thing that got me through.'

'I'm just so angry,' Sarah says.

'Pour it all onto the page. Be honest about how you feel. Above all, people want honesty in whatever they're reading.' Lily takes a deep breath and lets it out. She's surprised that went as well as it did. There were a few moments where they went off track, and she didn't get much from that Jack guy, but it was pretty smooth otherwise.

Next, she's going to try to have them work on a writing exercise. It's an exercise that her favorite writing teacher, Emily Bielanko, used to make her classes do. Just two characters talking. No description, no action, just dialogue. About a page. She asks them to take out paper and a pen. Most of them have remembered to bring those things along, as she directed them to on the phone. The couple who didn't – Shelley and Dino – borrow some from Jenny and Jack. The hard thing is that there are no desks, so there's nothing to lean on as they write.

Josh gets up and finds a box of missals over in the far corner of the room. He brings a stack back and hands them out to everyone.

'Is it blasphemous to use these?' Jenny asks.

'I think it's fine,' Lily says.

They put the paper on the books and begin work. Josh, Shelley, Sarah, and Jack get right to it. Jenny and Dino seem to struggle, staring at the ceiling, making a big show of their effort. Lily is doing the exercise too. She's not going to get too much into her personal life with them, but what she's writing is a conversation between her and Micah. If anyone asks it's fiction, just her imagination, but she's obviously writing from a place of fear.

Why are you harassing me?

I like that you can't think about anyone but me.

I'm only thinking of you because I'm scared.

I like that.

What she's feeling is really there. Maybe it's too much. If she shares it with the group, she should probably tone it down.

After about ten minutes, they go around and each takes a turn reading.

Jenny is shaking as she reads dialogue between a man and woman meeting on top of the Empire State Building after a long time apart. It's *Love Affair*, *An Affair to Remember*, and *Sleepless in Seattle* rolled into one.

Shelley doesn't really read anything. Instead, she talks them through a conversation she had with a patient who'd lost his wife of fifty years and was now visiting prostitutes in Coney Island. It's actually pretty funny. She keeps doing the guy's voice. He's an old, half-deaf Jewish man who screams everything he says. 'If I want to be with a hooker, let me be with a hooker. I'm hurting who?'

In Dino's piece, two men are arguing over the price of something. It's not clear what exactly they're arguing about. One keeps saying, 'Things were cheaper with Clam Man in charge.'

Josh has imagined a conversation between two Vikings in the ninth century. Lily holds in a laugh, not because his writing is bad but because she's looking around at the faces of the others and they seem puzzled, especially Dino, Jenny, and Shelley.

When they get to Jack, he seems particularly uneasy about sharing what he's written, but then he starts reading and she's taken aback by the power of it. He's written a conversation between a father and a daughter. It's clear that the daughter is dead. The father is missing her. Jack fights tears as he reads. Lily finds herself crying. The other women are crying too. Even Dino is teary. Only Josh is unaffected.

Cornacchia. Jack's last name clicks into place for Lily. That was the last name of the girl who died in the horrible accident at the Bay Parkway off-ramp back in 1996. Lily had just turned sixteen at the time. It was the summer between her junior year and senior year at Bishop Kearney. She'd skipped a grade in elementary school, and she was feeling ahead of everyone. She was very serious about colleges. All of the colleges she was going to apply to were in Massachusetts and Pennsylvania, for some reason. She was going to go wherever she got the best scholarship. That wound up being York. She and her mom were still living with her stepdad and stepbrother at that point. Looking back, things were clearly falling apart between her mom and Danny then. Lily remembers reading the story about the accident in the papers, hearing everyone talk about it at school and after church and on shopping trips to Eighty-Sixth Street and at the summer camp where she worked part time in Sunset Park. They knew two kids throwing rocks at cars had caused it, but the cops never caught them. A rock had flown in through the open passenger window and hit the girl in the head, making her lose control and go careening into oncoming traffic. What was her name? She'd gone to Fontbonne, Bishop Kearney's main rival. She was a year or two older than Lily and had just graduated. Lily remembers seeing her yearbook photo in the *Daily News* and *Post*, tracing her finger over the stranger's face and thinking how it could've been her. Lily remembers how, selfishly, it had launched her into an existential crisis. Every bus she got on, every subway car she boarded, every time she got in her mother's Lumina or Martha's Jetta, she'd go into panic mode. *What if this is it? What if a rock comes crashing down on me next?*

Jack's dialogue exchange ends when the father tells the daughter that he wishes he could go back to that moment and change it somehow, how he wishes there were a way to peel back the layers of time and fix things. He says he knows there isn't and that's what kills him the most, the permanence of her absence. They deserved so much more time. She deserved it. She deserved a whole life.

Silence after he's done reading.

'Wow, Jack,' Lily says. 'That was really beautiful.'

He puts the missal down on the floor, folding the piece of paper he's written on and laying it on top of the book. He wipes his eyes with the heels of his hands. He's about to say something, maybe just a simple *thanks*, but then he stops himself.

'What is it?' Lily asks.

'I'm just, you know... I'm sorry. I don't mean to saddle a bunch of people I don't know with my grief.'

'Don't apologize.'

If the others know his story or recognize his name, they don't let on. People can live in the neighborhood, even on the same block, and not know each other at all. It always amazes Lily. Maybe they heard the story back when it happened, but unless they know Jack well from church or somewhere else, chances are they haven't connected the dots.

'You lost your daughter?' Shelley asks, unable to contain herself. Jenny gives her a swat on her thigh.

'Yes,' Jack says. 'Five years ago next month. She was in an accident.'

'I'm so sorry.'

'Not that kid down by Ceasar's Bay?' Dino says.

Jack nods.

'That's terrible. Jesus Christ. What a world. They never caught the little shit who threw the rock, huh?'

'No. People saw a couple of kids run off up the bike path, but that's it.'

'A tragedy.'

'What was her name?' Jenny asks.

'Amelia,' Jack says.

That's it, Lily thinks. She knew it was something unusual for the neighborhood. Not Melissa or Daniella or Stephanie or Lucia, the kinds of names all the girls she'd gone to school with had. *Amelia*.

Sarah has to follow Jack. It's not easy. Everyone's having a hard time staying focused on what she's reading, Lily included. They're all hung up on poor Jack. What Sarah's written is angry, but even she's finding it hard to think about her own troubles in the face of Jack's. There's a quiet consensus that nothing's as tragic as losing a kid.

Lily intended to read what she had written for the exercise, but she finds herself staring down at the paper now, unable to make the words make sense. She looks up at the clock on the wall over the stage and sees that it's been an hour. She regains her composure and gives them their first homework assignment.

A two-to three-page story. They can write about anything they want, but it needs to be typed and – if it's possible – she'd like them to bring copies of their stories for everyone in the class as well as for her. She says there's a copier around the corner at Main Pharmacy and one at the library, but – if they're really in a pinch – maybe Father Andy will help them out.

After that, Lily says it was nice to meet everyone and dismisses them. They put the missals back in the box where Josh found them. She asks Jack to stay after class. The others linger for a few minutes, but then they scatter off into the night. The basement is quiet. It's weird to be standing there with Jack. She's not sure why she asked Jack to hang back, but she knows she was very moved by what he'd written.

She goes over to the table with the coffee urn, picks up a Styrofoam cup, and fills it. She asks Jack if he wants any coffee. He shakes his head. She takes a sip. It's lukewarm and weak. She puts the full cup down on the table. 'What you wrote today,' Lily says to him, 'was really beautiful.'

'Thank you,' Jack says.

'Have you always wanted to write?'

Another shake of his head. 'Amelia was the writer. That's what she wanted to go to college for. I've always been a big reader, but I was never much for writing. Sure, I wrote a few stories and poems back in high school but nothing that was any good. Amelia was really talented. I know she would've made it, written the books she wanted to write. I saw the flyer for the class and I thought it might help, you know. To sit down at the typewriter where she used to do her work and try to make something out of all this grief. Five years next month. I can't believe it. Five years without my little girl. The last decade was tough. I lost Janey, my wife, then I lost my parents, and then I lost Amelia. Just like that, over a five-year stretch, everyone I had was gone. I'm still trying to figure out what that means. I feel hollow most days. Why am I here? What's keeping me here?'

'Writing can help,' Lily says, suddenly unable to say what she wants to say. Why did she even ask him to stay? Does she want to tell him he has something to actually say, a purpose as a writer, and most writers she knows would kill for that? Most writers she knows, even the ones who spin gold with their sentences, don't really have anything at all to say. But she can't find the words, and she worries that they'd come out all jumbled anyway, that she'd regret suggesting that his daughter's death has given him purpose as a writer and is an excellent subject matter.

'Yeah, it seems like it,' Jack says. 'It felt good to imagine I was talking to her. It felt like she was here. She would've liked you. She could've been like you, you know? Winning awards for her stories. She was working on a novel too.'

'I'm thankful you shared what you shared. I feel like I know Amelia.' Her name is somehow difficult to say. Four long syllables that Lily barely manages to drag out. Maybe she shouldn't have said it. Her head is spinning with regrets and worries. She doesn't want to drive Jack away. She feels like – despite what he's saying about the exercise helping him – he might not return to class. When the dust has settled, it's possible he'll think it was too much to put his broken heart on a plate for strangers.

'I'll never get over her being gone,' he says. 'I don't have my job anymore. I don't have anything. I'm driving around on an empty tank. For a while, I played private eye and tried to figure out who the kid was who threw the rock. I don't know what I even wanted, to kill him or forgive him.' Jack steps forward and gets a cup of coffee for himself. 'Whoever it was, he's probably not even a kid anymore. I'm sorry for rambling. I don't talk much to anyone these days.'

On a selfish level, Lily's thinking of how she might use Jack in her own writing. Not now, of course. Maybe years down the road. A man touched hard by tragedy. A man who is all alone in the world. A man who wound up in this sad St. Mary's basement in her class, pouring his guts out.

'Well, I think it's really great that you're here,' Lily says. 'I'm happy to have you in the class. It takes a lot to sit down in a room like this with a bunch of people you don't know and share your work – I realize that.'

Jack smiles. 'Two to three pages on the homework, right?' he asks.

'Right.'

'That seems like so much. I don't know how people write whole stories, let alone books. All those words. People like you and Amelia amaze me. The discipline it takes to sit down and do that.'

'I know it can seem like a lot when there's nothing. Getting going can be the hardest part.'

Jack says good night and that he's really looking forward to their next class. He wanders out of the basement with his cup of lukewarm coffee.

Lily stays behind and puts the chairs back in a neat circle. She throws a couple of empty coffee cups in the trash. She can't finish the cup she poured, so she brings it to the dark little bathroom next to the stage, turns on the fluorescent light, and pours it into the toilet.

It's quiet in the basement. She swears she can hear the church breathing. She stuffs her notebook in her backpack and then hurries out, flicking off the light switch on the way.

In the parking lot, she pulls the door shut until she's sure it's locked. She stands there, alone. It's dark. Was it still daytime when she'd gone in? She can't remember. She takes out a cigarette and lights it. Across from her is the school. A window full of construction-paper cutouts catches her eye. That was the very room where she had her second-grade class. Mrs Scarsella. They'd probably hung very similar things in the window then. She wonders if Mrs Scarsella is still teaching. She was Lily's favorite. She encouraged her to write stories. She read aloud to the class daily. She had even given Lily a copy of her favorite book, *The Little Prince*, at the end of the year, saying that she knew some day Lily would write a book just as beautiful. Those were easy days. There was no such thing as bad news. Her dad was still alive. She loved nothing more than watching the Mets with him. Pizza was her favorite food. The little park up the block from their apartment building was heaven. She wonders if she should swing by the school one afternoon and drop in on Mrs Scarsella. Maybe she can read a story to the kids.

She walks out of the lot, headed for home. She takes a long sizzling drag off her cigarette, watching the smoke billow out in front of her. She thinks about Jack again. She thinks about how alone he is. Not just Amelia gone but his wife and parents too. She's always been a lonely person, but she's never been that alone. She still has her mom. She still has friends she feels a deep connection to. Not many, but a few. She thinks about how close so many folks are to being that alone, though. Lose a few people and, suddenly, there's no one left. Her cigarette just about done, she knocks the cherry off and stuffs the filter in her pocket.

It's a short walk back to the apartment. The blocks are all telephone wires and streetlights and shadows. It's a soft summer night, the best kind. No madness in the air. A train rumbles by on the Eighty-Sixth Street El, sounding like thunder.

When she gets inside, the apartment is dark. She can't think of it as home, not really, just as 'the apartment.' The fridge is humming. It's like any apartment in the neighborhood. Her mom hasn't done anything to set it apart. No cool art on the walls, no Christmas lights up year-round, no shelves full of books. Just knick-knacks and framed pictures. A newish TV from P.C. Richard & Son. A glass ashtray sprinkled with potpourri. The worst thing is a sign on the wall that reads LIVE LAUGH LOVE. Lily hates it. One day, when she has too much vodka, she plans on ripping it off the wall and throwing it out her window into the alley below. She wonders why people hang tacky things like that on a wall so they see them daily. What comfort or joy does it bring? Not just her mother. The fucking masses. There's a huge market for shit like that. People just like to stare at it and be reminded that the purpose of life is to live *and* to laugh *and* to love. So goddamn dumb.

On the kitchen table, there's a note from her mom, held down by a stress ball she got for free at the bank when she opened her new checking account. The note says that she and Dave have gone out to the Marboro to see a movie. Under the paper is a ten-dollar bill she's left for takeout. Lily's not that hungry, but she thinks she might order Chinese in a while. She throws her backpack on the floor next to the table. Her mom will scold her for that later, which is why she does it in the first place. 'I could've tripped and broken my neck,' her mom will say, anguished.

The answering machine is blinking on the counter. That horrible little orange light. Since she's been back with her mom, that little orange light has come to represent Micah and nothing else. It's as if he's trapped in the answering machine, like a genie in a bottle. Sure, others call and leave messages – Dave when he's not around, the Santangelos, telemarketers, her mom's office, Martha – but it's mostly Micah now. And tonight's no exception. There are ten messages from him. They start out with him just saying, 'Hi, Lily, it's Micah. I hope you're okay. Please call me back.' But they get increasingly troubling. He's crying, begging for her to talk to him, saying he's going to hurt himself. In the last message, he says he's coming to Brooklyn to see her whether she likes it or not. They need to talk. Part of her knows she should call the cops and report this, but the smarter part of her knows they won't do shit. She can hear some thick-necked beat cop now: 'It's just messages. He'll get over it.'

Instead, she deletes all the voicemails. It's intensive and boring, having to delete them individually. She thinks she should maybe save them as evidence, but she just wants them to be gone. She stands there, leaning against the counter, hovering over the machine and pressing the buttons she needs to press to make Micah disappear.

When she's done, she goes into her room and puts on a CD she got at the record store in York before she left. *Dogs* by someone named Nina Nastasia. It was on her favorite employee's recommendation shelf. Her name was Rachael, the employee. Lily liked the picture on the cover of the CD. She's been listening to it a lot lately. It fits her mood. She opens her window, sits on the bed, and the noise from the street competes with the music. Horns, voices, sirens. The messages from Micah had killed whatever she was feeling after meeting Jack. She hopes Micah's threat to come to Brooklyn remains just a threat. She's not sure what she'll do if he actually shows up.

Charlie

'I need you to hold something big for me,' Charlie says to Max Berry.

They're sitting in Max's cramped shithole office in Bay Ridge. Charlie has the black duffel bag at his feet. The bag that he snatched from Junky Greg. He's brought it to Max's for safekeeping because he needs to tie up Greg and Rainey's loose ends and Max's is where he always brings his money. Since Charlie got back from Florida last summer, he's come to depend on Max more than ever. Max is his bank. Charlie's never had this much. Plus, there are the drugs. He certainly can't stash it at his apartment. The trunk of his car would be exceedingly stupid too. He considers Max's place a haven. A lucky spot. Sure, people come around, but nobody messes with Max because he's protected. The irony isn't lost on Charlie. Max pays Stacks Brancaccio for protection, and Charlie just killed Stacks's no-good junky son, stole his score, and is now squirreling it away in Max's office where it will be safe because of the protection provided by the Brancaccios.

Max is fidgety. He has one of those small milk cartons he swears by on the desk in front of him, and he's taking nervous swigs. All the things he'd hoped for out of the day, Charlie bringing extra drama into his life probably wasn't one. 'What're we talking about here?' Max says. 'I don't need trouble.'

Max has a new kid working for him. Probably about eighteen or nineteen, fresh out of high school. He's sitting cross-legged on the floor behind the desk, packing CDs into padded shipping envelopes. He's wearing headphones, bopping his head to some droning hip-hop. As long as Charlie has known Max, he has some kid or another working for him. Usually fifteen or sixteen years old, a student at Our Lady of the Narrows, where Max went to school. Max is an atheist, but he looks back longingly on his Catholic schooldays and seems to want to relive them by inviting these boys to work with him. Max vibes weird, off in some way, but Charlie's pretty sure he's not a kid-fucker or anything. This one's older. The son of a guy Max had gone to high school with is what he'd said when he introduced the kid. 'Tell your little pal to take a walk,' Charlie says.

Max turns on his chair, reaching out and tapping the kid on the shoulder.

The kid lowers his headphones, presses stop on his Discman. 'What's up?' he asks.

'Bobby, do me a favor,' Max says. He digs a twenty out of his pocket and hands it to the kid. 'Run over to Key Food. Get me four or five of my milks, a bag of Twizzlers, and a Twix. You get something for yourself too. Charlie, you want anything?'

'I'm good,' Charlie says.

Bobby stands up. He tucks the twenty in his pocket, puts his headphones back on, and heads out the door, chugging along to the rhythm of whatever he's listening to.

'Good kid,' Max says. 'Dumb maybe, but good. I already told you Danny Santovasco's his old man, right? You know Danny? He went to OLN with me. We ran track and did stage crew together. Hard to believe I ever ran track.'

'I don't know the guy, and I can't picture you running track.'

Max nods, takes another swig of milk. 'I'm afraid to ask, but what's the trouble?'

'I need you to hold this bag for a while, that's it. I've gotta go to Jersey to take care of something.' He knocks on the arm of the chair he's sitting in.

'That's not wood you knocked on,' Max says.

Charlie taps his crotch. 'I got some wood right here. Perpetual wood. You ever walk around with a chubby all day long? That's my conundrum. I got these nonstop good ideas, and my wang stays inflated over them.' He picks up the bag at his feet, nodding his head in the direction of the black safe on the table in the corner. 'Just throw this in there.'

'What're you getting me into here?' Max asks.

'You're not involved. You're just holding something. You know this is my lucky spot. You know I trust you more than I trust anybody else.'

'Come on. You've got nowhere else to go. You've burned every bridge there is to burn.'

True enough, Charlie thinks. The last decade of his life has felt like one big burning bridge. First there was his wife and his wife's family, then there was everyone and everything in Florida, and now, back in Bay Ridge, he's managed to make enemies where he didn't even know there were enemies to make. Max is the only one he can depend on.

Charlie's intention, after getting out of Florida alive, was to come home and make a different kind of name for himself. He didn't want to just be the guy in the papers. The money he'd inherited from his wife after she died hadn't lasted as long as he'd hoped – it'd bought him the place in Florida, a car, a boat, and many good nights on the town, but it went fast, and he got tied up with guns and drugs and was locked up for a stretch. After he was released he came home and started plotting. As a kid, he'd dreamed of being big like Stacks Brancaccio. But he keeps running into brick wall after brick wall. All he wants is to rise in the ranks, bathe in dough, have one of those mansions with cement lions at the end of the driveway, a new wife (preferably a non-English-speaking Russian), maybe a fleet of cars, some guys taking orders from him. Instead, he wound up loan-sharking, with shitbags like Greg his only clientele. Dreams and reality are two different things – that's all he's learned in his thirty-seven years on the planet. Still, here he is with this score. It's not everything, but it's something big.

'You gonna tell me what's in the bag?' Max says. 'Or you expect me not to look?'

'You can look,' Charlie says. 'Nothing unusual. Not a bunch of hooker scalps or anything. Good old-fashioned dough and drugs.'

'And I get raided by the FBI, what happens then?'

'You're not getting raided by the FBI. Come on. That was gonna happen, it would've happened already. It's definitely not gonna happen in the next few weeks.'

'A few weeks is how long you want me to hold this stuff?'

'Probably not that long. A few days. A week or two tops.'

'And who's looking for this stuff? Not the Brancaccios, I hope. You know I pay them off. Stacks sends a guy once a month. It's usually Fleabag Freddie. Maybe they sniff out you were here.'

'Nobody knows we know each other from before Florida.'

'That's what you think.' Max drains the last of his milk. 'What's in Jersey?'

'Swamps, Springsteen, Whitney, the Devils.'

'Good one, smart guy. You said you're going to Jersey to take care of something.'

Charlie considers how deep he actually wants to get with Max here. After taking the bag and leaving Greg shot full of poison, he tracked down Rainey in Owl's Head Park. Charlie wanted to know where exactly the bag came from, whether or not Don and Randy were even real. Greg had said they were rich kids they'd blackmailed, but Charlie didn't trust anything Greg said. He knew Rainey to be slightly less scuzzy. He was a wannabe Brancaccio from way back, but Stacks wouldn't give him the time of day. It made sense he figured this bag was his way through the gates officially. He was pissed, like Greg said, but he was also a man whose allegiance could easily be shifted. Rainey could be convinced that Charlie was making a big move, that he needed someone at his side. Rainey just wanted to feel

important. Charlie made him feel that way. He promised him a
seat at the table. He said to forget Greg and to hop on board the
French Express. Rainey liked that kind of talk. He wanted in. He
gave up everything he had on the guys in Jersey. Full names and
last known addresses. Rich kids indeed. The sons of politicians.
Wrapped up in some scheme. He and Greg had lifted a hard
drive full of sensitive info. The guys were somewhere in Atlantic
City, hiding out. When Rainey finished talking, Charlie shot
him, left his body on a half-pipe ramp in the park. Dumb fuck.
Charlie's plan now is to eliminate Don and Randy so they don't
come hunting for their money. Rich kids get ideas. They hire
people. They're probably hiring people right this second. Those
people find out Greg and Rainey are dead and start digging
around hard, they might show up at his door. Killing Don and
Randy cuts off trouble at the pass. 'Nothing you need to concern
yourself with,' Charlie says to Max now.

'One more question,' Max says.

'Shoot,' Charlie says.

'You get pinched or killed, I got this package here, what do I
do?'

'That happens, and it's a long shot, you hold it for my ghost,
okay? I'm just kidding. Buy yourself a lifetime supply of milk
and Twizzlers. Or whatever you spend all your dough on. Buy
your little Bobby a corsage and take him out dancing.'

'It's not like that.'

'I'm busting your chops. I'm not getting pinched or killed.
Remember, back before I split for Florida, I did you that favor.
I paid a visit to that guy who hassled you. I tracked him down.'

'You didn't even have to do anything. He was a wreck. Half
dead.'

'Still, a favor's a favor. Consider this a favor. Above and
beyond.'

Max stands up. He comes over and takes the bag, unzipping
it to confirm what Charlie's just said. He brings it over to the safe

and spins the combination dial, making the stops he needs to make. Click. He opens the heavy door and stuffs the bag inside. It's a tight fit, but it's in there with whatever else he keeps hidden away. Some dough, sure, but Charlie bets he has some illicit nudie shots in there, maybe blackmail material of his own. Who knows with Max? Guy could be into anything under the sun. He closes the door and spins the dial wildly to make sure it's nowhere near the last combo number.

'There,' Charlie says. 'That wasn't so hard.'

'I got my limits,' Max says.

Bobby comes back in with a white plastic shopping bag drooping from his hand. Discman tucked in his shirt pocket, headphones down around his neck. 'I went to Chico's on the corner instead of Key Food,' he says to Max.

'Key Food's cheaper,' Max says.

'I know, but the place on the corner is closer.'

'Chico's is no good.'

Bobby shrugs. He plucks a tall boy of Rolling Rock from the bag and gets back to his stack of CDs and shipping envelopes.

'That's what you got yourself?' Max asks. 'A beer? That's your lunch? You're a growing guy. You need nutrients.'

'Twizzlers and Twix – that's nutrients?'

'The milk's got everything I need.' Max reaches into the bag for another carton. He peels open the cardboard and drinks.

Charlie gets up. He does have a chubby. He wasn't lying about that. He gets very excited over things. Now he's thinking about Jersey. He's thinking about eliminating trouble. He stuffs his hand down his pants and readjusts. Bobby has his headphones on again. 'Thanks for being my guy,' Charlie says to Max, giving him a high sign.

'Sure,' Max says.

'You still got that piece in your desk, right? Just in case.'

Max nods, focused on his milk.

Charlie leaves and goes out to his car, double-parked at a

hydrant, unticketed. He gets behind the wheel. His gun's in the trunk in a toolbox, a silencer nearby that simply gets screwed into place. In the cup holder there's a matchbook from the Bridgeview Diner, where he had breakfast after a night of not sleeping. He's going to Atlantic City now. He'll get a motel. Scope things out. Move smart. Be clean and efficient. Erase the problem before the problem comes to him. The stuff's safe with Max.

Maybe he'll gamble too. He took thirty grand from the bag for spending money. It's in the toolbox with his piece. He's thinking about slots. Lights spinning. Sitting down at a poker table. Seeing a show. Flirting with waitresses. A few drinks. Mixing what might be perceived as work with pleasure. He heads for the Verrazano now. In a few minutes, he'll be across the bridge in Staten Island and then he'll be in Jersey. He has the future to think of. When this is done, when he's back in Bay Ridge and has retrieved the money from Max, the next step will be clear. Everybody's going to know his name.

Jack

The writing class has opened something up in Jack. When he'd seen the flyer for it, he thought of Amelia. That was why he'd decided to give it a shot. He's always been a reader but he never really tried to write anything other than letters here and there. After Amelia died, he took to writing her letters every week. He'd bring them to her grave and read them to her and then he'd hide them in a shoebox in his closet. It helped. He figures more writing can't hurt. Plus, he likes Lily. She reminds him of Amelia. She's what Amelia could've been. A neighborhood girl who went to college with the dream of writing, and it paid off. She'd won a contest. She'd published stories. She's working on a novel. He wonders if that was what Amelia would be doing right now, plugging away on a novel. He wonders if she might've really finished the one she'd been working on. He can't imagine that many high school kids do.

Jack's feeling just how alone he is again. The house reverberates with his aloneness, seems to be deteriorating by the second as a result. It was run-down when Amelia was alive. Now, it's worse. Broken windows, crumbling porch, leak in the roof, faucets that drip, mold that grows, sad smells emanating from forgotten spaces, collapsing ceilings. He has to remind himself to try to do basic things. When a light bulb blows, it stays blown. When a handle breaks, it stays broken.

All of Jack's time is in the house these days, except for daily walks to Coney Island to get some air in his lungs. He quit his job with Con Ed after Amelia died. He survives off the cash he'd saved to set her up, payments for the services he provided, stashed in that safe-deposit box at the bank. He stopped drinking at the Wrong Number, choosing to drink at home with the TV or radio on. He stopped his side work too, letting Max Berry be and never following through with Mary Mucci. Max had figured out who he was and sent a guy – Charlie French – to talk tough to him regarding the Mucci situation. This was maybe three weeks after the accident. Jack let himself take Charlie's threats, told the empty-eyed bastard he was out of the picture, forget it. It signaled the end. Nobody else bothered him with jobs. They knew the tragedy he'd gone through, the hand he'd been dealt.

Jack goes into Amelia's room now. He hasn't touched a thing since the day of the accident. The blinds on the window have grown dusty. The yellow walls somehow yellower. He looks at the posters taped over her bed. A couple of that Irish band she liked, the Cranberries. One's the cover of her favorite record, *No Need to Argue*. The other's from the show she'd gone to at Jones Beach in 1995. She liked that singer a lot. Then there are pages ripped from magazines. Bands, movie stars. Most of them unfamiliar to him then and still unfamiliar to him now. He knows that one actor she loved, River Phoenix. A big foldout poster of him hangs crookedly over her headboard. She was broken up when he died. And there was that actress, Winona Ryder. Amelia used to rent *Mermaids* all the time. Even he liked that one. There's also her map of the world, pinned with all the places she wanted to visit.

The bed is just as she left it. Unmade. Checkered quilt that Janey bought at some stall on Eighty-Sixth Street bunched close to the wall. Yellow sheets ruffled. Boots on the floor at the foot of the bed. Three identical pairs of those Doc Martens she liked so much.

His mother's old Royal typewriter – the one he'd taken up for Amelia from the basement – is on her desk. The same page she was working on rolled in there. Not much written. Just a few sentences: *May hated Matthew for what he'd done. She wanted to blow up his house and blow up his car. She wanted to poison his mother.*

On one side of the typewriter, there's a boombox and a stack of CDs and cassettes. The Cranberries, Hole, Sinéad O'Connor, Erykah Badu, Soul Asylum, Natalie Merchant. On the other side is a tower of books. Kathy Acker, Katherine Dunn, Hubert Selby Jr., Irvine Welsh, William S. Burroughs, Sam Shepard, Jim Carroll. He'd heard some of the names along the way, mostly from her, but he doesn't really know what most of them are about. All the times he's come in here in the last five years, he's looked at the books and tapes and CDs and thought about reading them and listening to them as a way of communing with Amelia. What'd she like about them? What was there for him to learn about his daughter that he didn't know hidden in these books and songs? Then he'd be reluctant to touch them, to move or change a single thing. He's wanted everything to remain just as she left it.

He traces his fingers over the spines of the books again. Thinking now is finally the time. The book on top is Kathy Acker's *Blood and Guts in High School*. What a title. He remembers Amelia talking about that one. Maybe he'll start there. He'll bring the book down with him to the living room later and pour himself some whiskey and try to connect with her across this great distance through a book she'd read and liked.

He opens the top drawer of the desk. It's neatly organized, split into two compartments. A thin package of typewriter paper and a fresh ribbon in a box on the left side. Some typed pages next to that. He's looked in this drawer before but he could never bring himself to read what Amelia had written of the novel. It felt like it might be some sort of betrayal.

Now, finally, he decides to read it. Something about the class. It's more on May and Matthew. Their whole story, from meeting at a bowling alley to their first date at the movies to sleeping together to dinners with their parents to breaking up. It moves, really moves. She was so good. A natural. He wonders how a kid could even write the kinds of things she was writing at eighteen. Her mother dying gave her some kind of wisdom that most kids lacked, he guesses. She was an old soul. It shows in her writing. He wishes she'd been able to write her whole life.

He takes the piece of paper out of the typewriter and puts it in the drawer with the rest of the novel. He feels like he's rattling the cage of heaven, but he knows Amelia won't mind. He rolls a fresh piece of paper into the typewriter and taps the carriage return. He closes the drawer, and scooches closer to the desk so his forearms are leaning against the edge and his fingers are poised over the keys of the typewriter. He's going to work on his story for Lily's class. Probably the ribbon's dried out, but he'll give it a shot, see if this old dusty bastard has any life left in it. It feels good here, sitting in Amelia's room with some purpose.

Lily said two to three pages, which seems like a million pages to him.

The words start coming. They just keep coming, one after the other, appearing in front of him on the page. They're coming from his mind, through the tips of his fingers, clattering from the keys up through the spindly strikers and onto the page in faint (but not too faint to see) black ink. He doesn't know anything about how to format a story, so his lines are tight, his transitions nonexistent, his margins wild. It doesn't look like Amelia's novel – all that white space and neatness.

The story he's writing is from the point of view of the kid who threw the rock that killed Amelia. Jack's calling him Nobody Boy. He tries to feel empathy for him – it had to have been a kid. There were no leads other than some boys spotted running away, no good witnesses. Anyhow, who else would do that except a kid who doesn't understand the world?

A feeling of peace settles over Jack at first. He wonders if this is what Amelia felt when she was writing, if it was a way to quiet the pain of losing her mom and her grandparents.

When he's done with the first page, he unspools it and gets going on the second.

He tries to keep feeling that empathy but, the more he writes, the more that feeling of peace dissipates and instead he gets angry. Angry with God. Angry at the purposelessness of the world, at how cruel and terrible it all was and is. Angry on the page. He's typing hard. He's seeing the world through Nobody Boy's eyes and it's not the world he wanted to see. He's laughing when the rock hits Amelia. He's laughing when her car thunders into traffic. Jack's crying.

So much anger and sadness. He imagines Nobody Boy's life past that moment, not giving a shit what he'd done. If Jack can't have revenge in life, he can have revenge on the page. He puts Nobody Boy through hell. He's a fuckup. He has a rotten old man and a mother who won't give him the time of day. Teachers who think he's a piece of shit. Jack writes through the anger and comes out the other side. He starts feeling bad for Nobody Boy. All of that led him to Amelia. All of that made him throw the rock.

When Jack's done, he pulls the second page out of the typewriter and places it under the first. He rereads it all and notices a bunch of mistakes. Typos, wonky keystrokes, wrong punctuation. He's not sure if it's even a story. It doesn't look like a story. The two pages are just crowded with lines. There are no paragraphs. They look like walls of words.

He thinks about Lily. Should he be embarrassed to turn this story in to her? Is it too ugly, too raw? She seems like a nice kid. He likes the way she handled everybody in the class. He wasn't sure what to expect from a writing teacher. When he first saw the flyer, before he talked to her on the phone, he'd imagined a guy in a sport jacket with corduroy patches on the sleeves, wearing a turtleneck under that, maybe a beard, thick-rimmed glasses. He'd seen movies with college writing classes, and the teachers were usually something like that. Big drinkers who'd let their talent wash up on the shore. Lily's barely done being a kid. He likes her enthusiasm and kindness. She's genuine, to boot. No trace of her being a smartass. The crew in that basement could've been a joke to her. She could've laughed her way through that meeting. Instead, she was sweet, lovely. Just as he imagined Amelia would've been if she'd made it that far. Not exactly, though. Amelia would've left room for sarcasm. She wouldn't let the tracksuit wannabe-mobster guy, Dino, off the hook so easily. She would've had him pegged as a bullshitter right off.

Jack looks through his story one more time. He's embarrassed by it. He holds the pages up and tears them lengthwise and then crumples them into a ball and tosses them into the wastebasket next to the desk.

He looks around the room. He's trying to notice something he hasn't noticed before. Some little detail he's missed. A brown towel hangs from the hook on the back of the door. Amelia had used it after her shower that last morning and then hung it up to dry. It's stiff and faded. He's noticed that before. It's not new to him. Nothing's new. Nothing ever changes in here. He keeps hoping that something will change or shift, keeps hoping for some sign from Amelia. He's not even sure he believes in that kind of thing, but he wants to. He knows that, if there's a way, Amelia will tell him something, anything.

He decides he'll try again with the story later. He wants to make Amelia proud. He wants Lily to be as impressed as she was with what he'd written in their first meeting. This isn't that. He takes the Acker book, goes downstairs, and pours himself a mug of Seagram's Seven. He flops on the couch, tries to read but drifts off to an uneasy sleep.

Bobby

Bobby graduated high school from Our Lady of the Narrows a couple of weeks back. He's been working for his dad's friend Max Berry in Bay Ridge since. He's headed to Max's now by bus, his headphones on, listening to *Supreme Clientele*. He took the same bus to school every day, so it doesn't feel too far from normal. He'd woken up late after another long night of video games and pizza and weed and music, pretty much his routine since school let out. He has a hard time getting to sleep before 4:00 a.m. these days. His dad had come home with his new girlfriend at around one thirty. Her name was Gloria or something with a G. Bobby couldn't get his headphones loud enough to cover the sounds of them banging in the next room. He almost wanted to whack off to Gloria's noises but his dad kept ruining it by grunting as if he was moving heavy furniture.

Sometimes Bobby feels like a loser for being nineteen and living at home with his dad. He has no interest in college and isn't sure what else to do. The last five years have been tough. Ever since the rock he threw killed that girl, he'd stopped feeling things. He hadn't known it was his rock until he played the scene on repeat in his mind. Zeke knew. He said he didn't but he did. His rock was way off. They'd split as soon as the rock hit her. Bobby didn't know it'd wound up as bad as it did until later that night when he saw the news. He didn't cry. He just stopped feeling anything.

He and Zeke made a pact the day after it happened. They met in the alley behind Giove's Pizza, where they sometimes drank forties and broke bottles against the wall. They agreed they'd never talk about what they did, not to each other, not to their folks or siblings or anybody. And they never did talk, as hard as it was. No one had seen them somehow. Some people on the news said they saw kids running away up the bike path but they didn't have anything solid to go on. A kid's not a crazed adult – it's hard to give a solid description of two boys in the summer. They're like fire hydrants, just *there*. They could've been any kids from the neighborhood.

It got harder not to talk when the story stayed in the news. The girl was just a few years older than them. Bobby can't even bring himself to think her name. They saw pictures of her dad. Jack Cornacchia. He wanted to know the whole story. He was begging for information. Bobby didn't tell Zeke this but he went to the funeral mass at St. Mary's. Well, not to the actual mass itself, but he stood in the bank parking lot across the street and watched as they put the girl's coffin in the hearse, watched her father collapse on the sidewalk. What could he do? He couldn't say it was him. He couldn't say it was an accident. It wasn't. They knew they could do damage, but they didn't think they could kill someone. He's even thought about going to visit her grave, but he knows that'd be stupid.

Bobby and Zeke pretty much stopped hanging out and talking in their sophomore year. The secret had created this boiling tension between them. It was worse for Bobby. Sure, they'd both been throwing rocks, but he'd thrown the one that killed the girl. Zeke could've folded at any time. But he didn't. They both wanted to forget, to pretend it wasn't real, like it hadn't happened. Turned out the easiest way to do that was to stop being friends. It was weird at first, but then it was normal. And it definitely helped. Zeke started dealing drugs junior year, and he was a natural. The day after graduation, Zeke moved to this little hippie college town upstate. Not to go to school in the fall or anything. Just to become a kingpin in this crunchy granola town. Bobby had heard that from Johnny Nardulli, who he bumped into on his way to Max's one day. Johnny had become Zeke's best pal sophomore year. He said Zeke had it all planned out, said he got the idea from some other dealer he knew and scouted out towns upstate. Johnny said that Zeke said dealing to hippies was the easy life. They were dumb and happy and had trust funds from their parents. Bobby just nodded the whole time.

Bobby's stepmom and stepsister had bailed in '98, and that was fine with him. They'd moved somewhere new, while he and his dad stayed in the old apartment. He never liked them much, especially Lily, who thought she was such hot shit. She went away to college in Pennsylvania or some other dumbass state. He still sees his stepmom around now and again. She lives only a couple of blocks away. He bumped into her once at an Optimo on Eighty-Sixth Street, and they caught up for forty-five minutes on the sidewalk outside. She's not really that bad. Better than any of the women his dad's dated since. Bobby almost told her that day that he'd been thinking a lot about committing suicide. This was late in '99, in the middle of his junior year. It was a phase. He couldn't stop thinking about taking pills and jumping off bridges and slashing his wrists with razors in the bathtub. Seemed to be the only thing that brought him any peace. But he didn't tell her. Instead, he mostly just listened to her rattle on about Lily, who wanted to be a writer, *blah blah blah*. The suicide phase passed.

During his last couple of years of high school, every once in a while, Bobby would walk out of his way and go past Jack Cornacchia's house to see if he could catch a glimpse of him. The last time he walked past, it was April. Jack's place is falling apart. It's the house of a man who's given up. Bobby never did see Jack on any of those walk-bys. Just the house. And he thought about the girl, how she should still be alive, how she should be in college and coming home on weekends and during the summer to bring light into that shitty wreck of a house. Bobby wishes he could go back and change history. He dreams of having a time machine. He'd go back and he'd put that rock down. Better yet, he'd steer himself and Zeke away from their rock-throwing spot and push them to do something, anything else. Bowl, shoot pool, waste a million quarters on pinball, whatever.

Bobby gets off the bus on Fourth Avenue in Bay Ridge and walks toward Max's office. Max and his old man had gone to high school at Our Lady of the Narrows together back in the late seventies and early eighties. Max runs some kind of 'financial services' business called Options Incorporated. He also sells CDs by mail, but that might just be a front. Bobby doesn't really understand what the guy does. It seems kind of like a bank. He gets people to invest with him, at least a grand, and then he promises them higher interest rates than the banks. Twelve or thirteen percent. He has a ton of investors. He had some problems a few years back – not being able to pay people off – but it seems to have mostly cleared up and his reputation's on the mend.

If Max is making money, though, it doesn't show. He drives a beater car and his office is a dive, full of overflowing file cabinets and over-stacked CD shelves. He wears cheapo eyeglasses and shirts with holes in them. He lives with his parents in a rent-controlled shithole on Third Avenue. He drinks milk. Tons of milk. There's a safe where Max keeps some cash – Bobby's not sure how much but a decent amount – and he's got a gun in his desk because there have been more than a few times, he says, where his investors got pissed at him when they couldn't get their money fast enough or at all. The last week, Bobby's been daydreaming about robbing Max, pulling that gun out when he's not expecting it and taking whatever's in the safe.

Max is a big-time atheist and a big-time Republican too. A weird mix. He loves Ayn Rand books. He's been trying to convince Bobby to read one called *The Fountainhead*. Bobby has evaded the big shitty-looking book repeatedly. All he likes to read is comics. *The Punisher, X-Men, Batman*.

Job-wise, Bobby doesn't really do anything too complicated. He files stuff, occasionally types something up, packs CD shipments, and goes to the post office to mail them. Mostly, it just seems like Max enjoys having him around. Someone to talk with. Max tells him mob stories. He knows many mob guys, including Stacks Brancaccio, and he even knew Gentle Vic Ruggiero, back before he was gunned down on his front stoop. Bobby loves hearing all the stories. The guy who came around the day before was named Charlie French. He wasn't a mobster per se, more of an ambitious loner according to Max, but he had a real wild card feeling about him. As soon as Charlie was out the door, Max told Bobby his whole story. How he killed his wife and got away with it and then moved to Florida and started selling guns and drugs, wound up busted and behind bars in some hothouse Florida jail for a stretch. Now he's back, and he's got his hands in a lot of different pies.

When Bobby knocks on the door, Max opens up almost immediately, carton of milk in hand. 'There you are,' Max says at top volume so Bobby can hear him through his music. 'I figured you for dead.'

Bobby presses stop on his Discman. 'What do you mean?'

Max motions to the clock on the wall. 'Look how late it is.'

'Sorry. I thought whenever was fine. Didn't you say whenever was fine?'

'Yeah, but I want to take you to lunch. I've got to talk to you about some stuff.' Max pulls the door shut behind him, making sure it's locked, and pushes past Bobby onto the sidewalk.

They walk down Fourth Avenue a few blocks to Max's favorite dive pizza joint. Bobby doesn't even know the name of the place. The sign fell off at some point, and they never put it back up. Slices are a dollar. Cheapskate Max can bring folks to lunch there and spend six or seven bucks tops.

The owner is about five feet tall with an anchor tattoo on his forearm. He wears a white paper hat. His name is Artie. The other guys who work there – there are about three of them with different shifts – are really tall. It's a funny thing, this short guy who hires all these tall guys. It's like he loves feeling even shorter. The pizza's bad. Worst Bobby's ever had in Brooklyn. Only worse pizza he ever had in his whole life was when he was in Maryland with his dad, visiting some cousins. A cousin he'd never met had graduated college. Bobby doesn't even remember his name. Bobby's dad stopped at some pizza parlor connected to a gas station because he didn't trust his aunt's cooking. The pizza tasted like a communion wafer covered in jarred sauce and bland, rubbery cheese. Artie seemed to use regular ingredients but his pizza was almost as bad. It had this funk to it Bobby couldn't quite place. Like drinking a soda somebody ashed in.

Bobby and Max order slices from Artie. No small talk. They take a booth in the back, over by the *Jurassic Park* pinball machine. Artie brings them their slices on paper plates. Bobby gets a Coke from the fridge. Max knows Artie doesn't have milk, so he doesn't even ask. He used to, and Artie would make fun of him. 'A grown man drinking milk?' he'd say. 'You want it in a baby bottle?' Now, Max just gets tap water in a Styrofoam cup and only sips from if it he chokes on his pizza.

Bobby blows on his slice. 'What'd you want to talk to me about?' he says, nibbling the edge. Every time he eats here, he burns his mouth.

Max folds his slice and takes a monster bite of pizza, orange grease streaming onto his paper plate. He chews noisily. Bobby's never really noticed how big his mouth is. It seems like he could get away with cramming the whole slice in there. Max holds up his hand, signaling that he'll talk when he's done with this bite. He finally swallows and then dabs at his mouth with a napkin yanked from the dispenser in the center of the table. Bobby notices milk crust on his upper lip. This guy's however old he is, in his early forties, and he's got a goddamn milk mustache. 'I'm gonna start taking you on recruiting runs,' he says.

'Recruiting runs for what?'

'For investors. That's how it works. This person tells that person about Options Incorporated and then I go over and pitch them on it, let them know it's legit, let them know this is the interest rate, they get monthly statements, make them feel at ease about giving me their money.'

'Is it legit?'

'It wasn't legit, you think I'd be here right now? I'd be locked up. But I get why people think it's a scheme, and that's why I talk them down. "Start small," I say to them. "Give me a grand. See how it goes." They see the interest they get on that little amount, they get hungry for more. There's no risk, only benefits, only more dough in their pockets. I want you to learn the business. I think there's a real future for you in it. A few months maybe, things are going good, you can start making recruiting runs on your own.'

Bobby shrugs. 'Okay. Cool.'

'We'll start today. I've got this woman, Victoria, and her mom lined up. Victoria works with this investor of mine, Stan Caraballo. He's been with me from the start. You'll see him. He usually comes by once a month to make an appearance. Always picking between his teeth with a coffee straw. You know who he looks like? You ever see that show *Just the Ten of Us*? He's a dead ringer for the dad, Coach Graham Lubbock.'

Bobby remembers watching *Just the Ten of Us* when he was about seven or eight. He watched everything. It was a spinoff of *Growing Pains*, which he loved, so of course he watched. He remembers having crushes on all the daughters. He can picture the actor Max is talking about just as easily as he can picture his own old man. He used to wish he had one of those TV dads, the kind who sits his kid down on the couch and talks about serious shit. 'Sure, yeah, I remember that show,' he says.

'I had such a thing for Jamie Luner. She played Cindy. She was so hot. I made a shrine to her in my room. No kidding. I had all these pictures I'd cut out of magazines, and I'd light candles.'

'You made a shrine? How old were you, like thirty?'

'I was in my late twenties when that show ran. She was on *Melrose Place* more recently, like '97–'99. She still looks good. Who do you like? Actresses, I mean. I keep a running top ten list of who I think the hottest are.'

'I don't know.'

'Come on. No one?'

'You ever see *The Craft*?'

'Of course. I have it on tape.'

'I like Fairuza Balk.'

'Okay, wow. Goth Catholic schoolgirl thing, huh? Good for you.' Max pauses, returns to his folded slice and crams a hunk into his open mouth. When he's done chewing, he continues: 'You thinking about the future? You taking a year off and then going to college? We should talk about this stuff. I wanna know if I've got somebody here I can count on for the long haul.'

'I don't want to go to college. You can count on me.'

'That's what I like to hear. College is for chumps.'

After they finish their slices, they leave the pizza place and go back to the office so Max can grab his car keys. He has a dumpy silver Chevy Citation he parks up the block under an oak tree. Someone's taped a sign for a missing cat to the tree. The sign's been there for as long as Bobby's been coming to the block. Max gets in on the driver's side, leaning across to unlock Bobby's door. He pulls it open, and there's a loud squeaking noise. Bobby hesitates to sit because the seat's covered in statements and magazines. 'Don't worry about that stuff,' Max says.

Bobby sits. He reaches for the seat belt, but it's gone.

As if on cue, Max says, 'No seat belt. Had to remove it. Almost strangled my mother. I'm a safe driver. I take the streets. I rarely go over forty.'

Bobby nods.

The woman they're going to see lives on Bay Thirty-Fourth Street in the same house with her mother and daughter. It's not far from where Bobby lives. He's wondering if he can just go home from there. He'd hate to have to go all the way back to Bay Ridge when they're done and then catch the bus again. He won't ask yet. He doesn't want to come off as too anxious. When they're done at this lady's house, he'll ask Max if he can just go home. He'll say the pizza didn't sit well with him if he has to.

Bobby hasn't been in the car with Max before, and he is – true to his word – a very safe driver. The slowest Bobby's ever seen. He not only avoids the Belt Parkway but avenues when he can, staying on side streets all the way except when he's forced briefly onto an avenue by a dead end or one-way. He's got the radio tuned to some right-wing talk show. The host has a nauseating voice. Bobby opens the window to drown him out.

When they turn onto Bay Thirty-Fourth, Max parks in front of the house he identifies as Victoria's. He says he's driven by a few times just so he knew where it was when it was finally time to come over. It's a small, cramped two-story house. Falling apart, possibly condemnable. They get out of the car and go through the open front gate to the door. Right over the bell is the mailbox. The names dimaggio and clarke scrawled in black Sharpie on a piece of masking tape with curling edges just under the latch. Max rings the bell.

'Follow my lead,' Max says.

A woman answers the door. She's about Max's age, maybe a little younger. She looks more normal, dressed in gym shorts and a loose Yankees T-shirt, her hair up in a ponytail. She's barefoot, some crawling ivy or something tattooed on her right calf. 'Max Berry?' she says.

'Victoria Clarke?' he says, smiling. His teeth are clomped with pizza. 'It's nice to meet you. This is my apprentice, Bobby Santovasco.'

It feels weird to hear their last names said all in a row like that. Bobby hasn't heard anyone say his last name since the end of school. He didn't even hear it at graduation. He'd gone to the ceremony downtown, wearing nice new clothes that his dad bought him at Kings Plaza under his robe, but he bailed early, crumpling his robe and throwing it in a corner garbage can and then trying desperately to get served at a bar on his walk home. A grizzled bartender at a place called Willy's Ale House finally pulled him a beer and let him sit at the bar with the old timers. He left when they started riding him about his goofy-ass clothes.

Victoria shows them in. The house doesn't look as bad on the inside as on the outside. A long hallway with black-and-white family pictures on the wall leads to a living room. All the furniture covered in plastic. A gaudy lamp spreading dull light on a brown shag carpet. Beyond the living room is the kitchen.

'My daughter and I moved back in with my mom after my husband passed,' Victoria says, her back to them. 'We lost our apartment on Sixty-Fifth Street.'

'I'm sorry to hear about your husband,' Max says. 'How old's your daughter?'

'She's eighteen. Francesca. She's upstairs right now. Sleeping her day away. You know these kids. Just graduated from Lafayette.'

'I do know these kids,' Max says, nudging Bobby.

In the kitchen, an older woman – probably in her seventies – sits at the table doodling on a notepad, a plate full of cut squares of coffee cake in front of her. 'This is my mother, Eva. Eva DiMaggio. That's my maiden name. I have my husband's name.'

Eva stands, but she's wobbly.

'Please, stay sitting,' Max says, his voice suddenly louder. 'It's nice to meet you. This is Bobby. He works for me.' One thing Bobby has noticed is that Max will always pitch his voice higher when he's talking to anybody who could credibly be perceived as a senior citizen. He thinks they're all deaf. He talks like a person speaking careful English to a foreigner, as if that will help them understand. It's embarrassing.

Bobby and Max sit opposite each other at the table. Eva crashes back into her chair. Victoria stays by the stove, turning the gas on under a small percolator. 'Coffee?' she asks.

'Sure, thanks,' Bobby says.

'Just milk, if you have it,' Max says.

'A glass of milk?' Victoria says.

'That'd be great.'

'Are you a serial killer? I've never seen a grown man ask for a glass of milk.'

Max smiles. He's heard it all. 'Nope, I just like my milk.'

'Weird.'

'Oh, leave him alone,' Eva says. 'Where's the sin? How about some cake?' She pushes the plate of coffee cake in his direction.

'Don't mind if I do,' Max says, reaching out and taking a piece. He sets it on a napkin and picks at the edges. 'So, Victoria, you work with Stan, right?' It's a question Max already knows the answer to, but he's obviously trying to get the conversation moving.

'I do,' she says. 'We both teach at PS Forty-Eight. I teach language arts. Stan teaches English as a second language, but he's really the enforcer in the cafeteria – that's why we keep him around.'

'I'll say right now that I don't trust Stan,' Eva says.

'Stan's okay.'

'From the second Bill died, he's been trying to be your best friend. That's not right. Bill and I had our problems, God knows, but Stan should know better.'

'He's getting old,' Max says. 'He's been single his whole life. Probably panicking. He sees a beautiful woman who's back on the market – excuse me for being crude – and he figures he has nothing to lose.'

'Are you married, Max?' Eva asks.

'I'm not.'

'I don't trust an unmarried man.'

'I'm married to my job.'

'And is this your son here?'

Max laughs. 'No, no. Bobby's the son of a friend of mine. He started working for me a few weeks ago when he graduated from Our Lady of the Narrows.'

'He's awful quiet.'

'He can talk.' Max turns to Bobby. 'Come on, kid, show them you can talk.'

'I can talk,' Bobby says.

They all laugh. Victoria brings Bobby his coffee and asks if he needs anything for it. He shakes her off and says he's good with it black. She then brings Max some milk in a wineglass, almost reluctantly, and takes the last seat at the table.

It's even stranger to see a man in his forties drink milk from a wineglass. 'Okay, let's get down to brass tacks,' Max says, rubbing his hands together. 'Stan's probably filled you in to a certain extent, but what questions do you have about Options Incorporated?' He's keeping his eyes fixed on Victoria, trying not to engage unnecessarily with Eva. Bobby can tell that Max thinks Eva's trouble.

Eva's the first one to jump in: 'Is it a scam?'

'It's not a scam,' Max says.

'How is it not a scam? I hear about these Ponzi schemes. Guys like you, they take money from hardworking people like my daughter and they say they're investing it, doubling it, whatever, but then the money gets locked up, inaccessible.'

'I'm not a guy like that.'

'You drink your milk and keep your nose clean, huh?'

'Exactly.' Max raises a glass to that.

Victoria explains that she doesn't have much money right now, but she got a bonus for working at PS 48's summer camp and she wants to turn it into something more. Max clarifies how it all works. Smooth talk. Bobby still doesn't really get how it's not illegal, but he knows he's not that smart. Must be fine. Max has been doing it for almost twenty years, since he graduated college. Bobby's dad invests. Not much, but a few grand. He gets his interest in monthly checks. Victoria says it all sounds too good to be true, wants to know what the rub is.

'No rub,' Max says.

'I'm against it,' Eva says.

'That's your prerogative,' Max says. 'And I'm certainly not twisting anybody's arm. I don't need a decision today. You decide you want to do it tomorrow or next month or next year, I'm here.'

'That's good to hear,' Victoria says. 'I don't like to be forced into anything.'

'Believe me, I'm not forcing.'

The girl who must be Victoria's daughter, Francesca, comes wafting down the stairs, rubbing sleep from her eyes with the heels of her hands, yawning dramatically. She's wearing a white T-shirt with Sade on it. Bobby knows because he had *Love Deluxe* on cassette back when he was about eleven, and the T-shirt has the cover of that album on it. Francesca's also wearing frayed jean shorts that have been signed all over in marker.

'There she is,' Eva says. 'Sleeping Beauty. Just like her old man. No big thing to sleep the whole day away.'

'Leave Bill out of it,' Victoria says to Eva. Then she turns to Max and Bobby. 'This is my daughter, Francesca. And this is Max Berry and his assistant, Bobby.'

'He's an apprentice,' Max says, motioning to Bobby. 'It's nice to meet you.'

Bobby gives a shy wave.

Francesca yawns. 'Are they insurance agents or something?'

'I'm an investment counselor,' Max says. Bobby's never heard him use that term to describe what he does.

'I'm going outside to smoke,' Francesca says.

'With these cigarettes,' Eva says. 'She must want lung cancer, that's all I can figure out. Her whole life ahead of her, she ruins it with sleep and cigarettes. Why don't you have something healthy? I bought some nice grapefruit juice. There are almonds in the pantry. Skip the cigarettes.'

As if she's accustomed to ignoring her grandmother, Francesca doesn't blink, yanking a package of Drum tobacco from her pocket and heading down the long hallway to the front door and the front yard. Bobby imagines her leaning against the fence, rolling a cigarette with great concentration. He's always been jealous of people who can roll cigarettes. He had a teacher in high school, Mr Atkinson, who was aces at rolling cigarettes on his breaks. Principal Aherne hated him over it because he knew all the students figured Atkinson was rolling joints.

'I'm sorry for my daughter's behavior,' Victoria says. 'She's a touch antisocial. Ever since her dad died, things have been tough.'

'Nothing at all to apologize for,' Max says.

'She's just like him,' Eva says. 'Her father, that is. He was a big moper. Always seemed like he had somewhere better to be. He didn't like me. He didn't like the neighborhood. Black guy. Everybody looked at him sideways. Everybody looked at *them* sideways.'

'Ma, please,' Victoria says.

'What? I'm not writing a book. I'm telling our guests the way things were. He hated me.'

'Of course he did. You were cruel to him.'

'Cruel? Come on. I fed him. I let him marry my daughter against my wishes. I could've called Eddie Ingrassia and had it broken up in a second. "The world's changing," my daughter says to me. "You love who you love. Wake up." Well, I got news for you. The world doesn't change. Change is just an illusion.

You make things harder than they need to be, don't be shocked when you're bitten on the ass at every turn.'

'Enough, Ma,' Victoria says.

Max takes over control of the conversation by getting back to business. He talks more about his services. He mentions the names of many satisfied clients. He says to ask them. Go ahead and have them talk about the monthly interest checks they get. Or how some of them just let the interest build up and they've doubled, tripled their money that way. He says there's no reason to trust banks, there never was. Banks are fragile. There's nothing personal about a bank. This is him, that's it. This is personal. He cares. He watches out for his clients. It's a good spiel. Restrained and convincing. Victoria buys it hook, line, and sinker. She goes upstairs to get her checkbook.

Bobby's crushing hard on Francesca. He wants to talk to her. When Eva starts seriously bending Max's ear, railing against Francesca's dead old man again, Bobby excuses himself and goes outside.

Francesca is surprised to see him. She's just finished rolling a smoke. Probably her second in the time she's been out there.

'Can I have one of those?' Bobby asks.

'You know how to roll?' Francesca says.

He shakes his head.

She gives him the one she just made and rolls a new one for herself. She lights both with a yellow lighter she keeps in the tobacco pouch. 'So, what's your story?' she asks. 'What's this Max Berry's story? He looks like the kind of guy who comes around to collect after someone dies. The funeral director or whoever. A couple of guys like that came around after my dad died.'

Bobby shrugs. 'I just started working for him. He's friends with my dad. I don't really get what he does, honestly. Seems kind of like a private bank or something.'

'Sounds illegal.'

'I'm sorry about your dad.'

'Thanks.' Francesca pauses, looks out at the street. A guy on a motorcycle zooms by, seeming to rattle the air.

'Your mother said you just graduated from Lafayette?' Bobby says, trying to find a way to continue the conversation.

Francesca nods. 'Yep. You in college?'

'I just graduated high school too. Our Lady of the Narrows in Bay Ridge. I'm nineteen, though. I got left behind one year in elementary school.'

'I always hated that phrase. *Left behind*. Like, who leaves a kid behind? Sounds so mean when it's put that way.'

Bobby's never thought about it, but he agrees. He hates that he had to repeat a grade, and he's kicking himself for even bringing it up. She's definitely got him pegged as a dummy now. 'I went to St. Mary's for elementary school,' he says. 'Where'd you go?'

'PS Forty-Eight, where my mom teaches.'

'Are you going to college?'

'I'm taking a year off.'

'Me too. Maybe a few years off.'

Francesca laughs. 'Honestly, I want to get the fuck out of Brooklyn.'

'Where do you want to go?'

'I don't know. Los Angeles maybe. I want to make movies, but I'm not really sure how to crack into that world. I love movies. I've got a camcorder. I shoot little things. My mom around the house. My grandma, even though I hate her guts. The streets. My friends. Like the most boring documentary stuff. I just like to see it through the lens. Then I try to edit stuff, but I have to do it with two VCRs I got at the Salvation Army and everything looks like shit. Sorry, that's boring.'

'Not at all,' Bobby says.

'I wish I could write a script or knew someone who could. I'm a terrible writer. I can't get anywhere. But I see things. I see the way I want things to look.'

'My former stepsister liked to write,' Bobby says, remembering

Lily scribbling away in notebooks and tapping the keys of an inherited word processor.

'Once a stepsister not always a stepsister?'

'I guess.'

'I take it you're not close?'

'Never really were, but now I don't see her at all.'

'Too bad. I'd like to meet a writer.'

Bobby mistook her for shy and standoffish in the house, but now she seems downright outgoing. He wants to seize the moment. He's not usually quick on his feet but something about this girl is prompting him to act fast. 'Do you want to go out sometime?' he asks. 'We could go see a movie in the city. I like movies too. I mean, I don't know anything about how they get made, but I like them.'

She takes a deep drag on her cigarette. These little hand-rolled jobs sizzle better. He loves the sound of her long inhale. She smiles through smoke. 'You're asking me out?'

'Yeah, I am. I mean, if you want to go. If you don't, I guess I'm not asking you.'

That gets a good laugh. 'What are your favorite movies?'

'This a test?'

'Not really. Maybe.'

'I like *Saturday Night Fever* and *Goodfellas*.'

She nods. She doesn't seem impressed.

He continues: 'I like *Scarface* a lot. And *Rocky*.' He tries to think of something more unusual, something not every ginzo from the neighborhood would list. He draws a blank. A couple of years ago he rented some weird movies from Wolfman's. One was this artsy vampire thing. The other was this Brooklyn crime movie where everybody was screaming at each other the whole time. He's trying to remember the names. He can't. He knows he's flopped here. He's thinking there's no goddamn way she'll go out with him now. He's not cool enough. His favorite movies are boring. He wishes he'd paid more attention in his religion class junior year. The dude who taught it, Brother George Musso, showed them all sorts of foreign movies, French and Italian mostly, and Bobby remembered some of the images, the beautiful women in black and white especially, but he couldn't stand reading subtitles. If only he could've surprised her by saying some foreign movie from the sixties.

'It's okay,' Francesca says. 'I'll go out with you. What do you want to see?'

'It's your pick,' Bobby says, flicking the last little bit of his cigarette over the gate. 'What's your number?'

She gives it to him. He's lucky he's got a pen in his pocket. He doesn't usually keep pens in his pocket. Must be fate. This one's from the dentist's office where he's gone his whole life. Dr Hecker. He used it to sign some form his father asked him to sign the other day. An insurance thing. His father asks him to sign something, he signs without reading. He writes Francesca's number on the palm of his hand. When he gets home, he'll transfer it to paper and tack it to his wall.

Max comes out just then, letting the door slam behind him. 'What the hell are you doing?' Max asks.

'Talking to Francesca,' Bobby says.

'Don't do that, okay? Don't just leave.' Max is laser-focused on him. He's refusing to even look at Francesca at first, who's still got her cigarette going, didn't burn through it quite so fast. But then he does. He gives her a once-over that's simultaneously gross and dismissive, as if he – an ugly, soft Irish numbers guy – is judging her in a beauty contest and deciding she doesn't pass muster.

'Sorry,' Bobby says.

'You should be sorry. I'm teaching you the ropes here and you throw it out the window to come sweet talk a gal.'

'I'm right here,' Francesca says. 'Why don't you boys take this elsewhere?'

'Excuse me,' Max says, bile in his voice. 'I'm talking to my employee.'

'Hey, Max, I'm sorry, man,' Bobby says. 'It's no big deal.'

'"No big deal" is how people wind up dead on the side of the road.'

Francesca can't help but laugh.

'What do you mean?' Bobby says.

'Come on. Let's go.' Max storms out of the gate, headed for the car.

Bobby mouths an apology to Francesca. She raises her eyebrows, as if to say, *What the fuck's wrong with this guy?* Bobby shrugs and holds up his hand, showing how neatly and carefully he's written her number there. 'I'll call you,' he says.

Another long sizzle. 'Okay,' she says.

He follows Max out the gate and back to the car. Max's behavior has thrown him off. He'd forgotten all about asking if he could just walk home from there. If he'd done that, maybe he could have run back out and had a few more minutes of conversation with Francesca. Or maybe they could've just gone on their date now. He didn't do that, though. He trails after Max and takes it as Max berates him further in the car.

Then, he listens as Max goes off on Francesca, saying she's not even that hot, what's he thinking, that she's clearly nothing but trouble.

Bobby's not answering him. All he can think about is Francesca. The Sade shirt. The way she pinched her cigarette as she smoked. Her eyes.

Max is talking about Francesca like he's jealous of her. He's flushed in the way that only a pale Irishman can get flushed. Splotches of red on his cheeks and arms. Bobby's embarrassed for him. A fortysomething guy responding this way about a girl of eighteen. Maybe he's jealous that there's no scenario where he gets away with talking to her. Maybe he's wishing for a youth where he might've had the guts to ask someone like her out. Maybe he's a racist fuck. Or maybe it's just that Bobby's attention's divided. Maybe he likes having Bobby to himself.

'You asked her out?' Max says.

'Yeah,' Bobby says.

Max laughs. 'You're a kid. Don't fall under the spell of a girl like that.'

'A girl like what?'

'You can just see she's got some tricks up her sleeve. I hate to use the word, Bobby. I hate to use it, but I'm gonna use it. She's a slut. No doubt. Girls like that, they give off these fumes that blind you. Just like that, you're down on your knees. Nothing else matters. You're powerless. You let yourself get pussy-sick, there's no coming back from it.'

Bobby cringes at Max's use of that word. It's not so much the word itself as the way Max says it, like he's using it to sound hip. Max, who's probably never even gotten close to a girl. Maybe that's it. Maybe the jealousy – or whatever it is – is rooted in the fact that not only would he never have been cool enough to talk to someone like Francesca, but he's never even been laid, the poor bastard. Look at the guy. He's out of central casting. Pocket protector. Drinks milk. Lives with his parents. The movie of his life would be *The Guy Who Never Got Laid*.

Bobby's been laid. Three times. There was Gina, who he went with for two weeks, when he was fifteen. She was two years older and had been around the block. That's the other thing bugging Bobby. Max calling Francesca a slut. First off, he doesn't know that. How could he? Second, who cares? Bobby respects experience. Every other way in life, people respect experience. A girl sleeps around, she's a slut. Nope. She knows her stuff. He likes to learn from people who know their stuff. He didn't get that virgin/whore complex handed down in his Italian blood. After Gina was Sandy. That was a one-time deal at a party. She had knockers like wrecking balls. She almost crashed in the side of his head with them. He can still remember her breath. Cool Ranch Doritos. Then there was Ally. They dated for two months but they had nothing to say to each other. They slept together once in his bedroom when his dad was out and it was sad. Ally was a sad person in general. Nice but sad.

Max continues: 'Okay, Bobby? You listening? Stick with me, I'll take you places. Get rid of her number. Focus on work. You see how I handled them in there?' He takes his eyes off the road for a second and pulls a folded check from his pocket. 'I was masterful. They had a question, and I had an answer. Victoria was eating out of my hand. Was I trying to bang the broad? No way. Come on. I could've if I wanted to. I could've taken her upstairs to her room right then.'

Bobby sputters out a laugh.

'What? You don't think so? I know I don't look like much, but she could smell the money on me. Believe it. Anyhow, my mind was set on one thing. *Get the investment.* That's it. And that's what I did. Because I'm a pro. I'm great at what I do.'

Bobby nods along.

They're headed back to Bay Ridge. Max puts on his right-wing radio show again. The host's still prattling on in his sickly voice. Hell is listening to this shit for more than two minutes. Bobby looks at Francesca's number on his hand. He says it over and over in his head. That way, if it gets rubbed off, he's got it stored in his memory. He wonders if it's the landline at her house or if she's got a cell phone.

More and more, people have cells. He doesn't, but he wants one. He saves up enough dough working for Max, that's the first thing he's getting. Not that he has that many people to call. He just likes the idea of carrying it around. No more payphones. No more beepers. Someone needs him, there he is.

He has the number down cold. He's wondering when he should call. Today's pathetic. Tomorrow's too soon. He can't wait too long or she'll forget him. Somewhere between three days after meeting and a week tops. A week might be stretching it. He's worried Max ruined it for him. All Francesca's going to remember is that Bobby's taste in movies is pedestrian and that his boss is a gross jerk.

It's okay. He can watch some movies in the next few days that might make him look better. He'll ask Wolfman for some recommendations. Foreign shit. Weird shit. He should've asked her what her favorite movies are. He's kicking himself over that.

'You're still thinking about her, aren't you?' Max shouts over the voice on the radio.

'I'm not,' Bobby says, just loud enough to be heard. But he is. Big time. He's thinking about kissing her fingers, smelling the tobacco on them. He's thinking about how she rolled that cigarette. He's thinking about her voice. Her arms. The way she leaned against the fence. He's reliving their whole encounter on a loop in his memory, wishing he'd said some better things, wishing he'd come off as more memorable. He's also thinking about smashing Max's head into the windshield and busting it open like a piñata. He imagines Max's head is like an eggshell, easy to crack. He bets the fucker bleeds milk. Bobby hasn't really liked him from the start but now he hates him.

'I'm telling you. Steer clear.' Max beeps at the car in front of him, pounds the wheel.

'Right. I will.' Bobby rolls down the window and listens to the noises outside. An engine backfires somewhere nearby. Men yell at each other. Horns blare. Voices drift from windows.

The music of the neighborhood makes things better. He forgets about Max, forgets that he's in this beater car going back to that dreary office in Bay Ridge. Forgets that the radio's blasting this shit talker. The music of the neighborhood tells him there's a shot that Francesca's thinking about him too. He's not sure why he feels that way but he does. Something in all the terrible noise reassures him.

Francesca

Francesca Clarke crumbles the last little bit of her cigarette between the tips of two fingers, dusting it into the front garden. One thing she likes about hand-rolled is no filters. No filters means no guilt over dotting the sidewalk with trash. She always thinks of birds pecking at butts with filters or putting them in their nests, and she gets bummed.

That strange Bobby kid and his creepy boss have just driven away up the block, and she's feeling the kind of weird she feels when someone she doesn't know has just asked her out. She wonders if he knew from the second she came down the stairs that he was going to ask her on a date. She wonders what it was about her. It couldn't have been anything she said at that point, so it must've just been a physical thing. Or maybe he didn't know until they shared that smoke. Whatever. She probably shouldn't have said yes, but there's something she likes about him. He has this kind of Matt Dillon quality. Not how he talks or even how he looks but the way he carries himself. Cool and anxious at the same time. Steady and shaky. She's thinking if she ever manages to make a movie, even just a short, he's somebody she can use. Everything about him screams of the neighborhood.

She goes back inside. Her mom and grandma are fighting. She gets a drink of water from the tap. It's not long before the attention turns to her. 'What were you and that boy talking about?' Grandma Eva asks.

'Nothing,' Francesca says. 'Movies.'

'Always with the movies. Too bad you didn't care about school the way you care about movies. Did he say anything about his boss? Your mother just threw away a thousand dollars. A thousand dollars that could've bought a new stove or washing machine or fixed the roof. Nope, why do anything like that? Instead, she gives it to this bum Max Berry in the hopes that he's gonna double her money or triple it or whatever he promised.'

Victoria throws a dish towel over her shoulder, fed up with being second-guessed. 'Ma, you should hear Stan talk about the money he's made with Max. How do you think he affords those trips to Vegas and Paradise Island? And that new car he drives? On a teacher's salary?'

'So, how's it work? Magic?'

'He told us. He invests. He makes money off our money. That's how he's able to offer such high interest rates.'

'You ask me, it stinks. You might as well have set that money on fire.' Grandma Eva turns her attention back to Francesca. 'And you, look at yourself, would you?'

'What?' Francesca says.

'Leave her alone,' Victoria says. 'How'd you sleep, sweetie?'

'I slept okay.'

'We've got these strange men in the house and you dress like that,' Grandma Eva says.

'I didn't even know they were here,' Francesca says. 'What's wrong with the way I'm dressed? A T-shirt and jean shorts.'

Grandma Eva throws up her hands. 'Ah, you make me nervous.'

Her grandmother hates her. She hates that Victoria married her dad, Bill. She hated Bill when he was alive. Everything she did told him she hated him. She hated that he was Black. She hated that her daughter had married him, and she hated thinking that others in the neighborhood disapproved and talked behind their backs. She hates that her only granddaughter is half-Black. She's racist but mostly it's rooted in what others will think, which is a truly cowardly form of racism. The first thing she'd said to

Victoria when she brought Bill home was, 'What would your father say?' Grandma Eva's husband, Grandpa Natale, had died a couple of years before that. His kidneys had gone haywire or something. Victoria loved him, but he wasn't particularly good to her. He hated everyone who wasn't Italian, not just Black people but Irish, Polish, German, Jewish, and on down the line. Her whole childhood, Francesca has heard Grandma Eva say things about her like, 'What are people gonna think when they look at you?' or 'What boy's gonna want to marry you?' She constantly insinuates that the way she dresses is trashy, that the way she acts is trashy, and that these faults come one hundred percent directly from her no-good old man. It still bothers Francesca, but she's gotten good at ignoring it. The day will come where she leaves and she doesn't have to deal with Grandma Eva anymore. Having to move in here after they lost their apartment was the second worst thing that's happened to her after her dad dying. Victoria tries to make things okay, but there's not much she can do. Victoria has a good heart. No wonder she went for this money thing. She's always thinking about ways to try to get them their own place again.

'There's nothing wrong with the way she's dressed,' Victoria says.

'She dresses like a puttana. No brassiere? Come on. She shows everyone everything. Why pay for a ticket when you can see the show from outside the gates? And who signed those shorts? The men you've been to bed with? God help me.'

Francesca laughs.

'Don't talk to her like that,' Victoria says, her voice forceful and yet defeated. Francesca knows that her mother can't really throw punches in a fight with Grandma Eva, can only take them. She's been absorbing those punches her whole life.

'It's no wonder, really,' Grandma Eva says. 'She gets it from you. All those saloons you used to go to. The outfits. The hair. I'm lucky I didn't have a heart attack then.' She blesses herself.

'I'm just glad your father can't see her. A granddaughter like this would give him nothing but agita.'

'I don't need this,' Francesca says. She runs up to her room for her wallet and her boots and then escapes down the fire ladder into the backyard. She knows going out the front door means Victoria apologizing for Grandma Eva, making excuses for her, and Francesca doesn't have the patience for that right now. She just wants to get the fuck out of the house.

Her old man was too good for this. He deserved more than being stuck in this small world. Victoria is okay – she really loved Bill and they were great together – but she couldn't let go of Grandma Eva. She had and still has that old Italian sense that family is family, blood is blood, you can't walk away no matter how bad they are to you, no matter how toxic. If she'd had the guts to stay in the East Village the way Bill wanted to, maybe things would've been different. Maybe he wouldn't have even died. Maybe he would've had a regular music gig. He played double bass in jazz bands for a while before giving it up and taking whatever construction jobs he could get. He died in an accident on a nursing home site when Francesca was twelve. Taken out by falling debris. What a way to go. It was Victoria who insisted on moving back to her neighborhood once they were married and Francesca was on the way, going for her teaching certificate and getting a job at PS 48. It was Victoria who pushed against living the bohemian life they both wanted, settling instead for what she knew, trying to fit round pegs into square holes or whatever the fuck.

Her dad was from the Bronx but had moved to the East Village when he was seventeen. He met her mother at a bar called Long Eddy's one night in 1981. Aside from playing double bass, he was a painter and a poet. He typed poems on index cards and sold them for a buck each in Washington Square. His paintings were abstract. He used spray paint and found objects and lots of glue. He left them behind when they moved back to Brooklyn, to the apartment on Sixty-Fifth Street right before she was born. Art, poetry, and jazz weren't paying bills and certainly weren't going to help support a family. They got married at city hall – Grandma Eva was not happy about that – and he vowed to get a steady job. That's when he started in construction. Victoria always says the joy started going out of him then, and she still feels bad about that. He loved Francesca and he loved Victoria, but he didn't have anything else. He played softball on the weekends to help clear his head, but it was a beer league and most of the guys were assholes, except for one or two he liked. He never found purchase in the neighborhood, heard whispered slurs and not-so-whispered slurs, was made to feel like he didn't belong.

Francesca wishes he had some family she could contact, but there's not really anyone. His parents died when he was in his twenties, before she was born. He didn't have any siblings. The few cousins he had moved down to Virginia, North Carolina, and Georgia in the late nineties. She wrote a letter to one of them and never heard back. It was an old address.

Moving through the world, she feels really close to Bill, feels guided by him somehow. She lets him guide her now, away from Grandma Eva, away from the crumbling house on Bay Thirty-Fourth Street, and into the city, where things tend to make more sense for her as they did for him.

The subway ride is slow, lots of stops and starts. The conductor makes a few announcements that sound like long electric buzzes. Francesca watches out the window. Rooftops at first and then tunnel walls. Graffiti. Trash.

A woman enters the car at Thirty-Sixth Street and comes around with a plastic soda cup. She's silent. PLEASE HELP IF YOU CAN, I'M BROKE AND PREGNANT written sloppily on the cup in blue marker. Francesca gives her a dollar. She can just hear Grandma Eva: 'Why would you do that? She'll just use it on drugs.' Francesca gives her another dollar.

Passing over the East River on the Manhattan Bridge is her favorite part of the ride. It always makes her feel like a kid. She figures only a kid gets excited about going over a bridge on a train, about studying the way the sunlight hits the water. She'd like to use that in a movie someday, a lonely woman watching the river out the scratched-up window of a train.

In the city, she gets off at Broadway-Lafayette. She's thinking about the movies at first. It's always such a big relief to come into the city to see a movie. All the theaters in her neighborhood are closed or on their way out, and they were shitholes for a long time before that. Last time she was at the Marboro on Bay Parkway, one of the only theaters still standing in Southern Brooklyn, a rat scurried under her feet in the middle of whatever she was seeing. She loves coming to the Angelika and Film Forum, where it feels like movies still matter. She wonders what's playing. *The Anniversary Party* maybe. She loves Jennifer Jason Leigh. She'll try the Angelika first. She'll decide what to see when she gets there.

Standing in front of the Angelika, she decides against a movie. A bunch just started, and there's nothing she hates more than walking in late, even if it's still during the previews. She thinks maybe she'll go get a falafel at Mamoun's on St. Mark's Place. She wishes she had more than the fortysomething bucks she has in her pocket. Maybe she'll go to the Keyhole Cocktail Lounge while she's at it. The Keyhole's the easiest place to get served. She started drinking there when she was sixteen. The old Ukrainian bartender – he's the best – is always drunk as hell. Sometimes he charges people double for drinks, but sometimes he doesn't charge at all. Age is irrelevant there. She's seen kids maybe fourteen or fifteen get served beers. Last time she was at the Keyhole, it was one for the books. She made out with this painter from Red Hook right on the bar. The old man bartender sang them Sinatra while they kissed. When they walked outside for a cigarette a while later, it was snowing. This must've been back in February or March. There's nothing better than snow in the city. Fairy-tale shit. She'll miss it when she's gone, eventually, wherever she goes.

She thinks about stopping to call her friend Andre. He lives right nearby, on East Sixth Street. Maybe he'll come out with her. She got to be friends with Andre just from hanging out in Washington Square Park. He goes to LaGuardia High School. He's a singer. She wishes she'd gone to LaGuardia. It's one of the best high schools for the arts in the country, that's what she's heard anyway. The kids who go there, they go on to be professional artists. They have it figured out young. They get the right help. They learn the stuff she doesn't even know yet. The version of her that went there has already taken basic film-making classes, is about a hundred steps ahead. But Francesca's got nothing, just a camcorder and whatever she's figured out winging it around and trying to edit between two half-busted VCRs. Lafayette, where she just graduated from, is known for its baseball players. Back in the old days, some famous actors had gone there – Paul Sorvino, Rhea Perlman – and she'd heard that the screenwriter and director Richard LaGravenese had gone there in the seventies, but that was more chance than anything else. It isn't a place that nurtures artists. In fact, Francesca barely made it out. It'd become more and more dangerous in the past decade, and it's now – she thinks she read this somewhere – the lowest performing high school in the city. People see you went to LaGuardia, they think you're something special. Lafayette, that's nothing. A hot turd on the cracked sidewalk. Once she saw a list of notable alumni from LaGuardia and she got so jealous she puked in her lap. She wants to be on a list like that one day. She feels like she'll never be.

Since she's allowing herself to be guided by her old man, it occurs to her that she should chuck out all the stuff she'd normally go for – movies, the Keyhole, Andre, falafels – and what she should do instead is head to one of the places Bill used to hang out, see if anybody remembers him. That'd be fun. Ghost after him. She can't believe she never thought of doing it before. She wishes she had a picture of him, so she could show it around like a private detective.

Long Eddy's is on East Second between Avenue A and Avenue B. That's where the story of Bill and Victoria started, so it's where Francesca decides she'll go first. She knows that it's still there. Andre has talked about going with an older crowd, making out with a leathery junky poet or two in the bathroom.

Francesca knows there were also a few jazz clubs where Bill liked to go. The main one was Marbled Sigh. And there was this café, Memoir, where he went to open mics to read his poems. She's not sure if any of those places are still around. She can get the scoop easily enough. She thinks about staying out all night. Grandma Eva would go off on her when she got home, but she'd also make Victoria sweat. She thinks about calling Victoria and letting her know she's hanging in the city. She can lie and say she's staying at Andre's. She's eighteen now. Victoria will understand. Grandma Eva won't and she'll give Victoria hell over it, but that's a burden Francesca chooses to live with.

Francesca wishes she had a cell phone. Many people have them now. It's not a thing that people only have in movies like it was for a while. She can't afford it. She stops at a payphone on the corner of Broadway and Bond, dropping a quarter into the slot and dialing home.

Grandma Eva picks up after one ring. 'Who's calling?' she says.

'Can I talk to Victoria, please?' Francesca says in a deep voice, almost making herself giggle.

'Francesca? Is that you? Where'd you run off to?'

'I joined the circus, Grandma, and now they want me to bite the heads off chickens.'

'What?'

'Can I talk to my mom?'

'I think we need to have a very serious discussion about your future one day soon.'

'Okay, sure.'

There's some bickering on the other end of the line now, Victoria wrestling the phone away from Grandma Eva. 'I'm sorry,' Victoria says, taking over. 'You know I can never get it first.'

Francesca gives a little laugh. 'I might stay in the city,' she says. 'I just wanted to let you know. I didn't want you to worry. I'm not sure yet, but if I don't come home, that's why.'

'With Andre?'

'Yeah, probably.'

'You're a grown-up. You just take care.'

Grandma Eva is yelling in the background. 'She only thinks she's a grown-up,' she says. 'Wait until the world bites her in the ass.'

'Ignore her,' Victoria says.

'I always do,' Francesca says.

'Call me if you need me.'

'I will.' A beat. 'Can I ask you something?'

'Shoot.'

She wants to ask something about the night she met Bill at Long Eddy's. *What was the weather like? What was on the jukebox? Who was bartending?* Something. Anything. She wants more details. She wants to ask a hundred questions about the places they went, about their old apartment and the friends they had before going back to Brooklyn. She wants to ask about the best nights and the worst nights. But they've talked about some of this stuff before, and it always makes Victoria so sad. It was another life. It probably doesn't even feel real in some ways. She knows how much her mother regrets pulling her father out of it and into the small world of her neighborhood. 'Forget it,' Francesca says.

'What is it? You can ask me anything.'

'It's nothing. Really. I'm okay. It's okay. I'll see you tomorrow.'

'I almost forgot. That boy called for you. The one who was here earlier. Bobby.'

'Already?'

'I guess he really liked you. He seems sweet enough.'

'He left a number?'

'He did. You want it?'

'I guess.' She finds a pen with a chewed cap on top of the phone.

Victoria reads her the number.

Francesca writes it on the back of her hand, asks her to repeat it, and then says thanks.

'You gonna call him back?' Victoria asks.

'I don't know yet.'

'Well, call if you need me, okay? Don't be dissuaded by Grandma picking up.'

More yelling from Grandma Eva in the background.

'Okay,' Francesca says, placing the receiver on the hook, thinking about how strange it must be to get older, to have all of this past behind you and this future, flat as a plain, unknowable and yet unchanging, ahead. She knows that Victoria – even when she's not thinking directly about it – is weighed down by the decisions she made that led them to where they are, is haunted by a life that could've been, happiness that could've been. Francesca sees that life too. They still live in the city. Bill's alive. She just graduated from LaGuardia. She's going to film school in the fall. The air of regret that emanates from Victoria is contagious.

Long Eddy's looks like it's been around a hundred years. A weather-beaten hand-painted sign hangs over the front awning. The riot gates are down, though the place is open. Neon beer lights fizz in the foggy windows. When Francesca gets there, she knows it's the kind of place that might serve her. There's always a shot in the old-man bars, and it's not that late in the day. Inside, tinsel covers the walls. A thick tangle of Christmas lights chokes the jukebox. Music is playing. Jazz. Francesca doesn't know enough about jazz to identify who it is. On a folded open card table across from the shuttered payphone booth in the corner, a Virgin Mary statue with no head is propped on a stack of phone books next to a steaming hot pot full of chili and a pyramid of small Styrofoam bowls. A few old-timers sit hunched at the horseshoe bar. The bartender is wearing an eye patch and an oversized green flannel shirt. He must be in his forties, with graying hair and a kind of alcoholic tenderness to him, a dead ringer for the actor Joe Morton. Francesca's thinking that maybe he knew Bill, maybe they were friends.

She takes a seat at the bar.

The bartender comes over, dishrag clenched in his fist. 'How old are you?' he asks.

'Twenty-one,' she says.

'You got identification?'

The lies come smooth and easy. 'I lost it.'

He nods and smiles. 'Okay, well, might be best to move on then. This place ain't exactly full of excitement anyway.'

'I don't need a drink,' she says, surprised he's chosen not to serve her but not hurt by it. She is, after all, underage. Could be he has a good eye for it. Could be he's just not old enough to not give a shit like the bartender at the Keyhole. 'Can I ask you a question?'

'You want to ask *me* a question?'

'My dad used to drink here back in the day. Bill Clarke. You didn't know him, did you?'

The bartender comes closer. 'Sure, I knew Bill. You say you're his daughter? Who's your mother?'

'Victoria DiMaggio. She used to come in too.'

'Man, what a blast from the past. I knew Bill well. He was a good pal. Lived a few blocks over from me. I was here the night he met Victoria. Wasn't working the bar then. Just hanging out. She came in with some friends. They were all punked out. They'd been to a show at Coney Island High. Bill had eyes for her right away.' He pauses, leans on the bar. 'What's your name? I'm Pierce.'

'Francesca.' She extends a hand, and they shake. 'You said my mother was all punked out?'

'She was a fireball, yeah. I can see her in you. Bill too. You really twenty-one? Now that I know you, I'll serve you.'

'I'm eighteen,' she says, unable to continue the act.

'Close enough. It'll be our secret. You, me, the walls, and these bums.' He motions to the drunken regulars. 'Don't think anybody will throw up any roadblocks.' He plucks an icy beer from a cooler under the bar, setting it on a napkin in front of her.

Francesca takes out a crumpled ten and pushes it toward him.

'You keep your money,' he says. 'Just tell me how Bill is. Last thing I remember, they were dating. He brought her around a lot. One day, they just stopped coming.'

'My dad died six years ago.'

'Goddamn, I'm sorry to hear that. That's way too young. He couldn't have been older than me.'

'He was working construction. There was an accident.'

'Bill, working construction? I always figured him for teaching art or music. He was good at both.'

'I'm just, I don't know,' Francesca says, starting and not sure exactly what she wants to say. She drinks some of her beer. 'I come into the city all the time and I've never come to this place, even though I know he hung out here. I've never been to any of the places where he played in bands or read poems.'

'Most of those joints are closed. Everything's banks and frozen yogurt shops and Starbucks now. Marbled Sigh, that was a good one. I bet your mother mentioned it.'

Francesca nods.

'Bill Clarke's girl,' Pierce says, shaking his head. 'Nuts. Where in the hell do these years go? Poor guy. So, what'd he do? Move back to Brooklyn with Victoria? I remember them talking about getting hitched, but I wasn't sure it'd happen. Black guy, Italian girl. Lots of things still stand in the way of that, never mind twenty years ago.'

'Yeah, they got married and had me and went back to Bensonhurst. My mom started teaching third grade. He worked construction.'

'Bill Clarke in Bensonhurst. Jesus Christ. I'm sure he loved your mother a lot, but that must've torn him up. He loved living down here.'

'It did.' Francesca takes out her tobacco and rolls a cigarette. Pierce watches her. She has it down to a science. 'Can you tell me a story about him? Anything. The years are passing, and I'm getting further away from him. I don't know. It was so hard after he died but that grief just kind of numbed me. My mother can't really talk about him without crying.'

'I got plenty of tales,' Pierce says. 'You know your daddy was a prankster?'

Francesca smiles. She has many flashes of him from when she was a kid. He was always sweet to her and he tried to make her laugh, but he was also guarded, quiet, and melancholy. It makes her happy to think of him having fun, goofing off.

'One time, we were in here, drinking. The bartender at the time was this guy we called Mickey Fluff. He was about six-foot-six, barely seemed to fit in this joint. Made the ceiling seem even lower than it is. Mickey Fluff's thing was he had to piss constantly. And he was always complaining about how hard he pissed. How forcefully. Cracked me and Bill up to no end. Mickey Fluff would come out of the can and he'd say, "Man, it's like I was going to war on the water in the toilet." We'd be dying. A lot of times he'd complain his piss was sudsy. We'd be like, "Sudsy, what the fuck you mean?"'

Francesca is laughing the hardest she's laughed in a while. She doesn't know Mickey Fluff, but she can picture him perfectly. It's twenty-plus years ago. The East Village in its prime. Bill is happy.

Pierce continues: 'So Bill gets it in his head that he's gonna pour a bunch of dish soap in the toilet. Next time Mickey Fluff squirts his mean piss in there, the thing goes wild with bubbles. He comes out of the can, freaking. You'd think a rat crawled out. He's hyperventilating. "I pissed so hard, there's a million bubbles," he says. "They're coming out everywhere. Big, soapy bubbles. Something must be wrong with my pissing parts." He said that. *Pissing parts*. Bill hits the fucking floor, I shit you not. I thought he was gonna have a heart attack. We quoted that shit every day for the next year. If Bill was alive and he came in here, I'd say it and he'd be rolling.' Pierce is laughing, his eyes teary.

Francesca's still laughing too but now it's tinged with sadness. She never saw her dad laughing like that or at least doesn't remember if she did.

'That was your old man,' Pierce says. 'We had a lot of good times.'

'What happened to Mickey Fluff?'

'Motherfucker won big in Atlantic City one weekend. Last anybody ever saw of him.'

'I'm glad I finally came in here,' Francesca says.

Pierce tells more stories about her father. All bar stories. If he knew him much outside the bar, it's not exactly clear. It's all pranks and buffets and late nights. Crashing in a booth after hours. Carrying each other home. That New Year's Eve where they slept in the back of Oily Rudy's cab. He stops occasionally to pour drinks for the old glaze-eyed regulars.

Francesca finishes her beer, and he brings her another. It's silly, but she feels light, a bit buzzed. Pierce asks her about herself. Is she going to college? What's she want to be? She get the art thing from her old man? He reiterates that Bill was good at everything he did – poems, paintings, music. He says there wasn't even an ounce of him that was capable of selling out, which is why he never got anywhere. She tells him she wants to make movies. He says she should go to film school at NYU, as if it's that easy, just *go*, walk right on in, no money or application necessary. He says she should make a documentary about Long Eddy's. He says he knows it doesn't look like much but, every night, he can see the whole range of human emotions on display. Elation, love, euphoria, hate, anger, despair. All of it, maybe in the same face over a short stretch of time. A glorious dive. Part Garden of Eden, part apocalyptic hellhole.

She nods. One thing she's learned is that when you tell people you want to be a filmmaker, they tell you their great idea for a movie and it's never great, it's always horrible, barely an idea, more like a sliver of an idea wrapped up in the blankets of bullshit. But Pierce's idea isn't terrible. Of course, she wouldn't know how to shoot it or even have the guts to shoot it. How would she get a room full of drunks to behave like there wasn't a camera there? How would she pick out strands of narrative to follow so it didn't all feel random and boring?

At a certain point, Pierce starts doing shots of bottom-shelf whiskey, which is all that Long Eddy's has. There's no staggering selection behind the bar, just a small gathering of dusty bottles next to the register. Cheaper than the cheap stuff. He asks if she wants a shot. 'Why the hell not?' he says. 'For your old man.'

'Okay, sure,' she says.

He pours it for her, whiskey slopping out of the glass and onto the bar top.

'For Bill Clarke,' Pierce says. 'A beautiful guy. He knew that the rat's ass end of midnight held all the answers.'

She clinks glasses with Pierce. More spilled whiskey. She tries not to look at his eye patch. She throws the shot back like a pro. She hasn't done many shots but she's done enough to know to do it fast, not to sip, to just suck it down and hope like hell she doesn't puke. The whiskey is medicinal, edged with a bitter tang. It lights her up.

Pierce asks if she wants another, but she says she's good. She focuses on her beer.

'I've got these glue traps in my apartment for the mice,' Pierce says, his good eye gone pissy. He looks like just another regular now, drunk and unsteady. 'The other night, a mouse gets caught in one in my kitchen. I'm in the living room, on the couch, and I hear it trying to get free. It's an awful noise, like a baby trying to get off a fucking paper party hat, and I'm just sitting there, staring at the ceiling, going like, "This is terrible. Get up and do something." But I just stayed right where I was and I couldn't sleep because, you know, a mouse was dying in my kitchen and I was responsible. It's my fault it was stuck in the least humane trap you ever heard of.'

Francesca nods along, unsure where Pierce is going with this, unsure how they got to this mouse in his kitchen from Bill. The few shots he's taken have turned him into a slobbering rambler. He has that glare that drunks get when they start telling a story that might never end. Or it might end with them breaking down or trying to kiss her or giving her fifty bucks for her future because their future's lost.

Pierce continues: 'For five hours that mouse dragged itself and the trap from one end of the kitchen to the other. I was awake through it all. I went in to check at first light, and the thing had finally crapped out by the fridge. I swept it into a garbage bag. It was still alive. I took that garbage bag out into the hall and threw it into the chute that goes down to the incinerator. Then I went back into my apartment and thought about how I'm just like that mouse, except instead of one night it's been forty-three years of me dragging the glue trap I'm stuck in across this city. You know what I mean? Someday I'm gonna be by that fridge and I'm gonna realize, "That's fucking it. I can't pull myself anymore." And someone's gonna pick me up, bag me, and toss me in the fire.' Tears in his eyes now. He does another shaky shot.

Breaking down it is.

'I don't want to die,' Pierce says. 'I don't want that to be all life is. Your old man shouldn't have died. I'm sorry. He deserved a whole big life. He deserved to see you grow up. It's not right.'

'Thank you,' Francesca says. She can't think of anything else to say.

'You sure you don't want another shot?' Pierce asks.

'I'm okay. I'm gonna use the payphone, if that's cool.'

'You need quarters?' Pierce turns and opens the register. He takes out a thick roll of quarters and puts it on the bar in front of her. 'Here's ten bucks. Call everybody you know. I'd let you use the house phone, but the line's disconnected. Payphone's all we got.'

Francesca says it's okay, she has a few quarters left. She goes to the payphone booth, pushes the accordion door open, and then pulls it shut. It's dark and dingy in the booth. Smells like piss and beer. Maybe a hint of puke. Graffiti fills the walls around her. FOR A GOOD TIME CALL TEDDY BEAR CHUCK. FUCK BUSH. FUCK GIULIANI. 'JESUS CHRIST DIED FOR SOMEBODY'S SINS... NOT MINE!!!' More Patti Smith lyrics scrawled in red paint marker. A heart shot through with a cartoon dick instead of an arrow. It's quiet in the booth, and she notices the music from the jukebox has stopped.

She reaches into her pocket for a quarter, realizes she actually doesn't have any, and goes back to get the roll from Pierce. She thumbs the rounded top edge of the wrapper open and gets one out.

Nestled back in the booth. Things are spinning. Not a ton, but the shot was a bad idea. She needs some food. She thinks of that pot of chili on the table out there. Disgusting, sure, but it could be enough to get the job done. Two beers and a shot on an empty stomach wasn't smart.

Just as she's about to drop the quarter into the slot, Pierce passes in front of the booth and knocks on the glass. He motions for her to watch what he's doing. He dances over to the jukebox and puts in a handful of quarters. He punches some numbers. The first song that comes on is Sade's 'No Ordinary Love.' He dances back past the booth again and points in at her. She shrugs. He points more aggressively at her. The shirt. She nods and gives him a thumbs-up, acknowledges that she knows he played the song for her. He smiles and goes up behind one of the fragile drunks leaning over the end of the bar and tries to coax him to stand. The guy waves him off but then they fall into a sloppy slow dance in the center of the bar, rocking back and forth mechanically, the Christmas lights puddling behind them.

Francesca drops the quarter in. She looks at the number on her hand and dials slowly, careful not to get it wrong. She notices blood smeared by the coin release on the phone. 'Is Bobby there?' she says to the voice on the other end of the line that picks up.

'This is Bobby.'

'It's Francesca from today.'

'I didn't think you'd call me back. I thought I fucked up, calling so fast. I figured I should've waited a couple of days at least.'

'You want to come into the city?' she asks. 'I'm here now.'

'Sure,' he says. 'Where?'

She gives him the address of Long Eddy's, and he says he'll be there as soon as the train can get him there, probably an hour. After she hangs up, she opens the door. Sade on the jukebox sounds good. It makes her happy to see Pierce and the other drunk still dancing. She wonders if she would've called Bobby if she hadn't had those drinks. Probably not. She spoons some of the chili into one of the Styrofoam bowls and finds a coffee can full of plastic spoons. She takes the chili back to her seat and tries to eat some. Rubbery hot dogs float amid the mushy beans, which is disgusting, but otherwise it tastes just like canned chili.

She hopes it'll be enough to absorb the booze, so she can drink more when Bobby gets here. She's not sure what the night holds, but she's excited to see. Sometimes the city feels like everything's possible.

PART 2

Lily

Lily's in the church basement again. A lot has happened in the last week already, but right now she's focused on talking about writing and listening to her students read their first assignments. It feels good to be there. She feels like a professional at something. It's the same group. She'd hoped or expected that a few others might join for the remainder, but she's happy at least that she didn't lose anyone, that they didn't deem it not worth their time and money. She nods at lines that she likes, taking notes as she reads, as she'd seen her own teachers do. Everyone brought copies. No hitch there, which is nice.

Most of the stories so far have been terrible. Sarah's was simply a rant. Jenny wrote about her childhood dog. Shelley attempted to build a story around her grandmother's recipe for struffoli, which could've worked, but it fell apart badly when it became more about the actual recipe and less about the story she was trying to tell through the recipe. Dino wrote about two mobsters arguing over soda. That was it. A basic Coke versus Pepsi thing. The one mobster loved Coke, and the other one loved Pepsi. It was like a surrealist commercial that went nowhere. If it had been a self-aware comedy sketch, it might've been incredible, but it played out as an exercise in banality.

Of course, Lily didn't say anything bad about any of the stories. She kept it civil and cordial. She tried to mask her feelings with very specific critiques, opening up the stories and picking out moments where the writer might have added a vivid detail or improved characterization somehow. No one took notes. In that way, it was very unlike the classes she'd attended in college, where her fellow students seemed genuinely interested in getting better as writers.

Josh is reading now. He's written a tale about a bunch of Vikings turning into cannibals when they're stranded on an island and they run out of food. She did tell them they could write about anything they wanted to – she hates the idea of imposing limits – but how could she ever have expected a Viking cannibal story? The way Josh reads makes it even worse. He thinks he's a genius, that's clear, and he reads very dramatically, like he's written something so true about the human condition that they should all collapse in the circle and kiss his bare toes through his stupid goddamn sandals. They're the kind of sandals that men wear when they like to imagine themselves as wanderers, on a long mission through a desert or over mountain trails, when all they do in reality is sit in their parents' house and play video games or board games and eat chips and pizza. Who's she to talk? She lives with her mom again. She spends most of her time cooped up in her own imagination.

The best thing about Josh's story is watching Dino's reactions to it. It's like Josh keeps farting. Dino squints, scrunches his nose, makes his lips thin. He might not know good writing, but he knows that this is somehow foul.

When Josh is done reading, Dino's the first one to ask a question: 'So, all these football players, they're stranded on an island and they start munching on each other, right? They wearing their uniforms? That makes it better, to imagine them in those silly purple uniforms, you know?'

'It's not the Minnesota Vikings I'm writing about,' Josh says, again making the clarification. 'It's the Norse people from Scandinavia who raided and traded centuries ago.'

'Oh, right,' Dino says. 'I forgot. That changes the whole thing. I was picturing all these beefy football players. I mean, clearly the big guys, the offensive linemen and the defensive linemen, they'd eat the placekicker or the punter first. Some of these kickers are really tiny. It's like you start off by eating a bird instead of a cow, you know what I mean?'

'But I didn't write about football players eating each other.' Josh is getting defensive, slouching awkwardly in his chair. Lily doesn't like the feeling he's bringing to the class in this moment. A tension rooted in some expectation or sense of entitlement that the others lack. He seems pissed. He wants alms thrown at his feet. He wants to be crowned king of the geniuses.

'I really didn't like how graphic it was,' Shelley says.

'It turned my stomach,' Jenny says. 'When they eat the poor guy's – excuse me – pecker, I was like, "Do we need to hear this?" Last thing I expected tonight was to hear about a Viking toasting a pecker over a campfire like a marshmallow. Excuse me for saying "pecker". I hate the word "penis."'

'Lorena Bobbitt, that's who I thought of,' Sarah says.

'Okay, let's rein this back in,' Lily says, trying to redirect the conversation and actually address Josh's story. As bad as it was, she doesn't want him to leave here feeling like he got made fun of. He is, after all, still a kid. She tries to find some nice things to say. She talks about his descriptions of the island, saying his writing was particularly strong in those stretches (it wasn't). She also compliments him on some of the dialogue between the Vikings, saying it felt really real (it didn't). Jack speaks up and says there was a line about the sky looking like it was on fire that he really liked. Lily appreciates his effort to join in on saying nice things. The tone of the class is reestablished. Some of the tension that Josh had created with his slouch and his uneasy response to the initial comments dissipates. Lily asks if he has any questions or comments.

'I'm good,' Josh says. 'Thanks for the feedback.'

They move on to Jack's story. He reads it aloud. His hands are shaking, his voice quavering. Everyone else reads along on the copies he's given them. Within a couple of lines, it's clear that it's a story told from the point of view of the kid who threw the rock at Amelia's car. Jack's imagined a whole life for the kid, everything that led up to his picking up that rock and throwing it into traffic. He's imagined that the kid had it hard at home. Parents who ignored him when they weren't yelling at him. He's imagined that the kid had all this anger and sadness in him, and it just boiled to the surface and he was trying desperately to find a way to rid himself of it, and that's why he chucked the rock. It's the only acceptable version of events to Jack. It's as if he's telling himself a story to live. He can't see it another way – the kid did it as a joke and never looked back and never thought about the consequences of his actions or, even worse, the kid wanted something bad to happen, wanted to hurt someone.

Lily's amazed at Jack's capacity for empathy. And his imagination. It took a lot of guts to imagine the story from the kid's point of view. He calls him Nothing Boy. He could've given him a regular name but Nothing Boy is so much more effective. Lily cries at the end when Nothing Boy sees what the rock has done, how it's caused this terrible accident. Jack has the kid wanting to kill himself over it, but then it's as if he – Jack, the writer – talks his daughter's fictional killer out of suicide. It's a really touching ending.

Again, Lily thinks about what it must have been like for Amelia to have her world stopped just like that. A girl with her whole life ahead of her. A girl from the neighborhood who wanted to be a writer, who *was* a writer, just like Lily. She wonders if she was listening to the radio. She wonders a million things about the moment.

'Wow, Jack,' Lily says when he's done reading, unable to hide her admiration for his work, especially compared to what she's just heard from the others.

Shelley, Jenny, and Sarah are crying again.

'Very moving,' Dino says. 'Very.'

Josh is uncomfortable because of all the positive attention Jack's getting. He thought it'd be his work that people would respond to this way.

Jack clears his throat, 'I wrote it another way too,' he says, turning the page.

'You want to read it?' Lily asks.

'If it's okay,' he says, and he starts reading.

It's the same story but told from his point of view. In this version, he's there, on the scene, and he sees the kid throw the rock. He's nameless this time, the kid. Jack watches the accident happen. When the kid bolts away, Jack chases him down, beats him to a pulp with his bare fists. It's cathartic, an exorcism on the page, all of his anger filtered into this fictional violence. He describes every blow, every laceration, as if writing it this way can bring Amelia back to life.

The version of him in the story is relentless, cold. Lily doesn't buy that he would've chased after the kid instead of running to Amelia, but that's not the point of this. In a story, the revenge he can't get in life is there for the taking. It's as if Jack wrote it the other way, empathetic to the kid, and then needed to purge this feeling, the one that was haunting him, the desire to trade blood for blood.

In the story, as Jack beats the kid, he keeps saying, 'Take it back.'

It's devastating, this yearning to make the kid somehow turn back the clock.

When he's done, the group sits in shocked silence.

'I had to write it that way too,' Jack says.

'I get it,' Lily says. Now she's taken aback by his ability to imagine violence. She's thinking that to write it that way, it must live inside him. How could something awful not grow from what he'd been through?

'You gave the bum what he deserves,' Dino says.

'It was tough to listen to,' Shelley says. 'But I agree. I started to not see him so much as a kid as you were reading, and more like an idea that you were trying to kill.'

'That's interesting,' Lily says. 'What do you mean by *an idea*?'

'I don't know exactly. I think the first story was all about seeing him as a kid but in the second story, he was just an idea that you could do something bad for fun and get away with it – *that's* what Jack's trying to kill. I'm not sure if I'm making sense.'

'I think you are.'

Sarah connects it to her own story, also born of rage.

'Why's he get to write two stories?' Josh asks.

'Well, it was really two takes on the same story,' Lily says, trying to snuff out his jealousy.

Jack gazes down at his lap, nervous and embarrassed. Lily can tell that he regrets reading the second story.

She moves on. There's not much time left, so she wants to make sure she gets to their assignment for next class. She points to the clock on the wall. 'You see that clock?'

They all nod. Sure, they see the clock. What would she do if one them said, *I don't see any clock*?

Lily continues: 'Okay, I want you to write a story called "The Clock." It can be about anything as long as it's called "The Clock." Let's say three to four pages this time.' She's ripping off another assignment from Emily Bielanko. She remembers Emily talking about how Anton Chekhov was once asked where he came up with ideas for stories and he picked up a nearby ashtray and said he'd write a story called 'The Ashtray' by the next day. Or something like that. Lily can't remember it exactly – it's all written down in some long-gone notebook – but that's about the gist of it. Pick something. Use it as a jumping-off point. She thought of the clock on the wall because she'd watched this old movie with Judy Garland called *The Clock* a few nights ago on cable, and she thought it was as if the writers had started in the same place and built something beautiful from it. She rambles on about all of this – Emily, Chekhov, Judy Garland, and *The Clock* – to her class and they seem like they get what she's asking for.

'My grandmother had a clock in her kitchen,' Dino says, 'and this thing would drive you fucking nuts – excuse me, frigging nuts. This little figurine thing came out on the hour, scooting on a track, and made all this noise. It sounded like a dwarf screaming bloody murder. Nothing against dwarves. I had this guy, Three-Dollar Vito, I was good pals with – he was a dwarf. Just, you know, this figurine had this high-pitched munchkin voice. I don't know what it was supposed to be. I mean, I've heard of chickens crowing and all that cuckoo bird shit, but I don't know what this thing was getting at. I asked her one time, "Grams, where'd you get this thing?" "The waterfront," she says. What kind of ominous answer is that? What am I supposed to say?'

'There you go,' Lily says. 'That's a whole story right there. The origins of your grandmother's clock.'

Dino nods, impressed with himself.

'When my father was dying, he had this clock on the table next to his bed,' Jenny says. 'Just a regular alarm clock you could buy anywhere. He never used the alarm, though. It just went tick-tock all day. Only noise in the room. I'd sit with him for hours and I'd just stare at that clock.'

'Save it for your stories,' Lily says. She gathers the copies of everyone's work and stuffs them in her bag. 'I'm going to reread everything from tonight over the next few days and give you some written feedback next class.'

More nodding from everyone.

Lily dismisses them.

The others scurry away, but Jack hangs back again. 'You okay?' he asks.

'I'm fine,' Lily says. 'Thanks for your stories. That really saved the day. Between you and me, it was pretty ugly before that.'

'You seem like you're worried about something.'

'Me? I don't know. Not really.'

'It's just reminding me of the way Amelia used to carry herself when she was upset, like when she was trying to be normal but something was getting to her under the surface.'

Lily suddenly wants to tell Jack about Micah. All the calls. How he showed up out of nowhere a few days ago. He came down from Westchester and knocked on her front door like it was nothing, like she hadn't told him *no* a million times. He left without throwing a fit. He called again and told her calmly he was staying at a motel in Coney Island and he wouldn't leave until she promised to see him. She told him no, told him she was getting a restraining order, even though her lawyer cousin had told her getting a restraining order could be tough. Everywhere she goes, she feels like he's there watching. She feels his eyes on her right now. She wants to tell Jack all of this because there's no one to tell except her mother, who just keeps saying to ignore Micah and he'll go away. With guys like that, she insists, if you give them an inch, they take a yard. Just don't give up the inch, that's her mother's way of looking at it. It's amazing to Lily that Jack can somehow see she's upset under this teacher veneer she's tried to craft. 'You want to go get a coffee or something?' she asks him now.

They wind up at the Roulette Diner, where Lily has been coming since she was a little girl. Jack says he used to bring Amelia here after her CYO basketball games, and she'd always get a milkshake and disco fries. He used to come here after softball games too, which was kind of strange, the whole Brooklyn Battlers team taking over the back of the diner. He and this one guy, Bill, they'd get Rusty Nails and sit in a booth by themselves while the others drank pitchers of beer and ate burgers and flirted with waitresses.

Lily's memories of the Roulette begin with her dad bringing her here. Every Saturday morning for a while before he got sick. The earliest time she can remember is when she was five, wearing overalls, her hair in braids. Probably around 1985. The place had looked a lot less run-down than it does now, at least in her mind. She remembers not knowing what kind of place it was at first. So much blurry action. The lights. Mirrored walls. Booths that swallowed people up. It was as if she didn't take notice of the plates of food on all the tables, the waiters and waitresses carrying around big trays. The smell of frying oil must've been what finally made her aware. She sat in a booth with her dad, and he told her to order whatever she wanted. She got a grilled cheese and apple juice. For dessert, a slice of apple pie with ice cream. She remembers being so happy.

Every time there with her dad was like that. The memories become more vivid around age six and last until she's eight, when he couldn't go one Saturday because he wasn't feeling well – he'd fallen a few times – and then he wasn't feeling well all the time. It took him over a month to see a doctor. She doesn't like to think about the news he got then. He was only in his mid-thirties, but it was Lou Gehrig's disease. It's rare for it to hit someone so young is what she's since learned. He deteriorated quickly. His mind was still sharp but his body quit on him. Eventually, he couldn't eat. It was very hard to see, and her mother shielded Lily as much as she could.

Her dad's name was Matty. Other than those Saturdays at the Roulette and seeing him splayed out in his bed, dying, sipping blender food from a straw, she barely has any pictures of him in her mind.

On the year anniversary of his death, her mother brought her to the Roulette for lunch. They cried, remembering that he always ordered the same thing: a cup of black coffee and an 'All the Way' jumbo bagel with lox, cream cheese, red onions, tomato, cucumbers, and capers. They both ordered the same thing that day, picking at the edges of their bagels, scraping off the capers, pressing the tines of the fork into the salmon to confirm it was okay to eat.

After that, they made it a tradition to come to the Roulette on the anniversary of her dad's death. For four years, anyway. Until Lily's mom met Danny and they stopped going to visit her father's grave every month, stopped coming to the Roulette to order an 'All the Way' bagel and coffee in observance of his death, stopped talking about him altogether. A few weeks into dating Danny, Lily's mom took down all the pictures of her dad that were up on the walls, hid the photo albums full of their family pictures, and moved on, dragging Lily with her, out of a past that no longer existed and into a present that was off-kilter, as if they'd entered a new timeline. It turned out Danny was very jealous. He'd been over to the house a few times and hated seeing pictures of her dad, and that was what had prompted her mom to begin the act of erasing her dad. Lily's not sure if she meant to erase him totally right from the start or if it just happened naturally after those first acts acquiescing to Danny, but he was as gone as he could get.

Lily started coming here on her own in high school. She'd bring a paperback from the library and a journal, and she sat at a table by the kitchen, reading and writing. She'd come to love the unchoreographed madness of the place, its wild card vibe. Instead of journaling about school and extracurriculars and boys, she was describing the people she was seeing at the Roulette. What they were wearing, what their voices sounded like, what cigarettes they smoked, what tattoos they had, what their hair was like. Sometimes she'd just order coffee. Other times, she'd get French toast. She was going through a big French toast phase then.

After she graduated from Bishop Kearney, she stopped coming. There were new diners out in the world for her to explore – she got to know the ones in York well – and the Roulette's sad magic had all but evaporated. She didn't feel her dad here. It's been at least four years since she's set foot inside.

It's strange to be sitting in a booth with Jack. It's not the same booth she sat in with her dad, but it's not far off. The diner is more ragged than it was four years ago. Tears in the Naugahyde. Smudges on mirrors. Dust on the blinds. And there seems to be a new slowness to everything. The wait staff moves as if drugged. The people eating at tables and booths bring food up to their mouths, halting along the way as if they need to be oiled, Tin Man-style. Even the couples scattered around seem to be languid in their bickering.

Jack orders coffee and a bowl of lentil soup from the waiter, who has the biggest ears Lily's ever seen. She remembers him. He's been here forever. His name tag reads PETE but everyone calls him Bimsy. She used to puzzle over what Bimsy could mean. A shortened version of his last name? A nonsensical nickname? A reference to a private joke? She never asked, deciding it was better not to know, to keep wondering. She's almost always found this to be the case. It's just better not to know, to maintain the mystery.

She orders a grilled cheese and a Russian Roulette, which is just a Black Russian – vodka and Kahlúa – with splashes of Coca-Cola and cherry liqueur. She hasn't really looked at the cocktail menu closely. This was the first one she saw. But she knows she needs a drink. It's the first alcoholic drink she's ever ordered here. She almost laughs, thinking that. Booze has been so much a part of her life the last few years, it's hard to imagine a time when it wasn't.

Bimsy wanders off to put the order in, taking a detour by the register out front to sweet talk the squat old woman perched there, wearing a tuxedo vest, a pen with a paper marigold taped to its cap tucked behind her ear.

'You come here a lot?' Jack asks.

'I used to with my dad, before he died,' Lily says. 'And then with my mom. In high school, I'd come here to work in the afternoons a lot.'

'I'm sorry about your dad.'

'Thanks. I was young. He had ALS.'

'That's tough.'

Lily picks at the edges of her napkin. She takes a sip of water. 'How'd you feel about class tonight?' she asks.

'Yeah, good,' Jack says. 'I can see why you like to write. And why Amelia liked it so much. It really helps. You get to spill all these emotions onto the page. I don't know what I'm doing, but this is the closest I've felt to alive in a while.'

'That's good to hear.'

'You lost your old man, so you know. Grief is a nasty thing.'

Lily nods. She looks all around. Micah. She forgets and then remembers. She gets a flash of him sitting in a booth across from them and then realizes it's someone who looks totally different – long hair, scraggly beard, mangled teeth. Micah is country club soft. Pale. He wears cargo shorts, polo shirts, and Birkenstocks. Maybe that's why Josh's sandals made her so damn uneasy. What did she ever see in Micah? He was different from the Brooklyn boys she'd known. He came off as reserved and polite at first. She imagines him outside now, staring in through the glass from the sidewalk, wondering what she's doing with this middle-aged man. She can hear his scrummy voice in her ear: 'Are you fucking this old man, Lily?'

'You got something you want to talk about,' Jack says, as if reading her mind, 'we can talk about it. You remind me so much of Amelia, I feel like I can listen to you. I don't feel like I can listen to a lot of people anymore. No one, really.'

Bimsy brings their drinks, his hands quaking. Some of Lily's cocktail slops over the rim of the glass onto his wrist, and he licks it off as he walks away. She tastes the Russian Roulette. It's vaguely medicinal.

Jack sips his coffee. He gets back to what he was saying: 'No pressure, obviously.'

'Thanks,' Lily says. She takes a long pull off the Russian Roulette. It's getting better, this madness in her glass.

She's come to really enjoy the relief that comes with her first drink of the day. It's weird to think that in high school she'd barely had alcohol at all. While other girls she knew snuck pints of schnapps into class, soaked their tampons in vodka, and, on the weekends, drank beer at parties, she was sipping the occasional wine cooler and they just didn't do much for her. It wasn't until college that she had beer and hard liquor. At the start, cans of Yuengling didn't do much for her either. Things clicked when her friend Rhonda bought her a vodka soda one happy hour. It was fancy vodka. Fancy to Lily anyway. The kind of stuff that was thirty or forty bucks a bottle at the store. The vodka she'd come into contact with previously was the cheap stuff that came in big plastic handles for ten bucks – it smelled like rubbing alcohol and she could never bring herself to try it. But that one good vodka soda made her really enjoy drinking, and she started doing more and more of it, branching out, finding things she liked and could afford. There was a three-week stretch before Micah where she drank every day and then she had a seven-month streak of boozing after she managed to split up with him. She found that she was capable of functioning in classes and at work with a hangover, a blessing.

'How's that drink?' Jack asks. 'Sounds like it could go either way.'

'It's pretty good,' Lily says. 'You want to try it?'

'I'm good with coffee, thanks.'

'You don't drink anymore?'

'I'm not on the wagon. I drink. Whiskey. I have some days where I really get lost in a bottle, but I find I can't bounce back. The bad thoughts come faster. It's mostly not worth it.'

Lily studies Jack's hand on his coffee mug. His fingers curled fully around it. Rough skin. Dark hair. A vein that seems to pulse. She bets nurses have taken blood from that vein. He's still wearing his wedding ring, she notices. It's a simple gold band, tarnished and scratched, catching the light from the ceiling fixture. His wife died a few years before his daughter. That's so much loss. The coffee steams on. Beyond the tips of his fingers, there's the Roulette Diner logo, a golden roulette wheel emblazoned on the black ceramic. Under that, a tagline: YOU NEVER LOSE AT OUR TABLE.

'So, that second story where you wrote about catching the kid who threw the rock and beating him up, that was cathartic?' Lily asks, circling back to class. He's pretty much answered this question already, but she finds that conversation's smoother at first when she lobs some easy pitches.

'I guess,' Jack says. 'Maybe I shouldn't have read it. Maybe I should've kept it private.'

'If it was all you'd written, I might agree,' Lily says. 'But it really worked as a companion to the first story. It was like you had these two different things you were wrestling with, wanting to forgive and wanting to get revenge.' She feels like she's said something that's pretty smart. She takes another drink.

'When Amelia was younger, in middle school, there was this boy who'd pick on her. She was going through a tough time, and he was so mean to her. His name was Antonio Cuttitta. Just a complete little shit. Tortured her daily. Called her names. Drew on her uniform. Put things in her desk. A rotten banana peel. A rubber he found out on the street. A porno magazine. I'm talking the kind of awful you don't think kids can be until you witness it.' He pauses, stirs a spoon in his coffee even though he hasn't put in sugar or cream.

'That's terrible,' Lily says.

'This was while Janey, my wife, was real sick. Amelia was a wreck. She had to go to school, act like everything was normal, and then come home to Janey's cancer. But this Cuttitta kid couldn't even let things be normal at school. He set his sights on her. I wanted to kill him, no kidding. I dreamed about it. But Amelia wouldn't let me so much as talk to the nuns. She said things would get even worse if people found out she'd told.'

'What happened?'

'Nothing. She fought through it. Kept her chin up. They went their separate ways for high school. Janey died during Amelia's first fall at Fontbonne. She was such a strong kid.' Jack fights back tears. 'I saw Antonio Cuttitta on Eighty-Sixth Street a couple of months ago. He's the age Amelia would've been. Twenty-three. He seemed pretty much the same, honestly. Walked around like he owned the world. Catcalled some girl. Got into a fight with the Indian guy who runs the Optimo on Bay Parkway. I saw five minutes of him and it was all trouble. But *he* gets to live his life.'

'I'm so sorry.'

Lily's thinking that with a lot of men, this might be a ploy. Using a tragedy to try to get laid. It's a horrible thing to think, given Jack's state and all that he's written, but she's known enough men to know that even the good ones will sink to the lowest depths occasionally. They will stare at women's bodies, allow themselves to be driven by lust, utilize their sadness and pain in a way that makes them feel they're owed sex.

But that's not Jack. She can tell. He isn't being inappropriate with her at all. He isn't like most men she's met. There's seemingly no double meaning in his actions. She feels like he doesn't look at her the way most men do. He's not gross. His eyes don't wander down to her chest. He's kind, thoughtful, respectful. He could be her dad.

This isn't a date and doesn't feel like one, but Lily has been out with a couple of older men. There was Art, a grad student in his late twenties, who she met at an English department party at York. He wasn't that much older than her, but a world of distance existed between them. He was a didactic douche. They lasted three dates and even that was too long. He was the first guy she went out with after getting free from Micah. They didn't kiss or hold hands or even have a good conversation. She liked the idea of going out with someone who was more mature than boys her own age, who'd hopefully passed through his bouts of jealousy and possessiveness and juvenile behavior. Art was mature, sure, but that didn't mean he wasn't an asshole.

The other older man she'd gone out with was Nate. He was in his late thirties at the time, which means he was probably right around Jack's age, maybe a year or two younger. A carpenter. She met him at McMartin's Pub, where she'd waited tables briefly. He had long golden hair, a sunshiny beard, and wore clothes with labels that had names like Patagonia and Columbia. He was a rock climber. Lithe, sinewy. He loved the Grateful Dead. He and Lily hooked up a few times. It turned out he had about ten girlfriends at once and they were all young. It made her feel like she was part of some deranged hippie harem or something. She never called him back, and he wasn't the type to chase after her, which was, at least, a positive.

'You mind if I smoke?' Lily asks. She reaches into her bag for the pack of Parliament Lights stuffed below all the folded stories.

Jack shakes his head.

'Want one?'

Another no.

She lights her cigarette.

Bimsy brings their food, even shakier than before. Lily thinks about ordering another Russian Roulette, but she decides against it. She doesn't want to come off as too much of a lush. Her grilled cheese is about the saddest thing she's ever seen. It looks like a toy rubber sandwich that comes with one of those kitchen playsets kids have. It's pale, not buttery and golden like she remembers. The cheese dripping from the side is neon orange. A soggy pickle, which seems drained of its green, is next to it on the plate. Lily picks up half the sandwich, holding her cigarette away from her, and takes a bite. She wonders if it's always been this bad, if she's developed actual taste in the last few years, or if the Roulette's gone so far downhill that they can't help but fuck up a simple grilled cheese. She pushes the plate away and focuses on her smoke.

Jack spoons some soup into his mouth and seems unimpressed.

'I dated this guy Micah in college,' Lily says, finally ready to talk about what's been on her mind. 'We didn't go out long. He was okay at first and then he was terrible. He lives in Westchester. That's where he's from. I guess he found out I was back in New York after graduation and he started calling me a bunch. Kept threatening to show up at my house. He finally did a few days ago. Said he's staying at a motel in Coney Island and he's not leaving until I see him. I feel like he's watching me all the time. As soon as I get home, he calls, which means he's either calling the whole time I'm out or he knows exactly when I get home.'

Jack looks around the diner. 'You don't see him here, do you?'

Lily takes a long drag off her cigarette and then takes a good look at the faces of the people occupying various booths and tables. 'I don't see him, but he could be outside. Even if he's not *following* me, it's too much that he's here when I told him not to come, that he's hounding me. I haven't given him the time of day.'

'Absolutely,' Jack says. 'He calls once, maybe twice, that's one thing. Take the no and move on.'

'I'm just so uneasy. That's what was going on with me in class tonight. I'm probably making more of it than it is. I haven't heard anything since yesterday. Maybe he smartened up and went back home. I'm sure it has to happen like that sometimes, right? It's not all like the TV movies where the guy goes full psycho.'

'How you're feeling is understandable.' Jack's speaking through gritted teeth. He seems angry.

Lily butts out her cigarette in the glass ashtray on the table. Inexplicably, a clown's smiling face is in the center of the ashtray, also emblazoned in gold. Under the face, in script, is another slogan: HAVE A LAUGH AT THE ROULETTE! Ashes smudged on the clown's nose and all over his hair. 'Jesus, these things are creepy,' she says, pulling it near her to take a closer look. 'Who puts a clown in an ashtray?'

Jack presses his spoon around in his soup, turning the yellow mush of the lentils even mushier. He takes the final swig of his coffee.

Lily continues: 'I never thought I'd have a stalker, you know? I guess no woman worries about it until it happens. I know it happens a lot – all these bad men – but I never thought it'd happen to me. I'm freaked out.'

'I can help you if you want my help,' Jack says.

'I don't want to get you involved. I didn't bring him up because I was hoping you'd offer to help, but it's really nice of you. My mother's pretty much brushed me off. Her new boyfriend thinks I'm overreacting too.'

Jack leans forward. Some smoke still lingers between them. 'I know we don't know each other that well, but I don't want anything bad to happen to you. Guys like this Micah are unpredictable. Yeah, some of them might finally come to their senses, but some of them get it in their heads that they'll do whatever they have to do to get what they want. I don't want to scare you more, but I bet a lot of women don't know it's the worst-case scenario until it's too late.'

She nods, nudges at her grilled cheese on the plate, considers taking another bite but decides not to. 'Thank you for saying that. Too many people would give him the benefit of the doubt. Say he's just trying to learn to process rejection or whatever.'

'You remind me so much of Amelia,' Jack says after a couple of seconds pass. 'Maybe our paths crossed for a reason, huh? I know that's a stretch. I'm not the most religious guy in the world or anything. I don't like when people say "God did this" and "God did that," but maybe God did bring us together because you need your father back and I need my daughter back.' He pauses, as if he regrets what he's just said, as if he knows it's just too much too soon. 'I'm sorry. That's a lot to put on someone you barely know. My world's real small. Please forgive me for linking you to Amelia. You're your own person. I just, you know' – struggling to make words now – 'never expected a second chance. I can help you.'

Lily thinks that what he's said *is* a lot, but it also feels true. She's moved. In this diner – where she used to come with her father – she feels suddenly like Jack's daughter. She's not really even sure what he means when he says he can help but she certainly appreciates his saying it. She's not sure how to respond. She reaches into her bag, pulls out another cigarette, and rolls it around between her fingers. She taps her nail against the edge of the recessed filter. 'I don't believe in God anymore,' she says finally, 'but I feel like maybe you're right. Maybe something brought us together.'

Francesca

That first night at Long Eddy's when Bobby showed up, Francesca didn't think things would go very far. She second-guessed whatever feeling she'd had that made her want to call him in the first place. When he arrived, they sat together awkwardly in a booth, each other's phone numbers smudged on their hands, and tried to talk. A candle burned on the table. The jukebox played songs she didn't know. Pierce kept serving them drinks, which loosened things up. She'd gotten mostly sober waiting for Bobby, refusing a few rounds, but when he was finally there, her nerves got the best of her and she started really putting them back again. Beers, shots, whatever Pierce brought over. Bobby, also clearly nervous, did the same. Within an hour, they were dancing.

They left the bar around 3:30 a.m., stumbling, not knowing where they would go. They got slices at a pizza joint that was still open. The slices weren't very fresh – the cheese was marbled, the crust crispy and cracked – but, in the moment, it was just about the best thing she ever tasted. They sat on the sidewalk against the wall of the pizzeria, smelling piss and bleach in the air. Bars around them were starting to close down. Staggering adults and staggering kids passed in front of them. She's surprised she remembers as much as she does. It was the drunkest she's ever been. When she left Long Eddy's, Pierce made her promise she'd come back.

After finishing their slices, Francesca scooched closer to Bobby, sitting there against the wall, putting her head on his shoulder. They sat like that for a while. They talked about outer space. She said that sometimes she liked to imagine hurtling through space. Swimming through all that silence. Bobby said he had a dream that he was living on a colony on Mars once. After a while, they kissed. His lips were rough. He tasted of the pizza.

They decided to walk around. Bobby said maybe they could find an all-night diner and get coffee. That's just what they did. She doesn't remember the name of the place or what street it was on. She remembers neon and chrome. A bright spot in the dark night. A crinkling vinyl booth. A bathroom with graffiti on the mirror. Squatting drunkenly over the toilet, trying not to touch the seat. They ordered coffee, yes, but they also ordered dessert. He got cherry pie. She got a hot-fudge sundae. Their server was sweet. A blur of red hair and perfume. She asked if they were married. They laughed. It had somehow become one of her favorite nights ever.

After the diner, they wandered around until the sun came up. They got coffees to go and drank them on a bench in Washington Square Park. She talked about movies. He said they should stay up until the theaters opened and then go see a movie. She agreed. She slept with her head on his shoulder for about an hour. When they got up, she grabbed a *Village Voice* from a newspaper rack and checked the listings. Ten was the earliest show. He said for her to pick. He didn't know about any of the movies. She chose *Sexy Beast*.

They both loved it. She felt sure Bobby would fall asleep after being up all night, and she thought that might kill the magic, but he munched popcorn and stared wide-eyed at the screen. Despite the coffee and all the wandering, they were both still drunk. The hangover took hold near the end of the movie. They finally kissed again during the credits.

On the train back home to Brooklyn, Bobby asked when he could see her next.

'How about tomorrow?' she said.

'Tomorrow, as in today?' he asked.

'Today, sure. Don't you have to work?'

'I make my own hours, pretty much.'

He walked her home. Victoria was at camp, but Grandma Eva gave her hell. She said she smelled like booze and the city, which was exactly what she smelled like and there wasn't much better. Grandma Eva said she was throwing her life away. Francesca ignored her and went to bed. It was almost two thirty in the afternoon.

A call from Bobby woke her up around eight that night. She felt lucky to have grabbed it before Grandma Eva or Victoria. He asked how she felt. Not too great, she said. Her head was spinning. She found some Tylenol in the pantry and drank it down with a full glass of water. It felt like the first glass of water she'd had in years. Grandma Eva watched her while she talked on the phone. Victoria gave her space. Bobby asked if she wanted to go out for dinner in the neighborhood. Maybe Chinese food on Eighty-Sixth Street. She said yes. Victoria asked if she was okay. She said she was great, that she'd had a great night, just too much to drink. Grandma Eva's voice got raspy and desperate. 'No granddaughter of mine's gonna behave like this,' she said.

Francesca took a shower and got dressed and met Bobby at a cramped little Chinese place next to a fruit stall on Eighty-Sixth Street. Chickens and ducks hung in the window. They sat at a booth in the back with a red tabletop and ordered egg rolls and lo mein. Bobby was hungover. He said he'd called Max, his boss, and told him he wasn't feeling well and couldn't come into work. Max was pissed. Francesca talked about her grandmother. The food helped with their hangovers.

The next night they went to a movie at the Marboro. *Evolution.* It wasn't very good. Bobby fell asleep this time, and she didn't hold it against him.

There were other dates that week too. A pool hall in Bay Ridge. An afternoon and evening of browsing at Kim's Underground and Bleecker Bob's and Other Music and Mercer Street Books and Generation Records. Drinks again at Long Eddy's, though Pierce wasn't tending bar this time. They shared one of Francesca's hand-rolled cigarettes under the awning outside. The next night they got drinks at the Keyhole Cocktail Lounge, and the old Ukrainian bartender was the drunkest she'd ever seen him. They stayed until four and had to help him close. They brought him upstairs to his apartment – he lived right over the bar – and tucked him into bed. He passed out cold and they were standing there in his strange apartment, full of tchotchkes and framed family pictures, the smell of leftover coffee in the air, and Bobby kissed her, really kissed her, and she felt happy. They went back to the same all-night diner, not quite as drunk as last time but still pretty drunk, and got dessert again. The next day was another throwaway. She got home around noonish, Grandma Eva really railing on her. Bobby skipped work again.

Last night, they met at the Roulette Diner, splitting a plate of disco fries. Bobby asked if she wanted to get a room in the city and she knew what he was really asking. He said he realized it hadn't been that long but it'd been such an intense week and he was feeling strong feelings for her, the kind he'd never felt. She felt like she knew him as well as she'd ever known a boy. Better. 'Yes,' she said. He said he'd find a place if she wanted or they could just wander around until they found somewhere. It was New York City and there had to be hundreds of hotels and motels, though they'd both never paid much attention to stuff like that. There was the one on St. Mark's they both knew of. They didn't know how much it or any place would cost, though. Could be a lot. She said it was better to wander and let fate guide them. They'd wind up where they were meant to wind up.

Now, after a week she never could've anticipated, she's headed back into the city with Bobby. She's not sure she believes in fate. Not at all. But it felt like the thing to say in the moment. She'd never had a thought like that before. She'd never spoken of fate.

Was it fate that her father died? That a big hunk of concrete and rebar fell on his head? Was it fate that her mother made her father move to Southern Brooklyn? Was it fate that her parents met at Long Eddy's? Was it fate that Francesca's path crossed with Bobby's via Max Berry on a dumb nothing afternoon when the world seemed like it might be dull forever? Maybe she does believe in fate.

She looks over at Bobby now as the train rumbles underground between Thirty-Sixth Street and Pacific Street. If she had to explain to someone what she likes about him in a couple of sentences, she's not sure she'd be able to say it coherently. He's different from any boy she's ever been interested in. Not as showy. Not as swaggery. He has these heavy, sad eyes. She likes the way he's sitting there, bent over, his elbows on his knees, tapping his foot. His hair's effortlessly messy, like he planned it that way. He's wearing a white T-shirt and blue jeans. She usually likes tall guys, but he's about her same height, maybe an inch shorter. He has nice lips. If she had a camera, she'd focus on his lips. She'd also focus on his hands. He has soft hands. He flexes them a lot, opening and closing them, stretching his palms and fingers wide. He says they hurt when he doesn't do that, he's not sure why. They've been holding hands the last couple of days like it's sixth fucking grade and it's been wonderful. Those lips have kissed her neck and her ears. She asked him yesterday if he'd ever seen *Drugstore Cowboy*. He said he hadn't. She said they should rent the tape. She said he really reminded her of Matt Dillon in it. It isn't that he looks a lot like Dillon – the thought she had right after first meeting Bobby – but there's something about his cool aloofness that rings the same bell. The name of Dillon's character is Bob in that movie too. She had the poster up on her wall for a while, salvaged from Wolfman's video store when he dumped a bunch of stuff he previously had in the windows. Dillon's Bob was hugging Kelly Lynch's Dianne, his head against her chest. She always remembers it as such a romantic movie. Grandma Eva ripped down her poster because she said it was promoting drug use. To push Grandma Eva's buttons, Francesca told her she'd never shot heroin, but that she'd sure as hell try it given the opportunity.

'You ever think about getting out of Brooklyn?' Francesca asks now, daydreaming suddenly of a life on the run. Moving from motel to motel. Dust caught in the shafts of sunlight streaming in between the heavy curtains. Those beds, walls, and sad carpets. Watching movies on a motel room TV with crackly reception. Thinking of *Drugstore Cowboy* led her down this path. What would they be running from? What would they be running to? She pictures them as Bonnie and Clyde types, robbing a bank, pouring money out on the bed. Neither of them even has a car.

'All the time,' Bobby says.

'Where would you want to go? You know, if money wasn't an issue.'

He doesn't even hesitate. 'Vegas.'

She thought she knew him a little and then he says something like *Vegas* in response to that question. She's not sure what response she was expecting, but it certainly wasn't Vegas. All those lights. Casinos. Showgirls. Hookers. Drinking yourself to death like that Nicolas Cage movie. That's what she thinks of when she thinks of Vegas. 'Really? Why?'

'I don't know. I had a dream once that I was gambling and winning at a casino in Vegas. I don't even know how I knew it was Vegas. It was just sort of written into the dream. Anyhow, I was really happy in that dream. It's dumb. I've never even gambled in real life. I could start, though.'

'Good to know. I didn't figure you for a Vegas type.'

'Where'd you think I'd say?'

'I guess I figured you'd say you never really thought about leaving New York. Like most people.'

'What about you? Where would you go?'

'I mentioned Los Angeles when we first met. If I really want to make movies, I need to be out there, I think.'

They pass over the bridge and get off at Broadway-Lafayette. They begin wandering around. Victoria gave Francesca thirty bucks the other day, and she has that in her pocket. Grandma Eva yelled that she had to stop giving her handouts. That the kid was done with high school and needed a job. That didn't stop her mom, who was always good about passing her a few bucks if she had it to spare. She asks Bobby if he has any money and he says he does. Max just paid him in cash, and he's got a hundred fifty bucks tucked into his sock. It's something she should've thought about earlier, but she assumed he had things taken care of since it was his idea.

Their first stop is the hotel on St. Mark's. She realizes she doesn't really know the difference between motels and hotels. Truth is, she hasn't stayed in many. The only time was on a trip to Florida when she was eight and her dad was still around. They drove to Disney World, staying in roadside places along the way, and then settled at a Motel 6 in Orlando. She didn't remember much about that trip. Pools. Stained walls. Water that tasted like matches. Many meals at Denny's and Shoney's. The hot glow of Disney. Flashes of rides. Her father sweating. Her mother eating soft serve ice cream over her palm.

Bobby runs in to check the price on the St. Mark's Hotel while she stays outside and watches people filter into Mondo Kim's. He's figuring it'll be too much. He doesn't want to blow all the money in one place, says he would like to save some so they can get a nice romantic meal too. He comes out, shaking his head.

Francesca rolls a cigarette for each of them. Bobby lights them both with a book of matches from the Roulette. They talk about which direction to head. They walk south on Second Avenue, back toward where they got off the train. They don't see anything.

Finally, as they come up on Grand Street, on the edge of Chinatown, they see a place. It has a white sign that simply reads hotel. Under that, there are Chinese characters. The hotel seems to be three stories and takes up one-third of a building that stretches half the block. Next door is a dry cleaner. Next to that is some kind of language school.

This time, they walk in together. The lobby is dingy. The clerk is behind glass. He's smoking, another cigarette waiting behind his ear.

Bobby says they'd like a room.

The clerk speaks in Chinese. He holds up four fingers.

'Forty dollars?' Bobby asks.

The clerk nods.

Bobby reaches down into his sock for the money and manages to pull out two sweaty twenties without showing his whole roll. He stuffs them through a door under the glass into a metal tray, and the clerk snatches them up. He passes back a key with a tag that's just a square piece of cardboard: room 7 written on the cardboard in shaky black print. The clerk motions up.

They climb the stairs to the second floor. There's no room seven there. They try the third floor and find it. Bobby pushes open the heavy door. The carpeting in the room has bald patches. The bed is sunken in like a cake taken out of the oven too soon. Bobby turns on the light next to the bed, and it flickers. There's no TV. Only the silence of the room. A small window looks out over Grand Street. The wallpaper is peeling at the edges. A mirror by the bathroom is smeared with some kind of haze.

Before they sit on the bed, Francesca insists on removing the bedspread. She saw a documentary once where they ran a black light over a hotel bedspread and the results had been disturbing enough that she hadn't forgotten. Bobby bunches the spread up and throws it on the floor in the corner.

'I guess this'll do,' Bobby says. 'I'm sorry it's not nicer.'

'It's fine,' Francesca says.

They sit on the bed. The sheets are starchy and surprisingly clean. 'Where'd you tell your mom you were staying?'

'With my friend Carrie. Did you tell your dad?'

'He doesn't care. He's happy to have the apartment to himself. He's probably overjoyed I'm out for the night.'

'Can I ask you something?'

'Sure.'

'I know why I like you. Why do you like me?'

'You serious?'

'I'm serious.'

'This has been the best week of my life. You make me feel like I belong in the world. Like it doesn't matter my mom ran off when I was six. Like none of the ways I've fucked things up matter. And I think you're really pretty.'

'You're sweet.'

They lie back on the bed. Bobby takes her hand. A fire truck passes on the street below. She didn't know she was capable of distinguishing between sirens from fire trucks, police cars, and ambulances, but, apparently, she is. Bobby asks her if she wants to go get some booze first. She says she's okay for now.

He turns to her, and they kiss. They both taste of her hand-rolled cigarettes. A bitterness on their lips, passing between them, a shared bitterness. The light is still flickering. Some kisses are wrong. She's had plenty of wrong kisses. Every kiss with Bobby has felt right. This one feels especially right.

He has his hand on her side. His mouth travels away from hers and finds her neck. She remembers getting hickeys in sixth grade, having to cover them with scarves so her mom and dad didn't see. That was the year before her dad died. Bobby sucks her neck now. His hand moves down to her hip. She puts one hand on his chest.

'You okay?' Bobby says.

'I'm great,' Francesca says.

They scooch further up on the bed, their heads finding the pillows. They both still have their shoes on. Francesca doesn't want to rush. Bobby doesn't seem to want to rush either. That makes her happy. The worst thing that could happen – the way this could go truly bad – is for it to end too quickly. Some guys don't know patience. It happens too fast for them, maybe even at a touch, or they think it's just about the one thing. Her first time, with a guy named Ben Gely, had been the worst time for that. Over in a minute and then they both sat in the fogged car, and he was ashamed of himself and she was sad because she knew it was a memory she would always have. It could've been special but it wasn't. Sex had since remained something she mostly associates with sadness.

This is different. There's an electricity between them.

He helps her off with her shirt. She helps him off with his. She imagines that they're in a fancy motel in Vegas, where he dreams of going. A motel decked out with western shit. Instead of looking out at Grand Street, the view would be of a courtyard with a pool. Women in bikinis on chaise lounges. Leathery old people slathered in suntan lotion. The dinging of slot machines from nearby casinos. That's how she pictures Vegas. Casino sounds everywhere. Blinding sun. Summery bodies, ancient and youthful.

This room is fine as it is. Vegas wouldn't be better. No place would be better. This room is theirs. Even if this hotel is gone in two years, even if someone knocks down the building, this room will always be theirs. Something guided them here. The last week has led them here. Francesca's skin is goose-pimply. She's embarrassed about her bra. It's the nicest one she has, but it's cheap and plain. Bobby fumbles with the clasp.

His hands on her are tender.

It's barely evening. Feels like it should be later. Sunset light streams in between the slats of the crackly blinds. Shadowswirled light. Francesca thinks of the geography of the city. The island they're on. The concrete and streetlamps and skyscrapers and millions of bustling people. This one small part of it. This room. Them.

Charlie

Charlie's been comped a room at the Tropicana, where he's spent a few days gambling. He's lost enough that they gave him a suite on the top floor. He'd initially struck out with the old addresses that Rainey had given him for Don and Randy. Condos. They'd moved on. Rainey had said they were hiding out somewhere, but Charlie needed to confirm that. His first thought was that maybe they were content to chalk up getting ripped off as a loss or simply unwilling to go after a Brancaccio, no matter how much of a pinhead Junky Greg was. Even if that's the case, he knows they need to be dealt with. Trouble incubates.

He'd put out feelers. Paid a guy he knew via some old Florida connections to do the legwork so he could gamble and make moves on waitresses. The guy's name is Rufus. He's just had Charlie paged over the casino's PA.

Charlie meets him at reception, nursing the last of a Rusty Nail brought to him by a waitress named Dolly with green eyes and sparkly makeup and shoulders that looked to be carved out of stone.

Rufus is a tall man, maybe six-four or six-five, and he's wearing a laser-red windbreaker and a cap from a blueberry farm in South Jersey. He has on one leather glove and shoes that don't match.

'You found them?' Charlie asks.

'Sure did,' Rufus says. 'They're hiding out from their families at a motel called the Sandbar on Arctic Avenue. Room nine. Look like real yuppie types, but they're slumming it. Must be on the skids. Think they're still gonna get that call from your man, Junky Greg.'

Charlie thanks him. He reaches into his pocket and comes out with a fold of bills, counting off five hundreds and passing them to Rufus, who pockets them and then turns, limping as he walks away, disappearing into a crowd of bused-in old timers.

Charlie stops at a payphone and calls information and asks for the Sandbar Motel's number. They come back with it and want to know if they should patch him through. He says that'd be good, waiting through a few rings until someone at the Sandbar picks up. 'Yeah?' the woman says, her voice grizzled and lonely and angry.

'What's your address?' Charlie asks.

She says the numbers and then wants to know if Charlie needs a room.

'I'd like that. I need room eight or room ten. Can you do that? I'm on a lucky streak. Those are my numbers.'

'Bud, the joint's mostly empty. You can have either. Just not three or nine. Which will it be? Eight? Ten?'

'Give me eight.'

'How you paying?'

'Cash. I'll be there soon.'

'I'll be waiting with bells on,' the lady says, and then she's gone, the line dead.

Charlie goes up to his suite and punches in the code on the safe. He gets out his gun, screwing the silencer into place and puts it in the deep inner pocket of the light summer jacket he's wearing. It's a new jacket. He bought it at a fancy shop in the casino. Linen.

He closes the safe – that's where the rest of the spending money is stashed – and makes sure it's locked. He goes over to the bed and sits down, finding the remote and flicking on the television. He flips around. He likes the noise. He likes the dumbest shows, the ones with canned laughter. He settles on some sitcom he's never seen. Two guys and a girl in a living room, wearing tight clothes, cracking corny jokes. He likes how ugly it all is. The actors are sleek and glossy, models dressed up like goofballs, but everything's so goddamn ugly. He watches until the credits roll and then turns up the volume and leaves the room.

Outside, he sees a woman in a yellow bikini leaning against a yellow sports car. A man in frayed jean shorts is photographing her. Some heavy-duty lights aimed in her direction. It's dusk. He's been inside so long, it's weird to be out in the world.

Charlie stops with a crowd of dirty old men and watches the bikini girl drape herself across the hood of the car. The dirty old men are going nuts. One of them says he's going to have a heart attack. Charlie thinks it would be funny if he said that and then actually had a heart attack and the other guys just stood around, torn between helping their pal and continuing to ogle the girl. But it doesn't happen. They just drool and slobber. They stink. They smell like ass and old cigars and about a million regrets. Dirty old bastards like that, they'll whip their peckers out at dusk in the sad American night and go to town. They don't care. Charlie moves on.

He walks the few blocks to Arctic Avenue and checks the numbers on the buildings he passes to see how far off the motel might be. It's not far. A couple of blocks.

The neon sign out front reads SA DBAR MO EL, the tubing blown on two letters. He goes into the main office. The woman he spoke to is at the desk behind bulletproof glass. She's playing solitaire and drinking something from a gigantic gas station cup. She's a laundry pile of a woman, all frizz and static. 'You're who I just talked to?' Charlie asks.

'You Mr Cash?' she says.

'That's me.'

'Be forty-two dollars and twenty-three cents for the night.'

'What a steal.' Charlie takes out a fifty, shoves it into the tray under the glass, and tells her to keep the change.

She plucks up the bill and considers it closely, trying to decide whether it's counterfeit. She seems to settle on it being legit. 'You been winning?'

'Born lucky.'

'Must be nice. All I was born with was fucked-up feet. All my toes webbed together. Called me Lobster Girl in school. Fucked-up feet is better than no feet, anyway. My mother used to tell me it could be worse. I could be hopping around on my ankles like a Human Pogo. That'd hurt, no doubt. Need some sort of padding.'

'Can I see?'

'See what?'

'Your feet.'

'Get the fuck out of here. I got sickos coming out of my ass. I don't need another one.' She passes him the key to number eight and tells him to keep it down.

Back outside, he walks the length of the long, squat building, passing each of the rooms. The lights are on in room nine, but the curtains are pulled tightly shut. A little light seeps out around the edges. He can hear voices in there.

He goes into his room, struggling with the ancient key at first but then bursting through the door into darkness that smells of lemon cleaning spray. He turns the floor lamp on. The walls are wood paneled. The TV chained to the dresser. A Bible illuminated on the nightstand.

Charlie sits on the creaky bed. He puts the room key down on the pillow. He tries to hear what the voices next door are saying. Don and Randy. What dumb fuckers.

A door connects the two rooms, but it's locked three ways. He sees a black pubic hair coiled on the rose-patterned quilt. This is no normal motel bedspread. It looks like the kind of quilt some tiny woman in glasses worked a long time on. A nice touch. He stands up and goes to the adjoining door, pressing his ear to the cheap wood and listening closer.

The voices are a low hum. He can't make out a single word. He knocks. 'Keep it down in there,' he says. 'I'm trying to rest.'

Silence. A few seconds pass. Then a voice thunders back through the door, close on the other side: 'What was that?'

'Keep it down,' Charlie says again.

'Go to hell, buddy.'

Charlie takes a few steps away from the door and then leaves the room, going back outside. He looks around. No one is in the lot. The office lady with the fucked-up feet he'll never get to see isn't watching from her little back window. He knocks on the front door to Don and Randy's room.

Silence again on the other side. Probably confusion too. Charlie's not sure what to expect from these two, but he's not worried. He flattens his thumb over the peephole.

The same voice comes through the door: 'Who's there?'

'I'm next door. Can I have a word?'

'You're the one who just told us to keep it down?'

'How'd you ever figure that out?'

Whoever it is doing the talking – Don or Randy – opens up, the chain still on. Charlie can only see a sliver of him, but he's skinny and tall, wearing a black suit, his black tie undone. He has red hair and freckles and clean white teeth. 'What do you want?'

'You Don or Randy?' Charlie asks.

'I'm Randy. How do you know our names?'

Charlie decides to get right to it. 'Greg Brancaccio sent me,' he says.

'Greg? That motherfucker.' Randy unhooks the chain and pulls the door open wide. Behind him, the guy who must be Don is lying on one of the two twin beds in his boxers and a Tyson-Holyfield II T-shirt. He has a banker's haircut and rich boy skin. Looks like he's never shaved a day in his life. He sits up. Junky Greg's name is what they've been waiting to hear.

'Where is Greg?' the guy on the bed says.

'You're Don, I take it?' Charlie asks.

'Yeah, I'm Don. Where is Greg? We did what he said and then crickets. No call. No hard drive. We've been looking everywhere for him. Going crazy. He says one thing, he says he's gonna give us the hard drive back, and then he's gone in the night. Him and Rainey both.'

Charlie walks into the room, shutting the door behind him. 'Greg's sorry,' he says.

Red Hair Randy retreats to the other bed and sits down. He puts his elbows on his knees and sinks his head in his hands. He starts crying, really going at it, like his grandmother just died and he didn't say what he needed to say to her. His pale skin turns red as he cries. All that red. He looks like a tomato dressed up in a black suit. 'That was everything,' Randy says. 'He took everything and he didn't even hand over the hard drive. That fucking junky! Why'd we ever trust him?'

'Take it easy, Little Orphan Annie,' Charlie says. 'No need for Niagara Falls. Greg's still got what you need.'

Randy's cries die down to sniffles. 'Yeah? I figured he took us for asswipes.'

'Not at all. He just sent me for reconnaissance. We need to know where you guys got the dough and the drugs, so there's no trouble down the line.'

Don chimes in: 'What are you talking about? The money's ours. We cleaned out our trusts. The drugs we scored from a supplier friend of mine in Princeton.'

'You stole them?'

'Yeah, pretty much.'

'You pretty much stole them?'

'Right. Greg *made* us.'

Charlie plays dumb. 'What's the endgame? I don't get it.'

Don leans over to the nightstand between the beds and grabs a pack of American Spirits that's on top of their Bible. 'Greg is blackmailing us,' he says. 'He was supposed to give us back a hard drive he stole that has a bunch of incriminating shit on it. You work for Greg and you don't know this?'

'I'm new,' Charlie says. 'I'm a bit cloudy on the whole situation, to be honest. What's on this hard drive?'

'Man, fuck you,' Randy says. 'You don't know who we are? You don't know who our fathers are? The phone's right there. Call Greg. Tell him to get that hard drive over here. I go to my father, it's gonna be hardball time.'

'Hardball time, huh? Your father knows about Greg?'

'Not yet, but he will.'

'What about this Princeton drug guy? He knows about Greg?'

'No,' Don says, butting his half-smoked cigarette out in a glass ashtray behind the Bible. 'He doesn't even know it was us who ripped him off. He'd never expect it from me. We go back to grade school. I never would've done it either, if Greg hadn't threatened to go public with everything. We'd be fucked, sure, but our fathers would be done in politics forever. You know Senator Mack Fitzgerald? That's Randy's dad. Paul Ambrosino is my dad. Mayor of Newark. You might've heard of him. They could be in the White House in ten, fifteen years. President and vice president. That's what they're going for. And we went and screwed the pooch.'

'There's videos of you two fucking animals on this hard drive, huh?' Charlie asks.

'Come on. You know what's on the hard drive!'

'I don't know anything. I know my job. Report back on where the contents of the package originated, that's what Greg said. I don't know your fathers. I don't know Jersey politics. I don't know jack about hard drives. I don't even have a typewriter.'

'It's records,' Don says, his guard down. He still believes Junky Greg's coming through with the hard drive. 'A charity thing we set up. Forget it.'

'Money laundering?' Charlie says. 'Embezzlement? Good shit.' He reaches into the deep inner pocket of his linen jacket and takes out the gun with its silencer. He shoots Don on one bed and Randy on the other. Both square in the forehead. Don's body slumps forward, while Randy's falls to the side. Nice quilts on these beds too, Charlie notices. Different colors. A lot of hard work in those quilts.

He looks around the room to make sure no one is hiding anywhere. He uses his sleeve to open the bathroom door. Nothing. He uses his sleeve again to push open the closet. Pillows and an ironing board.

He hasn't touched anything else. It's a clean operation. The score is purified now. The politician fathers don't know shit. The Ivy League drug guy doesn't know shit. The hard drive will surface and these will look like righteous killings. The office lady won't remember anything about the guy next door except he paid cash and wanted to see her fucked-up feet.

Charlie takes the do not disturb hanger off the interior knob with his sleeve. He turns the bolt mechanism, also with his sleeve, and then pulls the door shut behind him as he leaves, confirming it's locked. He puts the hanger on the exterior knob, careful not to brush it with his fingers.

He doesn't go back to the room next door. The key is still on the pillow, the door unlocked. Consider him checked out. He's not sure how long Don and Randy paid for. Could be a day or two before they're found with the hanger on the door. Could be a week before the housekeeper notices the stink and gets a key from the office.

Instead, Charlie walks back to the Tropicana. Maybe a few more nights of gambling and fun are in order before heading back to Brooklyn to retrieve his prize from Max.

Jack

When Jack and Lily are done at the Roulette, it's after eight. They walk home on Eighty-Sixth Street. A warm summer night. Cugines cruising in big cars under the El with their windows open, techno booming. Sidewalks packed with people rushing home or to the gym or out to eat. Commuters getting off the train late. A deep ease to it. The kind of night where things don't go wrong. The weather's too nice. A rare vibe of contentment in the neighborhood.

They stop for Italian ices at Lenny's. Lily gets chocolate. Jack gets lemon. She asks what he's doing now, saying she doesn't want to go home. She doesn't want to get home and see that there are ten messages from Micah. She doesn't want to get home and find that her mother is out with Dave. She hates an empty apartment. She hates the silence of it. She can't even drown out the silence with music, but she usually tries. She feels safe with Jack. She hopes that's not weird to say.

It's not weird. It makes Jack happy. He hasn't felt happy in five years. He hasn't had an Italian ice in five years. 'You can come back to my place, if you want,' he says. 'I have tea, coffee. I don't sleep too well, so it's not like I'm some old-timer who goes to bed at nine.'

'You sure?' Lily says. 'I'd love that. I'd love the company.'

As they walk, they both keep an eye out for Micah. There's been no sign of him so far. It's scary to think he could be watching. It's scary to think he's holed up in a motel in Coney Island. It has to be the Luna Motel, but that's the type of joint where prostitutes bring johns. Jack can't picture this

Westchester County psycho hiding out there. Maybe there's a place he can't think of, a new little motel tucked on the corner of some block he never goes down, but he doesn't think so. He goes to Coney Island often on his walks. He likes to sit on the Boardwalk and watch the water, see the bodies mashed together on the beach. Gleaming, oiled bodies. The summer crowds. The voices. The whir of it all. The deadness in winter. The apocalypse feeling.

When they get back to his house, Jack can feel Lily taking it in. He can sense that she feels bad for him. He's lost his wife and daughter and parents in the last decade. This ramshackle house is what's left of his life. It's like something from a fairy tale, where the house has come to resemble the state of his soul. Ravaged.

It's dark inside. He turns on some lights. They pass through the living room to get to the kitchen. Lily looks at the pictures of Amelia and Janey that fill the walls, dust streaked on the glass in the frames. Janey on their honeymoon. Amelia, at seven, with a fishing pole down by Gravesend Bay. All of them together at Nellie Bly. All of them together at Coney Island, the Cyclone behind them. A dream of what was. The past laid out neatly. Pictures of his folks too. Their wedding. In front of St. Mary's, a crisp fall day in 1955, a year he hadn't known, wasn't around for yet. He was almost in the world. Almost made.

He flicks the kitchen light on and invites Lily to sit at the table. She puts her bag down on the floor by the radiator and sits on the chair closest to the wall.

'You can smoke,' Jack says.

She thanks him.

'It's a sad dump I live in, I know. You don't have to stick around if it's too much.'

'I wasn't thinking that at all,' Lily says. 'I was just thinking that it feels alive with memories.'

'There are a lot of memories, that's true, but it's dead every other way.' Jack goes over to the stove and puts the kettle on. 'You want some tea?'

'Sure.'

'I have coffee too. And booze.' He grabs the half-empty bottle of Seagram's Seven that's on the counter and holds it up. 'It's not expensive stuff or anything.'

'Oh, wow,' Lily says. 'I'll take some of that.'

He shuts the gas and removes the kettle from the burner and then gets two highball glasses out of the cabinet over the sink, pouring whiskey for Lily and some for himself. The glasses are dusty. He can see that now. Everything in the house is dusty. 'Ice?'

'Okay.'

He sets the glasses down on the table. He opens the freezer and breaks a few cubes from the tray. A loud snapping sound, as if the tray's cracked. Jack's always hated the noise of getting ice. It always rattles him. Always feels like one of the loneliest sounds in the world.

He brings over a handful of ice cubes, dropping two in her glass and two in his. He sits across from her. They clink glasses.

'I actually have a Seagram's Seven story,' Lily says.

'I'm all ears,' Jack says.

'My second year of college, I bought this used car for five hundred bucks. It was a Volkswagen Fox. White. Stick. I couldn't even drive stick before I bought that car, but I learned real fast. My friend drove it home for me. I stayed up all night that first night, just driving in parking lots and on back roads, learning how not to roll at stop signs, how not to burn out the clutch.'

'That's impressive.'

'I have my moments.' She takes a drink. 'It wasn't that old, the car, but it had something like three hundred thousand miles on it. The previous owner had driven it back and forth across the country a bunch. So, the summer after my sophomore year, I get it in my head that I'm going to drive to the Grand Canyon.

Alone. This wasn't going to be a road trip with friends or anything. I was imagining just me in my new old car, windows down, radio on, shifting gears, seeing the country. My plan was to sleep in the car, maybe camp out.'

Jack knows that Amelia was probably only a few months away from the desire to make trips like that. It hit most people around her age, the need to be out on the road, to see all of the country. He wishes she'd had the chance. He would've worried, but that's life. She should've had the chance.

Lily continues: 'So, right after classes ended for the semester, I started packing and planning. I left the next week. I had two bags of clothes in my trunk. A cheap tent. Lots of granola bars. Some tapes – this car had a tape player. I also brought a bottle of Seagram's Seven. Someone had given it to me, this girl Andrea I used to know. She'd stolen it from the liquor store where she worked to bring to a party but then didn't go to the party. I figured it couldn't hurt to have a bottle of whiskey. I imagined sitting around a campfire in a national park, making new friends, sharing the bottle. I'd just read *Into the Wild*.'

Jack likes that Lily seems to assume he knows what book she's talking about.

'Anyhow,' Lily says, swishing the ice around in her glass, 'I made it into Ohio and my car broke down. It was the middle of the night, and I was on this deserted stretch of highway. I didn't know what to do. There wasn't a payphone anywhere. I didn't have a cell. No one was passing to flag down, and I don't think I would've done that anyway. I was lucky I was able to get the car over to the side of the road behind some tree cover. I'm not even sure how I managed it. I crawled into the back seat and I found that bottle of Seagram's Seven. I'd brought along this little Gettysburg shot glass someone had given me too. I kept pouring shots for myself. I don't even know how many I did. Maybe seven or eight. I've never blacked out so fast. I woke up the next day around noon, sweating because I hadn't opened any windows, with this monster headache. Whatever was left of the Seagram's Seven spilled on the floor. That's it. That's my great story.'

'What happened with the trip?' Jack asks.

'I didn't make it. I hitched to a rest stop and called my mom and she gave me the Triple A information. I got towed to a garage. The mechanic said I needed a new engine. My mom had to come all the way to Ohio – she got there at nine that night – and helped me unload my stuff. I junked the car.'

Jack's thinking about Lily's sense of adventure. To him, just the fact that she wanted to do something like that – especially alone – speaks to some great nobility of character. A lot of people, they'd be too afraid. They'd get hung up on everything that could go wrong, like breaking down in Nowheresville, Ohio in the middle of the night. They'd shrivel at the thought of being alone with all these mistakes you don't even know you're going to make.

Jack asks if he can show Lily some of Amelia's writing. She says she'd love to see it. He goes up to Amelia's room and gets the first few pages of her novel. No one else – not that he knows of anyway – has ever read any of this. Maybe a couple of Amelia's friends from Fontbonne, but he doubts it. She was secretive about her work. He only read it for the first time the week before. It feels good to be able to share it with someone who knows her stuff, someone who will recognize the talent that was lost.

When he gets back, he pours more whiskey for Lily and hands her the pages. 'I don't want to overwhelm you,' he says. 'That's just the start of this book she was working on.'

Lily reads the pages. She pauses once to take a sip of whiskey. She seems wrapped up in Amelia's words. 'This is so good,' she says. 'She was really talented, especially for eighteen.'

'That means a lot. She would've liked your class.'

'Yeah?'

'Absolutely.'

'How much more of this is there?'

'Not a lot. Maybe fifteen pages. She also wrote some stories for school.'

'I'd like to read it all some other time, maybe when I haven't had a few drinks.'

Jack nods. 'That'd be great.'

Lily takes out her cigarettes and lights one. 'You sure you don't mind?'

'Of course not.'

Lily puffs smoke at the ceiling. She's a natural smoker. She has the posture for it, the angles. Some people look all wrong with a cigarette. They hold it strangely. They slump. They make a mess of looking cool. Lily looks cool, like she's in an old movie. That makes Jack realize that she does, in fact, have some of the qualities of a classic actress. He's thinking Lauren Bacall or Lizabeth Scott. Something in her voice – her halted, determined way of speaking – but also her look. He imagines her being interviewed on some talk show about the novel she's written, picking tobacco from her lip, blowing smoke away from the camera. She's hard and gruff and yet lovely.

'The food at the Roulette was particularly bad tonight,' Jack says. 'You hungry at all? I don't have much, but I could make you a sandwich if you want.'

'I don't have much of an appetite,' she says, alternating between her smoke and her whiskey. 'But thanks.'

'I probably shouldn't ask this, but do you have plans for what's next? Are you sticking around the neighborhood? Are you moving?' He's asking because, selfishly, he hopes that she'll be around for a while. There's the class to look forward to, sure, but he also feels like they're building a friendship that will endure beyond that.

'Oh, boy. I really don't know. I feel so lost since I graduated. I wish that were all I had to deal with, but the Micah thing on top of it is too much. I don't know about next moves. Next moves

freak me out. I can only plan about six hours ahead at the most.'
She laughs.

'Nothing wrong with that.'

'I know I'm writing,' Lily goes on. 'That's the only thing I
know. I'm putting in the time. I'm getting words down. It's been
harder in the last week, but I'm keeping at it. You're a talented
writer, Jack. Really. I've got some talent too, but you've got
experience behind what you're saying, which is something I just
don't have yet. Not enough anyway. I'm okay with sentences and
I've written some good stories, but I haven't lived enough. I keep
trying to live more but I can't quite figure it out. I don't know
if I'll have the chops to finish my novel or to teach writing for a
living. I guess I should go to grad school.'

'You're a really good teacher,' Jack says.

She blushes and thanks him. 'I'm sorry for talking so much
about myself.'

'I asked.'

'I feel like I know Amelia now, but can I ask you more about
your wife? Janey, right?'

He hasn't heard someone else say her name in so long.
He goes into the living room and gets the picture from their
honeymoon, showing it to Lily. They hadn't gone far on their
honeymoon, just a small inn on the Jersey Shore. It was the off-
season and they spent their time wandering around on empty
beaches and eating good meals and tangled up together in bed.
'Here she is,' Jack says, tracing his finger over her smiling face
behind the glass. She's wearing a white sweater and blue jeans.
He remembers the exact moment he snapped the picture. He'd
said something silly to get her to smile. It worked. They'd just
come from an Irish pub where they'd had a great lunch.

'She's so pretty,' Lily says.

'She had this light shining from her. All the time. She cheered
up every room she was in. She used to volunteer at nursing
homes. She'd go sit with these old-timers – some of them were

miserable, abandoned by their families, really and truly on their own – and she'd come in with a deck of cards and they'd just feel it right away. She brought happiness with her.'

Lily looks like she might cry.

'You okay?' Jack asks.

'Yeah, it's just nice to hear you talk like that about your wife.' She pauses and a tear does fall down her cheek. She catches it with the heel of her free hand and lets out another little laugh. She takes a drag off her cigarette. 'I'm sorry. Whiskey makes me prone to crying. Do you have an ashtray?'

Jack gets an old Atlantic City mug from over the sink and says it'll have to do.

Lily taps her cigarette into the mug, her long ash crumbling instantly. 'I'm so sorry,' Lily says.

'Sorry why?'

'Sorry you lost Janey and Amelia.'

'We all lose people. I'm sorry you lost your dad.'

'It's clichéd, I know, but it really seems like the only people we lose are the good ones. All these bad people out there keep right on chugging along.'

'It does feel like that.'

Jack can't remember the last time he talked to anyone like this. Not even Amelia. Not really. She was still a teenager when she died. Though he didn't outwardly irritate her and they rarely fought, she was still angsty, detached, and secretive. They didn't really sit down and have big conversations about life. He tried, especially after Janey died, but Amelia was even younger then and he hit a brick wall with her. He's also probably better now at articulating his own thoughts than he was five years ago or ten years ago. He's had nothing but time to sit with them, to reflect.

'Like Micah,' Lily says. 'He'll probably live until he's ninety. He's a demon that's been feeding in the darkness for the last couple of years, waiting for me to come home. In the meantime, there are probably good people everywhere dying. Kids with cancer who never really got a chance to live. People who feed the homeless. Whatever. But Micah makes it his life mission, suddenly, to hunt me. It's not even like we just broke up. It's been two years.' She pauses. 'I swear, I should've known from day one. You know what his favorite record was? Hootie & the Blowfish, *Cracked Rear View*. That's some *American Psycho* shit.'

Jack considers telling her about what he was doing on the side before Amelia died, his revenge business. He's never told anyone before. He knows he can trust her. He knows he can be open with her. He wants to tell her because it's a service he can provide to help her. He can find and take care of this Micah, no charge.

But he doesn't say anything. She shouldn't have to live with that knowledge. Plus, it'll change everything between them. This nice talk they've had, this evening of feeling alive for the first time in forever, it'll come to a grinding halt. 'Wait, what? You killed people for a living?' she'd say. 'Are you offering to kill Micah?' She'd see the house differently. She'd think of him as a hired killer, not a surrogate dad. Maybe it wouldn't bother her at all. Maybe she'd feel a great sense of relief. Maybe she'd say, 'Yes, please take care of Micah. Please, before things get even scarier.' Maybe. Probably not. Probably she'd be freaked out. Probably she'd feel unsafe. Probably she'd run screaming from his kitchen.

Lily continues: 'I don't know. Maybe I'm being stupid. Maybe he's just being persistent. You watch all these eighties movies, and it's like the guys are rewarded for being stalkers. You grow up with that, the message seeps in. *Don't take no for an answer. She just doesn't know she loves you yet.* He expects this switch is gonna just turn in me. I don't know how to be clearer. I'm sorry. I've rambled on about Micah so much. I shouldn't waste my breath. I'd rather hear about Janey.'

'You're scared,' Jack says. 'It's understandable.' He was going to say *I can help* again, but he figures it might come off as too ominous, too strange a thing to say twice. She'd probably be wondering how on earth he could help. He could go see Micah, talk to him, and threaten him? Jack decides that instead of offering help, instead of talking about it anymore, he'll just take care of it. He will get Micah out of the way for her because the risk is too great. He's not going to let Micah get away with snuffing out her talent and her spirit. He'll have to play it by ear and see what it'll take. Maybe the guy just needs some sense scared into him. The way Jack sees it, it's almost like someone's giving him the opportunity to go back in time and stop the kid who threw the rock that killed Amelia. Making that connection is kind of a crooked road, a stretch, but it doesn't seem that far off to him. The world loses nothing if it loses this version of Micah. It loses everything if it loses Lily.

'Can I ask you something?' Lily says. 'It might be weird. You can say no.'

'Of course,' Jack says.

'Can I spend the night? I don't need a bed. I can sleep on the couch. Even the floor's more than fine. I just don't want to go home. I'm sick of that apartment. I'm sick of my mom. It's just that I feel really safe here.'

Jack doesn't take it the wrong way. He doesn't make the mistake of reading what she's asking as an advance. She's a daughter without her father, and he's a father without his daughter. 'I'd love the company,' he says. 'This house is so empty and quiet, it's nice to have some youthful energy around. If it's not too strange, you can take Amelia's room.'

'That's too much. I'll just sleep on the couch.'

'Really. It's a nice room. The bed's not that old.'

She agrees. She asks if she can call her mom, which she does on the phone in the far corner of the kitchen. It's a mustard-yellow rotary. A circular picture of Amelia as a toddler fitted into the center of the dial.

Her mom picks up after a few rings. Lily says she's staying

with a friend and then gives one word answers. She says 'Uh-huh' a few times. She hangs up and comes back to the table, slugging the rest of her whiskey and then pouring more. Her ice isn't even melted.

'She didn't give a shit,' Lily says. 'I mean, why would she? I'm old enough that she doesn't have to anymore. Her boyfriend was over. She was drunk, I could tell. She sounds like an idiot when she's drunk. She gets that baby shower voice.'

'What's a baby shower voice?' Jack asks.

'You know, that phony voice women put on when they're pretending to be excited about everything. "Here's a plastic ring for your baby to chew on." "Oh wow, that's *amazing*!" She's trying to pass as happy around Dave. Dave's her boyfriend. He's a runner. He claims to have irritable bowel syndrome. He's forty-seven years old and he eats Yodels and Ring Dings every day. That isn't adult food. And it's probably not the best stuff to eat if you have a spastic colon. I bet my mom's had six glasses of chardonnay by now. I didn't even ask if Micah called. She probably hasn't checked the machine. She doesn't want to admit something's wrong with him. I don't get it.'

They drink more and then Jack shows Lily up to Amelia's room. It's not late, but he can tell that the whiskey's hit her hard. Woozy, she looks around at the typewriter, the posters on the wall, the books and tapes. 'Amelia was so cool,' Lily says, slurring her words.

'She was,' Jack says.

'I'm sorry I got drunk on you.' Lily sits on the bed, elbows on her knees, head in her hands, and lets out an exhausted sigh. 'I'm a mess. I'm sorry. I shouldn't have let you see what a mess I am.'

'You're not a mess.'

'I am.'

She falls onto her side, pulls her feet up onto the bed, and curls into a ball. She exhales again. Her eyelids are fluttering.

'There's an unopened toothbrush from Rite Aid in the bathroom drawer,' Jack says. 'Bathroom's at the end of the hall.'

She can't hear him. She's asleep. He takes her boots off and covers her with a light blanket that he finds in Amelia's closet. He opens the window so she has some fresh air. The window hasn't been opened since Amelia last opened it. The sounds of the night filter in. Distant radios. A vibrating breeze. Cars honking. The brakes of a bus whispering somewhere on the avenue. Kids outside the deli on the corner, making a racket. He shuts the light off and leaves the room, keeping the door open a crack. The house feels like a home again.

Bobby

'You know,' Bobby says, as he and Francesca lie naked on the hotel bed, 'if we had some money, we could move out west. Maybe stop in Vegas on the way to Los Angeles.'

'I have the money in my pocket and that's about it,' Francesca says. 'I have maybe seven or eight bucks left in my checking account. You have any money?'

'Just what's in my sock. But.'

'But what?'

'I know where we could get some.'

'You're crazy. Do you know how much we'd need just to get started?'

'I'm serious.'

Francesca sits up, leaning on her elbow. Streetlight filters in through the slats of the blinds, speckling her body. Bobby can't believe this is real. It seems like he's known her for a year, though it's only been a week. He feels like a man here in this room with her. For the first time in his life. If they run away together, maybe they can maintain this feeling. Stay free. Start a life that's new. Leave the ghosts of the neighborhood behind. It's possible. It has to be possible. People have made crazier shit work. 'You're serious?'

'I'm serious,' he says again.

'You barely know me.'

'I feel like I already know you better than I've ever known anyone.' He thinks it sounds romantic to say it that way. 'I'm so sick of my old man and my apartment and everything.'

'I'm sick of home too.'

'We could be on our own.'

'Tell me what you're thinking about doing.'

'You met Max.'

'Your creepy boss?'

'I told you he's kind of like a bank. That's what he does. I don't know exactly what he does, not really. The ins and outs, I mean. He takes deposits, gives people interest. There's tons of money on paper. I don't know where all that money is, but I do know there's a safe in the office and there's always some money in it.'

Francesca smiles. 'You're kidding. You're definitely kidding.'

'I'm not.'

'Number one, he can have us arrested. Number two, he's gotta have some security.'

Bobby looks up at the ceiling. Brown water stains blossoming under the light socket. Dust on the bulbs. Dust on the fixture. He thinks about what he's saying here. It *is* crazy. But it's doable. Fuck Max. Max is some kind of thief. At worst, he's been stealing from people for years. At best, he's been taking advantage of vulnerable marks for his own gain with a limited return for them. Taking money from him would be not only justified but righteous. 'He doesn't have any security,' Bobby says. 'It's unbelievable. He doesn't even have cameras. I mean, he does, but they don't work. They're just for show.'

Francesca puts her hand on his chest. 'I can't believe we're talking about this. We've definitely made each other crazy.'

'He has people he pays for protection, I think, but they're never around. It's more of a symbolic thing.'

'That means they'll come after us.'

'They won't know where we are.'

'They'll come after our families.'

'They won't even know about you or your family,' Bobby says. 'Max won't tell them. And he won't go after my dad. They've been friends forever. He'll make up a story. I know Max. He'll find some local thugs to pin it on.'

Bobby's really just figuring things out as he talks, but he's realizing how plausible it actually is. He knows where the gun in Max's desk is. Walk in, trusted as he is, put the gun on Max, tell him to open the safe, fill up a bag with dough. Sure, he's never done anything like it before, but everyone starts somewhere. Life is too slow. Life is not giving him enough. What's the option? Stay working a scrub job for Max and hope Francesca doesn't get bored? This just speeds things up. Makes things exciting. They can go straight to the airport and get a flight to Vegas. Buy a cheap car when they get there for the trip to Los Angeles. Maybe he can convince Francesca to marry him in one of those dumb chapels. Elvis performing the ceremony. An old woman in a rhinestone suit their only witness. A honeymoon at a motel with a heart-shaped bed and a Jacuzzi. Lovers on the lam. Francesca likes movies so much, she has to be into this. Goddamn American dream.

Maybe he should hold back. Maybe he should give it more time. A week isn't very long. But this week feels immense, in a good way. He's in love. Really. He's never known love. This is it. He wonders if she can see it in his eyes, feel it emanating from him. He wonders if she's ever been in love. If someone had asked him what love was before meeting her, he's not sure how he might have answered. What even was love to him before Francesca? A concept. He guesses he loves his father, but that's nothing. A dull light. He'd been excited over other girls, but it always passed very quickly, was never steady like this and was certainly never accompanied by this heavy feeling of aliveness and purpose.

This week has been staggering. He couldn't have imagined, meeting Francesca that day at her house, that things would've gone the way they have. Their connection so fierce, so immediate. Whatever made her call him back that first night from Long Eddy's, he's thankful. He felt stupid calling so quickly after meeting her – he knew that was against protocol and chances were good she'd be freaked out – but he followed his heart and it paid off. He couldn't have anticipated the best night of his life. He'd grown up in Brooklyn and he'd been to Manhattan hundreds of times, but he'd never experienced it like that. The booze had softened everything, but the magic was real. Light coursed through his veins. That diner. Their feet on the sidewalk, moving in time. Wandering. Kissing. Seeing a movie. The eternal music of the city. He felt like they'd been walking through photographs, like they were part of a story being told by a great storyteller.

And the days that followed. The magic somehow sustaining itself. He couldn't have imagined that they'd open up to each other the way they did. Her about her father. Him about his mother. He was even almost tempted to tell her about the rock he threw and how that had haunted him, but he couldn't bring himself to say it. He couldn't let the boy he was ruin this. The fact that he's proposing to rob Max is risky enough. He doesn't need to layer a dark patch of past thickly over the present. Stuff like that kills dreams. And this is a good dream, a dream come to life.

Bobby remembers longing for moments like this. Crushing on an actress in a movie and wondering what it'd be like to love her and be loved by her. Like with Fairuza Balk. He'd imagined scenarios where they met and talked all night and melted into each other. This is a million times better.

Francesca gets up. She puts on her shirt and underwear and then rolls a cigarette. She yanks up the rickety blinds, a blast of brightness from the streetlight right out front exploding into the room, and opens the window, leaning with her elbows up on the sill and blowing smoke outside, occasionally raining ash down onto the sidewalk below. 'After you rob Max, maybe we can start sticking up banks,' she says. 'Be a regular Bonnie and Clyde. Get some bandanas. Pick up a poor lowly getaway driver somewhere.'

'You still think I'm kidding. I'm not kidding.'

'Should we get something to eat? Are you hungry? It's late but not that late.'

'Definitely. What do you want?' He sits up, his back against the flimsy headboard. He covers himself with the sheet, which feels like an adult thing to do. He's slept with girls but he's never been naked in a hotel room with a girl. He's never watched a girl in her underwear smoke out the window.

'Maybe Indian?'

'Sure.'

Francesca seems to be staring at something down on the street. She breaks her gaze and finishes her smoke, bringing the butt into the bathroom and flushing it. They get dressed. They talk about going over to that block where all the Indian restaurants are. Francesca says she bets they're open until eleven or midnight. Bobby doesn't even know what time it is. Maybe nine thirty or ten. He's still thinking about that money in Max's safe and what they could do with it, where they could go, the world burning with possibilities, but he lets it go for now. He'll try again to convince her over dinner. He'll make the future come to life.

Lily

The next morning, when Lily wakes up in Amelia's bed, she's hit with a rush of embarrassment. She shouldn't have had so much to drink. She shouldn't have talked to Jack so much. Her head is pounding. Her mouth is dry. She knuckles her temples as if she can just push the pain away. She looks at the posters on the wall over the bed. The Cranberries, River Phoenix, Winona Ryder. A map of the world. All the books, CDs, and tapes stacked on the desk. So much stuff she loves too. She would've been friends with Amelia. Could've been if their paths were allowed to cross.

She sits up and listens to the silence of the house. She goes to the window. Pink light hovers over the neighborhood. Telephone wires cut against the pink. Dark roofs. The edge of the sun blazing on the horizon. It must be very early. She's not even sure what time the sun comes up on a summer day like this. Maybe five thirty. She doesn't understand enough about the mechanisms of the world. She wishes she knew more about this pink light. She could live inside light like this. An early-morning gloom settles on her. She's prone to feeling heartsick when regret and shame flood in.

She sits at Amelia's desk and touches the keys on the massive typewriter. She imagines Amelia writing here, a high school girl hungry to make sense of the world, walling herself in behind books and music and movie stars. She feels overcome with emotion. She cries. It feels strange to have slept in her bed. She feels suddenly as if she's been asked to play the part of Amelia. An understudy who's been waiting in the wings. Maybe it's just the hangover making everything feel so wrong, so depraved. She's sure that wasn't Jack's intention.

She picks up her boots and leaves the room, hoping to escape without waking Jack. In a way, this all feels as weird as a one-night stand, though nothing like that happened between them. She tiptoes downstairs and finds her bag right where she left it in the kitchen. She sees Jack asleep on the couch in the living room. She slips out the front door, opening and closing it with a whisper, and then pauses on the front stoop – the concrete cool through her thin socks – to put her boots on, the laces untied.

On her way home, she begins to feel bad about leaving that way. She thinks of Jack waking up, excited to have company. She read the situation the wrong way, she's sure of it. He wasn't having her *be* Amelia. He just gave her a comfortable bed to crash on, a quiet room. She can always lie and tell him she had an appointment. An early cleaning at the dentist she forgot about. Or something. She didn't want to wake him, that was it. She has a Rolodex of lies and excuses in her mind.

Back at home, she finds a bottle of Tylenol in the cabinet over the kitchen sink and washes down three pills with a tall glass of water. She can hear that her mother's in the shower, getting ready for work. If Lily plays this right, she can get into her room, crawl back into bed, and totally avoid her mom and Dave, if he's here. Maybe Dave's already out running. The bastard likes to put on his little shorts and hit the streets early. She thinks of her mother sleeping with Dave and feels grossed out.

She sneaks into her room, again achieving a whispery opening and closing of a door, this time in the service of a clean entrance instead of a clean exit. She opens the window for some fresh air, finds her Discman, puts the headphones over her ears, and presses play. The CD that's playing is a burned mix her friend Loretta made for her at York. It starts with Joni Mitchell's 'Coyote.' It occurs to Lily that the song that follows 'Coyote' on *Hejira* is 'Amelia.' Lily got her vinyl copy of *Hejira* at a thrift shop. She hasn't listened to it in a long time. The song that comes after 'Coyote' on the mix, though, is Jonathan Richman's 'You Can't Talk to the Dude.' Loretta loves Jonathan Richman. Every mix she's made for Lily – there have been three – has at least four Jonathan Richman songs. Sometimes it's the solo stuff. Sometimes it's the Modern Lovers. Lily loves Jonathan Richman too. Something about his voice settles her nerves.

Her head still hurts, but the music is helping. The water definitely helped. Maybe the Tylenol is kicking in already. She lies down on the bed and closes her eyes. She'll worry about brushing her teeth later.

She doesn't sleep. She keeps her eyes closed for a while but then she opens them and studies the ceiling. So much time spent like this, staring at the ceiling, headphones on. Through the music, she hears her mother and Dave out in the hallway. They don't even know she's here. They're making an early-morning racket. Her mother is particularly terrible in the morning. Frenzied. Soon enough, the front door slams and they're gone. She's alone in the apartment.

She gets up and goes into the bathroom, brushing her teeth while peeing, the Discman balanced on her thigh. Cyndi Lauper is playing now. She should take a shower but she'll wait a while. She sets the toothbrush on the edge of the sink, clips the Discman to her shirt, and wipes. She pulls up her pants and looks at herself in the mirror over the sink. Heavy smudges under her eyes. She runs the water and catches some in her cupped hands, rinsing out her mouth, and then washing her face.

In the kitchen, she makes a piece of plain toast. She tries to eat it, but she doesn't have the appetite. She finds tomato juice in the fridge and her mother's stash of good vodka and fixes something that comes close to a Bloody Mary, dosing it with Tabasco and pepper but leaving out the Worcestershire and skipping the olives and celery and whatever the hell else a bar would dump in there. She sucks it down and instantly feels better. Hair of the dog.

She sees a blinking light on the answering machine. She takes off her headphones, setting the Discman on the counter and coiling the headphone cord over it. She presses play on the machine. There are eight messages from Micah. In the first one, he speaks. He says only that it's him, that he'd like her to call him back at the motel. He leaves the number. The other seven messages are hang-ups, but she knows it's him, and he lets the line crackle for twenty or thirty seconds each time before disconnecting. Her mother hadn't even checked the machine. She lets out a gusty breath and deletes the messages.

Feeling bad about how she left Jack's so unceremoniously, she picks up the phone, dials information, and asks the operator for his listing. She has to say his name a few times and then tries to spell it. Finally, the operator finds it and gives Lily the number, asking if she'd like to be patched through. Lily says okay. She wanders into her room with the cordless handset as Jack's line rings.

Four rings. Five. Jack picks up. 'Hello?'

'It's Lily,' she says. 'I got your number from information. I hope that's okay.'

'Of course.'

'I'm sorry I snuck out. I was feeling bad. Too much to drink. Thanks for everything.'

'There's nothing to apologize for. I figured you were just an early riser and you didn't know when I was going to get up, so you skedaddled. Probably for the best. All I had for breakfast was stale crumb cake and an old orange.'

Lily laughs. She goes over to the window. A nice mild breeze from outside. 'I just wanted to thank you for letting me crash.'

'No problem at all. Like I said, it was nice to have some life in the house.'

Lily's window is on the third floor of the three-family house where their apartment is. Her eyes search the windows of the house across from them for movement. One time she saw the couple who live in the third-floor apartment there fighting naked. Really going at it. All sorts of angry hand motions. Whisper-yelling. Banging doors. Now all she sees is a pigeon perched on their windowsill. Her eyes go down to the narrow alley between the houses. Micah is standing there, hands in the pockets of his cargo shorts, looking up at her. She gasps and says, 'Oh God.' She backs away from the window.

'What is it?' Jack says.

'He's here. He's watching me.'

'Your ex-boyfriend?'

'Yes. I went to my window, looked down at the alley, and he was just standing there, looking up at me.'

'What's your address?'

She edges close to the window, double-checking that Micah's actually there, that she hasn't simply hallucinated him. He is. 'Come on outside, Lil,' he says. 'Or let me up. I just want to talk.'

Lily stumbles back to her bed and sits down. 'I'm so fucking creeped out.'

'What's your address?' Jack asks again. 'I'll come over and chase him off.'

'Yeah?'

'Yeah.'

She gives him her address.

'I'm coming now.' He hangs up immediately.

Micah calls her name from the alley. Twice. And then there's silence. She goes back to the window and sees that he's gone. She brings the phone back into the kitchen. She runs the tap and drinks another glass of water. The bell to the apartment rings. She shudders. The good news is that there are two doors. One on the first floor where the bell is, leading to a staircase that bypasses the second-floor apartment where Nancy and Stan McGuire live, on the way up to the front door of Lily and her mom's apartment. Micah can't get through the first door without a key or unless someone lets him in. She at least has this barrier between them, both doors and the staircase. He rings the bell incessantly.

She goes to the front door and looks through the peephole at the empty staircase. Her greatest fear right now is that he finds a way through that first door and then he'd suddenly be there, fish-eyed on the other side of the glass, so close she would hear him breathing. She checks the locks on the door. The slide latch, the deadbolt, the knob lock. Luckily, her mother is big on locks. Lily trembles.

The bell keeps ringing. Now Micah alternates by banging on the outside door. Lily wonders if anyone downstairs is home, Nancy or Stan, or even the landlords, Mel and Sandy Merolla, who live on the first floor with their bullmastiff, Duke.

She can hear Micah's muffled voice.

'Lil, please let me upstairs,' he says. 'I just want to talk.'

'Please go away,' she says, barely loud enough for herself to hear. She's not talking to Micah so much as she's talking to the universe, to God if there is a God, to take control of the situation, to pull this unhinged boy away from her, away from the house, away from the block, away from the city, just away.

She scrambles to the window in the living room that overlooks the front of the house and peeks between the blinds. She can see the top of Micah's head. He's ringing the bell with one hand, pounding intermittently on the door with the other. He gazes up as if he senses her there.

'I love you, Lil,' he says, his voice muted through the glass but clearer now, like when he was in the alley. 'I love you so much. I just want you back. I want another chance. Give me another chance. I've made a lot of changes since we broke up.'

'Go the fuck away, Micah,' Lily says. 'I don't want to see you. I don't want to talk to you. I don't know what's going on, but you're sick. You're sicker than before.'

'I'm gonna kill myself if I can't see you. Please.'

She doesn't say anything. She notices a few passersby on the sidewalk taking the situation in. They stop and stare but keep moving. She remembers reading all about Kitty Genovese. How people heard and saw her murder and did nothing. She wonders if that's what might happen to her.

'I'm gonna kill you and then I'm gonna kill myself,' Micah says in the most matter-of-fact way possible. It's chilling.

'I'm calling the cops,' Lily says.

He doesn't respond. He keeps his finger on the bell.

A loud screech overtakes the buzzing. Tires spinning to a halt on blacktop. A car has pulled up fast at the hydrant out front. The driver's side door flings open. Jack gets out. He's holding an aluminum bat in his hand. He approaches on the sidewalk. 'You Micah?' Jack says.

'What?' Micah says. His finger off the bell now.

'You're the Micah who's harassing Lily, right?'

Micah scurries down the stoop and runs around the side of the house, back down the alley. Jack follows him. Lily runs into her room so she can see what happens from the window there. Jack is about fifteen feet behind Micah, the bat clutched in his hand like a club. Micah hops the chain-link fence out back and disappears behind an overgrown fig tree in Mr Romandetto's yard. Jack leans over the fence and looks for him but has lost him in a maze of possible escape routes. Either way, he's gone. Jack heads back to the front of the house.

Lily goes down to meet him. She stands on the front stoop, tears in her eyes. 'I was scared,' she says. 'Thanks for coming.'

'Of course,' Jack says. 'I'm sorry I didn't catch the bastard.'

'Maybe it'll be enough now that he knows someone's watching out for me.'

'Maybe.'

'I like your bat.'

Jack holds it up. 'Used to call it "Wonder Boy" like in *The*

Natural. I hit plenty of dingers with it in my stupid softball league, which doesn't mean shit.'

'Do you want to come in? I can make some coffee.'

'Why don't you come back to my place? He doesn't know to look for you there. You can hide out. I've gotta go run some errands. You can work on Amelia's typewriter, if you want. Have some peace and quiet. Not worry about this guy showing back up.'

Lily did feel very safe at Jack's place, and she's shaken by this encounter with Micah. 'Okay,' she says. 'Maybe that's a good idea. Let me leave my mom a note and get some stuff.'

Bobby

Bobby and Francesca had a late dinner on Curry Row, picking one of the many Indian restaurants. A place called Gandhi. After that, they bought a couple of bottles of wine with screw-off tops at a liquor store and a package of rubbers at a bodega – he'd only brought a single rubber with him, never needing more than that before – and then they went back to the strange little hotel room, drinking and laughing, talking more about Vegas and California. Bobby professed his love. He said he wanted to hit Max's as soon as they got back to Brooklyn. They kissed. They went to the bed. They let their bodies tangle again. They rocked that flimsy headboard. Bobby had seen movies where people were sweating while they fucked, but he'd never sweated while he fucked. The handful of times he'd previously done it, he figured he looked stupid as shit. Grunting, pounding. With Francesca, he felt beautiful. Bodies glistening in the sad hotel glow. Cheap wine coursing through their veins. The fantasy of it all. This beautiful girl and him, Bobby Fucking Santovasco, lucky enough to be in her arms, wrapped up with her on the crisp white sheets of this Chinatown bed. They were all motion. All love. They felt like a good song on the radio. This time with Francesca had been a way Bobby didn't know life could be.

In the morning, they got coffee and bagels and kissed on the sidewalk outside a storefront with black mirrored windows. On the subway home, holding hands, sipping coffee, Bobby said, 'Let's do it now.'

'Do what?' Francesca asked.

'Let's go to Max's now. Let's go straight there. Transfer to the R and go right to Bay Ridge.'

'You're serious?'

'I've been serious.'

'You're gonna actually rob your boss and then we're gonna go to Vegas and Los Angeles?' A glimmer in her eye. He could tell she still didn't quite believe him but thought that the sentiment was romantic.

Bobby laughed. 'That's the plan.'

'Okay, let's do it. The guy does seem like a scumbag, and it sounds like he's running a Ponzi scheme, stealing from my mother and everybody else.'

And so they transferred to the R and now they're coming up on Fourth Avenue and Eighty-Sixth Street in Bay Ridge, a couple of short blocks from Max's office. Francesca smokes as they walk. Bobby takes a drag off her cigarette. She asks him if he wants his own. He says no, he just wanted some of hers.

'What are you gonna say?' Francesca asks.

'I don't know,' Bobby says.

Outside Max's office, Francesca knocks the cherry off her cigarette and puts what remains back in her tobacco pouch. 'Let's just go,' she says. 'I like you, Bobby. We don't need to do this. We can just let things play out the normal way.'

Bobby smiles. He's not even nervous. This feels right. He knocks on Max's door. A voice echoes inside. Frustrated, agitated. It's Max, but Bobby can't quite make out what he's saying.

When he finally opens up, Bobby's shocked by Max's appearance. White tank top, unbuttoned slacks, no shoes or socks. Bobby's never seen him dressed down like this.

A rush of hot air floods out of the office. Max is drenched. Sweat dotting his forehead like beads of hot glue. His face flushed. Pink splotches map his pale arms. He has a big glass of milk in his hand, ice floating in it.

'Oh, look who decides to show his face,' Max says. 'Everything's going haywire – the air conditioner's busted, there's a backlog of CDs to be shipped, I've got twenty investors breathing down my neck about their interest, I'm almost out of milk – and the kid's AWOL, nowhere to be found. "Where's the kid?" I keep asking myself. "I could sure use the kid about now," I keep saying.' His eyes travel over to Francesca. 'Now I know where you've been.'

'I wanted to show Francesca the office,' Bobby says. 'Thought I might pick her out a couple of CDs. Can we come in?'

'You wanted to show Francesca the office, huh? You've gotta be kidding me. What'd I say to you? I said don't get pussy-sick. What's the first thing you do? Huh? You get yourself good and pussy-sick.' Max eyes Francesca inappropriately, his yellow teeth gleaming between his wormy lips, milk crusted on the corners of his mouth. 'Now, she looks nice, pal. Don't get me wrong. I wish I could take a sniff.'

Bobby looks over at Francesca. She doesn't look so much disgusted as angry. The worse Max is, he figures, the easier it'll be for Francesca to realize that they're making a chump of a bad man.

Max moves to the side and extends his free hand as if he's welcoming them to his home. 'Come on in, both of you,' he says. 'Take the tour. I've got nothing more important to do.'

Bobby leads the way and Francesca follows. Max closes the door behind them. The office is stifling hot. The front window is lodged shut. Max has a desk fan going, but it's not doing much.

'I'm sure Bobby told you, me and his old man go way back. Went to Our Lady of the Narrows together. Where'd you go to school? Public school, right? You just graduated?'

Francesca nods.

'She doesn't say much, your girl here,' Max says to Bobby. 'That's good. Seen and not heard. I'm a big proponent of that. Guys must've had it made back in the fifties. Nowadays, almost every broad you meet runs her mouth off to no end. Generally speaking. So, I do appreciate your silence.'

'I should tell my mom how you talk,' Francesca says, breaking her streak of quiet. 'Maybe she'll want her investment back.'

Max smiles. 'You won't tell your mom anything.'

Bobby goes over to the desk and opens the top drawer, lifting a couple of file folders and taking out the gun that Max keeps hidden in there. Cute little bastard. Max's just-in-case gun. He's never had to use it, but he always says he's had to show it to a few people. Always loaded since the one time it wasn't when he needed it. Bobby points it at Max now.

Max laughs and puts his hands in the air as if it's an Old West stickup, milk slopping over the rim of the glass as he holds it up. 'Oh no,' Max says. 'You got me.'

'Can you go over and open the safe?' Bobby says. He's sweating now too.

'You're funny, kid.' Max puts his hands back down and takes a sturdy slug of milk, draining every drop, the ice rattling. He sets the glass on top of a stack of nearby boxes. 'Now put the gun down before somebody gets hurt. You can take your girl upstairs and show her where I've got all the CDs. Let her pick out a few. On me. Consider it a gift since her mom's an investor.' To Francesca: 'What kind of music you like, sweetie?'

'I'm not kidding,' Bobby says. 'Open the safe.'

Max looks to Francesca for confirmation that this is a joke. She shrugs.

'You're gonna try to rob me?' Max says to Bobby. 'One of your father's oldest friends? Knowing the people I know, the people I pay for protection? You've gotta be shitting me.' His skin turning from splotchy pink to raging red.

'Quit talking and open the safe,' Bobby says.

'What do you think is in there? There's nothing in there.'

Francesca seems scared and uncomfortable. She's looking away from Bobby with the gun. This was a week of tenderness and falling in love, and Bobby guesses she doesn't like this other side of him that she's seeing. He knows this side's always there, the side that's ready to burst, ready to break down walls, but he contains it. He doesn't want to contain it anymore because that's gotten him nowhere. He wants to take control of his fate. He wants to be far away from here with Francesca. He wants everything to be new.

Max continues: 'I'm serious, Bobby. It's empty except for some files. You're doing this for nada. Zilch. All I've gotta do is make a quick call and you're a goner. You want to be a goner? You ever think about what that means? People think a lot of things about death. They think either you wind up in heaven with everybody you ever loved or you wind up in hell shoveling coal into a furnace. You know what it is really? Just an eternity of staring at a blank screen. That's it. That's what you want?'

Bobby makes a move on Max. He comes up on his side and nudges the gun against his arm. 'Go now,' he says. 'Open it. And give me the keys to your car too.' Then to Francesca: 'Will you look in the bottom of that filing cabinet over there?' Motioning to the opposite corner. 'I think there are a couple rolls of yellow duct tape. Get them for me, please.'

Francesca scurries over to the filing cabinet and finds the tape. She holds it in her shaking hand.

'Just hold on to them a sec,' Bobby says to her. 'When he's done at the safe, we'll tape him up, okay?'

She nods.

'The keys to the car are on the desk,' Max says. 'How far you gonna get with my shitbox? I haven't had the oil changed in a year.'

Bobby pushes Max toward the safe on the table in the corner, and he finally budges. When he gets there, he really starts dripping sweat. He does one quick rotation to the left on the combination dial and then pauses, saying, 'Don't do this, okay? There's a real future for you at Options Inc. You can still be my right-hand man. I can forget about all of this, forgive you, and chalk it up to you being under the sway of this girl. She's driven you to this. The brain does crazy things when a woman like her shows up. You're not the first to go apeshit over a bit of strange.'

'Keep doing the numbers,' Bobby says, mashing the gun against Max's spine.

'You can still walk away,' Max says. 'Just put the piece down and think this through. You what, need a loan? I'll give you a loan.'

Bobby tells him to shut up again. 'A future for me in this? What is it even? You collect suckers and take advantage of them. Your days are numbered anyway.'

'This isn't that,' Max says, spitting as he talks. 'I'm a good man. I do a service for people. I'm helping them make their lives better. That's what I'm gonna do for *her* mother. I've been doing it for your old man forever. Every gift you ever got is probably because of the interest he gets from me.'

'Do the next number.'

Max rotates the dial to the right and stops on a higher number. 'This is it. I do the last one and there's no turning back. I open this and you're the bad guy.'

Bobby knows that Max's hesitation to open the safe must be a good sign. He wouldn't make this fuss if it was empty today. He'd spin the dial, throw open the door, and say, 'See? There's nothing.' Bobby and Francesca would leave with their tails tucked between their legs. But the score must be big. Maybe Max just got a bunch of dough out of the bank and is stashing it here to hand out to his investors or whatever mob guys he pays off for whatever services. Bobby's hoping the beater car can make it to the airport at least. He's dreaming about Vegas. A pocket full of dough. Francesca on his arm. A room with a hot tub. That chapel. She wants movies? This is the stuff of movies. Meet, fall in love, rob a guy, get hitched. The future's the open road.

'Do the last one,' Bobby says, really pressing the gun deep into Max's back.

Max winces. 'Your old man's gonna cry when he hears about this. He's always been disappointed in you, but this will make it something else. What's worse than disappointment? Regret. Regret he ever shot the load that brought your dumb ass into the world. There's not anything for you now. You're a weed someone needs to pull.'

'Open it.'

Max spins the dial to the left one last time and there's a click. He opens the door slowly, trying to shield Bobby's view of what's in the safe.

Bobby pushes past him and sees inside. The safe is crammed full of stuff. Bobby's never seen it so overloaded. A black duffel bag is up front, taking most of the space in the deep, wide interior. Bobby recognizes it as the bag that Charlie French had with him last week. He must've asked Max to hold it for him. Bobby pulls the bag out and drops it to the floor. He kneels, yanking on the zipper with his free hand, keeping the gun on Max with the other.

'You know who that belongs to, right?' Max says. 'You saw him drop it for me to hold. Charlie French. He'll kill you without hesitation. He'll kill your old man and your old man's girlfriend. He'll blow up your whole block. He'll blow up the church where you got baptized.'

Bobby finally gets the zipper to move. The bag is full of banded stacks of cash and bricks of heroin. He can't believe it. He laughs. 'Holy shit,' he says.

'What is it?' Francesca asks.

'It's better than I could've guessed.'

Max tries to make a move. He jostles two steps backward and gives Bobby a karate chop on the shoulder.

Bobby barely feels it. He stands up, leaving the bag at his feet. He turns the gun over in his hand and clocks Max with it. Right on the cheek. Max wails like the milk-drinker that he is. Bobby can smell the milk on his breath. His hands go up to his face.

'Jesus Christ,' Max says. 'That really fucking hurt. Really. I'm gonna be one big shiner.'

'Bring the tape,' Bobby says to Francesca. 'Please.' He keeps remembering to be polite to her, even in the midst of this nutso shit.

She's staring at Max, who's clutching at his cheek with both hands, as if he's trying to peel the skin back.

'Start with his wrists. Just have him cross them behind his back and tape them tight. Then do his mouth.'

'You're gonna pay,' Max says, his voice crumbling.

Francesca holds the tape out. 'Can you do it?' she asks.

'Okay,' Bobby says. 'But you'll have to hold the gun.'

She swallows hard and then nods. She's so nervous. She's even more beautiful nervous. Bobby's thinking this was made to be.

They switch places. Bobby has the tape now, and he's getting to work on Max's wrists behind his back, really binding him. The bruise on his cheek, once revealed, is bad, already purpling. The gun is wavering in Francesca's hand. She's earthquake shaking, just totally rattled.

Max keeps talking: 'Charlie French will skin you alive. He'll find your mother, wherever the hell she's hiding, and he'll skin her alive too. It's over for you, Bobby. I can't help you now.'

Bobby affixes a fat piece of the yellow tape over Max's mouth and finally shuts him up. Max makes muffled noises under the tape, protesting. The next step will be to get him on the floor and wrap his legs. Then Bobby will put him in the chair and tape him to it. Just tape him fully to the chair, using every inch of tape, so he can't move, can't do anything other than fall over in the chair and writhe around on the ground. It'll take a while. He shuts the desk fan because he finds the noise too distracting, his hand brushing across the cover of a Yellow Pages directory stacked on top of some files.

'Can you believe how rich we are, baby?' Bobby says to Francesca.

'No,' Francesca says from behind the gun.

'Well, believe it. We've got it made.'

More pointless muffled wailing from Max, the bruise on his cheek seeming to blossom up from under the tape.

'You shut up and get all the way down on the floor,' Bobby says to him. 'I've gotta do your legs.'

Jack

Jack brings Lily back to his house and sits with her in the kitchen over coffee. He's made it his grandmother's way, boiling the grounds with eggshells, and Lily says that's a great detail she's going to steal to use in her book. He's set the bat down on the counter next to the sugar bowl.

'You want to call your mother?' he asks.

'She'll just claim this is normal boy stuff,' Lily says. 'That it'll die down. But you saw him – that's not normal, right?'

'Definitely not.' Jack's thinking of Micah's face, how deranged he looked, and how scared Lily was. He knows this is the kind of thing that doesn't just go away. He's known guys like this before. Abusers. Many times it's the ones you least expect from appearances, not just the tatted, muscled-up tough guys that look like they've done stretches in prison, but instead a country club kid like this, cargo shorts and a polo shirt, a privileged little turd. 'You want to call the cops?' he asks.

'What's the point? I know they won't do anything. Maybe they go over to this motel he's staying at and knock on the door. Then what? He technically hasn't done anything.'

'Maybe that's enough. Maybe it'll scare him into leaving and not coming back.'

'I doubt it. Micah can play the game. He'd have those cops thinking I'm the crazy one within a minute.'

'You'll be safe here. You can stay as long as you want. A few hours. A few days. Whatever. Amelia's room is yours. You can use her typewriter to work. Take what you want from the fridge – there's not much – and use the phone whenever.'

Lily fiddles with the handle of her coffee mug. 'Thanks so much, Jack.'

'I have to go out and do some work,' Jack says. 'I'll probably be gone most of the day. You feel okay staying here alone?'

Lily nods. 'I do. I don't think he knows I was here last night.'

'There's no way to know that for sure, so I'm gonna show you something. Bring your coffee.'

Jack gets up and waits for Lily to stand. He leads her down to the basement and shows her where he keeps the gun hidden, wrapped in a cloth and nudged behind a pipe in the ceiling over the oil burner. He hasn't used it since Amelia died, but he keeps it in decent shape. He wonders if she'll be shocked or upset by it. He hopes not. He just wants her to feel secure.

His intention is to go straight to Coney Island and find Micah. There's likely only one place he could be staying, the Luna Motel, and it's the kind of dive where you can crash into a room and mash a pillow over a psycho's face without drawing too much notice. That's what Jack's going to do. Lily needs to be out from under this. Even if Micah doesn't follow through on stalking her or hurting her, Jack knows guys like this don't change and he'll continue to torment women until he does do some terrible damage. Jack wiping him out would be a service not only to Lily but to whoever would come next for this guy, as well as the kids he won't have a chance to fuck up.

Still, Lily could be wrong about Micah not knowing about his house – he very well could've followed her last night – and Jack wants her to be prepared just in case wires get crossed and Micah comes here while Jack goes to the Luna.

He takes the gun out and holds it in his palm, folding back the edges of the cloth. 'This is where this is, if you need it,' Jack says to her. 'I don't want you to be scared, but I want you to be ready on the off chance he does know you're here. I'm not a gun nut or anything. It's just for protection. I've never even used it.'

Lily nods. She prods at the grip. 'I've seen guns before. I've worked in restaurants.'

'The bullets are in that cookie tin, but you won't need them. Just pointing it at him would be enough.' He puts the gun away.

They go back upstairs. He shows her where he's hung his car keys – on a hook by the front door under a tattered Brooklyn Dodgers cap he used to wear when he played softball with the Battlers. He's taking the subway where he's going, he explains, so if she needs the car, desperately or otherwise, it's there in the driveway for her. He tells her that the lock's broken on the passenger side and not to roll down the driver's side window and that there's a hole under the gas pedal if she wonders where the whooshing noise is coming from. He says the radio works fine but the cassette player is on the fritz so just ignore the shoebox full of cassettes on the floor, not that he has anything she'd want to listen to anyway. She nods and says thank you and says she's sure she won't need the car or the gun but she's glad both are there. She says she might go lie down, if that's okay. Her head's spinning. She took some Tylenol and drank a Bloody Mary but the hangover she has is exacerbated by the anxiety. He says sleep's the best thing to feel better. She goes upstairs to Amelia's room and shuts the door.

Jack walks around the house. He checks the windows to make sure they're locked. He rinses the coffee mugs they just used. He looks in the fridge and throws out the most embarrassing stuff, a two-week-old container of Chinese takeout, some ancient mustard, packets of soy sauce and duck sauce that have been in there since his parents were around. He pushes the bag of eggshells behind everything else. He doesn't have much for Lily if she gets hungry, but there are cold cuts and he's got a fairly fresh loaf of semolina bread he leaves out on the table. He locks the back door, putting the chain on, and then goes out the front door, using the key in his pocket to lock it. He heads through the front yard and around the side of the house to the backyard. It used to be neat here. Janey had a garden once. Now it's all weeds and cracked concrete. The fence is falling down. The small garage in the back corner of the yard on his end of the shared driveway is decrepit, the wood rotten, the roof on the verge of caving in. He pulls open the door. It sounds like chains dragged inside a dumpster. He hasn't been in the garage in years. He sees wooden chairs laced in cobwebs, a couple of Amelia's bikes from when she was little, one of his bikes from high school, his father's toolbox, and a lawn mower that must be fifty years old. Next to the lawn mower is a crate that contains his softball stuff. A first baseman's mitt that's fuzzed with mold. His cleats and stirrups. Bunched wristbands. A tattered scorecard. Two different pairs of batting gloves, one red and one blue, the colors the Battlers wore.

Bringing his old bat – that he's kept in the hall closet of the house all this time – to Lily's is what made him remember the crate. What he's here for is the batting gloves. He leans over and plucks up the red batting gloves, cramming them in his back pocket. He stands, steps out of the garage, and pulls the door shut.

He walks to Twenty-Fifth Avenue and takes the subway to Coney Island. It's two quick stops. He's alone in the car, looking out over the neighborhood through a scratched window. The dark tops of buildings. Graffiti. Busted fences and overgrown yards. Pigeons.

He gets off at the Stillwell Avenue station, coming out on the sidewalk on Surf Avenue. Big groups of people cross the avenue, thundering toward the Boardwalk and the beach. He heads in the opposite direction, up Stillwell, cutting a left on Mermaid. The Luna Motel is a few blocks away, on the corner of Mermaid and West Sixteenth. It's been there for as long as Jack can remember, a remnant of a different Coney Island, but now – even though Coney's starting to get cleaned up and revitalized – it's still mainly a place where hookers bring johns or where junkies hole up for weeks at a time. Jack read a story just recently in the *Daily News* about a pimp gunning another pimp down in one of the rooms.

The Luna is an L-shaped one-story corner building. The sign in front was once classic, a neon beauty casting its glow on Mermaid, but it doesn't work anymore, just blown empty tubing that no one even seems to notice. Jack remembers its glow. He remembers its pinks and reds spilling out on the blacktop.

The main office itself isn't accessible. There's a window with a grate in it where you talk to the clerk behind bulletproof glass. A small parking lot edges up close to the rooms. Space for about eight cars. Hand painted lines on the concrete. Weeds grown up ankle-high between cracked slabs. The doors to the rooms are dreary. Numbers missing. Weather-beaten.

The lot is half-full. Three junk cars and a nice one, a silver 2001 Buick LeSabre. The license plate is in a black frame that reads MASTERS BUICK GMC OF BEDFORD HILLS. It's not hard to guess that it's Micah's car, that he's right there in the room the LeSabre is parked in front of. Jack walks through the lot. He sees a couple of syringes on the ground. A used rubber. A card for a phone sex operation. He takes the red batting gloves out of his back pocket and puts them on.

Passing the LeSabre, he notices how clean the interior is. One of those club locks latched on to the steering wheel. A pine air freshener hanging from the rearview mirror. Jack runs his hand along the polished side of the car.

Room five. The holographic sticker with the number on it peeling from the edges. Jack knocks hard on the door. If his guess is wrong, he'll try the next room.

He's spot-on. The door opens, and Micah's standing there, shirtless, wearing only his cargo shorts. 'You,' he says.

Jack pushes his way in. Micah backs up, confused. Jack closes the door behind him. The room is dark, blinds drawn. The wallpaper is brittle. The carpet rubbed down to almost nothing.

A small TV with a bent antenna, set up on the dresser, shows a soap opera. Micah's bag is open on a desk in the corner. Dim light comes down in a cone from the ceiling fixture. The room smells like bug spray.

'What is this?' Micah asks. 'Who are you?'

Jack pulls up a chair and sits across from Micah. He doesn't say anything.

'You her new boyfriend? She going for old guys now? I always thought she might have a thing for old guys. Looking for a father figure, that kind of shit. Lily doesn't know what she wants. She needs someone like me to tell her what she wants.'

'Shut up,' Jack says.

'You think you're gonna scare me? You don't scare me. You know who my dad is? You know what kind of connections he has? I call him right now, he'll have somebody over here in no time flat to take care of you. He knows people in Brooklyn. He grew up here.'

'I heard you've got a nice life in Westchester County. That your family's got a lot of money. None of that's going to save you. You could've been good, but you chose to try to ruin Lily's life. Guys who do stuff like what you're doing don't change.'

'You're nuts. Look at you. You're nobody. You think you're gonna beat me up and I'm gonna just disappear? Touch me. See what happens. Everything you do to me I'll do to Lily times ten.' Micah stands up. He puffs his chest out. 'Go ahead. Touch me.'

Without even standing, Jack pops him in the face. A quick jab to his right eye. He was careful to keep it away from the nose because he didn't want a gusher of blood. Micah falls back on the bed, splayed out, holding his face where Jack hit him, yelping. Jack wonders if he's ever been hit like that. Probably not. Guys like this don't even get in bar fights. They run or they get someone to fight for them.

'I'm gonna call my dad,' Micah says.

Jack stands. He gets on top of Micah on the bed, holding

him down with his body. Micah wasn't expecting this, and he's writhing around suddenly, fighting to get free, smacking at Jack with his hands, kicking his legs wildly. Jack manages to keep him pinned to the bed. He grabs one of the pillows that's scrunched up by the dirty headboard and he puts it over Micah's face. The last thing he sees are Micah's eyes going wide.

He holds the pillow down tight, one gloved hand on either side of Micah's head, pressing into the mattress. Micah's still smacking at him, kicking to get free, but now there's a desperation to his movements as his air's cut off. The panic is good. The panic will make this go faster. More oxygen expended. Jack's done it this way one other time. It took almost five minutes, and he wound up bruised but it was clean and quiet.

A couple of minutes in. Micah's hyperventilating now, Jack can tell. The urge to struggle is fading. He's trying to save his breath. Maybe he thinks Jack's taking it as far as he can to teach him a lesson and then he'll let him go, hoping it's enough.

But Jack doesn't stop. This is Micah, who's tormenting Lily. He imagines that it's the kid who threw the rock at Amelia's car. That helps. No hesitation.

Five minutes in, Micah stops moving. Jack keeps the pillow pressed over his face for another couple of minutes just to be sure. When he's done, he rolls off of Micah and lies back on the bed, trying to catch his own breath. He's out of shape, hasn't done much that's physically demanding in a while. Those seven minutes felt like seven years.

The reality though is that very little time has passed between his leaving Lily and then killing Micah. About an hour. It's been years since his last job, but he's always surprised by how easy it is. Murder just isn't hard if you're half-smart. Worst-case scenario is it's sloppy. Best is a quiet expiration, like trapping a spider in a jar and letting it suffocate as opposed to smashing its guts all over the wall. Simply switch off the valves to life.

Jack gets up and finds the keys to Micah's Buick on the

dresser by the TV. He goes out and starts it, struggling with the club lock on the steering wheel but finally getting it off. He backs the car out of the spot, turns it around, and then pulls into the same spot again, in reverse this time, getting the rear end as close to the door as possible. He pops the trunk and keeps the car running. He looks around. No one seems to be watching.

Back in the room, he wraps Micah in the comforter and carries him outside, dumping him into the gaping trunk. He looks around again, before shaking the comforter free from the body since he doesn't want it to be traced to the motel. He slams the lid and returns to the room, flinging the comforter on the bed.

Jack finds the room key and leaves it on the chair by the door, zips Micah's bag shut and puts the strap over his shoulder. He looks around for any other sign that Micah has ever been in the room, finds toothpaste and a toothbrush propped on the edge of the sink in the bathroom and stuffs those in the outer pocket of the bag. He exits the room, leaving the door unlocked.

In the car, he turns on the radio. Micah's been listening to a CD. Dave Matthews Band. Jack ejects the CD and tosses it on the floor. He scans the dial until he finds oldies. His plan is to drive upstate. He knows Poughkeepsie is the last stop on the Metro-North line. He can be there in a couple of hours, maybe even less. Somewhere along the way, maybe at a Thruway rest stop, he'll empty Micah's bag in a dumpster.

He's been to Poughkeepsie before. For a wedding. A distant Bronx cousin who'd moved up to Dutchess County. He'll leave the car parked on the street a few blocks from the station, toss the keys, and then hop on a train back to the city.

All told, it might take five or six hours to be at his house with Lily again. He won't tell her, of course. She might not know for days. And – hopefully – she'll never know he had anything to do with it. Micah's family will have a tragic mystery on their hands. They might not even know about Brooklyn, about his fixation on his ex. They'll puzzle over Poughkeepsie. They'll look elsewhere for answers. Lily won't speak up. She won't say he'd been stalking her. She'll feel a wince of confusion but mostly just relief. Jack will rest easy in the knowledge that Micah can't ever hurt her.

Jack pulls out of the lot and heads for the Belt Parkway. He prays there's no traffic.

Francesca

Francesca is scared. She's not sure what she expected, but she didn't expect this. What Bobby had proposed seemed ridiculous at first, a joke, and then it seemed romantic. Now it seems real in a way she's not ready for. She figured there might be a few grand in the safe. There's so much more than that, and there are drugs. Someone else's drugs. Bobby has taped Max up. Max is buzzing behind the tape. He's jolting his body around. He manages to lean the chair back on its legs. Bobby is looking around on Max's desk for something.

'What are you doing?' Francesca asks.

'Hold on a sec,' Bobby says. He finds what he's looking for. A leather-bound address and telephone book. He stuffs it in the bag.

Max is going wild now, rocking the chair, his noises seeming to make the hot room vibrate. He tips the chair back and falls over.

Watching him is freaking Francesca out. 'I think you should leave the drugs,' she says to Bobby. 'Just take the money.' She's never heard the name Charlie French before today, but he must be somebody pretty big.

Bobby comes over to her, clutching the bag. He whispers, 'No one will know we took it. Max has cameras up in here, but they're just for show. No one really knows that I work here. Your mom and grandma, my old man, maybe a few others. No one they'll think to ask. We could sit on the money and drugs for a while, not run away yet so we don't look suspicious. You know? And then in six months, a year, we could take off.'

'And what about *him*?' Francesca whispers back. 'As soon as we're gone, he'll tell.'

'Go outside. I'm gonna talk to him. I can convince him. This isn't even his stuff.'

'You're crazy. This is really bad. Can we just go back to last night? Last night was so nice. This is all wrong.'

'Go outside, okay?' He kisses her on the cheek. 'Just go outside and wait for me.'

She chokes on her words and nods.

She goes outside and stands on the sidewalk in front of the office. She looks all around. Just a normal day. A breeze in the trees. A fire hydrant spraying water into the gutter. Cars flowing on Fourth Avenue. The sun glinting off the mirrored glass of the bank across the street. Junk stores with beach towels and floaties in bins outside. A market with flower stalls. A guy pushing a stroller passes her. An old blue-haired woman in the upstairs window in the building opposite Max's place, just hunched there, takes in the summer breeze through her screen. A loud thump comes from Max's office but it gets lost in the noise of the neighborhood. Voices. Screeching tires. Horns and sirens.

Fifteen or twenty minutes pass. Maybe more. Bobby comes out with the black duffel bag from the safe. The money and drugs. He's sweating hard. 'Walk,' he says.

They head for the corner. They cross Fourth Avenue. 'What happened?' she asks, as they're in the middle of the street. Sunlight reflecting off the hoods of idling cars. Music bouncing from windows and storefronts.

'We can't take his car,' Bobby says, leaning over and discreetly dropping Max's car keys into the sewer drain on the opposite corner as they're about to step over the curb.

'What happened?' Francesca asks.

They continue up Eighty-Fourth Street in the direction of Fifth Avenue. It's a quiet block. The breeze hangs in the trees. A couple of seniors sitting on stoops. Sneakers dangling from the telephone wire just ahead of them. A tree that's burst through the concrete. Rusted fences in front of row houses. 'He wouldn't listen to me,' Bobby says. 'I tried.'

'What do you mean?'

'He's not a good guy. He stole money from your mom and grandma. He's robbed hundreds of people.'

'What are you saying?'

'He wouldn't listen. I just hit him again, that was it.'

Francesca has to admit it was good to see Bobby clock Max with the gun that first time. Max is no doubt a creep. His eyes all over her. The swindle he runs. Milk, milk, milk. 'You hit him again, and what happened?'

'I set him upright in the chair and I hit him with the gun again. I must've gotten him right on his temple. I opened up this big gash. There was a lot of blood. I don't even know how I did it. I think I killed him.'

Francesca stops in her tracks. 'Jesus, Bobby.'

'It was an accident.'

'Where's the...?' She drifts off, can't say the word *gun*.

'It's in the bag. I wiped everything down. I locked the door from inside. It might be days before anyone finds him. People sometimes only come around once a week, if that. Mostly he goes *to* people.'

'What about this Charlie French? He'll come around looking for his stuff.'

'Maybe.'

'I can't believe this.'

'We could have a whole life. Your dreams could come true. We can get out of here. Like we were talking about. He wasn't a good guy.'

'What're we gonna do now?'

'Leaving's not smart anymore. This is a different score. We wait.'

'I mean *now* now. Where're we gonna go?'

'My dad's at work. We can go to my place and figure out where to hide all this.'

'What about the drugs?' she whispers.

'I know a guy who can maybe help. My old friend Zeke deals.'

On Fifth Avenue, they find a car service called Jimmy & Rita's Express. They pay in advance. One of the drivers is ready to go out front. He asks Bobby if he'd like to put the bag in the trunk. Bobby shakes him off and says he'll hold it.

They get in. The driver isn't chatty, which is nice. Bobby keeps the bag in his lap. The car starts moving. Francesca looks out the window. She's thinking about Max Berry in his office, less than a hundred yards from here, taped to a chair, bleeding from where Bobby hit him, possibly dead. She played a part in it. She didn't hurt him, but she went along with Bobby on this. She's thinking that it's fucking crazy how you can be pretty smart your whole life and then do one stupid thing because it seems like it will open up a new world. Money did sound good. So did escaping west. Blinders. She's not the first and she won't be the last to stumble dumbly into a situation like this. A few short hours ago, she felt like she knew Bobby better than she'd ever known anybody in such a short time. Now she feels like she doesn't know him at all. 'I'm so thirsty,' she says.

'We'll be at my place soon,' Bobby says.

The driver takes the streets instead of the Belt, which is less stressful if a bit longer. He makes a left on Eighty-Sixth Street and stays on that all the way back to the neighborhood. At every red light, he spits out his window onto the blacktop. He's listening to trance music. The car smells of grapefruit.

They get out at Bobby's place. It's a dinky building on Eighty-Third Street, split into about twelve apartments. Bobby and his dad live on the second floor. Francesca had imagined visiting under different circumstances.

When he takes her inside, she's hit by the bottled-up smell

in the living room. Man funk. Crumpled clothes that need washing. Dust. Mold. This all gives way to the scent of old food and a nasty sponge emanating from the tiny kitchen off to the right. Bobby puts down the bag and gets her a glass of water from the tap. She drinks it fast. He drinks a glass too.

Bobby picks up the bag and takes her to his room. It's not much. A single bed. A TV on the dresser with his Nintendo 64. A beanbag chair on the floor. A Discman on top of the dresser. Some CDs and Memorex VHS tapes on the small bookshelf screwed over the dresser. Patches of tape on the wall containing the torn edges of posters that hung there once. The room's maybe fifteen feet long and ten feet wide. Narrow. Cell-like, except for the window leading to the fire escape on the side of the building. Francesca likes fire escapes. They make her feel less trapped.

Bobby empties the bag onto his bed.

She doesn't look at the contents. She goes over to the window, opens it, and sits on the painted cast iron steam radiator below it. She's drawing in deep breaths and then releasing them. She takes out her tobacco and works on rolling a cigarette. Giving her hands something to do stops the shaking. She licks the paper, sealing it perfectly. She lights her cigarette.

Bobby, prostrated in front of the bed, says, 'I can't fucking believe this. There's so much.'

'Jesus Christ,' Francesca says. 'Who are you?'

'Don't you understand what this means?'

'You might've killed someone.'

'I think we should split the money and sit on it for a while. Six months, a year. In the meantime, I'll try to get the drugs to Zeke. He sells them, I split that money with him, and we have even more in our stash. Then we run away.'

'You're crazy,' Francesca says, blowing a stream of smoke through the screen. 'I don't want anything to do with any of it. You keep it all.'

Bobby turns his back on the money and drugs. He comes over to her, kneeling. 'What are you saying?'

'You keep everything,' she says. 'I won't tell anyone anything, I swear.' She's thinking if Bobby's capable of what he did to Max, who knows what else he's capable of? Feels like a lifetime ago that they were at that dive hotel in the city but they only woke up there this morning – they've simply cycled through to whatever this is.

'I did this for you,' Bobby says. 'For us.'

She thinks back to that first night at Long Eddy's, Bobby coming to meet her. The drunken joy. Staying up all night. Walking. Coffee. Dessert. All that somehow leading to this. She shakes her head. 'Don't say that,' she says.

His hand on her knee. Moving up her thigh.

A fleck of tobacco on her lip. The smoke bitter in her lungs. Everything feels like poison now. Everything is poison. Some days you see it, some you don't. His eyes are poison. His hands on her, poison. His breath.

Her eyes drift over to the bed. Stacks of banded cash. Drugs. The gun. More poison.

She swats his hand away. 'I just want to pretend like this didn't happen,' she says.

'What are you saying?' Bobby asks.

She doesn't say anything else. She picks the strand of tobacco from her lip and flicks it onto the radiator.

His hand on her knee now.

'This *didn't* happen,' she says, again brushing his hand from her. 'It *didn't*. None of it. I won't tell anybody anything, I promise. There's nothing to tell.'

He says her name.

She stands and pushes in the two little buttons on the bottom of the screen window, lifting it. She flicks what's left of her cigarette outside and then climbs up on the radiator and onto the fire escape. 'I don't know why I came back here with you,' she says. 'I'm leaving.'

'Please,' Bobby says. 'Don't go.'

She descends the ladder into the side alley, coming down on a patch of cracked cement strangled by weeds. She looks up at Bobby through the rusted metal grates of the fire escape landing. He's leaning out the window. She rushes up the block. She keeps seeing Max taped to the chair. She keeps seeing the gun in Bobby's hand. Whatever Bobby did to Max, she's glad she didn't see that. She doesn't have to lie. *I was outside. I didn't know what he was planning. I thought it was a joke until it wasn't.*

Home is only a handful of blocks away, but it seems so far.

PART 3

Charlie

Charlie French gets back from Jersey and drives straight to Max's office. He'd stayed in Atlantic City too long. Had lost track of days. Had gotten on a roll winning again.

Traffic on the block. Cars stuttering and halting. Drivers riding their horns. As Charlie finally makes it to Max's, he sees the place overrun with cops, both uniformed and plainclothes detectives. Yellow tape strung up from the telephone pole to the edge of the building, cordoning off the whole corner. The Kings County coroner's van parked at the curb behind a gaggle of police cars.

Stopped at a light on the corner, Charlie takes it in as much as he can. A papery Irish couple in their sixties or seventies stand off to the side, tangled together, in tears. Charlie pounds the steering wheel and curses. He has no idea what's gone down but something bad has happened at Max's. It's not hard to figure out that much. But what? No one knew he'd stashed the bag here.

Charlie looks all around. He notices an old woman sitting up in her window across the street. A real watchdog. Taking in all the action.

When the light changes, he makes a right onto Fourth Avenue and pulls into a spot at a meter in front of a Laundromat, right across from the market on the opposite corner. He gets out of the car and goes to a payphone in front of the flower shop next to the Laundromat. The phone is covered in silver graffiti. He picks it up, inserts a quarter, and dials Lou the Goon's number. Lou is his friend on the force. He rides a desk all day. He always answers when Charlie calls. Charlie is the closest he gets to feeling dangerous.

He greets Charlie with his trademark, 'What's the good word, chief?'

'What happened at Max Berry's?' Charlie asks.

'You're gonna need to elaborate since I have no clue whatsoever who the hell Max Berry is. This is Berry like *blueberry* or *strawberry*?'

'That's right. He runs an investment place called Options Incorporated in Bay Ridge.'

Charlie hears the tapping of keys. Lou covers the phone with his hand. Muffled voices. A woman talking loud at Lou. He comes back on the line: 'This guy was your pal?'

'Not really. We were working together on something.'

'He's dead, chief. Sorry. Someone robbed his joint and killed him. This is not information I should be telling you, by the way. Looks like somebody tied him up, emptied his safe, and plugged him. You knew him good?'

'Jesus fucking Christ.' Charlie bangs his hand against the wall next to the payphone. A man in the flower shop glares at him through the window.

'You hear your buddy Junky Greg OD'd?' Lou asks. 'Well, that's not accurate. Shot up rat poison. Suicide, they're saying. Suicide by fucking rat poison, you believe that? It's a first in my book. And his buddy Rainey got clipped in Owl's Head Park. Makes you think the suicide wasn't a suicide, huh? But nobody gives a shit. Except Stacks. He knows something isn't kosher. He's piping mad. A son's a son.'

'I've gotta go,' Charlie says. He hangs up the phone and just stands there. He'd wasted all that time in Atlantic City, stupid bastard that he is. It took him too long to find Don and Randy, and then he lingered another whole week, kicking up his goddamn heels. Keeping the money and drugs should've been his priority. He thought he was so smart. He thought hiding the bag at Max's was perfect. Maybe Junky Greg and Rainey were being tailed and whoever was tailing them knew it was him who'd killed them and stolen the score and followed him to Max's.

He thinks about the lady he saw before parking. Just up in her window, watching the whole scene. He figures the cops haven't gotten to that lady yet, if they get to her at all.

He opens the door to her building and goes up a narrow piss-stinking staircase to what must be her apartment door. He presses the buzzer.

Nothing.

He presses again and waits.

Some action inside. A voice calling out. Brittle, quavering, ready to talk.

The door opens slowly. The old woman stands there, holding herself up against the jamb. Summer housedress, bluish hair pinned sloppily, slipper socks, too much blue eye shadow. The heavy smell of cooking oil mixed with flowery perfume drifts out of the apartment. She has a loud fan going inside. The TV and the radio. A clawing of canned voices and heavy whirring blades. 'Are you a detective?' she asks Charlie.

'I am,' Charlie says.

'Come on in. Can I get you coffee?'

'That'd be great.'

She leads him through a short hallway overflowing with half-opened boxes. 'Excuse the mess,' she says. 'I don't get much company.'

The kitchen is small. Orange tiled walls. A stove that looks as old as she does. Two sinks, one clean, the other used for storage of pots and pans. Greeting cards taped to the wall tiles. Hundreds all around the room for every holiday imaginable. He wonders if they're actually from anyone or if she just buys them for decoration. Over one particularly intense patch of greeting cards, a mix of Valentine's Day and Thanksgiving, a large crucifix is duct-taped to the wall. He's seen crucifixes on walls his whole life, but he's never seen one duct-taped to tile. It looks disturbing.

'My name is Mrs Fonseca,' the old woman says.

'I'm Detective Mackey.' The name just popped into his mind. For some reason, he thought of a fighter he used to watch, Bub Mackey, who didn't have a great record but always took the best fighters the full twelve or fifteen rounds. He fought until he was fifty and then drank himself to death by fifty-six.

'Sit.' She points to the table, covered with church bulletins, scratch-offs, crumpled lottery tickets, catalogues, and circulars. A magnifying glass and scissors displayed prominently. He imagines her – like his grandma way back when – spending hours cutting coupons for Pathmark and Waldbaum's.

He sits at the table.

She puts a kettle on to boil and scoops instant coffee crystals into two chipped mugs. When the water boils – and it's fairly quick, as the gas is set on high – she brings the coffees to the table, setting one in front of him and one out for herself. She plods to the pantry and gets a jar of powdered creamer and a couple of sugar packets snagged from a bodega's coffee station. She pours a ton of the creamer into her coffee, stirs it with her finger, and then sits down. He shakes off the creamer and sugar, saying he takes it black.

'I guess you're here about across the street?' Mrs Fonseca asks.

'I am,' Charlie says.

'That Max Berry is a real bum. I say he got what was coming to him. He cheated more people than anybody I ever heard of. He was a bum and a thief.'

Charlie nods. 'So you weren't a fan?'

'A man in his late thirties or early forties – I don't really know how old he was – and he drank milk out of those cartons they give kids in school. What kind of man is that? I always suspected he liked boys. He had high school kids working for him.'

'Did you see anything over there?'

'I sit at my window day and night. I patrol the block. Mr Carsonetti says I'm better than any security system. I keep an eye out, you know? That's valuable. With Berry, it was only a matter of time. You know the nature of his work? He schemed people. A thousand-buck investment doesn't seem like much but you get enough people and it adds up. Then he pays interest for a while and folks get to thinking it's safe, so they "deposit" more. I'm surprised he didn't get clipped sooner, honestly. Cross that many people and your days are numbered.'

Charlie puts his elbows up on the table and leans forward. 'Anything recent that might indicate what happened?'

'Last action I saw over there was a week ago. Nothing too unusual. The kid who worked for Max showed up with some hot-to-trot little number. Thought she was the queen of something. Ass in the air. Dark-skinned. She came out after a while, waited on the sidewalk. Maybe twenty minutes later, he followed. Had a bag. They raced off up Eighty-Fourth Street. I didn't think much about it at the time.'

'What'd the bag look like?'

'Black, I'm pretty sure. He was holding it by the handles. I'm old, but I've got a good memory on me.'

Charlie's thinking about that kid sitting on the floor of Max's office, shoulders slumped, headphones on, stuffing CDs into envelopes. Going to the store and bringing back Twizzlers, Twix, and milk for Max. Maybe Charlie's been giving others too much credit. Maybe this kid's the one who stole the stuff? What was his name? Max said it, but he was a nothing kid to Charlie at the time and it barely registered. His old man went to high school with Max at Our Lady of the Narrows was the thing he mainly remembered. 'You know the kid's name?' Charlie asks Mrs Fonseca.

'Never met him. I don't know. Coffee's no good?'

Charlie takes a sip. It's lukewarm now, tastes flat and sour. 'It's great.'

'I've got some fruitcake, if you want it.'

Fruitcake in June? He shakes his head, puts up his hand.

He presses for more information, but she can't really think of anything else. The only other unusual thing is that she hadn't seen Max come out of his office at all the last week. Usually, she says, she sees him at least two or three times, in the morning and the evening especially.

Lines up that the day the kid and his girlfriend left with the bag was the last time Mrs Fonseca, the eyes of the block, saw Max alive. She saw him open the door for them.

So, the kid popped him and made off with Charlie's stuff? Must be. What other possible conclusion could he draw? He wouldn't think that scrawny-ass kid would have something like that in him, but sometimes a boy makes a move to be a man, or makes a move that he thinks will make him a man, but it gets him in deeper shit than he could've anticipated.

Charlie thanks Mrs Fonseca for her time. She's about to stand and show him out. He tells her to stay put, he can find his own way.

Back outside, he looks across the street at the bustling crime scene. Nothing else reveals itself. Mrs Fonseca is in the window above him again. He turns his head up to her and smiles.

Charlie goes back to his car. He didn't feed the meter and he's already got a ticket. He snags it from under the wiper, rips it to shreds, dropping the pieces in the street. He opens the door and gets behind the wheel, starting the car. He lets a long exhale fly. This is a big goddamn inconvenience. A hurdle he wasn't expecting.

He thinks about driving over to Last-Time Betty's, which is where he goes when he's angry at the world. It's in Dyker Heights. A residential mansion that doubles as a brothel of sorts. Last-Time Betty has three other women working there, but Charlie doesn't like any of them. He likes her, the Boss Lady.

How it goes is Last-Time Betty takes him up to one of her rooms, puts on a nun's habit she scored from some runaway nun and these black high heels he likes, sharp and pointy as hell. Then she makes him get naked and lie on his back on the floor, his legs spread, and she stomps his ballsack with the heels, pressing hard into the carpet, careful not to squash his nuts like grapes.

The fantasy started back in Catholic school, probably sixth or seventh grade. He didn't have crushes on nuns who wore regular clothes, but he liked the ones he saw in habits. That's what he'd think about when he was a kid tugging off. Over time, the heels came into it and then he realized he liked pain, and the rest of the picture came together.

Nobody does it right like Last-Time Betty. Others tried before her, both paid and volunteer work. She's one of the best things that's ever happened to him. All business, no bullshit. He loves to pay her. He'd really like to go there right now, find some relief. But having his balls stomped won't get his stuff back from this kid.

'Fuck it,' he says. He needs to clear his head before he hunts for the kid and his missing bag.

He drives to Last-Time Betty's joint, parking across the street. It looks like any other gaudy mansion in Dyker Heights. Cement lions out front. An ornate metal fence with detailed scrollwork. White columns on the porch. A front gate that's locked. To get in, he presses the buzzer and speaks into an intercom. A small security camera on top of the fence stays on him. He waves. A buzz lets him know he can push through the gate.

Last-Time Betty greets him at the front door. She's in her forties. Straight brown hair. Long nails painted red. A red business suit. Black flats on her feet. Gold bracelets on her wrists. A gold chain with a glass ball containing a dried flower dangling around her neck. If someone saw her like this out on the street, they'd take her for a no-nonsense divorce lawyer. He can just picture her pacing back and forth in front of a judge, flipping those nails into the air as she drives home good point after good point. 'Been a while,' she says.

'Had to go out of town,' Charlie says. It's quiet in the house. No sign of the others. It's fairly early, probably a pretty dead time around here. 'Now okay?'

She scrunches her chin and nods. 'Sure.'

They go up to their usual room. Charlie takes off his clothes and lies on the floor. Last-Time Betty goes to the closet, changing into the habit and strapping on the heels, careful she doesn't bust a nail.

Charlie's trying not to think too hard about the kid who probably stole his stuff. He can see his face so clear, and he knows that Max said his name, but there are a million possibilities sifting through his mind and he can't find the right one.

Last-Time Betty walks up to him, her heels clicking on the floor. It's as much about this sound as anything. The way it fills the room. In the habit, she's flowing, ghostlike.

'Sister, please don't,' he says. It's part of the act.

'Tell me what you did wrong,' Last-Time Betty says.

'I didn't do anything wrong, I swear.'

Then the heel is pinning his scrotum into the carpet. She keeps it like that for a while and finds a new angle, a new spot, and really drills down hard. The skin on his ballsack burning with hurt. The pain a thrill. He closes his eyes. He sees lightning storms on the black of his lids. He doesn't even need her to touch him. The stomping is enough.

He also likes the endurance part of it. He likes this to go on for as long as she'll let it. He lets out little yelps, and she tells him to say the Hail Mary.

He says the Hail Mary repeatedly while he looks up at her. The best thing about Last-Time Betty is she never seems disinterested or bored. She stays in character. Anger radiates from her. He's really someone who needs to be punished like this, and she's the only one to do it.

In high school, Charlie prayed for pain. The last time he was the praying type. He prayed for broken bones. He fantasized about getting hit by a car. He'd dig a screwdriver into his forearm to see if he could break the skin. His mother once caught him trying to burn himself with her hair dryer. By the time he was in his twenties, before he was married, he realized he liked pain inflicted on him. He asked women to strangle him, to pull his hair. Anything. It rarely went well. Least well with the woman who became his wife. Maybe that was the greatest pain she inflicted on him. Her obvious disgust with everything about him. The anger in him boiled over into something else then. The pain wasn't enough. Violence was the only way. He threw her down the stairs and made it look like a bad fall. He loved the way her body bent and her head cracked.

When Last-Time Betty has had enough, she steps away. Charlie gets dressed. He pays her, and she sees him out. She stays in character all the way to the door. She does this for him. He likes her to tell him that he's vile, that he's disgusting, that he's going to hell.

Back in the car, he really has to spread his legs to make himself comfortable. The soreness is a lot to handle. The soreness is a gift that stays with him sometimes for a couple of days. Every movement reminding him of the good pain.

His head clear now, the kid's name is on the tip of Charlie's tongue. He'll remember it, or he'll at least remember who the kid's old man was. Maybe he can go to Our Lady of the Narrows, look at a yearbook from when Max graduated, see if any last names ring a bell.

He shouldn't have trusted Max, that much is clear. He should've known somebody would eventually turn on him. The guy was juggling too much. He would've been better off hiding the bag in a vent in his apartment.

The trip to Last-Time Betty was as much about fending off panic as anything else. The bag's his future. The bag's all he's got right now. If the Brancaccios trace Greg's and Rainey's murders back to him, he'll be fucked, but he'll consider that the next thing. First, he needs to find the kid.

The panic is seeping in. What if the bag Mrs Fonseca saw the kid carrying wasn't his bag? What if some dirty cops had actually managed to knock off the safe when they discovered Max's body? That's way goddamn worse than the kid taking it home and hiding it in his toy chest or whatever.

He drives away. The pain he's still feeling holds him together. The pain builds a wall around the panic. For now.

Jack

Jack's been feeling peaceful for the first time in forever since he did what he did for Lily. They're back in class in the church basement. Lily seems like a new Lily. She's so relieved she hasn't heard from Micah in a week but doesn't have any idea what's happened to him. It's possible he hasn't even been found yet. She'd stayed with Jack for a couple of days and then decided to go home. She said she thought just seeing Jack with the bat must've scared the life out of Micah. Jack acted reluctant about letting her go, said she was safer with him until she knew for sure that Micah was gone, but he knew she was in fact fine now, so he didn't put up much of a fight.

Jack hasn't written anything for class this time. He just couldn't bring himself to do it. Nothing about the clock prompt set him off. He listens to the others. Shelley reads a great story she wrote about a woman dying of cancer who buys a boat and just drifts out to sea to die. Josh's is another Viking thing. Dino details a mob hit in a building with a clock tower to the point where it definitely sounds like he's the guy who did the hit.

Jack's started thinking he might've written everything he's capable of writing. He knows Lily will say that's nonsense, everyone feels like that at some point, but he can't figure out a way to put more words on the page.

After class, he and Lily walk out to the parking lot together. Lily tells him she's been getting some great work done on her novel. She says it all started in Amelia's room. She says she's going to dedicate the novel to Amelia if that's okay with him. She says she knows it's ridiculous or at least presumptuous to dedicate a novel that might not ever be published to someone, but she doesn't care. She's always dreamed of typing out a simple dedication page. 'If Amelia can't write her own book, at least she can have one dedicated to her,' she says, and then she feels bad about it, asking Jack if that was the wrong thing to say.

He shakes his head. 'I love the idea of you dedicating the book to Amelia. She'd be flattered.' He's not sure he's ever used that word. *Flattered*. It's just a thing to say. How would Amelia feel about it? Having feelings about it at all would require knowledge of her death. No sense in any of it.

'I'm thinking I should apply to MFA programs,' Lily says. 'Just in case. If I finish this novel and I send it to that agent and he's not interested, then what? What do you think?'

'I don't really know what an MFA program is,' Jack says. 'I'm sorry.'

'Just graduate school for creative writing. If I get into a fully funded program, I won't pay tuition. It's really just a way of studying with great writers and throwing yourself full-time into the writing thing. I've had a couple of teachers push me toward doing it. A few others have pushed me away, saying it's a worthless degree. I don't know. I'm so confused. If I apply, it'll be for next year. I'd apply to all the big schools. Iowa, UC Irvine, Michigan, Virginia. I think Cornell is good too. I haven't really done my research. I don't even know if I'll get in.'

'What will you do if you don't apply?'

'That's the million-dollar question.'

'You going home?' Jack asks.

Lily nods.

'I'll walk you.'

'It's okay. Micah's not here anymore. He isn't following me. I guess he went home.'

'I've got nowhere to be.'

They head in the direction of her apartment, walking slowly. It's warm, not too hot, getting close to sunset. The sounds of a ball game explode from the window of a house they pass. It's that Yankees announcer, the one with the deep voice. Jack doesn't watch baseball anymore, but he's followed this team in the papers the past five years. All the championships. The core group. If Amelia were still alive, maybe they would've gone to games. He remembers she watched some games in '95, Derek Jeter's rookie year, and she said how much she'd liked him. She watched a few games in '96 too, before she died. They won that year. The city was ablaze with their victory. It barely registered on him. They won again in '98, '99, and '00. Derek Jeter got older. Amelia stayed back there in the past, with her crush on a slim rookie. She probably would've grown out of having any interest in baseball.

'I guess I should be a teacher now,' Lily says, 'and ask you why you didn't write anything for tonight?'

'I'm sorry,' Jack says. 'I just couldn't. Nothing would come. I think I might be a one-trick pony. I think I might've written all I have to write. I've been reading this book from Amelia's stack. It's called *Blood and Guts in High School*. I don't remember the writer's name. I can't do that.'

'Kathy Acker's probably not the best writer for you to read. And don't even think about not being able to do what another writer's doing. Do your own thing. You have a great voice.'

'I don't know. I might be tapped out.'

'You just need to find some books that make more sense to you. That'll help get you going.' She pauses, turns to him. 'Can I tell you something? I'm nervous.'

'Of course,' Jack says, unsure of what to expect.

A smile. Electric. Beaming. 'I've got a date tonight.'

'Who with?'

'I went out in the city with some friends a few nights ago. Actually, I went to see about a job at a bookstore in the East Village and then I met my friends at Dojo and we got drinks at Seven Bar. One of my friends, Stacy, she brought along her

friend from when she studied abroad in college, Mairéad. She's
Irish. A writer too. Like *really* a writer. She's twenty-five and she's
already got a novel out. It's called *Girl in Amber.* We really hit it
off. We talked all night. It was like a movie. Like *Before Sunrise*.
We broke off from the group and wandered around, just talking.
She's really smart and funny. Like, it's overwhelming how smart
and funny she is. She's into the occult. She says she can talk to
spirits. We met for lunch yesterday too. She's from Dublin, but
she's been living in New York for two years now. She's never
been to this part of Brooklyn. I invited her here tonight. We're
going to get some pizza. She wants to see the neighborhood after
hearing me talk about it. She doesn't know how little there is to
see.'

Jack imagines Lily strolling aimlessly in the city with this
Irish woman, carefree, no longer under threat from Micah. The
feeling of peace in him intensifies.

Lily continues: 'I've never gone out with a woman before, but
this is the happiest I've felt in a long time. You know, Micah
disappears, stops calling, and then I meet Mairéad. It's like a
gift. I'm glad I can tell you because I can't tell my mother. She's
nuts about stuff like this. She hates gay people. She'd definitely
disown me if I said I was gay or bi or whatever.'

'I doubt that,' Jack says.

'You don't know Grace.' Lily nudges Jack with her elbow. 'So
how do you feel about it?'

'What do you mean?'

'I mean, you're kind of like – I don't know – you've kind of
become like this father figure to me the last few weeks. I don't
want to hang too much on you, but are you weirded out? Do you
have some good fatherly advice for me? Or bad? Are you going
to tell me it's "just a phase"?'

'I think you should do what makes you happy.'

'Yeah?'

'Yeah, of course. I would've been happy with Amelia dating

women too. Women are better than men. Way less terrible, at least. You probably feel a lot safer too. They probably won't pull the kind of shit Micah pulled.'

'You're funny, Jack. You always surprise me.' They turn onto Lily's block.

'Can I ask you one more thing?' Lily says.

'Shoot.'

'Would you want to meet Mairéad? Can we come over? I told her all about you. I told her about your writing, about Amelia. She's excited to meet you.'

Jack tries to picture the three of them sitting in his sad kitchen. 'You've been to my house. It's a dive. I'd be embarrassed to have this woman you're interested in over.'

'It's not a dive,' Lily says. 'It's a real place where a real person lives. It's not like one of these suburban model homes that people live in now. That stuff makes me sick. Anyhow, I can't bring her back to my apartment because of my stupid mom. Your house feels more like home now.'

'That's nice of you to say. You're really buttering me up here.'

'I'm trying.'

'Okay, come on over. What time?'

'I'm picking her up from the train on Twenty-Fifth Avenue in a half hour. We're going to get pizza at Spumoni Gardens. Then we'll head over. Maybe nine? Is that too late?'

'It's fine. I should stop and get some drinks. You know what she likes? Wine? Beer?'

'Whatever you have is fine. Don't go nuts.'

They stop in front of the house where Lily's apartment is. She looks up and sees the lights on and complains that her mother is home, of course she's home now and not out with her dumb boyfriend, and she'll have to answer questions about what she's getting dressed up for and who she's going to see. Her mother doesn't care most of the time – take Micah stalking her, for example – but then she chooses the most inopportune times to be nosy. 'She'll probably be able to sniff out the fact that I'm dating a woman,' Lily says. 'Okay, I've gotta go. I'm going to change and stuff before I pick up Mairéad.'

'Okay,' Jack says. 'I'll see you in a little bit.'

Lily goes in through the gate and up to the front door, keying it open.

Jack walks away from Lily's. He guesses he'll stop at a bodega and buy a couple of six-packs just to have them around in case this Irish woman wants beer. He has Seagram's at home, probably a dusty bottle or two of gin, definitely some ancient vermouth. Be nice to have some beer in the house. Beer feels younger.

Francesca

Francesca hasn't left her room in a week except to use the bathroom and go down to the kitchen for water and snacks. She hasn't eaten much, barely touching any of the sandwiches Victoria has made for her, instead bringing bowls full of chips and packages of fruit gummies up to her room. Bobby has called fifty times at least, but she's managed to ignore him. She's told Victoria that she's not feeling well, that maybe it's some kind of summertime sickness, and Victoria has been understanding. Grandma Eva has, as usual, been riding her about not going out to look for a job, saying she's faking feeling bad so she can avoid the responsibilities of the real world. She calls her lazy. She says she expects everything handed to her. Francesca avoids her as much as she can, which pretty much means that she tries to stay up super late and then sleeps away the day.

She's haunted by what happened at Max's. She keeps thinking about how Bobby made her hold the gun while he taped Max up. And then she thinks about the gun in Bobby's hand. The same hand that had touched her in the hotel. The way he'd gone from tender to scary. The way he'd looked emptying the money and drugs on his bed. Max with his milk. That slummy office, which certainly didn't look like the base of operations for someone who was stealing from old people. She thinks about standing out on the sidewalk while Bobby did whatever he did. She plays the scene repeatedly in her mind, as if on tape. Did she hear anything? A gunshot? Is what Bobby said about hitting him too hard or too perfectly by accident true?

What happened at Max's was finally on the news today. She's feeling extra uneasy. Likely, a robbery gone wrong or a mob hit, they said on Channel Nine. Bay Ridge rattled to its core. Max discovered by his shut-in parents who had finally ventured out of the house after a week and hobbled to his office. They were shaking. His mother said they thought he might've gone to Atlantic City for a few days with one of his clients, which he sometimes did, but they knew when he didn't call that something was wrong. He was a good boy, she said. He was always so good to them, helping with their medicine and buying their favorite snacks. Weeping. He was their caretaker. His father didn't say anything. He just stared blankly at the camera.

The cops are probably thinking it's a mob hit. Probably the last thing they'd guess is the nineteen-year-old kid who worked there. Bobby is right about one thing. Running away would make clear he did it. *They* did it. Staying put means the cops might show up at his door if they discover he was on Max's payroll (though Max paid him off the books), or if his father brings him in to talk when he hears the news. All he has to do is hold his tongue, play dumb, and the cops might pass him over. She wonders about his conscience. How can he just live with what he did?

Francesca is sitting cross-legged on her bed. The small TV on her dresser in the corner is playing a commercial. The news has just ended. Some movie's coming on. A black bar swims across the screen every few seconds. The reception on this cheap little TV isn't great. The antenna is wispy. She thinks about getting up and trying to adjust it but then just stays put.

A knock on the door.

'Who is it?' Francesca says. She's pretty sure Victoria is out on a date, so it must be her grandmother.

Grandma Eva doesn't answer, instead barging in and standing between Francesca and the TV.

'What is it?' Francesca says.

'This is ridiculous. A young girl like you, wasting away. Tomorrow you're going to get your act together. Or else.'

'Or else what?'

'You've got a smart mouth on you.'

'Can you please leave me alone?' Francesca asks. 'I really don't feel like talking. You can't just come into my room like this. I don't know why my door wasn't locked. It should've been locked.'

'Locked doors,' Grandma Eva says, disgusted. 'If my sister, Jean, or I locked our door growing up, we would've gotten the belt. Even at your age, my mother wasn't afraid of giving us a good whack. One time she hit Jean with the broom for talking back. It was a different time. A better time. Children feared their parents, not vice versa. You have your poor mother walking on eggshells around here lately. "I don't want to upset Frannie," she says. "Victoria," I says, "you've got to force her to grow up." I'm glad she went out to try to have fun tonight, even if it's with that dummy Stan. Your mother still has a spark in her. She's a DiMaggio, after all.'

'Please. Leave me alone.'

'You know what your grandfather used to say to your mother when she was in high school and got in the habit of snapping back at us? "Go find your own apartment, your own food, your own this and that," he'd say. "Pay your own bills. See what the real world's like." He'd say, "Aren't you ashamed?"'

Shame is big with Grandma Eva. She thinks Francesca should feel so much shame about who she is, about who her father was. She should feel shame because she doesn't mold herself into whatever Grandma Eva wants her to be. She probably prays to God about how ashamed she is of her own granddaughter. Francesca can't help but imagine God listening to all these awful people and their awful prayers.

'You know what?' Francesca says.

Grandma Eva stands there, hands on her hips, poised to do battle. 'What?' she says.

'Go fuck yourself.'

'Who do you think you're talking to with that mouth? I should call the cops on you.'

'You're gonna call the cops on me for telling you to go fuck yourself? What is your purpose in life other than to irritate me? You're telling me to go get a job? You need a job. Go volunteer somewhere. Please. Just leave me alone.'

'I want you out of my house right now,' Grandma Eva says. 'I let you and your mother move in here because your father died and left you with nothing, but I can't tolerate you under this roof anymore. You are an angry and aimless person. You have no respect for me or for the rules of my house. Grandpa Natale's rolling over in his grave.'

'I'm done,' Francesca says, uncrossing her legs and getting up. 'You tell Victoria you kicked me out. See how she responds.'

'Stop calling your mother "Victoria."'

Francesca grabs a backpack and fills it with a couple of pairs of underwear and T-shirts, her favorite jeans, her deodorant, toothbrush, and toothpaste. She takes the few bucks she has hidden in her dresser. What's left of her rolling tobacco, which isn't much, just a skittering of tobacco flakes and the apple slice she put in the Drum pouch to keep it fresh. She's not sure where she's going to go, but she's a hundred percent on walking out of this goddamn ugly house right goddamn now.

'Where are you going?' Grandma Eva asks.

'What are you talking about? You're kicking me out. I'm leaving.'

'But *where* are you going?'

'None of your business. Maybe I'll go sleep in a park.'

'What park?'

'Any park.'

'You'll get raped and killed.'

'My blood will be on your hands, Granny.' *Granny*, like a fairy tale. Grandma Eva hates when Francesca calls her *Granny*. It makes her feel a million years old.

'Don't you ever –'

Francesca slings the backpack over her shoulder, pushes past Grandma Eva, and leaves the room. She stomps downstairs and out the front door and doesn't look back at the house as she walks angrily up the block, crosses the avenue, and then just falls into wandering around the neighborhood.

She looks at statues of the Virgin Mary and Jesus in the cramped front yards of run-down houses. She looks at garbage cans in driveways. She looks in windows. One house, a two-story job with yellow siding, has a tattered American flag out front on a proper flagpole. That's a lot of work, probably, putting up a real flagpole like that, sinking it in cement.

She's lost track of where she is, winding up and down the blocks surrounding Bay Thirty-Fourth.

A house close to the corner of Twenty-Fourth Avenue and Eighty-Sixth Street looks familiar. It's a house she remembers visiting for some reason or another when she was very young. Who lived there? Maybe a friend of Victoria's? That's it. Claudia Camarda, who'd been Victoria's best friend since grade school, lived there with her family. Francesca remembers Victoria saying that Claudia moved to Delaware a few years ago. Her dad had died and her mom had dementia, and the house was too much. Francesca wonders about Delaware. She's never been, never even driven through, that she knows of. It's a state she can't picture.

A sunset gloom has swallowed the neighborhood. The sky is pink and purple. She likes when the sky does this.

She's trying desperately not to think about Max Berry, toppled in his chair. His mother and father finding him. The cops. That open safe. What if there's security footage? What if Bobby was wrong about that? What if she's right there, caught on camera, handing Bobby the duct tape, standing by idly as he forces Max to spin the dial at gunpoint? What if, instead of telling Bobby to stop, the world sees her turn her back on the situation, just walk outside because she can't stomach it. She'd try to explain to the cops how great the week with Bobby had been, how she thought he was this sweet guy and then he talked about robbing Max to finance a trip west and she thought it was a fantasy until it wasn't anymore and it was really happening and she felt paralyzed.

If she's being totally honest, though, she'd also been a little thrilled. Part of her found it romantic, the idea at least.

On Eighty-Sixth Street, she finds a bodega she's never been in before. Not that she remembers, anyhow. The window's plastered with ads for canned iced tea and beer. The smell of the place hits her as she walks in. Some kind of sweet incense. The floor is tiled. A brown cat roams around, strutting down the long aisle, disappearing behind a display rack of shelves. A man is behind the register. Thirties, maybe. White shirt. Gym shorts. He has the Yankees game on the radio. To the right, a mostly empty rack with one *Daily News* left. It's today's, so the Max story isn't on the cover, but it might be tomorrow. Lotto cards on the counter, a few loser scratch-offs left behind by some furious gambler. Another man, a customer, is back by the beer fridge.

Francesca needs cigarettes. She hopes they have rolling tobacco. 'You have Drum?' she asks the counter guy.

'This look like a music store?' he says.

'It's a brand of rolling tobacco.'

'Yeah, I know. That was a joke.' He gets her a pouch from the wall of cigarettes behind him, tucked next to the Bugler tobacco. He drops it in front of her. 'Anything else?'

She shakes her head and pays.

The guy who'd been back at the beer fridge is now standing a few steps over from her, a six-pack of Guinness dangling from each hand, waiting in line. He gives her a half smile. She ignores it.

She goes outside, takes off her backpack, and sits on the edge of the little kiddie ride in front of the bodega. It's a train car with the face of a pig, covered in graffiti, slicked with grime. Drop a quarter in and it bops around for a minute. She can't imagine any parent putting their kid on this gross thing.

She remembers her father taking her to Coney Island one summer day when she was little. Tickets in her hand. A hot dog and orangeade. Most of the rides were awful, but she loved the Wonder Wheel. She also loved a display case that showed pictures and souvenirs of old Coney Island. The crowds. The lights. Tickets for rides. Ads. Flyers.

She rolls a cigarette with the fresh tobacco and lights it with a Bic she finds in the front pocket of her backpack.

The other guy, the one with the six-packs, comes out, his beer bagged, and he takes another glance at her. He's about to walk by but then he stops. 'You okay?' he says. 'You mind that I'm asking? You look troubled.'

'I'm just great,' she says, her voice all smart-ass tough.

'You look –'

'Let me guess. Like I'm not from around here. Like I don't belong here. Yeah, I get that a lot. I'm used to it. You want to see my neighborhood passport?'

'I was gonna say you look familiar.'

'Oh.'

'Maybe you just remind me of somebody.' He's about to say something else. A train rattles by on the El overhead. He holds up his hand, signaling that he'll ask what he's going to ask when the train's passed.

She drags on her cigarette. Looking at this guy, really taking him in for a second, she thinks that, actually, he looks pretty familiar himself.

The train passes.

'I don't make it a habit of chatting people up,' he says. 'I just wanted to say I'm sorry I bothered you.'

'I had a fight with my grandmother,' Francesca says. 'She threw me out of the house. You asked why I look troubled.

That's why, I guess.' She leaves out the part about Bobby and Max, of course. About being an apprentice to a murder. Not an apprentice. Jesus Christ. Her mind. An *accessory*. She's seen enough cop movies.

'You got nowhere to go?' he asks.

'I'll figure it out. I've got friends. I just had to get away.'

He nods. 'I'm Jack,' he says, extending a hand.

She reaches out and shakes it. 'Francesca,' she says.

'I'm telling you – not to harp on it or anything – but you're the spitting image of somebody I knew. I can't think of who. Who are your folks?'

'My mom's name is Victoria. Her maiden name's DiMaggio. My dad was Bill Clarke.'

Jack almost drops his six-packs. 'Bill Clarke. That's it. You look just like him.'

'You knew my dad?'

'We played softball together. The Brooklyn Battlers. I think you were probably at some of the games. I played first base.'

'No way,' Francesca says.

'I heard about Bill – I'm sorry. He passed away right around the same time as my daughter.'

'Your daughter died?'

'Five years ago. She was around the age you are now. Amelia was her name.'

Francesca connects the dots. She remembers that name. The girl getting off the Belt. She remembers the headlines in the *Daily News* and *Post*. Some random kid throwing a rock. Her car careening into oncoming traffic. Francesca's heart jumps in her chest. She mostly remembers her mother talking about it, and saying, "How terrible. What a tragedy." It didn't have any real impact on Francesca because she was already living in a haze of grief at that point. Her father's accident had happened a few months prior. It was too much to imagine a girl just on the other side of high school, dying young like that. She does remember that there was a memorial in the grass down by the off-ramp. Someone planted a white cross with her name on it. People brought candles and flowers. Amelia's classmates pinned pictures to the cross. It stayed up for a few weeks until the weather destroyed everything and someone came and respectfully gathered up the pictures, the candles, and the flowers. The cross remained until one day it was gone.

'What about your wife?' Francesca asks, figuring she split. She knows what death does. She figures Amelia dying broke the marriage up.

'She died a few years before Amelia, actually,' Jack says. 'She and your dad met a few times. They got along good.'

Francesca feels bad that she doesn't know what else to say to Jack. She knows humans are programmed to respond in certain ways, that she should say, 'That's terrible' or 'How awful' or 'I'm so sorry.' But her mouth can't make the words. She just looks at the cigarette between her fingers. White paper. Sizzle line. Stray tobacco flitting out from under the seal. Not a perfect roll. A very sloppy one. Shaky-handed. The cigarette's lumpy, misshapen.

'Me and your old man, we had some laughs together,' Jack says. 'We were in the same boat. We didn't like a lot of the other guys on the team. Meatheads. Bill had lived in the city for a long time, if I'm not mistaken, and he didn't like the neighborhood. Not a very welcoming place. How's your mother?'

'She's okay,' Francesca says. 'She teaches.'

'I liked Bill a lot.'

'Me too.'

'So, you in college yet or what?'

'I just graduated high school.'

'You got plans? You going away to college?'

'I'm not very good at plans. I didn't get my applications done. I'm taking a year off.'

'Nothing wrong with that. Kids rush to college, they're not

ready, they don't get the most out of it. What I hear, anyway. Learn the ropes. Work. Get some experience.'

'I want to make movies.'

'Really? Wow. What kind? Is that a dumb question?'

'I don't really know what kind. I guess just personal ones, you know? I'm not really good with ideas yet. I need to figure that out. But I can see in my head how I want them to look.'

'That's really neat. I wish I saw movies in my head like that.'

Francesca guesses that they've run out of things to say, that Jack will be on his way, plodding along with the six-packs under his arm, but he lingers, drifts a few steps toward the corner then comes back like Columbo. 'You've got nowhere to go, you want to come over to my place?' Jack asks. 'My friend Lily's gonna be there in a bit. She just graduated college. She's bringing this Irish gal. Showing her around the neighborhood. I've been taking this writing class with Lily in the St. Mary's basement. She's a good writer. She reminds me a lot of Amelia. Amelia was a writer too.'

'I don't know.'

'No pressure or anything. I just figured, you have nowhere to be, you're more than welcome. I've lived cooped up in my house alone the last five years. Having Lily over has brought some life back to it. I see you, you're more life. Another nice kid. My old acquaintance Bill's kid. It's nice to be around people who are on the way up, just starting out.' Francesca doesn't feel like she's on the way up. She feels stagnant.

The week with Bobby, she felt like there was some great, unknown future ahead of her but that shattered in Max's office. Now she's back feeling like she's waist-deep in a flood. Moreover, girls her age don't meet men in their forties and go back to their house. That's stupid. That's rule number one in the How Not to Get Croaked manual. She's seen enough horror movies.

But Jack doesn't have a skeezy vibe. He's not eyeing her the way most men do. He seems gentle and nice. And he's got beer. She bets he'll give her a few. She could really stand to have a few drinks right now. Might be interesting to meet this girl who teaches writing in the St. Mary's basement too. She didn't know people did things like that at the church. She can't picture it. A bunch of people on those hard chairs, grouped in a circle, talking about stories they wrote with that churchy smell in the air the whole time.

'You're a writer?' Francesca asks.

'No, not really,' Jack says. 'Amelia was. Or wanted to be. I saw the flyer for the class. I figured I'd do it for her. I'd never really talked about any of it. I had no one to talk to. I figured maybe I could get it out in writing.'

'Do you like it? Writing, I mean.'

'It's hard. The first couple of things I wrote just kind of exploded onto the page. I guess I had something I wanted to say. But now I've hit a wall.'

'I get that.' She knocks the cherry off her cigarette onto the sidewalk, and it flickers against the pale gray cement. She puts the little that's left of the cigarette back in the pouch. She stands. 'I'll come hang out for a bit.'

'Yeah? Good. You'll like Lily. She'll like you.'

They walk the few blocks to Jack's house on Bay Thirty-Eighth Street. Jack asks her what some of her favorite movies are. She says *Just Another Girl on the I.R.T.*, *Mystery Train*, *Do the Right Thing*, *Rumble Fish*, and *The Addiction*. She's not sure why those are the first five that come to mind. He says he hasn't seen any of them. She asks him what movies he likes and he says he doesn't really watch movies much anymore, but he always liked the old gangster stuff with Cagney and Bogart. She says her dad liked gangster movies from the thirties and forties too. He says she reminds him of her old man, the way he talked about stuff. He always had some book with him at softball. The other guys ragged him about it. He'd be reading in the dugout, while they were scratching their balls or hitting on each other's wives in the bleachers.

When they get to Jack's place, Francesca feels comfortable because the place is as broken down as Grandma Eva's. It's not fancy or anything. It's just a house where someone has lived for a long time and things are falling apart. She has an idea for a movie that's the story of the neighborhood told through silent portraits of houses. Crumbling yards. Religious statues with missing noses. Fences with holes. Roofs with missing shingles. Damaged siding. Weeds growing up through concrete. Busted windows. Cracked foundations. Clocks on the wall that don't tell time.

Inside, the quiet tells its own story. She knows what the apartment on Sixty-Fifth Street was like after her dad died, how it still seemed to contain his voice and his laugh, and she senses that here, Jack's daughter still alive somehow in the quiet. Part of Francesca has always wondered if the story Victoria told her about not being able to afford their old apartment and having to move in with Grandma Eva was even true, or if she just couldn't take it anymore, couldn't stand to live in the place where they'd all lived together as a family. Jack hasn't run away from it, clearly. He's let it swallow him up. Francesca respects that. This is the kind of house that's just right for her movie. A house that tells its own story.

Who's she kidding? She'll never make that movie. Such a stupid idea. Who wants to sit there and just look at all these silent shots of houses for ninety minutes?

Jack puts the beer in the fridge. He asks if she wants one, or if she'd prefer tea or coffee or booze. She says a beer is good. He says Lily and her friend should be over soon. He says he hopes Lily doesn't mind about him inviting Francesca back, but he'll explain who Bill was and how strange and random it was to encounter his daughter out in front of the bodega, stuck with nowhere to go. Lily's great, he says, so she'll understand.

Francesca is struck again by how unimposing Jack is. He doesn't want anything from her. There aren't any creepy vibes emanating from him as there so often are with men.

Jack grabs two beers for them, popping off the tops, and brings them back to the table. He hands one to Francesca. They clink bottles.

'To Bill,' Jack says.

'To Amelia,' Francesca says.

Francesca's backpack is on the floor between her feet. She takes out her rolling tobacco and asks if it's okay to smoke in the house. Jack says of course. She gets to rolling. He watches, mesmerized. She asks if he wants one and he says it's okay, but he likes to see her rolling her own. Reminds him of a western.

In the center of the table is a glass fruit bowl. A couple of manila envelopes are propped on top of it. Jack reaches out and grabs both. He opens the clasp on the first envelope and shakes out a stack of pictures. He looks through them quickly and then passes the stack to Francesca. 'This is my daughter, Amelia,' he says. 'I was going to give these to Lily. She feels a real kinship with my daughter. That's a stupid way of putting it. I don't know. A connection. She hid out in Amelia's old room for a few days last week, wrote on her typewriter, listened to her music. She wants to dedicate her book to her. I thought it might be nice to give her some pictures. I had doubles made. I like that somebody other than me is thinking about her. She had good friends in high school, but they don't stop by anymore. They forgot all about her. She's nothing but a story they tell. That tragic girl they knew.'

Francesca looks at the pictures, blowing smoke away from the table. Amelia on the beach at Coney Island, wearing jean shorts and a Sonic Youth *Daydream Nation* T-shirt, the Parachute Jump and Wonder Wheel in the background. She's maybe fifteen. Another shot, this one from a school play. Francesca can't tell what the play is. Some musical. Amelia's not a lead, more of a background person, and she barely looks like herself in strange clothes with all that makeup on. Then there are pictures of Amelia when she was younger. Her first day of school, third grade. Francesca knows that's what it is because it's written on the back in curlicue script. A picture where she's maybe four or five, being held by a woman who must be her mother. All smiles. No sense that they'll both be gone too soon. The woman has brown hair, bright eyes, and she's wearing a red St. John's T-shirt. 'Is this your wife?' Francesca asks.

'That's Janey, yeah,' Jack says, leaning in.

Francesca takes a pull off her beer. She taps some ash into the overturned bottle cap on the table in front of her. 'She's beautiful,' Francesca says.

'She could really light a place up.'

Francesca wants to say something about how it's nice to be around someone who understands loss so fully, but she can't figure out how to put it into words without coming off as stupid or selfish. Instead, she just says, 'I really like her smile.'

A few more pictures from Amelia's grade school years. Onstage at a spelling bee. Playing Mary Magdalene in a school play for Easter. Posing with her second-grade teacher, Ms Krauza, who Jack says Amelia loved so much. When Ms Krauza quit teaching to go work with developmentally disabled kids on Long Island, Amelia was proud of her but so heartbroken. She wrote Ms Krauza letters every week for a year, and Ms Krauza always answered, even if just with a short note or a drawing. Eventually, Amelia stopped writing her and it made Jack sad because it meant she was moving on and growing up.

Jack grabs the other envelope. He shakes out a sheaf of stapled pages. 'This is a story that Lily wrote. She won an award for it. She doesn't even know I read it, but I made copies at the library.'

Francesca can't picture this Lily, who sounds like she's become a kind of surrogate daughter for Jack.

Jack passes across the story. It's on slick copier paper, the small print a bit faded. It's from some magazine called *Spiral*, with a smudgy illustration of two girls sitting on an unmade bed at the top, the younger of the two clutching a huge teddy bear. The title of the story is 'North Until We Can't Go Further North.'

'You don't have to read it,' Jack says. 'I just wanted to show it to you. It's a great story. It's about these two sisters living in a motel in Pennsylvania. They're on the lam from their abusive father, but they've run out of money. It's sad. Lily's really good at sad. The older sister is seventeen. Her name's Moira. The younger one is six, and she's got this teddy bear she carries around with her. She's Lara. Moira lies about her age and gets a job at this roadside diner. She's trying to save enough money so they can catch a bus to Canada. She has this big dream about Canada. They have an aunt there who she knows will take care of them. One night at the motel, the power goes out during a storm. I won't tell you the whole thing, but that's basically it. It's about the characters.'

'Sounds good,' Francesca says. 'I'd like to read it sometime. They should make a movie.' She pauses. 'Don't you hate that? When people say "they" should make a movie? Who's *they*?'

'It would make a good movie,' Jack says.

She thinks about how that could've been her life with Bobby, living in motels, scared shitless. She can't believe her own naïveté. How she got all wrapped up in a fantasy and let it cloud her judgment. She sees a possible scene from the movie of her life. Nabbed by the cops. Questioned. An interrogation lamp. Sweating detectives. Tears. Her mouth making words: 'I didn't do anything. I tried to leave. When he snapped, I wanted out. I thought he was just going to borrow some money.' *Practice lying. Get good at it. Know your story.* Maybe they're coming for her. Maybe they'll find her here.

She downs her beer in a long throaty gulp. 'Can I have another one?' she asks Jack.

Charlie

Charlie couldn't get past the front office at Our Lady of the Narrows, and they didn't like that he was asking about Max Berry. Turned out Max had been a big alumni donor. They probably figured Charlie for a journalist trying to dig up dirt after the murder. He went to a pub a few blocks away from the school and talked to a couple of the Brothers who drank there on the sly. Oiled up with whiskey, they were more than willing to spill whatever dirt they had on Max. He was a weirdo. He liked hiring boys from the school. As a student, he'd been a booger-eater and chronic masturbator. Principal Aherne would never say a word against him because he'd donated tens of thousands of dollars, they confirmed. They didn't remember his pal from his school days. Charlie couldn't get his hands on a yearbook. That was all he needed. A quick glimpse. He'd followed a hunch to this dead end. It was especially frustrating because he knew Max had said both names to him, the kid in the office and his old man, and Charlie just needed something, a few letters even, to get his memory moving.

After that, he tried another tactic. Calling around to see if any of Max's clients knew the name of the kid who worked there. He didn't have a master list or anything, so he had to follow word of mouth. He checked in twice more with Lou the Goon, figuring the cops must have the kid's name, that his prints must be all over the place in the office, that he'd be one of the first people they'd want to question, not even necessarily as a suspect. He couldn't tell if Lou was lying or simply couldn't access the information. Maybe Lou felt wrong about giving out the name and address of a kid because Charlie couldn't get him to acknowledge there even was a kid. Charlie also subtly used Lou as a source of news about the Brancaccios, attempting to ascertain whether they were onto him for killing Greg and Rainey. Seems like he's still in the clear on that front, thank Christ.

He's having the desire to drink hard for the first time since Florida. He can drink almost anything and function okay, except for tequila. On tequila, he's an animal. Ready to throw down at the drop of a hat. Sometimes liking to be wasted and start trouble and get his ass kicked. That pain thing again. Just different.

He's at the Salty Salute on Fourth Avenue now, not far from Max's office. It's a dive bar with no TV, a broken jukebox, and sad alkies gathered at the bar like orphans waiting on their slop. It's quiet in the joint. Smells like dust and unwashed clothes. The bartender is a woman named Neely. She used to be a nurse. She has white hair. White like the bandage he wore on his arm as a kid after breaking it in a brawl with Clubby Cummings. Her hands are gentle. Liver spots like mushed raisins on her frail skin. Yellow teeth that remind him of melted butter pats. Bloodshot eyes. Wears a Red Cross pin. Still seems like a nurse. 'Haven't seen you in a while,' Neely says to him.

'I'm on the skids,' he says. 'Streak of bad luck.'

'What'll it be?'

'Double shot of tequila.'

Neely serves him the double. The glass has a crusty smear on it. It's cheap tequila and the smell makes him want to puke. Before he lifts it, he says, 'Can I ask you a question?'

'Sure thing,' Neely says. 'You looking to confess? I charge twenty bucks a confession.'

'People pay you to hear their confessions?'

'Everyone has their racket.'

'Maybe next time. Or maybe after a couple of these bad boys.' He motions to the tequila.

'Well, what's your question?'

Asking anyone there is to ask now: 'Did you know Max Berry?'

'Did I know Max Berry? Only since he used to get caught drinking holy water out of the fonts at St. Anselm. Wore diapers until he was eight. A shame he got taken out like that. Max wasn't that bad. There was an innocent kid in him somewhere. He just got greedy. Probably the Brancaccios did him in. Must've stepped on the wrong toes.'

Charlie doesn't touch his drink yet. 'Had you seen him around lately? Did you know the kid who worked in his office?'

'I'd see Max every once in a while, at the bank or Key Food. He'd just wave hello. I didn't know any of the kids he had working there over the years.' She picks up a pint glass and wipes it with a dish towel. 'What's your interest in Max?'

'We were friends. I'm trying to get to the bottom of things.' Then it hits him. Neely saying she'd see Max at Key Food sometimes is what does it. He remembers that day in Max's office a couple of weeks ago, the day he dropped off the bag for safekeeping. The kid was packing CDs in padded envelopes. Max asked him to go to Key Food for milk and junk food. The kid left and came back shortly after, saying he'd gone to the place on the corner instead. That place could only be the market catty-corner from Max's office across Fourth Avenue. He remembers Max saying he had a problem with the guy who owned it, but the kid had shrugged that off. He obviously went in there all the time.

Charlie stands. He downs his drink and leaves a twenty for Neely. He might take her up on that confession deal one of these days. He likes the idea of whispering his sins in her old nursey ears. He thanks her and rushes out of the bar, headed for the market across from Max's office.

It's only a few short blocks. He gets there and looks up at the white sign with black marquee letters: Chico's Market. He'd parked right across the street from it earlier when he called Lou the first time and went up to see Mrs Fonseca. He looks over at

Max's. Yellow crime scene tape webbed like decorations, making something memorable out of an unmemorable building. Still some stray action, Max's front door open, the lights on. People out walking and driving are stopping to look. Mrs Fonseca is up in her window. She doesn't notice him as he walks into Chico's.

A guy is behind the counter working furiously on a scratch-off. He's wearing a baseball cap with the Puerto Rican flag on it and a yellow muscle shirt that shows hair on his shoulders and back and flabby arms with sagging tattoos. A pinup mermaid. A bolt of green lightning. The place is otherwise empty. The refrigerators hum. Dance music plays low on the house speakers.

'Help you, bud?' the guy says to Charlie.

'You Chico?' Charlie asks.

'The one and only. How can I help you?'

'Did you know the kid who worked for Max Berry? He used to come in here, right?'

'The cops were in earlier asking questions. You, you're not a cop, right?'

Charlie fooled Mrs Fonseca but he can't play that game. 'Just a friend of Max's. I've gotta ask the kid a few questions. I don't remember his name. I know he used to come in here.'

'I don't know.'

'You don't know the kid's name?'

'I don't know nothing.' Chico puts his hands up.

Charlie reaches into the deep inner pocket of this linen jacket he got in Atlantic City. He's hardly taken it off this week. He takes out the gun and shows it to Chico.

Chico raises his hands even higher. 'Whoa, buddy, come on.'

'Just the kid's name, that's all I need.'

'Bobby Santovasco, okay?' Chico says. 'There you go.'

Charlie shakes his head. 'Santovasco,' he says. 'How'd I forget that? Used to have a memory like a steel trap.'

Chico doesn't say anything.

Charlie tucks the gun back in his pocket and heads outside.

He crosses the street and goes to the same payphone he was at earlier. He calls information and asks what Santovascos they have in Southern Brooklyn. There are a few, spread out between Gravesend, Bensonhurst, Bath Beach, and Midwood. He asks for first names. Danny is the one that clicks. Danny Santovasco. They ran track and did stage crew together, he remembers Max saying. Charlie can hardly believe his own stupidity. Stupid to forget the names. Stupid to leave the bag with Max. Stupid to stay in Atlantic City so long. But he does like pain, after all. Maybe this is another way of inflicting pain on himself. Anyhow, it's time to get the bag back. It's time to go see Bobby. He scribbles the address and phone number the operator gives him on the back of his hand with a pen he took from his room at the Tropicana.

He parked his car back by the Salty Salute. He walks there. The double tequila did him right. He feels the werewolf in him, ready to bust out, but he also feels in total control. He gets in the car, keys the ignition, and flicks on the interior light. He looks at himself in the rearview mirror. *Santovasco. You fucking mook.*

Lily

Before leaving to pick up Mairéad, Lily got a call from an old college friend, Ruby. Ruby asked if she had heard about Micah. She said she hadn't. Ruby told her they found his body in the trunk of his car near the train station in Poughkeepsie, ninety miles north of Brooklyn.

'What do you mean, his *body*?' Lily asked.

'I mean, he was murdered.'

All Lily felt in the moment was relief. She wondered if anyone from Micah's family would call her. She'd only met his mom and dad once. They took them out to lunch in York. She wondered if they knew he'd come to Brooklyn for her.

Her mind then went to the *how* and *why* of it. A brutal coincidence. He was in Coney Island and then he wound up dead in his trunk in Poughkeepsie. Her guess was he got involved with the wrong people. Probably drugs. She headed out to pick up Mairéad at the Twenty-Fifth Avenue station, feeling light and free.

Lily's showing Mairéad around the neighborhood. They're walking back on Eighty-Sixth Street from Spumoni Gardens, where they just got a square slice each and a cup of spumoni and Mairéad acted like it was the best thing she'd ever had. Lily's hardly even registered the news from Ruby. She's preoccupied. Knocked out by how beautiful Mairéad is. She seems even more beautiful here, in her neighborhood of ravaged souls and ravaged bodies. Pale skin, dark black hair, distinguished in crisp khaki shorts and a white sleeveless blouse. She's tall, maybe five-nine, with a lilting voice. That accent.

Lily hates to say it, but she hasn't met a lot of people from other places. Everybody she knows is from America. More specifically, everybody is pretty much from the Northeast. She knew one girl at York, Marnie, who was from Michigan, and a guy she knew, Ted, was from somewhere out west, but the only people from abroad she'd met before Mairéad were the Italian parents of some high school friends and that had only really been in passing. Her dad's grandparents grew up in Ireland, but she'd never met them. Ditto her mom's grandparents, who were both Sicilian. It makes her sad to think about that, how inexperienced she is, how little of the world she's actually seen. But those feelings of sadness are washed away by walking with Mairéad.

'What's that place?' Mairéad asks, pointing at the square brick building across from them. The hand painted yellow sign with red lettering over the door reads CHIFARI HOMING PIGEON CLUB. Only part of the elaborate coop on the roof is visible from the street.

'That's Zip Chifari's place,' Lily says. 'I don't know him, but he's got a tire shop on Stillwell and then he runs this pigeon club. I think he races them. I read an interview with him once all about it. I remember him saying the pigeons have these built-in compasses. Little metal fibers right over their beaks or something.'

'You should write about *that*.'

'I should. I'd have to do a lot of research. Research and I don't get along too well. I like just making stuff up.'

'Believe me, I understand. I'm sorry I even suggested it. I hate when people tell me what my next book should be about. Just tell me to fuck right off, okay?'

Lily laughs.

'So, next you're taking me to meet your middle-aged writing student whose whole family is dead?' Mairéad says. 'Sounds fun.'

'Well, when you put it that way.' More laughter from Lily. She's never met someone so forthright, so loudly funny, so confident.

'There's not much else to do in the neighborhood. Eat pizza and meet traumatized people.'

'You're funny. I'm usually the funny one.'

'Will it be difficult for you?'

'Will what be difficult?'

'Being in a house where almost everyone's gone. Maybe there'll be spirits.'

'It's not difficult so much as overwhelming sometimes. All these spirits with no one to talk to and then they find someone to listen. But, often, they're quiet. Often, I can see them but they don't say anything.'

'When did you know?'

'Oh, I was a very little girl the first time. Everyone kept telling me my great-gram Lucy was gone, but I could still see her and hear her.'

Lily nods. She's not sure what else to say. The cynical part of her thinks it must be bullshit – communicating with the dead – but the romantic part is so drawn to Mairéad that she can't help but feel mystified in the best possible way. She steers the conversation away from Mairéad's gift.

'Jack's been really nice to me the last few weeks,' she says. 'I guess I remind him of his daughter. The stuff he wrote for my class was incredible. So raw and true. I don't know if he has any real interest in continuing to write, but he should. He's got a lot to say.'

'I'm excited to meet him.'

'Anyhow, my mom's not worth shit. I'd rather introduce you to Jack.'

'Mom wouldn't be too keen on you dating a girl, huh?'

'I doubt it. When it suits her, she puts on this big Catholic act.'

'Oh, I get it.'

Lily changes the subject. 'I started reading your book,' she says.

'And?'

'It's great. Really great. I love the language. I should've bought a copy for Jack. He'd like to read it. I'm going to get one for him.'

'I'd like to read some of your fiction.'

'I don't know. I'm not there yet. I'd be embarrassed to show you any of it. You're a pro. I'm just starting out.'

'Don't say that. I'd love to read your work.'

They wander toward Jack's. The air is so different with Micah suddenly out of the picture. Lily's floating. She wonders if she's falling in love with Mairéad. She's never felt anything so fast.

When they get to Jack's house, Lily says, 'It's run-down, but I think it's really beautiful. His daughter's room is just the way she left it. He let me hide out there when things with Micah got scary.' She realizes what she's said. Mairéad has no context for it.

'Who's Micah?' Mairéad asks.

'No one. He's no one. Just this boy who was kind of stalking me.'

'"Kind of stalking" you? Jesus Christ. You okay?'

'Yeah, actually. Right before I met you at the station, I got a call from my friend Ruby. She told me Micah's dead.'

'Oh, good. So, did you do it?'

'Do what?'

'Kill the fucker?'

'The sick thing is I think you'd like it if I said I did.'

'I would. I'd be very impressed. I'd ask for details. I've always wanted to kill a bad man.'

'Well, I wish I could say I did it just to impress you, but it wasn't me.'

'What'd he do? Off himself? Couldn't have you and slashed his wrists? Jumped off a bridge?'

'I don't really know the whole story. Ruby said they found him dead in the trunk of his car at a train station in Poughkeepsie.'

'The plot thickens. Poughkeepsie's always struck me as a place where folks go to get murdered.'

They walk up to Jack's front door. Lily rings the bell. When

Jack answers, she's surprised by how upbeat he seems. 'Jack, this is Mairéad,' Lily says. 'Mairéad, this is Jack. I'm bad at introductions, sorry.'

Jack puts out his hand. He and Mairéad shake. 'It's an honor to meet you,' Jack says. 'I'm glad Lily brought you over to my dump. Show you what the neighborhood's really all about. Decay.'

'Wonderful to meet you,' Mairéad says.

Lily swears she hears something inside, someone moving around. 'Do you have company? We don't have to come in.'

'This kid I just met,' Jack says. 'I used to know her old man. Her grandma kicked her out of the house, and she had nowhere to go. I invited her back here. Figured I'd let her cool down. Thought it might be good for her to meet a couple of big-shot writers.'

They go into the kitchen. The girl is standing by the fridge, opening a bottle of Guinness. She looks troubled. Jack introduces her as Francesca. Lily wonders if he's collecting neighborhood girls who need help, if – fearing she's moved on with Mairéad – he's looking for someone else to fill the role of surrogate daughter.

They all say it's nice to meet each other. Jack asks if Lily and Mairéad want beer, booze, coffee, or anything else. They both say beer's good. He grabs a couple of bottles and hands them over. The whole crew settles back at the table. Lily thinks it's cute that Jack bought Guinness.

Even with the unexpected addition of this other girl, it's still more comfortable than taking Mairéad home to her mother. Lily marvels again at the fact that Jack's place feels so much like home. She looks at Mairéad and wonders what she's feeling about the house, if she's hearing voices, seeing ghosts, doing whatever she does.

'So, you're from Dublin?' Jack asks Mairéad.

'I am,' Mairéad says.

'It's stupid to bring this up, I guess, but my daughter, Amelia, loved the Cranberries and Sinéad O'Connor. That's about as Irish as things ever got around here.'

'Well, that's a good start.'

Lily looks at Francesca. Eighteen, probably. Slumped in her seat. Rolling a cigarette. A few beers in. 'Can you roll me one of those?' Lily asks, to try to break through the tinge of jealousy she's feeling.

'Sure thing,' Francesca says. She passes the one she's just finished to Lily and then starts work on a new one, drawing some tobacco from her pouch. Lily lights her slim little hand-rolled cigarette with a book of matches she finds on the table. It's strong. Hits her in the back of the throat. No recessed paper filter to smooth the taste down. Maybe what's she's feeling isn't jealousy as much as resentment. She wanted this meeting with Jack to be about her and Mairéad. She wanted to find some time to tell Jack about Micah. She had hoped Mairéad might commune with Amelia's ghost. Now she has to make small talk with a girl who's barely out of high school.

'I played softball with Francesca's old man back when I was the softball-playing type,' Jack says.

'He died a few years ago, my dad,' Francesca says.

'You and Lily have that in common,' Mairéad says. 'Your fathers both passing, I mean. And Jack, you lost your daughter and your wife. And both of my folks died when I was a teenager. Geez, there's a lot of loss at this table. I feel like we should toast all these dead people.'

Lily hopes Mairéad hasn't crossed a line.

Francesca doesn't seem put off. Maybe she likes people who don't just say the same clichéd things that every idiot says. She raises her bottle. 'To all these dead people,' she says.

Jack shrugs along. Lily knows he can be funny, but Mairéad's dark humor might be too much for him.

They all raise a toast.

Things have lightened up. Jack asks Mairéad a few more questions. They talk about her novel. Lily smokes the cigarette down to her fingers and then drops it into one of the empties on the table. Mairéad tells Jack that Lily's been raving about his work. She says how cool it is that the church allowed her to teach the class. Jack agrees. He says it's brought him back to life. He asks Mairéad about talking to spirits. He asks if she's a medium. She says she sort of is but she doesn't really like that word. She explains that she's mostly just tuned into the frequency of the dead.

Lily and Mairéad ask Francesca questions. She talks about wanting to go to film school but not having the grades or the money and just generally feeling stuck in the neighborhood. She stubs out her cigarette in a bottle cap already overflowing with ashes and immediately rolls another one. Lily is suspicious of her. She seems like she's hiding something. Still, to be nice, Lily tells her she was in that exact place a few weeks ago when she met Jack but things have crystallized, she sees the future more clearly now, says maybe Jack's a good luck charm. Maybe that's why they lucked into meeting each other. Tides can change fast.

Francesca gets up to use the bathroom, unsteady on her feet. Jack points down the hall to where it's located, a rickety little room with a busted ceiling fan and an off-kilter sink.

Lily's wondering how many beers Francesca has had and if that's okay. She's not that much younger. Lily was certainly drinking by eighteen. It's just sitting here with Mairéad, she knows how it might look, Jack facilitating and all. Instead of bringing it up with Jack, she starts talking about Micah. 'Did you see Micah other than the one time you scared him away?' she asks.

'Nope, that was it,' he says.

'He's dead.'

'What?'

'My friend Ruby called and told me. They found his body in the trunk of his car in Poughkeepsie.'

'Who knows what else he was into?' Jack says. 'Guys like that, trouble finds them.'

'Sounds like you should be celebrating,' Mairéad says.

'Yeah,' Lily says.

Jack lifts his bottle and drinks.

Lily remembers Jack disappearing for half the day after the confrontation with Micah. He said he had work or errands. A coincidence, surely. He's right. Micah liked to play tough, liked to believe he could swim in the deep end.

Jack points to an envelope in the center of the table. He pushes it over to Lily. 'Some pictures of Amelia,' he says. 'I thought you might like to have them. I have doubles. I don't know. It's dumb. I know you feel a real connection to her.'

Lily looks through the pictures. Amelia as a girl with her mother. In high school, less thrilled to be posing for a shot. Still, smiling. Bright. 'These are wonderful,' Lily says. 'Thanks, Jack.'

'It means a lot to me that you're thinking about her, that you're remembering her, even though you never met. I wish you had known her. I wish you'd gotten to be friends.'

Lily hands the pictures to Mairéad.

'This was your daughter?' Mairéad says. 'Oh, she's lovely. I'm sorry if I was flippant before. I've got a weird sense of humor, and I don't always have the best awareness of when I'm being inappropriate.'

'Nothing to apologize for,' Jack says. 'Amelia was the same way. She liked her jokes dark and strange. It was like *Harold and Maude* around here for a year or so. She staged a suicide as a goof. Fake Halloween blood. The whole works. This was maybe two years after Janey, my wife, died. I walk into Amelia's bedroom, and it's a horror movie. She got me that time. She really got me. I was pissed for about five minutes but then we laughed a lot about it.'

'That's brilliant,' Mairéad says. 'A girl after my own heart.'

'You don't see or hear her, do you?' Jack asks. 'I'm sorry. I was trying not to ask.'

'It's okay. I don't, I'm sorry. It's not all the time. It's not every house. Not every spirit. You know? It just happens sometimes. It's only happened a few times since I've been in New York.'

'I'm sorry.'

'No apology necessary.'

'What's in here?' Lily asks, tapping the other envelope in the center of the table.

'Don't be mad,' Jack says.

'What is it?'

Lily picks it up and finds her story from *Spiral*, winner of the Marsden-Bellwether Prize. She's moved to see that Jack has it. It's such a dad thing to do, like he's proud of her for it. Her mom treats her writing like a hobby. She shows no interest in it. Doesn't mean shit to her that Lily won that award and had a meeting with an agent, that she's working on a novel. All Grace cares about is income. 'Geez, where'd you get this?' Lily asks.

'The library,' Jack says. 'It's such a great story. I was just telling Francesca all about it. She was saying someone should make it into a movie.'

'I can't believe you tracked this down,' Lily says.

'I'd like to read it,' Mairéad says.

Lily stuffs it back in the envelope. 'I don't think so. Not yet anyway. I don't want you to think I'm a hack.'

'Stop.'

'One of these days.'

'You should write a story about how you killed your stalker ex-boyfriend.'

'I didn't do it!'

Mairéad puts on a cop voice, tips a mock interrogation lamp in Lily's face. 'Where were you on the day he went missing?'

Francesca comes out of the bathroom. They all get another

round of beers. The two six-packs depleted now. Jack brings out the whiskey, his Seagram's Seven. Lily thinks twice about telling her Seagram's Seven story. She hopes Jack doesn't bring it up.

Mairéad tells a story about how her uncle Colin back in Dublin tried to get out of going to some dinner he was supposed to go to by dropping something heavy on his foot. He wasn't a liar, couldn't bring himself to lie, so he figured if he actually hurt himself he could get out of the obligation honestly. This was her uncle who also kept a jar full of piss in his yard to ward off evil spirits. Anyhow, she goes on, the thing Colin used was a fucking anvil, and he should've gone with something much lighter because the anvil really smashed the hell out of his foot. 'It was like a cartoon,' she says. 'He tipped this anvil off his workbench and it just flattened his foot. Like comically flattened it.' Tears in her eyes as she tells it.

The music of Mairéad's voice. Lily loves listening to her.

'What happened?' Francesca asks.

'Well, first he had to call his wife, my aunt Beibhinn, to try to help him move the anvil, and then he wound up in the emergency department,' Mairéad says. 'He really, truly messed up his foot. I mean, there weren't many things worse he could've dropped. He had his leg up in traction for a month. He missed the dinner, so I guess he achieved what he set out to achieve.'

They all laugh.

Jack's tapped into the whiskey. He looks as happy as Lily's seen him in these few weeks of knowing him.

Mairéad keeps going. She has the floor, a born storyteller. 'I have another uncle who got into clowning. That was his big dream, to be a clown. But he was an alcoholic bogger. Uncle Jerry. Pissed in my grandmother's living room one night in front of the whole family. Himself, flute in hand, spraying the furniture.' This part she acts out a bit.

Jack's laughing so hard, he's doubled over the table. 'Anyhow, he shows up to my little cousin's Holy Communion in his clown costume,' Mairéad continues. 'It's a run-down costume. Secondhand wig, red foam nose, wrinkled yellow jumpsuit. His makeup job looks like a fucking Parkinson's patient did it. Forgive me for saying that. All the kids in the church are crying bloody murder. "Why's there a clown sitting in the pew?" they want to know. He's real calm. Just sort of slumped over. Probably hungover something awful at this point. The kids are wailing. Just wrecked. They either don't know it's Uncle Jerry or they don't know Uncle Jerry.'

'This is at the mass?' Jack says, astounded.

'Right. Now, my father, he is firmly against clowns, and he's had it up to here with Uncle Jerry's routine. My father, God bless him, gets up and starts beating on Uncle Jerry with my mother's bag. Just going to town on him. The Communion kids in all their dresses and suits start cheering. My father's lost his fucking mind. Uncle Jerry's making these little noises and they're not like I'm-getting-beaten-up noises, they're like sex noises. Grunting and moaning.'

'Oh my God,' Francesca says. 'This is amazing.'

Lily proudly watches Mairéad spinning her tale. She's again thinking what a genius she is. How melodious her voice is. The same voice that's in her novel.

'So, finally, Uncle Jerry is up on his feet, struggling to escape my father,' Mairéad says. 'The kids are watching a clown getting his ass beat all the way up the aisle. I'm sitting there thinking, *How could this possibly get better?* Enter Father James O'Rourke. This old demented fuck, they usually keep locked away. Ninety-four if he's a day. Looks like a skeleton hung with silver tinsel. But, somehow, on this day of days, he's escaped and he's sniffed his way to Uncle Jerry. What he does is he starts yelling like he's performing an exorcism. He has this echoey ancient voice. I'm sitting next to Granny Kath. When I tell you that she lets out a fart at this particular moment, you must be aware that I can't do this fart justice. It's massive. Brutal. Sounds like a chainsaw. It really thunders against the wood of the pew. And the smell. I mean, there's several waves. First, there's this burning onion quality but that only paves the way for the kind of diapery main stink that has enduring fucking potency. We're all choking. Gasping for breath. I tell you, I can't cope.'

Jack looks like he's about to have a heart attack, he's laughing so hard.

Mairéad pauses to take a drink. 'It's around then people start leaving. The smell's not going away. I'm looking around at my family like, *Did she poo her pants? I think she pooed her pants. Is Da still beating up Uncle Jerry? He is? Oh, good.* The Communion kids are at a fucking loss. All the ways they saw this day going, this definitely wasn't the outcome they desired.'

'Jesus Christ,' Lily says. 'Did your grandmother really shit her pants?'

'She sure did,' Mairéad says. 'It was kind of tar-like. Really soaked through the fabric. I heard they had to fumigate the church afterward.'

'And what about Uncle Jerry?'

'That's the best part.'

'You haven't even gotten to the best part?'

'Right. The best part is that Father O'Rourke – in the midst of all this madness, people filing out, choking to death on the stink – hops on Uncle Jerry and starts biting him. The fucking guy's got dentures. And Uncle Jerry's still making his sex noises. My father's disgusted. If there's one thing he never wanted to see in his life, it's an old priest biting a clown in a church.'

'Holy shit,' Jack says. 'You have a gift.'

'Is that the end?' Francesca asks.

'Pretty much,' Mairéad says. 'Someone came and collected Father O'Rourke. My mother took my father by the arm and brought him outside for fresh air. Uncle Jerry was fucking fine. He stuck with clowning for another year but he stopped showing up to family events in his costume. We had to hose Gram down, which you might think would be a vast indignity, but she seemed to like it. I said, "Don't get used to this, Gram. We're not hosing you down after every poo."'

'You deserve an award for that story,' Jack says.

'Well, thanks. I suppose I was lucky to have witnessed it.'

Lily's hung up on the way Mairéad says *think* and *thanks*, no *h*, like *tink* and *tanks*. Really beautiful.

'I wish I had a story about my grandmother shitting her pants in church,' Francesca says. 'I don't have much money, like a few bucks to my name, but I would give it all to see that happen.'

'You know, once they hit a certain age, odds are better than you'd imagine,' Mairéad says.

They drink and laugh, laugh and drink. Lily and Mairéad have a good buzz going, and Jack remains about as steady as he always is. Lily can't imagine him getting drunk and out of control. It was a good idea to bring Mairéad over. He seems very happy. Lily's thankful. She's thinking that this is what it should be like to come home to family. Everything revolving around laughter and booze. Never mind the state of the house or even the state of the world.

Meanwhile, Lily notices that Francesca's pretty wasted. Her eyes have gone droopy. Lily feels her pain. A few years ago, her tolerance was nothing. Now it takes an awful lot for her to get wasted. 'Can I tell you guys something?' Francesca asks. Her bottom lip is outturned.

'You tired?' Jack says. 'You want to lie down? You can take the couch in the living room.' He turns his attention to Lily and Mairéad. 'Same goes for you two. If you don't feel like going anywhere, you can take Amelia's room. I like having all this life in the house.'

'He killed the guy,' Francesca says. 'Bobby did. He killed Max Berry.'

'What's that now?' Mairéad says.

'He robbed him and he killed him.'

'Did you say Max Berry?' Jack asks.

Francesca nods slowly, drunkenly. 'I can't hold it in. I met Bobby a couple of weeks back. I fell for him. He said he was going to steal some money from this bad guy he worked for and we were going to go out west. It was just a dream.' The edges of her words warped.

'Are you okay?' Lily asks.

Francesca shrugs. 'Max has this dumpy office in Bay Ridge. We went there. He was just going to rob the safe, Bobby was. Then we were taking off. That's what he said. He knew where Max's gun was. I thought he was bullshitting. And then we were there and it was happening and Bobby had the gun and there was all this stuff in the safe. It belonged to some other guy. Charlie something.' She chirps into her palm, a mix of a hiccup and a belch. 'I was handing Bobby duct tape. I was just there. It didn't feel real. I went outside. He came out and told me he killed him by accident.'

'When did this happen?'

'Last week. They just found Max. His parents found him. I saw it on the news. I didn't do anything. It was a mistake, being there. I didn't think Bobby was like that.'

'They found Max Berry dead today?' Jack asks.

Francesca nods.

Jack gets up, goes over to the counter, and turns on his little portable kitchen radio. He scans the AM dial, settling on 1010 WINS. A sad announcer voice booming. Weather. Traffic. Francesca is drifting off at the table. Jack puts water on to boil, probably figuring it might be good to get some coffee or tea in her. Lily wants to ask a million more questions, but she feels weird interrogating a drunk girl. Besides, she doesn't even know her. She could be a pathological liar. She could be anything. Of course, the name jumped out at Lily. Bobby. Her former stepbrother's name, but how many Bobbys must there be in the neighborhood, let alone Brooklyn? A fucking Bobby on every block. Two, three Bobbys. Bobbys crawling up out of the sewers.

The story gets mentioned on the news. Briefly, in passing. A murder-robbery in Bay Ridge. The body just discovered. They're not sure when the crime was committed. Cops suspect it might be mob-involved. Jack shuts off the radio. He mixes coffee grounds and eggshells into the boiling water and lets it go for a couple of minutes. When it's been long enough, he pours the coffee through a mesh strainer into a mug. He brings the coffee over to Francesca.

'I'm sorry I got so drunk,' she says.

'It's okay,' Jack says.

Lily prods anyway. 'Who's Bobby? Where'd you meet him?'

'Bobby works for Max. *Worked*. They came over to my house. My mother was "investing"' – she puts dramatic air quotes around the word – 'with Max.'

'Max Berry runs a Ponzi scheme dressed up as an investment firm,' Jack says.

'You knew him?' Francesca says.

'I've heard from a few people he screwed over. Took their investment, promised them high interest rates, delivered for a short time with small payouts, and then all their money suddenly became inaccessible, tied up in investments, whatever. A lot of old timers trusted him and lost their savings.'

'That's the guy. Big milk drinker too.' Another chirp into her palm. 'Anyhow, Bobby called my house later. I was in the city, getting drunk – I guess that's what I do now – and my mom told me he called when I got in touch to let her know I wasn't coming home that night. I called him back from a payphone at this bar and he came and met me. We just kind of fell in love, I guess. I don't know. I wasn't expecting it. I didn't even like him at first. It was just something to do. He was different from other boys, there was something intense about him. He reminded me of Matt Dillon in *Drugstore Cowboy*. You ever see that?'

That makes Lily's ears perk up. Her former stepbrother, Bobby, did in fact bear a slight resemblance to Matt Dillon. Those eyes. A look like he was always surprised. Lily has seen *Drugstore Cowboy* but she's thinking more of *The Outsiders* and *Rumble Fish* when he was even younger. Bobby did cruise the world with that same kind of dumbly beautiful strut. They never had much between them. He was a few years younger and the marriage between their parents didn't last that long. A step-brother's not a half-brother. A stepbrother's nothing when the marriage ends. Could Francesca's Bobby be her Bobby? The same kid who once roomed across the hall from her? The same kid she once walked in on cutting his thighs with a sharp kitchen knife and blotting away the blood with one of her mother's nice hand towels? When Lily asked what he was doing, he said he just wanted to see how it felt. 'His name isn't Bobby Santovasco, is it?'

'How'd you know that?' Francesca says, looking shocked, almost sober for a second.

'He was my stepbrother for a while,' Lily says. She used to look at him and wonder what on earth he could ever be. He was kind of a blank slate. If she usually defined people by what they loved – what books, what bands, what movies – she couldn't make heads or tails of him. To her, at least, he always seemed passionless. Maybe he wasn't. Maybe there was just too much distance between them. A distance that couldn't be bridged. They had their different lives already when their folks got together. They co-existed, but there was no bonding moment, no sense of warmth ever, not even a hint of rivalry for affection or otherwise. They were just on different tracks. Even if their parents hadn't broken up, there probably would have been very little to keep them connected.

Still, this idea that he could rob and kill someone, that doesn't seem right. Bobby did stupid things, pointless things, but she never got the sense he did or ever would do evil things. She's thinking, *People change, though. He's what, nineteen now?*

She's thinking, *Maybe these last few years have been really bad for him.* She's thinking, *Not only can't I picture him killing this Max, but I can't picture Francesca falling for him. Bobby, ick.*

'Wait a sec,' Mairéad says to Lily. 'This fella she's talking about, this is your stepbrother?'

'*Former* stepbrother.'

'Small fucking world.'

Francesca's just sitting there, her mouth open, booze-soaked brain on overload. 'Bobby was your stepbrother?' Seeming to say it just to hear herself say it. 'You know, I'm remembering he did mention having a stepsister at some point. Whoa.' She leans in and taps the envelope containing Lily's story. 'Even said she was a writer.'

'Bobby said that? I wouldn't even think he knew.'

'He knew. He said it sort of proudly.'

'Where is he?'

Francesca shrugs. 'I haven't seen him in a week. I went back to his apartment with him that day and then ran off. He's tried calling me a bunch, but I've avoided him. I don't know what to do. I shouldn't have said anything.' Francesca puts her head in her hands. 'Don't tell, okay?'

'Max Berry was a scumbag,' Jack says. 'Did he deserve to die? Probably not. What I'm worried about is the stuff Bobby stole. You said it belonged to a Charlie. How'd you know that?'

'Max said it.'

'Did he say it was Charlie French?'

She looks through her fingers like she's playing a drunken game of peek-a-boo. 'That's it. You know him?'

'I met Max once. He'd screwed an old lady I know out of her money and she asked me to go talk to him. He mentioned getting Charlie French involved like I should be scared. I knew Charlie's name from the papers. He supposedly killed his wife and got away with it. Her family had been loaded but there was nobody left except her, so Charlie got all that money. He came around as Max's strong-arm guy for revenge, but it was right after Amelia died and he saw he didn't have to do anything to hurt me.'

Lily's never heard Jack talk like this. It's a different him. Something in his eyes too. She had Jack figured as only one thing, a guy who'd lost his daughter and his wife, and she's realizing she doesn't really know anything else about his experience in the world.

Jack goes on: 'That was unusual. He's pretty relentless generally from what I hear, Charlie French is. Bobby's gonna have big trouble. Eventually, anyway.'

Francesca drinks more whiskey, shaking her head frantically at the burn in her throat.

'Maybe you shouldn't have anymore?' Jack says. 'That okay? I don't want to tell you what to do, but I think you've had enough. Drink your coffee.'

Francesca puts her hand around the mug and brings it up to her mouth, slurping away. She wiggles her nose at the coffee. 'I should go warn him to run away. Should call at least. We were going to run away together but then he said it'd be better to wait. He says he knows a guy who can sell the drugs, but it'll take time. I don't know. No matter what he did, I don't want him to die. What if this Charlie guy finds him? I should stop talking. What am I gonna do?' Wiping tears from her eyes with the backs of her hands now. 'Last week I was falling in love. Now I'm all tangled up in something I didn't do. I have this weight on my chest. I just feel like I can't fucking breathe.'

Mairéad reaches over and squeezes Francesca's shoulder. 'Don't cry, love. It'll be okay. You didn't know. You didn't do anything wrong.'

Francesca tries to stand up and staggers, almost toppling. 'I should go warn him.'

'Don't try to go anywhere. Not right now anyway. You've had too much to drink. You need to have a lie down.'

'I think that's for the best,' Jack says.

Francesca nods.

Mairéad takes her by the arm, guides her into the living room, and helps her settle on the couch. Lily follows, standing there, not doing anything. Francesca lies on her back, her head against the hard arm of the ragged green couch. Mairéad maneuvers her around until she's on her side, and she helps her scooch down away from the arm, stuffing a fringed throw pillow under her head. Francesca makes a noise of contentment. Her eyes flutter closed. Mairéad covers her with a red and black checkered wool blanket that makes Lily think of playing checkers with her father. The way they'd set the board up on the floor. The way he'd let her win three out of every four games but he'd really wreck her in the one game he allowed himself to have. They shut off the light in the living room and leave Francesca snoring in the dark.

'Holy shit, that was wild,' Mairéad says when they're back at the kitchen table. 'You two do not disappoint. A memorable evening in-fucking-deed. When I see the story in the papers tomorrow, I can rest assured I have the inside scoop. Five years from now, I'll tell everyone at a pub one night the whole mess and they'll think I'm lying. Plus, we have Lily's stalker dead in Poughkeepsie. Grand.'

'I can't believe this,' Lily says.

'I'm at a loss,' Jack says.

'I'm not sure if it's harder to believe that Bobby would kill someone or that a cute girl like her would fall for him.'

'I mean, she said he looked like Matt Dillon,' Mairéad says.

'A little bit he does, but there's no emotion in his eyes. Not much of anything. The kid I knew had zero character. Maybe he's changed drastically. That happens from the beginning of high school to the end, right? Maybe he got charming.'

'Maybe he got dangerous. Dangerous can be sexy.'

Lily never did see the blueprints for charming or dangerous

in Bobby, though. She thinks of the boy she knew. Slamming into the apartment and flopping on the couch. Slugging Sunny Delight in front of the open fridge in the kitchen. Eating grapes and leaving the seeds on the counter. His boxers hanging from the back of the door in the bathroom. The way he always seemed to smear the bathroom sink with his blue toothpaste. The way he never turned off a light in the apartment. The cologne he started wearing when he was twelve. Polo Sport. The same kind all the boys he went to school with were using. Gross. Little Bobby. Unbelievable. She guesses that, even then, he had a life she didn't know, couldn't know.

'Fuck,' she says. 'I feel like I should help him.'

Bobby

Bobby had taken Max Berry's address and telephone book in the hopes of finding Charlie French's number in there. He was thinking he could go to a payphone somewhere, call Charlie, put on a deep voice, and say it was someone else who'd stolen his stuff. One of the Brancaccios. Some client of Max's. Just anything to lead the trail away from the kid who worked in the office, in case that came up as an option. He thought he could then call the next day and the day after that, either talking to Charlie or leaving messages, and each time he'd pin it on someone else – a dirty cop, Max's folks, whoever – just to create more chaos. He'd even had the thought of saying it was Jack Cornacchia, but that seemed too cruel. He imagined Charlie's head spinning in all directions. He'd see everyone around him as the person who snagged his stash from the safe. The city itself would become a thief.

It was a good idea, except Bobby hadn't acted on it. Charlie's number was in the book, scrawled hastily in Max's demonic chicken scratch print, but Bobby couldn't bring himself to go outside and dial the number and hear Charlie's voice, even if only on a message machine. He's just been hiding in his room all week, tense, playing video games, waiting for the news to break, waiting for his father to ask why he hasn't been going to work, wondering how he'd explain the coincidence of his stopping work and Max's being found dead when the time comes.

Bobby's reconnected with Zeke upstate, which is cool, and he's planning on getting the drugs up there soon and then Zeke will sit on them for a while before slowly selling them off.

Whatever's made, they'll split fifty-fifty. In addition, there's all the other money. Fifty grand. He's sitting on that too for now. It's hidden, along with the drugs and the gun, in the bag up on the high shelf in his closet. He keeps trying to call Francesca, but she wants nothing to do with any of it. All those movies she loves – she lives in a world of fantasy. She's cool with talking about going on the run, living like Bonnie and Clyde, but when it came down to it the shit was too real. He guesses he understands. He scared her. He scared himself. What he's turned out to be capable of. Still, that week with her was the best of his life. He's just become something he didn't know he could be. He's proven himself to himself. Maybe this is his calling, being a badass.

Holing up with his Nintendo 64 is about all that's gotten him through the waiting. He's sitting on his red bean bag chair in front of the TV, his eyes pissy from staring at the screen so much. He's been eating cold pizza and cereal when he gets hungry, scrounging the cabinets for snacks that aren't stale. His dad has a new girlfriend, which explains why he's even more inattentive than usual. Her name's Jessica. She's from Midwood. They've gone out every night this week, which has worked out well. The timing's good. His dad, Danny, is at his best when he's just met a woman and he's trying to throw a lay on her. He leaves money for food, though Bobby currently doesn't need money for anything. He tries to act as if they're a normal father and son, living it up sitcom-style in this shitty apartment. He tries to act as if one wife of his, Bobby's mother, didn't disappear like a ghost in the night, having divorce papers delivered, and that the next, Grace, hadn't skedaddled once she had the real him figured out. He tries to act as if he's a prize, as if they're both prizes, when they're the opposite of prizes.

He hears Danny get home now, rattling through the front door. Bobby's not even sure what time it is. Probably after 10:00 p.m.

He's been staring at *Donkey Kong 64* for at least five hours. His stomach's rumbling. His mouth's dry. The room smells of his bottled up funk. He should open the window and go out on the fire escape for a stretch.

'Bobby?' Danny calls out from the kitchen. Bobby can hear that he's drunk. He can hear it in his voice but also in how he drops the keys on the table.

'Yeah?' Bobby says.

Danny comes thundering down the hall and knocks on his door. Hard. A cop knock. A drunk dad knock. 'Bobby?' he says again. 'It's fucking open, Danny,' Bobby says. 'Take it easy.'

His father turns the knob and pushes the door open. He stands there in his best cheap suit, plaid tie undone, and a sauce stain on his wrinkled dress shirt. He wobbles a bit and then props himself up against the jamb. 'Watch your mouth, huh?' he says. 'And don't call me Danny.'

Bobby shrugs. 'Sorry. You went out with Jessica again? Where is she? I figured you'd bring her home.'

'I got her a car service and sent her back to her place.' He pauses, burps loudly. 'Did you hear about Max? It's been on the news all day.'

'No. What about Max?'

'He was killed. Right there in his own office. Jesus Christ. It's terrible. His folks found him. They think it happened a few days ago, maybe even a week. The last time anybody saw him was at the bank eight days ago. When's the last time you saw him? You haven't been in to work, right?'

'He called me last week and told me he didn't need me right now, not to come in for a while,' Bobby says, not taking his eyes off the screen, thumbing buttons on his controller.

'The cops haven't called to talk to you?'

'Nope. I didn't even know until you told me. I've been playing my game. And I don't know if many people really know I work there. I mean, it's all under the table.'

'They'll come around. A few people must know. *I* know. He paid you off the books, right? You should call the cops. It doesn't look good otherwise.' Danny comes in and sits down on Bobby's unmade bed, the sheets and comforter crumpled against the wall. 'Jesus Christ. Who would kill Max? He was shady, sure, but he was a harmless guy.'

'Yeah.'

'What was your impression working with him this last little while?'

'I don't know. He was weird. He said weird things.'

'Weird like how?'

'Weird like he asked me what my shoe size was a few times. He also asked to watch me drink a carton of milk once.'

Danny scratches his head and then he undoes his tie and rips it off. Rumors had been out there that Max liked the boys who worked for him, that he said inappropriate things to them. Bobby's thinking he could arouse his dad's suspicions that Max might've been killed for a reason he hadn't even considered. Anyhow, those things are true. Max had said plenty of things to Bobby that were strange, played initially as a goof. Like asking to watch him drink a carton of milk. That was, Bobby first figured, Max trying to be funny.

'I can't believe he's dead,' Danny says. 'He was my partner in chem lab in high school. We worked stage crew and ran track together. He was a dork. That was it. A harmless dork.'

Bobby thinks about what happened after Francesca left the office to go outside, how – with Max taped helplessly in the chair – he held a yellow pages directory up to his head and shot him through it, the book muffling the noise of the shot slightly. Something he'd seen in a movie. It was the only way out he could think of. He hadn't planned on it, not at first anyway, but then he knew it was the only option. Leaving Max alive meant losing the money and drugs. There was no way Max wouldn't say it was him. Bobby never could've pictured himself shooting someone but then the gun was in his hand and he just found it incredibly easy, even thrilling. He didn't think about Max as a man. It was easy not to think about him that way.

'Are you okay?' Danny asks. 'I remember, when I was a kid, there was this guy I knew pretty well, Armond, who was killed in a hold-up. I must've been around twelve or thirteen. Since you're older maybe you know how to deal with it. I remember being so scared. I didn't sleep for months after that. I'd known old people who'd died of natural causes, but Armond was only in his forties and I was really naïve to the fact that something bad like that could happen to someone I knew. I used to sit at my window every night, waiting, thinking it was going to happen to Grandma or Grandpa or even me at Uncle Jules's hardware store, that one day someone would come in with a gun and that'd be that.'

'I'm fine,' Bobby says, really mashing buttons, pulsing along on his game, throwing pixelated barrels.

'You don't want to talk about how you're feeling at all?'

'Nope.'

His dad reaches out and takes the controller away. He gets up and manually switches off the TV. 'Come on, I'm trying to talk to you here. The least you could do is stop playing.'

Bobby continues to stare at the black screen. 'I don't know. I'm fine. I'm nothing. I'm not scared. Max was involved with some sketchy people. He definitely knew mob guys.'

'Yeah?'

Bobby nods.

'Huh,' Danny says. 'Whatever happened, it makes me scared that I got you a job there. What if you'd been there when this happened? What then? They might've killed you too. Maybe he knew he was in trouble. Maybe that's why he told you not to come in. Truth is, I guess I know what he does – what he *did* – isn't totally legal. He must've pissed off the wrong folks. I feel like I should call the cops. I feel like you need to talk to them.

Maybe you can think of somebody who came around who might've been planning this.'

'Just let it go. I don't know anything. They won't come here for me.'

A loud knock on the front door jolts them both. 'Maybe that's them,' Danny says.

Bobby shrugs. His mouth goes dry. He's sweating. Could be that he misjudged the situation and the cops found out about him and they're poking around, asking questions of anyone who might have a lead. Has to be. People so rarely knock on their door, unless it's the landlord or one of his dad's girlfriends. He's so stupid, believing that hardly anybody knew he worked at Max's. Of course people knew. He went into Chico's Market every day. He ran errands for Max at the bank and the post office and had to go to a law office on Fifth Avenue a few times. 'Maybe it's Jessica?' Bobby says.

'I don't think so. I put her in a car. Probably the cops heard from somebody you worked at Max's. Who else would come around this late?'

More knocking. Louder this time.

They go out together. Bobby stands by the kitchen counter as his dad looks through the front door peephole. 'Who's there?' Bobby asks his dad in a whisper.

'It's the cops,' Danny says. He asks who it is just to make them say it, and they identify themselves as Detective Chen and Detective Rinaldi. They say they're looking for Bobby.

Bobby's panicking on the inside, trying to prepare himself for the questions these detectives might ask. He worries that he left something behind, that his prints were somewhere, and then he remembers that of course his prints would be everywhere because he worked there and that would lead the cops to him no matter what. He feels so stupid that he hadn't thought of that. What else hasn't he thought of?

He knows he just has to play it cool. No way they have

anything on him. He just has to say Max was being weird and fired him last week. Maybe he can make it seem like he thought Max was in big trouble.

Danny takes the chain off the door, opens up, and lets the two detectives in. Chen identifies himself. Rinaldi doesn't. Danny seems sober now. He does the talking. He says they heard about Max. How goddamn awful. He says that Bobby didn't work there that long. He says that he went to high school with Max. He's the one who got Bobby the job. Bobby's taking a year off to figure things out after graduating from OLN. He seems to realize that he's rambling. He stops talking, blows on the back of his hand, and smells it, trying to confirm to himself that he's not coming off like an alkie.

The detectives turn their attention to Bobby. They ask when he was last at the office, if anything unusual had happened that they should know about.

Bobby looks past them and lies. He says Max told him to stop coming around. He says a strange guy came by and gave Max some trouble. He says the guy's name was Charlie Something. Charlie French.

The detectives both nod. One of them is taking notes on a small lined pad.

'What was in the safe Max had?' Rinaldi asks.

'I was never allowed to see,' Bobby says. 'Max always sent me out when he put stuff in or took stuff out of the safe.'

'My son's not a suspect, right?' Danny asks. 'Look at him. He couldn't hurt a fly. His prints are probably everywhere, but he worked there, so that's why.'

'We're just asking questions right now,' Rinaldi says.

They ask a few more. Nothing too difficult. Nothing that makes Bobby uneasy. Maybe they're just trying to get a read on him. He relaxes as the questioning winds down. Chen gives him a card and tells him to call if he thinks of anything else. He tells him not to go anywhere since they're probably going to need to talk to him again tomorrow. Danny goes and stands next to Bobby and takes the card. He laughs and says his son will definitely lose it so he had better hang onto it. Chen and Rinaldi leave.

Danny closes the door behind them. 'It's so nerve-racking talking to cops,' he says. 'Imagine how it feels if you actually did something.'

'Yeah,' Bobby says.

'Were you scared? It's normal. It's okay.'

'I wasn't really scared. I didn't do anything. I wasn't there. I don't care about Max.'

'That's not nice. Max was my friend. We weren't super close or anything, but I knew him a long time. You should be asking me how I feel. Am I doing okay? My friend was murdered.'

'You didn't even like Max. Not really.'

'That's no way to talk.' Danny goes over to the fridge, takes out a can of ginger ale, and chugs it. He belches and then finishes what's left in the can. 'You want a ginger ale? I needed that. The whole time I was thinking those detectives had me figured for an alcoholic. I could smell it on me. I'm sure they could too. Cheap wine's the worst. You want a ginger ale?'

'I'm going back in my room,' Bobby says.

'I'm here if you need me.'

Another knock on the door. Bobby's guessing it's Chen and Rinaldi. Maybe they forgot to ask him something. Maybe this is a tactic. Maybe they get him relaxed with softball questions and then they leave and come right back with the hard stuff.

'Who's there?' Danny asks.

From the other side: 'My name's Detective Mackey. I just have a few questions.'

Danny looks at Bobby. 'A different detective?'

Bobby shrugs.

'Two detectives were just here,' Danny says through the door. 'They talked to my son.'

'Oh,' Mackey says. 'Okay. Well, I just have a couple of follow-up questions for Bobby. Won't take me but a minute or two.'

'Yeah?'

'Just a second of your time.'

Danny looks over at Bobby, who shrugs again.

Danny puts his hand on the knob and twists it until the door opens in. Once the guy's inside, it takes Bobby a second to realize that he's no detective. He's Charlie French. He remembers him from that day in the office, the day he dropped the bag off. Add to that the fact that he doesn't really look anything like a detective. He's wearing an off-white linen jacket, a black cabana shirt with red piping, chinos, and tasseled loafers. He's trying to look like one of those guys you see outside the Italian social clubs, but he's not quite pulling it off.

Bobby's fucked. He's not sure what to do, what he even can do. He weighs his options. Bolt out the front door, forgetting the bag and taking nothing, or barricade himself in his room. That's about all he can come up with. Charlie French has him now. It really just depends how he plays it.

'How can I help you?' Danny asks, closing the door behind him. He looks the stranger up and down. Now that he's gotten a good glance, it seems to register that something's off. 'Like I said, Detective Chen and Detective Rinaldi just left five minutes ago.'

Charlie looks at Bobby and smiles. 'I've got a few questions for your son here. I think he knows why.'

'Look,' Danny says. 'Bobby wasn't trying to hide anything by not letting anyone know he worked for Max Berry. He hadn't been there in a while. Max told him he didn't need him around anymore.'

'That so?' Charlie asks.

'Max and I were friends from high school. That's how I got Bobby the job there. He doesn't know anything. He just told me he thinks Max might've been tied up with the mob. Maybe he crossed somebody?'

'Maybe. Why don't we let the kid talk?'

'Bobby?' Danny says. 'Anything for the detective?'

'He's not a cop,' Bobby says, anguished, almost choking on his words.

'What do you mean?'

'I wasn't sure you recognized me,' Charlie says.

His father's confused, scratching behind his ear. He moves a few steps back from Charlie. 'What's going on? What is this? You got a badge? Let me see your badge.'

Charlie takes a gun out from under his shirt. A silencer screwed onto the barrel. 'You want to tell your old man?'

Bobby stays silent.

Charlie's holding the gun in front of him, not pointing it at anyone yet, just kind of considering it. 'Seems like, as best I can piece together, your boy here took his badass pills and held up Max Berry. Must've been to impress the little chick he was with. Where is she? She hiding in your room? More importantly, where's my stuff? See, Bobby knocked off the contents of Max's safe, which I generally wouldn't give much of a shit about, but Max happened to be holding a very important bag for me.'

'Come on,' Danny says. 'You've got the wrong kid. My son couldn't hurt anybody. Look at him. He's shy as shit.'

'Took me a minute to find you,' Charlie says to Bobby. 'Couldn't remember your name. Even tried hunting down a copy of Max's high school yearbook to find your old man but had no luck. Chico finally came through.'

Bobby wishes that the gun in his closet was in his hand right now. At least that'd give him a chance.

Danny starts moving toward the phone on the wall. 'I'm gonna need you to leave,' he says, holding out the card from Detective Chen. 'I'm gonna have to call the real cops back here in a sec. They might still be outside.'

'Stay where you are,' Charlie says, putting the gun on Danny. 'Hands up.'

Danny stops in his tracks and puts his hands in the air. He's trembling. The gravity of the situation has him way past sober. 'Bobby, tell me this isn't true. Tell me this guy's wrong.'

'Go on and tell him,' Charlie says.

'I didn't do anything,' Bobby says to his dad. 'I don't know what he's talking about.'

'Okay, play it that way,' Charlie says.

'Listen, I won't call the cops,' Danny says. 'This is just a misunderstanding. Put the gun down. Please. Maybe Bobby can help you figure out who might've done this. He was in the office a lot before Max asked him to stop coming. Maybe he has a lead. Maybe he can remember someone casing the joint. Bobby, you told the detectives someone came around the office before you left. What was his name? Charlie Something.'

Bobby looks at his father, sweating, flustered. Charlie's gun is still on him. Bobby hadn't thought about his father in all of this, not once until Charlie walked through that door. 'This is Charlie French,' Bobby says.

'Oh,' Danny says.

'I'll give you ten seconds, kid,' Charlie says. 'Tell me where my stuff is or I'll plug your old man.'

Bobby thinks about the bag right there in his closet, maybe fifteen feet away or less. All he has to do is say where it is. Maybe that'll be enough. Maybe Charlie will retrieve it and leave. He doesn't need to murder them. He just wants his stuff back. Bobby feels like he might piss himself. He wants to keep it all. He wants to be rich the way that bag makes him rich.

'Ten,' Charlie says. 'Nine. Eight. Seven. Six.'

Bobby gulps. 'Wait,' he says. 'I don't know, I swear. I don't know where your stuff is.'

The phone in the kitchen starts clanging. That loud, cloying old school wall-mount rotary.

On the fifth ring, Charlie goes over, keeping the gun on Bobby, and picks up, saying, 'Who's this? Yeah. No. Bobby can't come to the phone right now.' He hangs up as hard as he can, shattering the top of the receiver. He bangs the receiver into the cradle a few more times until the mount loosens from the plasterboard and crashes to the floor.

Danny is shaking harder.

'Where was I?' Charlie asks. 'Right. Five. Four.'

'I don't know,' Bobby says. 'I swear. I don't.'

Jack

With Francesca passed out on the couch from too much booze, Lily takes Jack aside in the kitchen and says, 'Maybe I should go see Bobby, help him, convince him to give the stuff back to this Charlie French guy at least? What do you think? He lives in the same apartment. I can drop Mairéad at the train and go over. Francesca told us. Others must know already, right? I don't feel much for Bobby, but I don't think he should die over this.'

'He killed Max,' Jack says. 'He probably wasn't smart about it. It's only a matter of time before Charlie French or the cops are on his ass. Like you said, they might be already. You should stay out of it.' He had that one encounter with Charlie French, the day he came over to get revenge on behalf of Max and found only the shell of Jack Cornacchia, his house full of flowers and cards and pictures of Amelia.

'I should check in with him,' Lily says.

'Call him before you do anything. How about that? Start there.'

Lily nods. She goes over to Mairéad, who is sitting back at the table, sipping her whiskey. Lily says, 'I feel like I should help Bobby. He's so stupid.' The way she says *stupid*, the neighborhood really comes out in her voice, the *d* more of a *t*.

'It's a wild fucking situation,' Mairéad says.

'I'm gonna call him first but then I might go over. I can drop you at the train on the way.'

Mairéad reaches out and takes her hand. 'I think you should listen to Jack. I think you should stay out of it.'

But Lily can't let it go, which Jack respects. He's not sure if it's some sense of loyalty to Bobby. Probably not. It's just the goodness in her that won't allow her to sit idly by while Bobby is sucked down the drain. She knows that all it takes is one person trying to help. She knows he doesn't have that one person. And she's right. It could be the difference between him living and dying. Maybe there's more to the story between him and Max. Jack knows firsthand that, even five years ago, people wanted Max's blood. It wasn't like Bobby killed some saint. Jack should have sympathy.

Lily goes to the phone and dials the number to her old apartment, still automatic in her memory. Someone picks up after a few rings, a voice she doesn't recognize. It's definitely not her former stepdad. It's definitely not a girlfriend of his. 'Is Bobby there?' Lily asks. Jack can hear the hum of the voice on the other end. No doubt a man.

The line goes dead.

Lily hangs up. She tries again and gets a busy signal. She tries twice more. Busy signals both times. 'I think he's in trouble,' Lily says to Jack and Mairéad. 'I'm going over.'

'I think that's a really bad idea,' Mairéad says. 'Could be very dangerous.'

'I'm coming,' Jack says. 'Where is it?'

'Eighty-Third Street,' Lily says.

'I'll drive. We can be there quicker.'

'Do you want us to drop you at the train?' Lily asks Mairéad.

Mairéad gestures toward Francesca in the other room, snoring. A pained look visible on her face through the dark. 'I can stay here, keep an eye on Herself.'

'Yeah?'

'If it's okay with Jack.'

'Of course,' Jack says.

'Be careful,' Mairéad says. 'It's on the record that I don't think this is too smart.' She stands. She kisses Lily on the cheek.

Jack says he just needs a minute. He heads down to the

basement for his gun. He checks it and loads it with the bullets he keeps in the old cookie tin next to the oil burner.

They go out to his car, nestled back by his garage at the end of the shared driveway. He opens the passenger door for Lily and walks around the front, pulling on his door until it gives, the metal whining. He gets in behind the wheel. The gun tucked under his shirt, basement-cool against his skin.

'You brought the gun, huh?' Lily asks.

'I figured I'd better.' He pauses, turns to her. 'Listen, why don't you stay here too? Tell me the building and the apartment number. I'll go over myself.'

'No way.'

'You're on a date. It's going good. Irish is great. I'm gonna call her Irish because I can't pronounce her name. Why throw yourself into the middle of this? Your stepbrother – what's his name? Bobby? – made his bed. The cops could be there already. Charlie French could be there. What's the point?'

'I just feel it,' Lily says. 'He needs my help. He needs to see a friendly face. We were never really friends, but still. I just feel like he needs me to tell him it's okay to do the right thing, you know?'

Jack exhales. 'You're a good egg, Lily. The world's lucky to have you.'

'Thanks for saying that. Thanks for coming with me.'

They drive to Eighty-Third Street, the car making its whooshing noise the whole way. Lily points out the building. They park across the street, probably a bit too close to a fire hydrant, backing up against a neon yellow line spray-painted on the blacktop to mark a driveway boundary.

The glass front door of the building is supposed to be locked at all times, but Lily says she remembers that it's rarely locked, if ever. The glass is splattered with pigeon shit. Someone has scribbled tags on the upper half with a silver paint marker. The handle on the door is rusty, one of the screws that keeps it in place dangling out. Lily says it was a wreck of an apartment building when she and her mom lived there with Danny and Bobby, and it's even more of a wreck now. She continues: 'The landlord had a walrus mustache and smelled like cardboard and didn't fix shit. People would call and he'd say, "Uh-huh, I'll get right on that," and then he'd disappear back into whatever he was watching on the tube. I once saw him at Wolfman's Video, coming out from behind the saloon doors that led to the adult section, a stack of big porno VHS boxes under his arms. Sid, that's his name. He's probably still around. Guys like that don't die or retire. They don't go anywhere.'

The front door isn't locked. They go inside.

Lily says she's doesn't remember many other people from the building, which doesn't have a fancy name or anything like some of the other apartment buildings around. This isn't the Benson or the Carlos or the Cropsey Arms. It's just a nameless little runt of a building. Four stories. About twelve apartments. Drab hallways with threadbare carpets. An elevator that grinds when it's going up and squeals when it's coming down. Smoke detectors that don't work. A laundry room that could be a bondage den from hell. A rickety fire escape on the side of the building that comes down to a weed-choked alley heaped with garbage cans and empty crates. Old-timers on rent control, Lily says, occupy most of the apartments. Half deaf or half dead. A lot of them with Jamaican aides.

The apartment where Bobby lives with his dad is on the second floor. They take the stairs, bypassing the elevator, and come to a heavy rust-colored door at the end of a hallway bathed in vomit-colored light. The number six turned upside down over the peephole. The hallway is full of cooking smells. Frying oil, spices, gravy. The smells seem to be flowing from the other apartments.

Lily knocks on the door.

A few seconds pass. Nothing.

'Bobby?' Lily says. She tries the little buzzer under the peephole. 'Bobby, open up, it's Lily.'

Jack has a bad feeling. He's usually pretty good about sensing when something's off and he feels it in the air now, a ripple of bad vibes coming from behind the door. 'Let's go,' he says to Lily. 'Let's get you out of here.'

'Give him a sec,' she says.

When the door opens from the inside, Jack can see that he's right. Jack has never seen her former stepbrother, Bobby, but that's who he guesses has opened the door. It's confirmed when Lily speaks to him. 'Bobby, you okay?' she says.

Bobby's so taken aback by Lily's presence, he seems to not even notice Jack at first but then he does and he goes even whiter in the face than he already is. It's like he recognizes Jack from somewhere. Jack's never seen the kid. He could be anybody from the neighborhood, a punk or a saint, a kid on the verge of doing something great or doing nothing miserably forever.

Jack gets a glimpse of two other guys in the apartment, standing off to the side. He doesn't recognize the first one, not by sight, but he guesses that he's Bobby's old man, Lily's former stepdad. The other is none other than Charlie French. Jack knows him from that one visit, though Charlie's face has been cloudy in his memory all these years. Jack only saw him through a sheen of grief. Even if he'd never seen him, he'd know who he was. Something just screams Charlie French about this bastard. Maybe it's the way he's dressed. Maybe it's the swagger. Jack remembers Max saying back in '96 how Charlie likes rough games. He has one hand behind his back now, hiding something.

'Come on in and join the party,' Charlie says.

'What's going on?' Lily says.

'This your little girlfriend?' Charlie says. 'She's older than you, huh? I like older dames too.'

Lily ignores Charlie, focusing on Bobby. 'We met Francesca. She told us what happened.'

'You saw Francesca?' Bobby says. Then his eyes go to Jack. 'And, holy shit, what's *he* doing here?'

Jack's confused. Bobby isn't asking *who* he is. He's asking *what* he's doing there, again, as if he knows him, or at least knows of him, his presence especially unwelcome. That *holy shit* really confounds Jack.

'Come on,' Charlie says. 'Quit the chit-chat. Get them in here. Close the door.'

Bobby steps back. Jack and Lily enter. The apartment isn't much. It has the same kind of broken-down quality as Jack's place, except it doesn't feel like anybody was ever happy here. It smells of dust, mold, and wet towels.

The guy who Jack has pegged for Lily's former stepfather speaks: 'Jesus Christ, what are you doing here, Lil? Now, of all times.'

'I heard Bobby was in trouble,' Lily says.

'Bobby is in trouble,' Charlie says. 'Trouble of the outsized variety. You're what, related? And who's your friend? He looks very familiar to me. I've seen many faces. I throw away most of them.'

'I'm nobody,' Jack says, not bothering to explain the previous circumstance under which Charlie encountered him.

'I don't like nobodies. Nobodies make me nervous.' Charlie takes a gun out from behind his back. It has a silencer. He points it at Lily's ex-stepdad and talks to Bobby, who is standing close to Jack and Lily now. 'Let's get back to where we were. I've been patient with you, kid. You tell me where the stuff is, and I'll be on my way. You don't and, like I said, I start by plugging your old man here. Next, I go for the girl, whoever the fuck she is. I'll knock off Mr Nobody for kicks, though I don't guess he means much to anybody. Then I'll finish with you. A regular bloodbath. We don't need a bloodbath.'

'Christ, Bobby,' Lily says. 'Just give it to him.'

'I don't have it,' Bobby says.

Jack thinks about making a quick reach for his own gun, but he holds back. The last thing he wants is for Charlie to turn on Lily and fire at her.

Without hesitation, Charlie shrugs and shoots Bobby's father. The noise the gun makes is a pop. It doesn't match the effect of the bullet. Right in the chest. A moment of shock and recognition on the guy's face. He goes down hard on the linoleum in the kitchen.

Lily gasps.

'You thought I was fucking with you?' Charlie asks.

Francesca

Francesca wakes up with a start. She's lying on a couch in the dark. She forgets where she is for a minute. Light streams in from another room. Her head is pounding. She needs to pee and she needs a glass of water. She sits up. She remembers everything. Her mouth is so dry. She goes out to the kitchen. The Irish woman, Mairéad, is sitting at the table, reading Lily's story and smoking a cigarette. 'You're up already?' Mairéad says.

'I can't believe I passed out,' Francesca says. 'I have to use the bathroom.'

'Of course.'

She rushes to the bathroom, knowing she's been there already but not quite remembering where it is. She tries one door and it goes down to the basement. Another is a closet. Mairéad points down the hall and says she's pretty sure it's the last door.

Francesca goes into the bathroom and pulls her pants down, closing the door most of the way. She sits on the toilet and pees forcefully, feeling an intense burst of relief. As she pees, she puts her elbows on her knees and tilts her head back, looking up at the ceiling and a gross old light fixture full of dead moths and browned with dust. The light is buzzing, almost sizzling. She wonders what keeps old houses like this from burning down.

When she's done, she wipes, flushes, and stands, balancing herself with one hand against the tiled wall as she pulls her pants up. She struggles to the sink, washes her hands, and then splashes cold water on her face over the basin. She opens the medicine cabinet above the sink and looks at the ancient bottles of amoxicillin and St. Joseph Aspirin and Vicks VapoRub and two rusted cans of Barbasol shaving cream. Hidden behind a package of unopened Q-tips, she finds a small bottle of Tylenol Extra Strength, popping the cap and emptying three into her palm. She tosses them in her mouth and then leans over the sink, running the water and drinking straight from the tap to wash them down. She puts the bottle back, closes the medicine chest, and dries her face on a stiff blue towel hanging from the hook on the door.

She goes into the kitchen and sits across from Mairéad, who looks up from the story. 'Feel any better?' Mairéad asks.

'I feel like an idiot,' Francesca says. 'Some real rookie bullshit, huh?'

'Happens to the best of us.'

'Where is everybody?'

'They went over to help your friend. Bobby, was it? I'm worried. Could be a bad situation.'

'What? Really? Christ.'

Mairéad motions to the half-full cup of coffee on the table in front of her. 'Your coffee might still be lukewarm. You want me to heat it up for you?'

Francesca takes a sip. It's cold. 'I'll do it,' she says. She takes the coffee over to the stove and empties it into a small, clean pot already on one of the burners. She turns the gas on high. While she's waiting, she finds a glass in a cabinet over the sink and fills it with cold water straight from the tap. The glass is one of those collectibles from McDonald's. It has the Hamburglar on it. She drinks the water and thinks about Jack and his wife taking his daughter to McDonald's on Twenty-Fourth Avenue when she was a girl and bringing home this glass. She places it on the counter when she's done. The coffee boils quickly, and she pours it back into the mug. She drinks some on her way back to the table. She sits down, finds her tobacco, and rolls a cigarette. 'How's the story?' she asks Mairéad.

'Quite good,' Mairéad says.

'I can't believe they went over there. I can't believe this night.'

'It's my favorite thing about the world,' Mairéad says. 'Nights like this where there's nothing really, it's just plain, and then there's everything all at once.'

Francesca lights her cigarette. 'Do you really communicate with the dead? Or is that just something you tell people at parties?'

Mairéad laughs. 'Just something I tell people at parties. It's not hard to imagine what people want to hear from their dead loved ones. "Oh, I miss you so bad, Larry. Heaven's fucking great. Can you please send my sister a card?"'

'You're messing with me.'

'A little.'

'So, you do... talk to the dead?'

'Not on command or anything, but I've had my encounters. I didn't ask for it and I don't take advantage of people either, if that's what you're wondering. I'm not a con artist who charges people to get messages from their dead relatives. And I don't solve murders with it.'

Francesca takes a drag on her cigarette and exhales away from Mairéad. She drinks more coffee. The pounding in her head is getting lighter. She looks around at Jack's kitchen. Linoleum peeling up. Scuffed cabinets. An ancient, humming fridge the color of a faded lime. A clock on the wall, stopped at four thirty. She wonders when it stopped. She can feel time in the silence of the house. 'Can I ask you one more thing?'

'Sure,' Mairéad says.

'I'm sure you get this all the time and I'm sorry to ask it, but I don't want to regret not asking. Can you talk to my dad?' She pauses, blows smoke down at the table. 'Forget it. I'm sorry. It's not a party trick. I'm just like everybody else.'

'Asking is natural. I can't just switch it on. The situation has to be right.'

'Like a séance?'

'I don't do that stuff. It happens when it happens. I can't really predict it. Sometimes I see things. Other times I just hear things.'

Francesca nods. 'I'm sorry.'

'I was only half kidding before about being able to guess what people want to hear. Without even hearing from your dad's spirit, I can tell you he's proud of you. He's proud of the person you are. He's happy you think about him so much. He misses you. He wishes things had worked out differently.'

Francesca's crying. She drops her cigarette into an empty Guinness bottle and wipes the tears away from her cheeks with the heels of her hands. 'Yeah?'

'If I heard from him, that's what he'd say. I guarantee it.'

'You're right. That is exactly what I want to hear.'

Mairéad has let her cigarette burn down to a long line of trembling ash between her fingers. She tries to deposit it in a bottle without the ash scattering everywhere but doesn't have any luck. The ash flits out across the table, on Lily's story, little whispers of black debris among the dark bottles. 'Shit, I'm cooked now,' she says. 'Lily will know I read the story. Oh well.'

'So you believe in the afterlife? These people you communicate with sometimes, they're either in heaven or hell or purgatory and they tell you about what it's like there?'

'I don't know. I guess. But it's not like any afterlife I've ever heard of, not really. More a kind of bank of spirits. They're here. They watch. They listen.'

More tears. Francesca thinks of her father's spirit, floating around. 'I hope Jack and Lily are okay,' she says. 'I should've gone with them.'

Jack

Lily's about to move forward to help Bobby's dad but Jack puts his hand on her shoulder and tells her to stay back.

Bobby's on the verge of tears, his old man shot right there in front of him, the bad decisions he's made leading to this. It wasn't real at all – it was a fantasy he was living inside of – until Charlie pulled that trigger and dropped his father like dirt.

'I'm gonna puke,' Bobby says. He collapses to his knees. Charlie has the gun on him now. Bobby doesn't throw up. He just stays there, kneeling, looking like a sprinter who's stuck at the starting line, a failure who never even gave himself a shot.

'Puke's the last thing we need,' Charlie says. 'Get up.'

Bobby stands, wavering. 'It's in my room,' he says.

'All that for nothing. It's right here in your room? Jesus. You got it in your Mickey Mouse suitcase? Go.' He waves the gun at Jack and Lily.

Bobby leads the party into his room. Charlie has Jack and Lily lean up against the wall. He stands back, so everyone is in front of him. He keeps the gun on Bobby, who unfolds a pink plastic stool he keeps behind his dresser and places it on the floor in front of the closet. He stands on it and reaches onto the high shelf in the closet, a shelf up out of sight behind the frame, shooting a look at Jack as he rummages around.

Jack has the sense that Bobby's going for a gun, but there's no sign of that yet. Bobby tugs a big duffel bag out and drops it on the floor just to the side of him.

'Now you're talking,' Charlie says. 'Everything's there?'

'Yes,' Bobby says. He turns to Lily. 'How do you know *him*?' It's clear he's talking about Jack.

'He's in my writing class,' Lily says.

'You really don't know me?' Bobby says to Jack. 'You don't know it was me? I was there with my friend Zeke, and we were both throwing rocks, but it was me.'

What Bobby's saying hits Jack full in the chest. The room becomes a roar. Lily's saying something now. Charlie too. Jack's shaken beyond words. This kid – Lily's former stepbrother, Francesca's wild fling, the murderer of Max Berry – threw the rock that killed Amelia?

The roar settles into a hum. Lily says, 'What are you saying? You threw the rock that killed his daughter? You didn't tell anyone? Jack, I'm so sorry.'

'I couldn't tell anyone,' Bobby says.

Jack has thought about this moment nonstop over the years. Meeting the kid responsible for Amelia dying. What he'd say. What he'd do. He'd imagined every scenario. Different ways to kill the kid. Different ways to forgive him. And now here he is, confessing, under Charlie French's gun. 'You were what, fourteen or fifteen?' Jack asks.

'What the fuck's going on?' Charlie says. 'Open the bag. Let me see my stuff.'

'I was fourteen,' Bobby says to Jack. 'I'm nineteen now. I'm sorry. I don't want to die.'

'You're *sorry*?' Jack says.

'I wish I could take it back. I wish that more than anything. I can't, though. I was a stupid kid.'

'Looks like you still are.'

'Open the bag now,' Charlie says, waving the gun at Bobby.

The blood's drained from Bobby's face. He begins to unzip the top of the bag, struggling with it, the teeth caught in the fabric. When he gets it partially open, he reaches in, coming out with a small gun. His hand is shaking so bad, it's a miracle he doesn't drop it.

Without hesitation, Charlie fires at Bobby, seeming to have had a good read on the situation as soon as that zipper started moving. This shot's not as perfect as the one he pumped into Bobby's old man. This one gets Bobby in the upper arm and he flops forward over the bag.

The shot at Bobby gives Jack just enough time to draw his gun and return fire at Charlie. He hasn't used the gun in a long while, but it's still in decent shape. It's loud, his shot, filling the room, seeming to echo and reverberate and do whatever else it is that sounds do, settling over them, a boom that keeps booming. It's not a good shot. It goes over Charlie's shoulder.

Lily is terrified. She backs up further against the wall, trying to disappear into it. She keeps her eyes away from Charlie and Jack.

Charlie looks around like he can't believe Jack missed. He puts the gun on Jack. And Jack still has his gun on Charlie. He can see an ending for this he doesn't like, both of them unloading on each other. If he's going down, he's not missing again this time, Charlie's going down too. And maybe Bobby. Maybe that's what Jack wants. Revenge. An ugly end.

Bobby, sitting up now with his hurt arm dangling, fires at Charlie while he's distracted by Jack. It's better than Jack's shot. Gets him in the chest.

Charlie turns to Bobby and pops off a quick return shot. This one tears up Bobby's gut.

Lily cowers on the floor, hands crossed over her head.

Jack aims to plant his next shot right between Charlie's eyes. He squeezes the trigger and the shot goes low, catching him in the throat. Charlie drops his gun and puts his hands up around his neck, blood swarming out between his fingers, his breath halted. He falls hard.

Jack lowers his gun and tries to comfort Lily. She's scared.

He's about to put a hand on her shoulder but he stops himself from touching her. It's not his place to touch her. To be touched is probably the last thing she wants right now. 'Are you okay?' he asks.

Lily looks out from between her arms and focuses first on Charlie bleeding out on the floor and then she turns her attention to Bobby, realizing how badly he's hurt. 'Jesus Christ,' she says.

Bobby sits with his back against the opposite wall. He lets his gun clatter to the floor. He pulls the bag close to him by its strap. The first shot he took is in the fleshy part of his left arm. He's hunched in that direction a bit, as if that side of his body has sort of caved in. The second shot to his stomach has done the real damage.

Lily scurries on her knees to Bobby's side. 'How bad is it?'

'It's bad.' Bobby puts his hand on her hand in an effort to hold her in place but his strength is waning.

'This is a mess,' Lily says. 'I need to call an ambulance for you.'

'I can't believe you saw Francesca,' he says.

'I wish we hadn't,' Lily says. 'We never would've come here.'

Bobby's coughing blood now. He looks at Jack. 'I'm sorry. Take the money.'

Jack's seeing Amelia tangled up in all that metal. Part of him wants to lift his gun and finish Bobby off. Instead, he tucks the gun under his shirt. 'We should get help,' he says to Lily.

Lily nods. She's about to run out to the kitchen but Bobby stops her.

'Please stay,' he says.

'Okay, I'm not going,' Lily says. One of her hands is holding Bobby's right hand and the other is touching his face. She's crying. She has the hands of someone who would rescue a baby bird. She has the hands of someone who would tend to the sick. 'You're gonna be okay,' she says.

But Bobby's not going to be okay. He's pale. He's fading fast.

The bullet must've hit a major organ. He coughs more blood. He's having trouble breathing. He can't make words.

'Jesus Christ,' Lily says again.

And then Bobby's gone. Just like that. One last pained breath. Blood pooling on the floor around him. The kid who threw the rock that killed Amelia. A stupid kid then and still a stupid kid now. Stupid to steal this money. Stupid to risk Francesca's life. Stupid to get his father killed. And himself. Dead now, this stupid fucking kid.

Jack puts his hand on Lily's shoulder. 'We should go,' he says. 'We need to go.'

Lily

Lily follows Jack. She's not sure what else to do. They leave Bobby and Danny and Charlie French and leave all that money and all those drugs, climbing over the old steam radiator and out Bobby's window and rushing down the fire escape, which trembles under their feet. Jack has no hesitation about leaving. Lily does.

There are already sirens but she insists on going to the payphone on the corner. Her heart is beating so fast, she's sure she's going to die. She pictures it. A nuclear explosion in her chest. Disappearing in a thrum of light. She tries not to think about all the blood up in that apartment, about the dead bodies. She was there. She saw it all. She didn't see it all. She can't have. It's a dream she'll wake up from.

She says what she needs to say into the receiver to the 911 operator. She heard shooting. The address. It doesn't matter how fast the ambulances get here. Bobby is gone. She hangs up without answering any of the operator's questions.

She guesses that Jack took care of Micah. It hadn't seriously occurred to her, but it should have. Those long hours he was gone. She thinks of him hoisting Micah into the trunk of the car his rich Westchester County parents bought him, driving up to Poughkeepsie and leaving him there near the station. She wonders how Jack did the deed itself. She wonders what happened between them. Was there a fight? Jack probably believed that the only definite way to avoid danger with someone like Micah was to get rid of him.

She looks at Jack now. He's been so kind to her. She couldn't have known about Bobby throwing the rock that killed Amelia, but she feels somehow responsible. She couldn't have anticipated that trouble layered over the other, newer trouble. She feels so safe with Jack. He's the kind of person who makes things feel like they'll be okay, even if they hadn't been okay for him, which is why she didn't hesitate to go warn Bobby. They don't say anything to each other. Not yet.

They go to Jack's car. He opens the door for her. She settles into the passenger seat and he gets behind the wheel and they leave the block. She takes a deep breath, trying to regain some of her composure. She looks down at her right hand. A couple of spots of blood. Bobby's blood. She spits on the fingers of her left hand and wipes the spots away, circling over the blood with her thumb and forefinger until the red dissipates into a faint pink on her pale skin.

The moon has settled over the neighborhood like the fluorescent entrance to a tunnel-of-love carnival ride, spilling its light on the blacktop, on the hoods of cars and the Virgin Mary statues in weed-strewn front yards, on all the damaged windows and doors, on the cracks in the sidewalks and all the cracked hearts, on the rooftops, on the order and disorder, on all that's hidden and all that's out in the open.

As they drive past St. Mary's church in the dark, she blesses herself. It's an old habit from when she was a kid, but this time she's blessing herself for Bobby and Danny. Saying a prayer for them, she guesses, even if she doesn't believe in prayer anymore.

They drive down Twenty-Fourth Avenue where a shadowy apartment building on the corner has obscured the moon. The block is heavy with darkness. A shaft of light is up ahead. Seeming to point their way. Jack yearns the car toward it. The world has been hard, is hard now and only getting harder. Lily thinks of Bobby throwing that rock. If he hadn't thrown it, he wouldn't have killed Amelia and maybe he wouldn't have killed Max either. Maybe none of this would have happened. Events chained to events. She thinks of Amelia's final moments. She thinks of Francesca passed out at Jack's, and Mairéad waiting there. The future is a story she hasn't written yet, wilder and more unpredictable than she could've anticipated.

'Are you okay?' Jack asks, finally breaking the silence.

'I don't know,' she says. It feels so wrong, leaving like they did.

'We had to leave,' he says, as if reading her mind.

'Did you think about taking the money?'

'I thought about taking it for you. Could've made things real easy. But I figured you wouldn't want a life built on that. If you're good, and you are, it'd be hard to live with the shame.'

She nods. 'I'm so scared. I can't believe any of it. The timing. Us showing up right at that moment. Danny and Bobby getting shot. The bag of money and drugs. Bobby confessing to you. My God.' She pauses. 'Would you have killed Bobby if he wasn't already hurt so bad?'

'No,' Jack says.

'Because of me? Because I was there?'

'I wouldn't have done it anyway.'

'Did you kill Micah?'

'I didn't,' he says, but he's looking straight ahead at the road. They stop at a light. The red from the light is gleaming through the windshield onto his face. He's so steady he could be telling the truth, but she knows he's lying. There's a whole version of him she doesn't know, will never know.

The light changes. Green shining on his face now. He drives through the intersection. The moon is back.

At the house, he pulls into the driveway, getting as close to the garage as he can. He turns off the engine and the lights. They sit there in the dark car.

'What should we say?' Lily asks. 'What shouldn't we say?'

'Say no one was home when we got there. Say we knocked and knocked but no one answered. When the news breaks, they'll think we were lucky and got there too late.'

'You shot Charlie. Do you think the cops will come for you?'

'I doubt it. The bag's still there. They'll figure they took each other out.'

'Even though the bullet doesn't match Bobby's gun?'

Jack shrugs. 'I hope so. This isn't Sherlock Holmes we're dealing with. It's the Six-Two. They'll be happy to close the case.'

'We shouldn't tell Francesca about Bobby?'

'I don't think so.'

'I'm not a great liar. I get all red.'

'It's okay. She was sleeping when we left. Maybe she's still sleeping.'

They go inside. Lily is surprised to see Francesca back at the table with Mairéad. They're both smoking. Her short story is out on the table.

'Caught red-handed,' Mairéad says 'I read your story. I adored it.'

'Thanks,' Lily says, sitting at the table and lighting her own cigarette. 'You don't think I'm terrible?'

'I think you're a lovely writer. And I'm glad you're back.'

Jack disappears downstairs to put the gun in its hiding spot.

'Did you see Bobby?' Francesca asks.

Lily shakes her head. Looks away. She can feel the red rising in her. 'We knocked but no one answered. I'll call again tomorrow. Maybe he'll come to his senses.'

'I hope so.'

Jack returns and joins them at the table. He pours whiskey for himself and Lily. Mairéad says she'll take more too. Francesca says she can't.

'You know what this whole thing reminds me of?' Mairéad says. 'A folktale I read as a girl called "House of Daughters." An older man lives all alone. His wife and children died from the plague. Three girls on a long journey through the woods pass by his house. He's working outside. They stop and ask for water. He offers them water and a meal and beds for the night. The beds in his house are empty because his family is gone. The girls have been trained to be frightened of men – of all men because they are responsible for the evil in the world – but they can tell that this is a good man with a good heart. They have a fine meal and the girls even manage to make the man laugh and forget the tragedy of existence. He realizes that all we can ask for, in the end, is moments where it feels like living is okay, that it's not all for nothing. He feels comforted and surrounded by love for the first time in a long time. The journey the girls are going on is a hard one. They're going from a nothing town to a city in the hopes of making a new life. The man says they can stay with him instead, if they want. They can live as a family. They can have comfortable beds and food and help him farm the land. There's a town not so far away so they can meet people their own age too. It's not a city, but it's lively enough. The girls agree to stay. The man cries. He's so thankful for his new daughters.'

'Did you just make that up?' Lily asks Mairéad. She doesn't really mean to ask – it feels like a rude question – but it's just there on her lips suddenly. So what if she made it up? Lily looks at Mairéad, her black hair catching a glint of gold from the kitchen lights, the bright hunger for life in her eyes. Here is a woman who will never stop being exciting. Here is a woman who knows what stories do.

'I heard it as a girl,' Mairéad says. 'Hand to God. I was always taken by the message.'

'This is nice,' Jack says. 'It's nice having you all here.'

Lily downs her whiskey. Maybe it's wrong to be happy after what she's seen and what she knows, but she doesn't care. She's letting the guilt go. She pours more whiskey and gives herself permission to feel okay.

Acknowledgments

For their endless support and encouragement, thanks to my wife, Katie Farrell Boyle, and our children, Eamon and Connolly Jean. I wrote the first draft of this book during our lockdown summer when daily pillow fights to 'The Mercy Seat' by Nick Cave and the Bad Seeds helped us survive. I wouldn't have had the energy or ability to write it without their love keeping the lights on in my heart.

Thanks to my mom, Geraldine Giannini.

Thanks to Nat Sobel and Judith Weber and everyone at Sobel Weber.

Thanks to Victoria Wenzel, Claiborne Hancock, Tim Thomas, Maria Fernandez, and everyone at Pegasus Books.

Thanks to François and Benjamin Guérif, Simon Baril, Oliver Gallmeister, Marie Moscoso, Clotilde Le Yaouanc, and everyone at Éditions Gallmeister.

Thanks to Ion Mills, Geoffrey Mulligan, Claire Watts, and everyone at No Exit Press.

Thanks to readers and booksellers and libraries everywhere. Thanks especially to Richard and Lisa Howorth, Cody Morrison, Ted O'Brien, Bill Cusumano, Katelyn O'Brien, Lyn Roberts, Slade Lewis, and everyone at Square Books; Charles Perry and Tom Wickersham at the Mysterious Bookshop; Patrick Millikin at the Poisoned Pen; Scott Montgomery at BookPeople; and Pete Mock at McIntyre's.

Thanks to Megan Abbott, Jack Pendarvis, Ace Atkins, and Jimmy Cajoleas. Weekly calls with them kept me afloat during a tough year. Thanks also to my pals Alex Andriesse, George Griffith, and Tyler Keith.

Thanks to Willy Vlautin – I read *The Night Always Comes* three times while working on this book, and I sure hope some of its spirit rubbed off on me.

The title of this book comes from a Garland Jeffreys song I love. I'm really thankful for his music and for the words that inspired me here. Thanks to all the writers and filmmakers and actors and musicians and painters and photographers whose work sustained me during the making of this book. Some others that were at the front of my mind: Abel Ferrara, Zoë Lund, Ellen Burstyn, Lynn Shelton, Martin Scorsese, John Cassavetes, Gena Rowlands, Bill Gunn, Hong Sang-soo, Lydia Loveless, Helen Levitt, Spike Lee, Mickey Rourke, Steve Buscemi, David Lynch, Alan Rudolph, Guillermo Arriaga, Polly Platt, Larry McMurtry, Johnny Thunders, Bill Withers, Yukio Mishima, Thalia Zedek, Ralph Albert Blakelock, Charles Burnett, Frank Borzage, Edgar G. Ulmer, Charles Burchfield, Reginald Marsh, Kathleen Collins, Lou Reed, Jim Carroll, Eagle Pennell, and Joseph Stella. The road goes on forever.

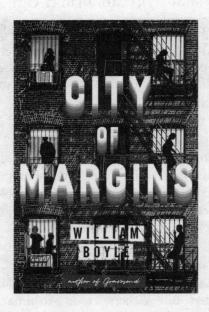

In *City of Margins*, the lives of several lost souls intersect in Southern Brooklyn in the early 1990s. These characters cross paths in unexpected ways, guided by coincidence and the pull of blood. There are new things to be found in the rubble of their lives, too. The promise of something different beyond the barriers that have been set out for them.

This is a story of revenge and retribution, of facing down the ghosts of the past, of untold desires, of yearning and forgiveness and synchronicity, of the great distance of lives lived in dangerous proximity to each other.*City of Margins* is a Technicolor noir melodrama pieced together in broken glass.

9780857304056   8.99

BECOME A
NO EXIT PRESS MEMBER